CW01033648

THE
TRAIL
OF
BLOOD

A.K. NAIRN

Copyright © A. K. Nairn

All rights reserved.

No part of this publication may be altered, reproduced, distributed, or transmitted in any form, by any means, including, but not limited to, scanning, duplicating, uploading, hosting, distributing, or reselling, without the express prior written permission of the publisher, except in the case of reasonable quotations in features such as reviews, interviews, and certain other non-commercial uses currently permitted by copyright law.

Prologue

OCTOBER 11TH, 1516

It was a body all right. They could see that now. But what was so strange about it? Why did it look so different from all the other cadavers they had seen round here, hacked to death on battlefields, stabbed in their homes or battered by the roadside? Perhaps it was simply the location – on a dismal island, right on the border between the two countries. Or maybe the morning light was playing tricks on their tired eyes. There was just something about it that sent an uncommon chill through their marrow.

The steam drifted up off the water as the two bailiffs rowed their little coble across to investigate. It had been raining, and the river was swollen. They had to work hard against the current. As they did so, they kept an eye on the banks and the island itself, for it was covered in thick scrub that could conceal any number of enemies. When they neared the shore, they paused to draw their swords and laid them against the thwarts. Then they carefully dragged the boat onto the shingle, ensuring it was stable before picking up their weapons and crunching over the pebbles.

Now they could smell it, that unmistakable stench that signalled the end of earthly life. And they were not the only ones: the flies buzzed around the remains in an ominous cloud, as if the soul were trying to escape. Slowly, the idea of any killer being nearby receded in the men's minds, so they relaxed their guard. Instead, they covered their noses and mouths as they crept forward, more fearful of disease than of attack.

Only once they had picked their way over the last line of rocks did they see what was wrong. They had not been mistaken: the body had been defiled. Or rather, its extremities had. For the body was all that there was left. There was no head. Or arms. Or legs. It was just a lumpen torso in a blood-soaked shirt.

"Well, this is a new one, even for this place," coughed the older man, trying not to gag through his sleeve. "We'd best tell the warden."

"What warden?" replied his companion grimly. "He's been chopped up, too, remember?"

Chapter 1

Antoine de Lissieu rode right up to the entrance of Holyrood Palace, as was his privilege. He had been summoned to Edinburgh at short notice, and as he handed over Carbonel to a stable boy, he mulled the potential reasons why. Over the years, he'd learnt that an urgent request was rarely a good sign, so while he dearly hoped that he might be released from his responsibilities in Scotland, he knew this was unlikely.

It wasn't that he hated his adopted country – although Hell's teeth, he would never get used to that icy wind which now whipped in from the German Ocean. The chaotic politics meant that there was always something to keep a man busy. The soldiers were generally dependable. And, of course, thanks to the long-standing alliance with his homeland, there was decent claret aplenty. But as he approached his fortieth year, his prospects surely required him to leave this boggy wilderness and return to Paris soon.

When Antoine reached the palace gates, the sentries saluted him and allowed him to pass without question. Two pikemen fell in behind him and followed him around the quadrangle to the governor's office, where they handed him over to Lord Albany's bodyguards. He noted that they were more numerous than usual. One went through the familiar ritual of knocking three times before waiting a moment and opening the immense, panelled doors. "The Chevalier de Lissieu, my lord."

While much of the palace was still under construction, this room was well-established, and there was no denying that it was impressive. Huge tapestries from Flanders hung on the walls, and an iron chamber clock from Germany presided over the hearth. On the far side, the window had been designed to showcase the great crag of Arthur's Seat.

Scotland's Governor sat in front of it, reviewing a stack of ledgers. He rose immediately and extended his arms – an action which, along with his thick furs, made him look even more bear-like than usual. "Ah, my friend, it's good to see you! You've come at the perfect time to rescue me from these tiresome accounts…"

Antoine noted Albany's jovial tone but took it as another ill omen. He had helped him clamber his way to power after the carnage of Flodden three years ago and knew that he often disguised his ruthless ambition to achieve his aims. He was being softened up, then. But for what end?

"I am glad to be of assistance, my lord," he said. "You deserve some repose after all the recent strife. Talking of which, what brings me here?"

Albany smiled and crossed the parquet floor to place a hand rather too heavily on Antoine's shoulder. "All in good time, my friend. As you say, we have been busy recently, so let us relax awhile before we turn to affairs of state."

The governor took Antoine by the elbow and guided him back to the door, where he instructed two of the bodyguards to escort them to the garden. It sounded like a delaying tactic to Antoine, but he had no choice but to follow all the way round the other side of the quadrangle and out through an iron gate. As the guards opened it, the cold hit him more forcefully, for the bitter wind was now laced with spits of rain. He believed that the local word for this particular combination was *yillen*, although there were so many terms for specific varieties of foul weather that he might be mistaken.

Undeterred by the elements, the party went down a trellis walkway, through a small herb garden and into a meadow that was being reworked in the modern style, for next spring. The trout pond had been drained, and the terracotta pots moved indoors, so there were few signs of life. However, as they passed through a newly made arbour, the silence was broken by a tremendous roar. Antoine instinctively reached for his sword, but when he looked to the guards, they were strangely relaxed. Albany gestured for calm. "Welcome to our new menagerie!" he declared, with a grand sweep of his arm.

They moved into the section beyond, where they encountered a group of labourers erecting a cage. In a nearby enclosure, a handful of monkeys huddled together in some straw, and in another, an antelope stood forlorn. Further on, there was a brick wall built at waist-height. Albany led the party to the edge and pointed down into a deep pit, where a lion was chained to a post. Its mane was tatty, and its ribs were visible through its tawny hide, but it still appeared magical enough to Antoine, who had never seen such a creature before.

"Well, what do you think?" said Albany. "This is just the start, of course, but one day, I hope we'll have a collection of animals to rival any in Europe."

"It is wonderful," replied Antoine, who was genuinely

enchanted. "A little bit of Africa in this icy kingdom. I only hope you're feeding it malmsey to warm its blood!"

"Ha!" said Albany. "It's a little weak now after its long journey. But it's a fighter, I can tell that. If it makes the spring – God willing – it will soon be roaring in the local tongue."

"Yes, it will be our own lion rampant," mused Antoine. "A symbol of all that you're doing to get this country back on its feet. But what about a humble beast like me? What role shall I have in the new menagerie you're building? I'm eager to learn your thoughts, for I doubt you asked me here just to display your new pet."

As the words left his mouth, he worried that they could be interpreted as impertinent, so he was relieved when Albany's fearsome temper did not show itself. Although perhaps he detected a slight sharpness in the Governor's reply, a signal that the true business of the day was about to be revealed?

"A new pet never dislodges a faithful friend. And you are something of a unique creature, with qualities that go far beyond our latest arrival's brute strength. Qualities which we need right now."

Antoine gave a modest bow. "These are trying times, my lord, but at least we are at peace."

"For the moment perhaps. But our truce with the English expires at the end of next month. On St Andrew's Day, no less! And to make matters worse, your own king does not wish to antagonise them by signing a new accord with us. So we are in a very delicate position. Potentially without friends – and with our enemies ready to pounce."

Albany turned to catch his eye. There was a coldness to his gaze that Antoine had not seen in him before, the look of a powerful man who was under threat. "That is why I have asked you here, in the hope you'll accept a new appointment. One that is crucial to this country and its very survival as a realm."

Antoine doubted that he would have much say in the matter but quickly went over the possibilities in his mind, just in case. The most favourable outcome would see him resuming his ambassadorial duties – this could enable a temporary mission to France, if not a permanent return. Alternatively, a naval position might afford similar opportunities. More likely, though, it would be an administrative role in Edinburgh – taking over those ledgers for which Albany had no appetite. He dreaded this prospect. But in fact, the news was far worse than this.

"To get to the point, I wish you to be the next Warden of the Eastern Marches and bring order to that lawless region, once and for all."

Antoine's whole body tightened. The Marches were a notorious hellhole, run by corrupt warlords and bandits, not civilised men like him. *Reivers*, they called them, for bereavement was their stock-in-trade. This was a position without prospects, a role without hope. Still, he had to tread carefully and cite objections that did not smack of self-interest.

"Sir, I am flattered by your proposal," he began. "But what do the troubles of one savage region have to do with the great affairs of state you mentioned a moment ago?"

"Everything," replied Albany. "It is a tinderbox at the best of times. Now, one spark could set Scotland and England ablaze. And France, too, if we're not careful."

Antoine frowned. "Even so, I can't help worrying that I am miscast. When you took off Lord Hume's head last week, I assumed the warden's job would go to one of his kinsfolk, as it always has. Or at least to a local we could control."

"There are no suitable candidates left," Albany muttered. "We took one brother's head the next day. The other brothers are exiled or cannot be trusted – and the rival chiefs are no better."

"But surely the appointment of a stranger will only rile the natives?"

"Who knows? After all, you can rise above their petty feuds in a way others cannot. Perhaps they will see advantages to having a foreigner at their helm?"

Antoine doubted it: many Scots already had misgivings about the number of strangers Albany was bringing in. However, he knew better than to mention this. He stroked his beard, now flecked with its first grey he had noticed recently. "And what about the English? Won't they be upset to see a Frenchman on their border?"

"Not if you play to your strengths," said Albany firmly. "You might be a war hero back home…"

"I hardly—"

"…but here you are a diplomat. The perfect man to pour oil over troubled waters."

The rain was getting heavier, and the two men drew their cloaks about themselves. "Very well,' said Antoine, hunching his shoulders. He had handled enough negotiations to see that the conversation was over and he must salvage what he could. "I will do my best, as ever, and just pray that Paris gets to hear of it."

Albany smiled like a hunter might on cornering a deer. "Listen, my friend – if you can stabilise the Marches at this sensitive time, King Francis will be very grateful. Not only will he call you home, but he will also give you great rank. And more coin than you can carry."

Turning back towards the palace, he fixed Antoine in

that cold stare again. "All I ask is that, before you feast at his table, choke down this one last meal for me. And do it cleanly. Otherwise, we will all be devoured."

There was another roar as the keepers threw a sheep's carcass over the wall of the den. The lion plunged on it greedily, chewing through the ribcage and then dragging out the liver, heart and lungs. Soon, the slippery flesh was smeared all over the animal's great maw and the muddy ground was spattered crimson.

Chapter 2

Antoine woke up in one of his sweats again, but for once, he had been wrestling with new fears rather than old ghosts. Most of all, he fretted about how long this position would last. Thinking back to last night's conversation, he realised that Albany had studiously avoided that matter. All he knew was that the Kings of Scotland and England had been trying to pacify the Marches for hundreds of years, so it was unlikely to be a short shift.

As he felt his black bile rising, it occurred to him that if Francoise had been here, she would have tempered his melancholic humour with her more phlegmatic disposition. But she was not here – would never be here – and thinking of her made things worse, not better. So he would have to put such foolishness aside. He rose, dismissed the bodyguard outside his room and went downstairs. Perhaps a further conversation with Albany would allay his concerns and allow him to make a plan of attack. A plan of escape, indeed.

The quadrangle was quieter at this time of the morning, without the queues of petitioners that built up during the day. However, as Antoine turned the corner, there was a commotion as some dignitaries were ushered into the governor's office, leaving their entourages milling around outside.

He pushed his way through the group and approached a guard. "What goes on?" he asked. "Is the governor able to see me, to complete some business of ours from yestere'en?"

"I'm afraid not, my lord. He sits wi' the Northern Earls and is not to be disturbed. He has asked that ye proceed to the Red Office, where Master Turnbull will meet ye."

"I see," said Antoine. He felt a pang of envy as he realised that other positions were being handed out. "But who is Master Turnbull?"

"One o' the new advisors, sir," said the guard with an eye-roll. "He arrived from the Marches this summer. I believe the governor has put him at your disposal, but I had better let him explain."

The Red Office was a small room at the end of the corridor. To many a visitor's confusion, the walls were whitewashed: the name came from the practice of dispatching messages from here, bearing the governor's vermillion seal. When Antoine entered the office, he saw a young man sitting at a bureau, surrounded by ink pots, parchments, sticks of wax, dispensing spoons and bronze matrices. The sweet, musky smell of warmed resin hung in the air.

"My lord!" said the boy, scrambling to his feet. He made a cursory attempt to tidy his desk. "Please allow me to introduce myself. Dod Turnbull of Lauder, at your service. Governor Albany has instructed me to accompany you on your travels, if you'll have me."

Antoine sized him up. He was a thin lad with unfashionably short hair and a face that radiated the eagerness of youth. On another day, Antoine might have admired this spirit and even recognised something of himself in the boy – but his earlier contemplations had soured his mood. Now, he saw only the likely failings of the lad. After all, the recent bloodshed had thrust forward a whole generation of young folk well before their time. They were red-raw, and their confidence typically outstripped their ability.

"That depends," said the Frenchman. "What counsel might you provide?"

"Any you care of, sir. In particular, there's one pressing issue which I must brief you on. A strange incident, the like of which I've never seen in all my years."

"I see. And how many years do you have, Dod Turnbull?"

"Twenty, sir."

"No, not your age, I mean your experience. For how many years have you been engaged in the work of men?"

"Ah, I'm sorry, sir," said Turnbull, flushing. "Just the three, I suppose. I studied at St Andrews, then took on the running of our estate when my father and brothers fell at Flodden. Our land was a terrible marsh, so I brought in engineers from the Low Countries, to help with the drainage. Since then, I've been helping the governor settle in other strangers as part of his improvements."

Antoine pursed his lips. So, despite Albany's praise for his outsider's perspective, he was obviously worried that a Frenchman would not understand the local ways. Although he had deployed this argument himself just yesterday, that had only been in an attempt to avoid this wretched position. Now that he had the job, the suggestion irked him.

"Ah, but I'm less of a stranger than you think. I've been a visitor to these shores since you were a babe. Or a bairn, as you might say. I have no need for a local minder."

"Let me try, sir," said Turnbull. "I'd do anything to learn from you: your exploits on the battlefield go before you."

Antoine looked away, as he always did when this topic hove into view. Still, perhaps having an aide was not such a bad idea. At the very least, the lad could handle all the administrative tasks a mission like this would require.

"So be it," Antoine said, pulling up a chair. "If you are to be of use, let us start." He cleared his throat. "First, we need a base. My current stronghold at Dunbar is too far away, at least for now. We need to make our presence felt in these early weeks."

"I have already anticipated this," said Turnbull proudly. "And have arranged for us to take over a tower near Dunse, which has been confiscated from the Humes: Black Rig. I've been assured it's in good condition and has room for forty men. A dozen will accompany us on the journey, and the others will join us within the week."

Antoine frowned, for these arrangements must have been made well in advance. The lad had clearly known about his appointment long before he did, but there was no point chiding him for this: the fault lay with Albany.

"You have guessed well," said the Frenchman through gritted teeth. "A good start. Next, we must inform the English Warden of my appointment."

"Also done," said Turnbull. "I sent a messenger to Lord Dacre at dawn. I imagined you would wish to recommence the monthly Truce Days, suspended since Lord Hume's arrest."

"Yes, that is so," said Antoine. At least this letter had only left today: it would have been humiliating if the English had heard his news before him. "Lord Dacre is a fox, and I would rather have him in my sight than chase after the feathers he leaves behind." He steepled his fingers. "Well, you have exceeded my expectations. But who have you forgotten in your haste to win my favour? Who should be the first person we meet, above all others?"

The lad's face fell. "I-I am at a loss, sir. Normally, I would invite the region's most powerful chieftain to attend upon you, but given the recent conflict with the Humes, that would be inadvisable."

"Not at all," said Antoine, wagging a finger. "The bad blood is exactly why we must meet with their new leader, George Hume. He will be all hellfire at his brothers' executions and will see this job as rightfully his. It would be better if we could cool his heat. Invite him to parlay, so that I can get his measure."

"As you wish, sir," said Turnbull, stiffly. "But first, I must brief you on this local matter, which might yield all the measure you need of him."

Antoine bridled at another suggestion that he didn't understand the native culture. "You've prepared the ground well, Master Turnbull, but do not over-reach yourself. If I do not talk to wicked men, I will have a lonely time in this role."

"Of course," replied Turnbull. He bowed his head. "But this incident is no ordinary one, sir. It involves a body that was found a few days ago: directly on the border."

Antoine furrowed his brow. "What do you mean? On which side exactly?"

"That is the first problem. The body was left on an island, right in the middle of the Tweed. On the very spot where the Truce Days are held."

"I see. That is odd, as you say. But who was the victim? I assume it *was* a murder, by the way? I hear the place is ravaged by disease as well."

"It was certainly a murder – unless some strange malady can take a man's head and limbs clean off, which brings another challenge: we do not know who it was."

"Urgh. That is a foul end. But are there no papers to identify him? No permit? Or his clothes, perhaps?"

Turnbull shook his head. "Nothing of consequence, I hear. A couple of river bailiffs found the body, so I've ordered them to visit us, upon our arrival. Meanwhile, I've just sent another letter to the scrivener who provisioned our tower. I've asked him to account for any missing persons and report to us forthwith."

"That is good," said Antoine, but in truth, he was getting tired of this singular focus when there were so many more significant challenges to address. "When we find out the victim's identity, we will no doubt be able to put a name to the killer, too. But until then, let's not dwell on this. And let's not cause trouble with the new Lord Hume before we've even started."

"Yes sir," said Turnbull. He bit his lip before going on. "I only mention him as I fear he may be sending us a message. Does not the mutilation echo the way we decapitated his brothers, just days before? Does not the location speak of a shameless reiver who intends to wreak havoc across borders? Perhaps he means to tell us – to tell you – that he means ill?"

"Perhaps," said Antoine, standing up. "Or perhaps it could be nothing but the fancy of a young man's mind. We shall have to wait and see."

Chapter 3

By the next morning, the rain had passed, but the savage chill remained. The ostlers had readied the horses good and early as it was a full day's ride to Dunse, and with the nights drawing in, the party wished to arrive before dark. Antoine led them off, with Turnbull on his shoulder and twelve men bunched behind. As he left the city by the great Netherbow Gate, he wondered how his career had taken him on this godforsaken path and whether he would ever get it back on track.

After plodding through the Lothians, they cut inland to Dalkeith. Albany's project was in full swing here, and the town thrummed with industry. Carts rumbled through the streets, carrying loads from the Italian brickworks at Tranent. Merchants from the Baltics touted their strange wares in even stranger voices. Pedlars bought up stock to take to Polonia, where ambitious Scots could apparently make a fortune. The air was thick with the stench of boiled leather, horseshit and men's sweat.

"It's exciting, isn't it?" said Turnbull as they nudged through the crowds.

"What is?"

"This age of marvels that we live in. Our ever-expanding world."

"You think so?"

"Oh yes, there seems to be no end to the discoveries men make these days – or the lessons we can learn from strangers."

Antoine did not respond to the latest attempt at flattery.

"Don't get me wrong," continued Turnbull. "I realise that the world can be a dark place and that the candle of wisdom does not illuminate every corner. Where I'm from – where we are going – it barely flickers. But perhaps this mission will let us bring it to the Marches, too?"

Antoine grunted. "The candle of wisdom is all well and good," he said, "but it is easily snuffed out by war and murder. Let's deal with those threats first, before we seek to enlighten anyone."

The Frenchman immediately regretted the way he had spoken. The truth was that he shared Turnbull's fascination for the new and considered himself the foremost advocate for Albany's improvements. But he was still smarting from the way his old friend – no, his master, he had to remind himself – had treated him. He knew he would need to depend on his young assistant, and he resolved to be more generous. For the moment, though, he said no more as the wind had picked up, making the soldiers' pennants flap noisily and rendering conversation impossible.

For the next four hours, they climbed up into the Lammermuirs. There were no landmarks from this point, save the ruins of the old hospital at Soutra – long since abandoned and ransacked for pieces of masonry. They met few travellers either, apart from the occasional drover, bringing cattle down from the summer shielings to the winter pastures. A vast grey sky hung over them, pierced by the odd buzzard circling for prey.

The further they went, the more Antoine could feel Carbonel's discomfort on the boggy surface. The other men seemed to have no such problems as they were riding the smaller hobblers that were indigenous to these parts: shaggy beasts with incredible stamina, they sloshed through the marshes without complaint. Antoine had been offered one at the palace but had refused on the grounds that he preferred an elevated view. This was true, but he was also reluctant to send any signal – to himself or others – that this new role would be a lasting one.

It wasn't until well into the afternoon that they started their descent into the Marches. They were at once relieved to escape the desolation of the moors and nervous about what might lie in store. The hills were smaller here but crested with peel towers and other crude fortifications. Many of these belonged to hostile warlords – or at least they had done, before the recent forfeitures – and the men became anxious to reach a warm hearth and lay out their bedrolls. They took a tighter hold of their reins and spurred their horses.

As the sun disappeared, the spectre of Black Rig rose in front of them on the Langton road. The fortress was perched on a rocky outcrop, looking down on the surrounding landscape like a vengeful deity. Its focal point was a single square tower, three storeys high, judging by the windows, which were tiny and barred with wrought iron yetts. Beneath this, a crenellated wall ran round the perimeter. The place was dark and bleak and foreboding: not quite the cosy haven they had been promised, but a good choice for a stronghold, Antoine thought.

The men dismounted and crept up the hill on foot to

avoid the sharp wooden stakes planted all over the approach. As they did so, they watched out for signs of an ambush: movements on the battlements, noises from behind, softness in the ground that might see them plunge into some hidden pit. They detected nothing, though, save the strong sensation of past violence.

Turnbull unlatched the gate, and the wind sent it flying back with a bang, making them jump. They walked through the barmekin, and were met by a swirling mess of debris, charred cloth and rotten food. They saw that the well had been filled in with huge pieces of timber too.

At last, they entered the barrel-vaulted hallway of the tower, where it became clear that the interior had been utterly destroyed. The walls were scorched black, the store cupboards had been smashed in, and some flagstones had been pulled up. In the middle, there was a trestle table, presumably too heavy to drag away – and on top of it, somebody had laid an enormous human turd.

Chapter 4

"They have slighted their own castle, to make it useless for us," said Turnbull, surveying the squalid scene.

"Yes, I think we can all see that," said Antoine, handling a piece of charred wood. He lowered his voice so that only Turnbull could hear him. "Who did you liaise with, to seize this place?"

"The scrivener I mentioned yesterday. A man named Meikle. He assured me the tower was in good order and would be ready for our arrival."

"Well, somebody has certainly readied it for us, all right. I would speak with your Master Meikle at some point, to see who he blabbed to. Now get some torches lit, and we'll assess the damage."

As the soldiers set off into the shadows, Antoine pulled up a couple of wooden crates and gestured for Turnbull to join him.

"I'm truly sorry," said the young man, shaking his head. "I should have ridden on first and secured the property before dragging you to this midden."

"It's not your fault," said Antoine. He was frustrated by this setback, but he was also tired from the long journey and felt that a reprimand would be of little use. "This is a bad business, but perhaps it provides a helpful warning. We will be able to trust nobody down here, so we might as well remind ourselves of this, right from the start."

"Thank you, sir. I will begin to make things good in the morning, I promise. Once our men have seen what's needed, I will away to Dunse to buy replacements."

Antoine nodded. "Make sure you take a couple of guards then – we're all vulnerable until the reinforcements arrive. When are they coming anyway?"

"That's a good question, sir. In theory, they should be here within the week…"

"Except?"

"I'm afraid I entrusted their recruitment to Master Meikle, too."

Antoine sighed. He was starting to worry that Turnbull might be a liability after all. But before he could say anything more, the soldiers returned with their report. Antoine had not paid them any great attention before, but he was now struck by how green they were. He doubted that any of them had been old enough to fight at Flodden, so they probably had little active service between them. They looked unsettled, scared even. The exception was the serjeant – an older, bull-necked man named Anderson. He seemed quite unfazed by the night's reversal, almost as if he were enjoying his young charges' discomfort.

"Well, those buggers have done a good job o' this, to be fair," he chuckled. "The ground floor is wrecked. The barracks are no' a pretty sight, either. The worst thing is the well, though. I'm no' sure whether we'll be able to save that – and if we cannae, we'll have to move as it'll take too long to dig a new one."

"We can send someone down to take a look," said

Turnbull, bringing out a quill and paper to make a list. "What about the higher quarters?"

"They're in better shape, sir. The roof's a' there, so we'll have some cover while we fix things up. The kitchen's fine, too – although they've built a trip-step intae the stairs, so ye'll have to watch out for that. Oh – and ye'll be glad to know there's a bed and truckle on the top floor which hasnae been touched, so at least ye'll have somewhere to sleep. I'll make sure these lads put their backs intae it all, first thing."

"Good man," said Antoine. "So there's nothing out of the ordinary for us to fret about? Nothing beyond the mess that we can see?"

"Ah, now," said Anderson, rubbing his stubbly chin. "There is one thing. A strange one, so it is. Burnsie, tell our master what ye saw. What ye found out the back, I mean."

A stringy youth edged forward, eyes down. "I think it's probably better to show ye," he said, leading them back out into the courtyard and round the base of the tower to a battered wooden door. "It was covered up wi' old barrels and the like, so I almost missed it in the dark."

One of the others passed Burnsie a torch, and he held it as he opened the door. Inside, there was a narrow staircase leading straight down. Antoine and Turnbull positioned themselves at the front of the group and peered into the gloom.

"Is it safe to go in?" asked the Frenchman.

"Aye, sir, but look at the floor," replied Burnsie, crouching with the torch. Antoine hunkered down, too, balancing himself with one hand on the cold, uneven steps. Turnbull craned over him. It took a little while for the men's eyes to adjust to the poor light, but when they did, they saw a trail of rusty marks.

Antoine motioned to the others to stay where they were.

Then he, Turnbull and Burnsie stood up again and continued downwards without saying a word. They bent low and kept their eyes on the trail as it led them into the bowels of the building. The air was freezing, and they could barely see the others' torches any more, just their own.

At the foot of the stairs, they came to a small hallway and two heavy doors. The first room was empty. It looked as if it had not been occupied for years. After a cursory examination, they left it and followed the drops to the other room. This one had a straw pallet in the corner and an upturned clay bowl beside it. A set of leg irons dangled from the wall on the far side. The bloody markings were no longer drips and smears but covered the rough stone floor.

Antoine felt his heart pound as memories from the past raced through his mind. Memories that rarely visited him when he was awake. It was all too much, and he feared that he might pass out. Instead, he made his excuses to leave. Casting one last glance around the room, he scrambled out backwards, feeling his way up the stairs in the dark.

Chapter 5

The next day, Turnbull went off to Dunse in search of provisions while the others cleared away the worst of the wreckage. After fishing out anything that could be repaired or put on the fire, they carried the rest outside and dumped it by the perimeter wall.

While doing this, they were alarmed to see two men ride up. They were clad in brigandines: canvas waistcoats with small pieces of metal sewn in. The soldiers could see swords swinging by their sides and put a hand on their own weapons.

"Good morrow!" called one of the visitors, an older man with a bald head and straggly grey beard. He dismounted and walked towards the soldiers, hands in the air. The younger man followed, clutching both horses' reins. "We are river bailiffs from Coldstream and have been ordered here by the new warden. We can show ye a letter, carrying his seal, if ye wish!"

Hands trembling, the old man reached into a pannier on his horse's flank and pulled out a parchment. Anderson allowed him to advance, and seeing that the seal appeared legitimate, he ordered his men to escort the pair to the barmekin while he fetched his master.

In truth, Antoine was a little irritated when the serjeant came knocking at his chamber door as he had been chewing over the scene they had uncovered the previous night: the icy cell, the leg irons, the gore. As he trudged downstairs, he tortured himself with the sickening familiarity of it all. It was only when he stumbled over that trip-step, which Anderson had warned him about, that he told himself to snap out of it. Picking himself up, he resolved to revisit the dungeon later, but for now, he needed to concentrate on the odd couple who shuffled before him.

"God bless ye, my lord," said the older man, bowing deeply. As he straightened up, Antoine could see that he hardly had a tooth in his head. "I am Thomas Heron, and this is my son, Cuddy."

"Ha! Heron's a fine name for a pair who watch rivers," said Antoine, who enjoyed such plays on words. He hoped to put the men at their ease, but the trick did not seem to have worked. "And who do you work for on the Tweed?"

"The Prioress of Coldstream, sir. The nuns own that stretch and employ us to mind it for them. They're Cistercians, so handle most o' the fishing and farming themselves but use us for some muscle."

"I see," said Antoine. "Well, you must have your work cut out, for most round here are not as godly as the good sisters."

"Yes sir," said the old man, flexing his fingers by his sides. "It's a constant battle."

"I can imagine. So tell me how you came to find this poor soul's body. Everything you know, mind. From start to finish."

The father and son exchanged awkward glances before young Cuddy Heron took up the story. "Well, we began work just afore dusk, as is our custom. We launched our coble frae the priory and lurked in the rushes there, but all was still, so when the Lauds bell rang, we decided to take a look upstream. There are some deep pools by the Truce Day Island, where the salmon gather for their autumn run."

"And where salmon gather, so do villains…" murmured Antoine.

Cuddy's eyelids flickered. "Aye," he said. "Indeed we'd no' been there long when my father nudged me and pointed to some lights on the river."

"That's how they do it here," interjected the old man. "They burn tar-soaked rags to bring the fish to the surface – then spear them wi' long forks."

"We made out a boat wi' three men in it," Cuddy Heron went on, apparently eager to finish his account. "They lurked over the pools awhile – like our namesakes, ye might say. Then they threw in their leisters – their forks – and quickly pulled their ropes back in to check for a catch. Maybe three or four times, they did this, although wi' nothing to show for their troubles. They were whispering as best they could, but ye cannae silence a splash, so we used their noise to push off frae the bank and glide a little towards them. We got about half-way over before they spotted us and made off."

"Did you get a look at them?" Antoine probed. "Or see which way they went?"

The old man was quick to reply. "No, we chased them downstream, but it was still an hour to dawn, and the light was poor. They likely got off at Wark – so I suppose they were English."

"Perhaps," said Antoine, tapping a finger on his lips. "I daresay they're unlikely to be our killers anyway. They'd hardly dump a body and then go for a little fishing trip afterwards. But we will search for them all the same."

Cuddy Heron clenched his fists. "Of course," he said.

"So let's get to this body. Could it have been placed on the island while you chased your thieves?"

"No, sir. We did not stray far and would have noticed another boat going across, for sure."

"What if the killer was already on the island and used your commotion to drag the body out?"

"No, we'd have seen that, too. Or caught him as he left the island. So I believe it must have been there all along, it was just that the darkness deceived us."

"Yes, I agree," said Antoine. "Most likely, it was ferried over between dusk and Lauds, while you were stationed at the priory. But wait – you said you'd chased the thieves downstream. What took you back to the island?"

The men looked at each other as if trying to decide who should speak first. After a pause, the young man continued in a faltering voice. "Sometimes the poachers come back for more... when they think the fish have settled and we have gone. So we made back to our hidey hole and watched again. Another hour or so went by, and then we heard the Prime bell ring for dawn. That's our signal to go hame, but just as we started off, we saw that... thing lying there. Bright red it was, like a butcher's carcass – which, of course, is just what we found when we went over, and..."

The old man came to his assistance. "It was truly hideous. A bloody chunk o' meat, a' covered in maggots and flies – like something the Devil himself might have roasted on a spit."

"Was the body stiff?" asked Antoine. "Or the blood sticky?"

"Neither, sir," said Cuddy. "It had loosened up again, and the gore had dried, as if he'd been deid a while. I remember that, because when we lifted it – him – intae the coble, our hands sank intae the flesh."

Antoine tutted. "What about the surrounding area? Did you see anything out of the ordinary?"

"No' that I recall, although I confess we didnae make a search until the next day. We wanted to secure the body afore the birds got it, so we took it back to the priory and the prioress had it buried."

"Well, we will have to pay the island a visit – and the prioress, too, by the sounds of it. But for now, I thank you for your assistance. We have many other matters to attend to, so I cannot guarantee that we will catch this killer, but we will certainly do our utmost."

Antoine bade the men a cordial farewell, but there was something about their account that did not quite tally. Perhaps Turnbull could talk to them again and make more sense of it. For his part, though, he resolved to rise above such trivia and engage men of his own station from now on. If he could pacify the Humes and form some kind of relationship with Lord Dacre, he would get home much sooner than if he went around conversing with toothless riverfolk about bits of rotten flesh.

Chapter 6

After the bailiffs had left, the men returned to work, and Antoine spotted his chance to revisit the dungeon alone. He walked around the base of the tower in a purposeful manner that would ward off conversation. Pausing at the entrance, he steeled himself and yanked open the door. It was still gloomy inside, but there was no need for a torch at this hour. The rusty marks were unmistakeable, but at least this time, he was prepared for the sight that lay in store.

As he entered the second cell, he took a deep breath, and his lungs filled with that same cold, damp air he remembered from another life. However, instead of allowing his imagination to drag himself back to those dark days, he focused on the present. He crouched by the pallet and waved his hands through the straw, but there was nothing there except spiders and mites. The clay bowl was similarly unhelpful: it carried no distinctive marks and had lost any scent it might once have had. Still, Antoine held it in his hands, turning it over as he walked around the room. He paid particular attention to the walls and floor, lest somebody had scrawled a name or message, but again, nothing – apart from the odd scrap of wool.

He began to relax. In truth, he had no idea how old the

blood was or how recently this place had been occupied. For all he knew, he could be raking over the ashes of a long-forgotten crime. He prepared to return to the surface, but just then, he heard the upstairs door slam shut, and he was plunged into darkness. A jeering laugh followed.

"Holy God," he said aloud and threw his arms out, dropping the clay bowl with a smash. It was pitch black, and he had no sense of his position in the room. He reckoned the door was behind him, but he had been so deep in thought that he could not be sure.

At the sound of more jeering from upstairs, he lunged forward, with greater urgency. Who could have trapped him this way? And what did they want of him? As he grappled with these questions, he barked his shin on something. It must be the pallet. Leaning over, he put both hands on a cold, slimy surface and felt his way around until he came to a more even plane. The cell's door? He was relieved that this pushed open easily and slid his right foot forwards to find the first step. Then, putting a hand on each wall, he came slowly up the stairs, fumbling for his sword as he reached the top.

He found the outer door in front of him. No doubt it would be bolted, but how sturdy would it be? He gave it an almighty shove with his left shoulder and was amazed to find that it swung wide open, causing him to fall forward. The tip of his sword clattered against the ground.

When he looked up, the shock on his face was matched only by that on Anderson's.

"What's happened, sir? I had nae idea ye were there."

"I could say the same to you," said Antoine as he picked himself up. A group of soldiers watched him nervously. "I was just taking another look at that dungeon. Who in the name of Jesu closed the door?"

There was an awkward silence until a youth named Wilson piped up. "We were clearing the rubbish away frae the entrance, and I thought it'd been left open by accident. I am sorry, sir."

Anderson clipped Wilson around the ear. "So ye should be, you clot. But if it's any consolation, sir, I think we've solved the mystery of a' that blood." With a grin, he reached into the pile of barrels by the entrance and pulled out a sheep's carcass. A few pieces of rancid meat still hung from its bones.

"It looks like someone slaughtered this beast, dragged it down there to butcher and then dumped the remains up here. They'd have got a nice fleecy coat and a tasty stew to boot. Meanwhile, our own muttonhead has got a new friend." He pushed the animal's skull up against Wilson's face, and the men guffawed: it was the same jeering laughter as before. Antoine remembered the pieces of wool he had found on the floor and allowed himself a wry smile. As Francoise had often said, overthinking would be his downfall one of these days.

Dunse was a destitute settlement on top of a windswept hill. It could hardly be said to have a centre, but in so much as it did, there was a little square with a tavern, a smithy and a couple of poorly stocked stores. Turnbull ordered his three men to dismount here and tether their horses to a flimsy wooden rail.

They entered the White Hart cautiously, half-expecting that it might be hiding an army of men, but it was quite empty. A tinker sat in one corner with a basket of scissors, needles and knives laid out beside him. Two old men played cards. A dog sniffed about the tables in the hope of being thrown a scrap. The innkeeper introduced himself as Richard

Purves and offered them some ale and pottage. When he brought it over, they invited him to join them.

"Ach, I'm no' sure about that," said Purves. "There's a lot to dae right now, so I must stay busy."

Turnbull surveyed the empty room. "A lot to do, eh? You look like you could do with some extra custom to me, so hear me out. I have a proposal that might interest you."

Purves waved a hand. "I really dinnae think so, although it's kind of ye to offer. I can see ye're after more than your dinner – ye had that look on your face when ye came in – but whatever it is, I'd rather no' get involved."

"Ah, don't be so hasty, friend. Will you not sit with us awhile so that we can say our piece?"

"Honestly, I—"

One of the men – a stout fellow called Nisbet – clapped the innkeeper on the shoulder. "We're with the new warden, and we're in a hurry. Now, pull up a stool."

Purves flicked his head to the tinker and the old men, who packed up their things and made themselves scarce. The innkeeper was a short fellow with a round face and a whiskery moustache – rather like a wildcat, Turnbull thought. No doubt he could be as vicious as one, too, if required. But for now, he exhibited a weary pragmatism.

"No disrespect to the new warden," said Purves, joining the table. "But the spirit o' the old one is still alive and well round here. The Humes may have lost a couple of castles, but they still have a thousand men on their side. And they'll be here long after ye go back to Edinburgh – or France, for that matter."

"I understand," said Turnbull. "We certainly lack numbers at this moment, but recruitment is next on my list. So I urge you not to underestimate my master. He comes here under direct orders from Governor Albany, to bring peace to the Marches. And I can assure you that we will be going nowhere until we have achieved this. As for the future, this is your opportunity to find favour with him and profit from it."

"How so?"

"We need allies. People on the ground who can ease our way."

The innkeeper narrowed his eyes. "How d'ye mean?"

"Well, for a start, we need someone who can supply us with food, drink, tools, timber and a host of household things."

The innkeeper rubbed the back of his neck, and Turnbull detected that he might be inhibited by the soldiers' presence. In truth, he had been vexed by Nisbet's intervention himself: he had felt it carried some implication that he could not handle the situation. He sent the men off to guard the doors and continued in more hushed tones. "As you can imagine, we will pay well for this. Enough to make it worth your while."

"There's nae point making money if it's just paying for ma funeral," said Purves. "If I wanted to dae that, I could collect the bodies when the plague's next in town."

"We can protect you. We're meeting Hume tomorrow and will tell him to behave. Otherwise, we will call in the full might of the governor's army."

The innkeeper tapped his fingers on the table, and Turnbull sensed that he was coming round to the proposal. The man sighed. "Very well, but we would have to be discreet. Come back here the morn and I'll have a plan. Then stay away after that."

"Of course. We'll keep this quiet."

"I won't be able to get it all on ma own, either. I'll have to involve others and they'll want a cut."

"That's your choice. We don't need to know."

"Then it will a' come down to coin. How much are we talking, and when can I have it?"

"We can discuss that later," said Turnbull, relieved that the momentum had passed to him. "But before we do, there is one other question I have for you. It's unrelated to our arrangement but important to us nonetheless." He raised his chin. "Do you know if anybody round here has gone missing this past week?"

The innkeeper looked at him slyly. "How d'ye mean missing?"

"Something out of the ordinary. A man who's not shown up for work or who's vanished from his home, say."

Purves wrinkled his nose. "The only person that fits that bill is a fellow called Blackeyed Bob, a swarthy sort wi' dark manners to match. He's fond o' an ale in here, but people are no' so fond o' him. He normally comes in every day, but we havenae seen him for a week."

Turnbull was excited by this unexpected intelligence. He could tell that his master had little interest in the Coldstream murder, so perhaps he could re-establish some favour with him by solving it quickly. Certainly, he had received no other suggestions of missing persons from that rogue Meikle. If he could clear this up himself, he could focus the scrivener on the more important task of recruiting some men.

"Well, at least we have a description of him and a sense of his character. But what's his full name, this Blackeyed Bob?"

Purves gave him an odd look, and Turnbull understood that he wanted payment. He took a silver coin from his purse and slid it across the table. The innkeeper reached for it greedily, but Turnbull quickly closed his hand. "You'll get it when you give me an answer," he said.

"Fair enough," Purves replied. He checked that the others were not listening. Then he leant across the table, his hand cupped around his mouth. Turnbull drew closer, too, his skin prickling with anticipation. But when the answer came, his heart sank to his boots.

"He's called Robert Meikle. He's the scrivener round here."

Chapter 7

That night, Antoine's first sleep passed peacefully enough. This was normal for him: he found that he could drop off relatively easily, no matter what troubles he had on his mind. Only during his second sleep would the Devil pay a visit. He had tried all manner of remedies for this – even sleeping straight through the night, as unnatural as that was – but he was rarely able to escape the storm clouds that swirled around his head in those hours before dawn. The only method which worked was work itself, and so while others spent their watch – the interval between their two bouts of slumber – talking idly or enjoying the pleasures of the flesh, he spent his with quill and parchment.

As was his habit, he began to set out his thoughts, by the dim light of an oil lamp. He looked at Turnbull, still asleep on his truckle, and had to admit that the lad had done well in finding a provisioner. His news about Meikle was troubling, though. If the torso in the river truly were the scrivener's, it would support the suspicion that dark forces were working against them. Currently, they were just inky shadows, sketched out in front of him with a murky concoction of oak gall, vitriol and gum arabic. But as he retired for his second sleep, Antoine had a feeling that his enemies would soon reveal themselves in flesh and blood.

The meeting with Hume had been scheduled for noon at Earl's Meadow, just outside of Dunse. It was a wide-open space with little opportunity for concealment. Anderson ensured they arrived early, to identify possible escape routes should the conversation turn ugly. After eyeing up a few alternatives, they agreed to take up position on the near side of the field, which would allow them to make off along the Langton road if necessary.

It was a bright day but still cold, and the ground was hard. The men wiggled their boots in their stirrups, and Antoine shivered, even though he was wearing his best miniver-lined coat. They looked towards the East, where the Humes' remaining strongholds were, but there were no signs of activity there beyond a few wisps of smoke from the outlying cottages. Then, gradually, there was a low rumble – from the south.

They turned to see a large group of men riding towards them, to their right. They were perhaps a hundred strong, although it was hard to tell as their steel bonnets flashed in the midday sun. They were moving at a steady canter, untroubled by the hard going, the noise building to a veritable thunder.

Antoine's men were in danger of being cut off from their route home. They wheeled around to face the oncoming horde but readied their spurs to make a break before it was too late. The other group was only a couple of hundred yards away and still moving at an unsettling speed. The ground shook, and individual faces became visible. Then, just as Antoine was about to give the order to move off, the others came to an abrupt halt. Both sides stayed still, and the only sound was the snorting of horses, causing clouds of hot breath to rise into the pale blue sky.

After a while, one man rode forward at walking pace. He was not wearing body armour but a leather jack. When he reached the middle of the field, he stopped and padded about on the spot.

"Is that Hume, do you think?" asked Turnbull.

"They're all Humes, that's our problem," said Anderson. "But I doubt it's George Hume if that's what ye mean. More likely, a lieutenant sent to sound us out. You or I should go to meet him."

Antoine waited for Turnbull to respond, but, for once, the young man seemed tongue-tied. Was that fear in his eyes?

"I suppose I'll go then," said Anderson pointedly, nudging his horse forward over the rutted meadow.

The others watched as he reached the middle, stopped a few yards from the other man and began to talk. They strained to hear the conversation or even detect its tone, but it was too far away, and neither side made any tell-tale gestures. Occasionally, Antoine would scan their surroundings to ensure this was not a distraction for some other mischief. The interaction seemed to take an eternity, but eventually, both parties turned and rode back to their respective sides.

"That was Hume's kinsman, Wedderburn," said Anderson on his return. "Hume asks for a face-to-face meeting wi' you, my lord. Just the two of you and no weapons. I thought that'd be permissible, given the circumstances."

"Yes," said Antoine. "We can hardly refuse. But tell me: what tone did their man take in making this request? Did he sound genuine, or is there trickery afoot?"

"Oh, he was as sweet as sugar," said Anderson. "That's what worries me."

Despite these misgivings, Antoine handed him his sword and set off for the middle ground. He watched a figure on the other side do the same, although it was only once he was almost there that he realised he still had no way of knowing whether this was Hume. Whoever it was, he was a small, sinewy man with a broken nose. He bowed extravagantly from the saddle, but his narrow eyes exuded malice.

"Bonjour to you, Monsieur Warden. Allow me to introduce myself: George Hume, the fourth Lord Hume. I believe you're staying in one of my towers."

"One of your former towers," Antoine corrected him. "Now requisitioned by our governor."

"Well, I hope it brings you all the comfort you deserve."

Antoine understood the hostile meaning but decided the wreckage of Black Rig was not worth a confrontation. "It's just as I expected, thank you."

Hume smiled. "That's good to hear. We wouldn't want you to feel unwelcome. We even came here light-handed as we'd heard you were small in number. Although we didn't realise just how small."

"I appreciate it," said Antoine, who could already sense that this conversation was unlikely to yield a miraculous reconciliation. "Ours is just an advance party, of course. We didn't want to rub your nose in it, given your family's recent losses."

For a moment, he wondered whether he had gone too far, but the warlord did not blink. Perhaps it was time for a more direct approach. "Listen, Hume," he said. "I understand that my appointment will not be to your liking. It's not necessarily to my taste, either. But I am here to offer you a fresh start. If you can help me enforce the law, or at least not stand in my way, you will be rewarded. If you obstruct me, though, things will end badly."

"That's a reasonable offer," replied Hume. "But you

must remember that the laws of Edinburgh and London count for little here. We've got our own code to settle things: the March Laws."

"I'm well aware of that. They're based on Leviticus, aren't they? A fracture for a fracture, an eye for an eye, a tooth for a tooth."

"Bravo, monsieur, somebody has schooled you well. Some see us as savages, but we have rules for everything: how many days we have to take revenge, how far we may go with our retribution, how much coin each life is worth. It's just that our laws are less about keeping the peace and more about managing the flow of blood."

Antoine shrugged. "It's an interesting distinction, but I would hope we could achieve both, in time. Perhaps with your help, we might do so – and we could prosper together?"

"Alas, we do not feel the urge to help right now. And as for time, you'll find people are impatient around here. They like their justice fast." A wicked glint flashed in Hume's eye, as if he were enjoying a private joke. "Indeed, it's just as well Bob Meikle had no friends, or they'd be banging down your door already."

Antoine was taken aback at the mention of the scrivener's name. He had not intended to raise the issue until later, but now Hume had done it for him. Was it a double-bluff designed to show his innocence? Or an act of bravado intended to provoke? Either way, the Frenchman found himself wrong-footed.

"What do you mean by that? Are you referring to this strange murder in Coldstream?"

Hume smirked. "You tell me. The corpse was discovered a week ago, but you still don't seem to know a thing about it. Apart from the fact it's likely Blackeyed Bob."

The man was taunting him, but Antoine was determined to stay calm. "And what's Meikle to you? You speak as if you knew him?"

"Of course, he was a well-kent face, if not a well-loved one. He had so many enemies, you'll look a fool if you cannot tie a noose around one."

"Then help me out if you know who might be responsible. Who would chop a man into pieces like that?"

Hume's face darkened. "Your master Albany, for a start. But as for others, you must work it out yourself." He paused to give a wolfish smile. "Or beg Lord Dacre's help."

At the mention of the English Warden, Antoine shifted in his saddle. Dacre had not even acknowledged his appointment yet, let alone shown any inclination to collaborate. It was a reminder that silence could be a weapon, as barbed as any insult.

Hume seemed to read his mind as he gave a dry chuckle. "No word from Dacre then? A shame." He gathered his reins. "Well, my only other counsel would be to question that sorceress Catherine Gray of Cheeklaw. But best do it quickly, before things are taken out of your hands."

Antoine was about to ask what he meant by that, but Hume had already turned his horse sharply, causing it to rear. Before the reiver returned to his men, he pulled back his cloak – to ensure the Frenchman saw the dagger hidden in his belt.

"Until the next time, warden," he said. "Au revoir."

Chapter 8

As the Humes thundered off again, Antoine updated the others. "I think it's safe to say that we can expect no help from him. Well, at least we have looked each other in the eye."

"Did you confront him over Meikle's disappearance?" asked Turnbull as they turned their horses around.

Antoine was about to snap that the lad should set aside this obsession with the river murder, but the way Hume had mentioned the case unnerved him. Especially how he had framed it as a test of his authority. Perhaps the case deserved more of his attention, after all.

"I had no need. He did it for me. He claimed no involvement with it, of course."

"Naturally. But did you believe him?"

"I am sure he intimidated Meikle – the slighting of our tower is the clearest proof of that. Whether or not he killed him is another matter."

"Aye," said Anderson. "It sounds like the scrivener didnae lack enemies."

Turnbull frowned. "But not ones that would despoil a body so. That's why the finger points at Hume, surely? Only he had a reason to send such a public signal – either to proclaim vengeance for his brothers or to threaten those who would help us. Probably both."

"I admit your theory grows on me," said Antoine. "But let's not close our minds just yet. Hume mentioned another name that we should investigate. A sorceress, apparently, named Catherine Gray of Cheeklaw."

Turnbull gave a little snort.

"Not a believer in such maleficence, then?" said Antoine with a wry smile. "I share your doubt. But I fear that few round here will. So I'd better take Wilson and Burnsie to check this woman out – you take the rest to Purves."

The path to Cheeklaw took them through an ancient oak forest. On the far side were a couple of simple dwellings made with strips of wood and earth. An old man was feeding chickens and seemed to stare at the soldiers as they approached. It was only when they got closer that they realised he was blind. With his milky eyes, pale skin and white hair, he looked like a ghost, and the two soldiers crossed themselves instinctively as they passed. Antoine asked the old man for directions, and he gestured to the other house before turning back to his fowl as they raked about the golden carpet of leaves.

The men dismounted at the second cottage and took in their surroundings. This house was better kept than the other, with freshly whitewashed walls and a neat little herb garden by the front door. Antoine recognised some familiar plants, such as rosemary, sage and lavender, but many others were strange to him. Without even meeting the owner, he could imagine how a house like this would be viewed suspiciously. The relief on the men's faces when he told them to wait outside was palpable.

He approached the front door and raised his hand to

knock, only for it to open and a woman to appear. Antoine was immediately struck by her eyes: they were as green as the forest itself and seemed infinitely deep. He obtained only a fleeting glimpse, before she averted them, but he thought he recognised the same melancholy that he sometimes found in his own countenance.

"Good day, mistress – we are looking for a Catherine Gray."

"That is me, sir. And I suppose you must be the new warden?"

Antoine was startled by her guess, and the woman smiled awkwardly.

"Do not worry – I am no soothsayer, whatever folk might say. I heard your accent. Ye speak well, but there's no' many Frenchmen round here."

Antoine was at once relieved and embarrassed by the false leap he had made: it was another caution against his tendency to over-contemplate. He looked at the woman again and found her pleasingly unremarkable: she had no warts or hairy lip as he might have expected. A white linen coif covered her auburn hair with the appropriate level of modesty. She wore a thick woollen kirtle down to her ankles and full sleeves. In short, there was nothing lewd or malevolent about her appearance – she seemed like an ordinary woman of about thirty. Or at least someone who was determined to present herself as an ordinary woman of about thirty.

"I have come to ask some questions about a vexing matter," Antoine said, collecting himself. "May I come in? My men will stay outside if that pleases you."

She welcomed him in, and he saw that the interior was as neatly appointed as the exterior. All the pieces of furniture were arranged at straight angles, in their own spots. A pot bubbled quietly on the open hearth. There was no clutter or even a speck of dust. Only a perfectly aligned row of jars on the kitchen dresser hinted at any industry.

The woman offered Antoine a stool by the fire, and he was glad to feel a little warmth in his bones for the first time that day. "Well, Mistress Gray, I compliment you on the order of your house."

She shifted her eyes again and spoke quietly but clearly. "Thank you, sir. I like to keep things tidy and in their place."

"And have you always lived here?"

She hesitated. "Since my parents died and my brother took on our house by Upsettlington. That would be over ten years ago."

"You don't find it lonely, living here alone?"

"No, old Gibb is a good neighbour – his heart is strong even if his eyes are no'. And I am surrounded by nature. I find the birds and the beasts make fine companions without subjecting me to the irksome demands of our species."

Antoine nodded, for he had often thought the same. "Yes, there is much truth in that. But how do you make a living out here?"

She arranged a fold in her apron so that it was flat against her kirtle, pressing it down three times. "I help folk wi' their ailments. There is no monastery for miles, so people come to me wi' their aches and agues. Sometimes wi' their animals, too. I cannot cure them a', but I do what I can."

"And how do you treat them?" Antoine was getting to the heart of the matter and spoke very deliberately, looking the woman in the eye as he did so. For once, she held his gaze and replied with equal precision.

"Using the herbs and seeds that God has given us. For as

it says in Genesis, He gave us dominion over all the vegetation of the earth, and He saw that it was good."

It was unusual to hear a woman quote the bible so expertly, almost as if it were a rehearsed defence. It unsettled Antoine, made him wonder where she had learnt to speak this way. "You are a good Christian then?"

"No, not at all," she said, leaving an uncomfortably long pause. "I am an abject sinner. That's why I pray to the Lord to forgive me, and I hope He considers my work penance of sorts."

"Well said, we are all sinners," said Antoine, his mind momentarily drifting to his own affairs. He tilted his head as if to empty those thoughts out. "But some more so than others. And it is on such a wicked matter that I come to you today. You see, I am investigating a murder in Coldstream – not far from where you grew up."

He did not intend those last words to be accusatory, but they hung in the air for a moment before the woman replied, those green eyes now looking weary. "I have heard of this. It sounds like a diabolical affair, which is no doubt why someone has pointed me out to ye."

Antoine laid a hand on his chest. "I swear I have no preconceptions, Mistress Gray. But of course, I must investigate when a new name comes to my attention. So tell me, do you know anything of this heinous act?"

She balled her fists. "No, I swear to ye on Christ's bones."

"Do you know who might be responsible for it?"

"I do not."

"Do you know who the victim might be?"

"I have nae clue."

Antoine looked hard at the woman. "And have you ever had any dealings with a gentleman named Robert Meikle?"

The woman fussed with her apron again; even though it was perfectly straight, she flattened it three times, as if it were folded. "I know of him. He's the local scrivener, but I've never had any need o' him."

"You have never quarrelled with him nor had cause to do so?"

"I've never even met him. Why? Is he responsible for this murder? I had thought him a bad man but no' a killer."

"He appears to be the victim," said Antoine, watching her face. "But you swear to me on everything that is holy that you know nothing of this?"

"That I can say."

Antoine reflected on the evidence in front of him. The idea of this slender, fidgety woman dismembering a man seemed fanciful – even allowing for some form of infernal assistance. There was something odd about her, though. Her fussing spoke to a troubled mind, and he felt there was something she was not telling him.

"Well, Mistress Gray," he said, standing up. "I will not detain you further. But I may return the morn if further questions occur to me."

As he left, he was not sure why he had said that. He should really get Turnbull to follow up if necessary. Did this woman remind him of Francoise? Was that it? There was surely no resemblance either physically or in temperament, and yet he was drawn to her somehow. He made a note to watch himself for any unhelpful emotions of this kind. This mission was proving difficult enough already without further complications.

Chapter 9

Turnbull was still churned up by the meeting on Earl's Meadow. He was embarrassed by how frightened he had felt and worried that it had been obvious to the others. Perhaps this was why Anderson had suggested he go forward to meet Hume's lackey. Old soldiers like him looked down on students, so maybe this had been his way of putting him in his place.

The truth was that Turnbull had always been keenly aware of his position in life. As the third son of the local laird, he had been destined for a clerical career from the moment he was born. His father had favoured his older sons, who shared his enjoyment of drinking, fighting and hunting – while 'Wee Dod' was cossetted by his mother. He was not strong, although he sometimes wondered whether this was the result of paternal neglect rather than the cause. Either way, his father did not bother to school him in the usual ways of being a man, and he was sent off to St Andrews at thirteen. A career in the church or the law beckoned until Flodden thrust him forward.

Now here he was, back in the Marches, where his studies in logic and geometry counted for nothing. With his accent long gone and his family mostly departed he was as much of an outsider as his master was.

This idea boiled away in Turnbull's head. The more he

thought about it, the more he determined that he must toughen up – or else he would be no use on this mission at all. So when he reached the Langton road, he shifted back in the saddle to bring Fogo to a halt. "I'll go on into Dunse myself," he said. "It might unsettle Purves if we arrive mob-handed."

Anderson drew his brows together. "I dinnae think that's wise, sir. All it takes is one peasant who's had a flagon too many, and then ye're in trouble."

"I think I'm capable of handling some fox-drunk carl," replied Turnbull. "Besides, we shouldn't leave the tower unguarded for too long. For all we know, the Humes are there now, wrecking it again."

"Then at least take a couple of men wi' ye, while I take the others hame."

"Really, there's no need. It might strengthen our hand if I go on my own because the locals will see we're not afraid."

As he said the words, Turnbull felt how hollow they were. But at least he did not detect any mockery on the men's faces. Reluctantly, Anderson agreed to the plan, and they parted company. Turnbull started up the hill, affecting a casual farewell as he did so. Once he'd turned his back, he closed his eyes and considered what he had just got himself into.

The town was much busier today as there was a market on. Dairy girls, buttermen, fruitmongers and brewsters shouted out to the goodwives who milled about the mercat cross. A flesher spread out some hides and scraped off slithers of meat into grimy parcels. A baxter sent his lad running alongside Turnbull, offering him fresh-baked oat bannocks for a ha'penny. He was persistent and Turnbull eventually relented, on condition that the boy minded Fogo while he was in the White Hart.

Turnbull entered the inn, which was also much livelier than it had been the day before. Groups of men sat drinking at the trestle tables. A gaggle of women – farmworkers, judging by their clothes – were having a heated conversation, punctuated by gales of saucy laughter. Turnbull felt a little exposed as he approached the counter. He surveyed the premises and saw that Purves was busy changing a keg of ale. When the innkeeper turned round, Turnbull was alarmed to see that his face was ruddy and violent.

"You again?"

Turnbull was not sure how to answer this question, as it had been Purves himself who had suggested the return visit. He settled on what he hoped would be an inoffensive reply. "Yes, I'm here to continue our conversation." He spoke quietly, to avoid attracting the attention of others.

"Ye've got a cheek." Purves spat the words out.

"I'm sorry?" Turnbull really was confused now.

"Aye, ye will be if ye dinnae leave my inn. I served ye some ale and pottage yesterday as ye'd travelled a long way. But I'll have no more to do wi' ye."

Turnbull began to protest, but by this stage, Purves had come round the counter and had him by the right arm. He was panicking, unsure how to react. He considered drawing his sword as a warning, but Purves held his elbow in a tight grip. Besides, that would only escalate the situation – the room was full of armed men who would likely take the innkeeper's side. And what did he know of fighting anyway? He felt the men's eyes on him, leering over the tops of their ales, and heard the raucous laughter of those farmgirls again.

"What the hell's got into you?" hissed Turnbull as he was

huckled out of the door. He could not believe the transformation in this fellow, the venom that he oozed. He could only imagine that thinking about Meikle had made him reconsider their deal, for fear of being Hume's next victim. He jerked his elbow in an attempt to free himself, but Purves had him by his collar and pushed him against the wall.

As the goodwives and traders stepped back from the struggle, Turnbull wrenched himself free, trying to use his superior height and reach to keep the innkeeper at bay. But again, Purves shoved him back, ramming his meaty forearm into the lad's throat. He wondered whether this was it: would he meet his end in this squalid town, in a foolish attempt to prove his masculinity?

Purves' face was so near that Turnbull could smell his fetid breath. The innkeeper leant in closer and closer, and Turnbull waited for a dagger to enter his ribcage or for the man's foul teeth to gouge his ear. But instead, Purves whispered something.

"Sorry about that, my friend. The place was full o' Hume's men, so we werenae safe. But someone will deliver the goods to your tower at dawn. Trust me."

Chapter 10

Sure enough, when the men woke, the provisions were waiting for them. They had been left outside the main gate in a messy pile as if the bringers had been in a hurry. Judging by their tracks, the nocturnal quartermasters had used an ox and cart, but apart from that, there were few clues as to their identity.

"Maybe a friendly sprite has come to our aid," joked one of the men as they began to ferry the goods to the tower.

"You're laughing," scolded another as he rolled a barrel of water through the gate, "but little folk called redcaps are known to live in places such as this. We should leave them a bowl o' cream as a reward. After all, we could do wi' all the help we can get."

Superstitions aside, the appearance of the provisions lifted the men's spirits as they looked forward to a decent meal for the first time since their arrival. The sound of whistling and laughter echoed around the walls. The delicious aromas of fresh bread, green cheese, game and stockfish filled the air. Turnbull ticked off the items as they entered the barmekin, and he made sure that nobody helped themselves. However, he did so with good humour, so relieved was he that his original mistake had been rectified.

Even Antoine's mood was buoyed as he observed the activity before him. Watching from his window, he reflected that they could now feed the troops and rebuild their home, so that some of the basic comforts would be in place. This, in turn, would allow him to focus on bigger challenges – and ultimately bring him closer to Paris.

It was in this fine fettle that the Frenchman rode out to Cheeklaw to finish his conversation with Catherine Gray. He took Wilson and Burnsie with him again, securing their presence with one of the newly arrived pigeon pies. The three of them tore into it as they rode and enthused about the feast they would have when they returned. They were still chattering merrily when they entered the woods, but as they approached the clearing, they heard a woman's scream: a single, piercing shriek.

All three men immediately fell silent and pulled their horses to a halt. Antoine put his index finger to his lips, and they listened for a moment, but nothing further came. In this heightened state, they became aware of every tiny movement in the forest. A cool breeze sent a shiver through the trees. A jay paused its burial of an acorn, looking directly at the men before resuming its scrabbling in the leaves. They soothed their horses and strained for further sounds.

The screaming started again. It was more insistent now, like the howl of an animal caught in a snare. Antoine felt sure that the woman's voice belonged to Catherine Gray, but he could also hear men shouting. He motioned Wilson and Burnsie to advance, and all three of them spurred their horses into a brisk trot. At this speed, they had to be wary of low-hanging boughs and overgrown roots. The journey was short, but it seemed to last for an age as their thoughts raced ahead of them to what they might discover.

When they reached the cottages, they pulled up again. Old Gibb was lying on the ground with a bloodied head. One hand fumbled at the wound to his face. A dark patch had spread around the crotch of his hose. Antoine bent down from his saddle to inspect him, but as he did so, he saw the source of the commotion – and no doubt the man's injuries – up ahead. Hume and half a dozen of his gang were crowded around Catherine Gray's cottage, dragging her out of the door.

Antoine and his two companions rode forward. "What the hell is going on?" the Frenchman shouted as he got closer.

Hume was still mounted while his troops manhandled the woman. "That's just what we've been asking this witch," he snarled.

Catherine wailed as one of the men pulled at her. She was bent double and clutching the top of her head as the fellow yanked her by the roots of her hair. Her coif had fallen to the ground, and her kirtle was torn. She cut a piteous figure, unrecognisable as the neat, articulate woman Antoine had met the previous day.

"Let go of her, you oaf," he said, but the man simply snorted and looked to his master for instruction. As the fellow turned his face, Antoine recognised him as Hume's kinsman, Wedderburn.

"Why would we let go of a murderess?" said Hume. "I told you she might be to blame for Meikle's death, but you would not listen."

"Do as I say," repeated Antoine. He dismounted and left the others to tether Carbonel. "I will not tolerate any interference with my duties."

"What do you know of duties? This sorceress has butchered a man like a pig, and you've done nothing about it."

"I have already spoken to Mistress Gray and am satisfied with her response for now."

"Then she has enchanted ye," said Wedderburn. "Or ye've failed to ask the right questions."

"That is for me to decide. Now unhand the woman and let me deal with it."

Hume looked at him intently, then gestured to Wedderburn to release Catherine. She continued to sob while she straightened her hair and rearranged her clothing.

"As you will," said Hume, a cruel smile flickering about his lips. "But once we've gone, perhaps you should ask her about her feud with Meikle. And why she has concealed it from you."

Antoine glowered at Catherine, but she was in no state to answer the charge. She just sat on the ground with her hands over her face. The Frenchman shook his head wearily.

"Just go, Hume. And stay out of this business. We will find the killer soon enough, you can be sure of that."

Hume's men mounted their horses and clattered off into the forest, shouting insults over their shoulders. Antoine inspected the wreckage that they had left behind. The cottage door was coming off its hinges, and the herb garden had been trampled over. Broken jars lay on the path, their lurid contents oozing out into the cold earth. Meanwhile, Wilson and Burnsie – who had barely moved during the altercation with Hume – had drawn their swords and stared at Catherine. Antoine did not like the glint in their eyes and sent Wilson to check on Gibb. He ordered Burnsie to stay outside the cottage while he helped Catherine to her feet and led her back inside.

The house was in an even sorrier state than the garden. "No, no, no!" Catherine groaned as she flung herself at the mess. Antoine attempted to help by picking up a stool that had been knocked over, but she snatched it off him and carefully put it back in the corner. She rearranged what was left of the jars on the dresser, only to cry with frustration and move them around again. Antoine was alarmed by the intensity with which she worked. She seemed possessed; there was no other word for it. Still, he allowed her to tidy the worst of it before putting a hand on her shoulder.

"Mistress Gray," he said softly. "We need to talk."

Reluctantly, she sat down, but she would not meet his eyes. "Those men are animals," she said. "They speak of justice, but they want only blood. Just look at my poor house. All is ruined, utterly ruined!"

"We will see to them in due course. But now I need you to calm yourself. They say that you have deceived me over your relationship with Meikle. Is that true?"

Her body stiffened. "Everything I said to ye was God's honest truth."

"So you maintain that you had no dispute with the scrivener?"

"I never claimed that. I said I'd never met him."

Antoine became uneasy. "What do you mean? I hope you've not been clever with your words?"

Catherine straightened her apron in that strange way of hers. One, two, three times.

"You asked me if I'd ever quarrelled wi' this man – and I told ye that I'd never met him. All of that is true. But Gibb had experienced some difficulties wi' him. Oh, tell me that my old friend is alive?"

Antoine frowned. "He breathes, although we will have to see how he fares. But pray stick to my questions and answer them straight this time. What was the nature of Gibb's dispute with Robert Meikle?"

Catherine hesitated again and cast about the floor. She reached over to pick up a piece of broken pottery and held it tightly in her hand.

"The scrivener had been attempting to swindle him out of his house. He tried to make him put his mark on some papers, but of course, Gibb couldnae read them so…"

"So…?"

"So he asked me to look at them."

Antoine jerked his head back. "You can read?"

The woman looked up for the first time. She wiped away her tears, but her eyes remained red hot. She spoke with a bitterness that took him aback.

"It's no' a crime, even according to the March Laws."

Antoine stared at her. "It is unusual, though. You should have told me this."

"I did. I said I had no need of a scrivener. No doubt ye assumed that was because a woman like me has no need of reading or writing. Whereas I meant that I have no need of someone else to do these things *for* me."

Antoine cursed himself as this was exactly how he had interpreted her comment. He wondered where she had done her learning but thought it better to press on with his interrogation.

"Either way, how did this argument develop? And how were you involved?"

"I could see the scrivener's trick and told Gibb no' to mark a thing. That made Meikle furious, and he came back one evening, to get his way."

"When exactly was this?"

"Just after Michaelmas. It was a Friday night, and he'd been drinking at the Hart. He staggered around our cottages, banging on our doors, but we kept them locked. As I say, I never so much as clapped eyes on him, but I heard him, good and proper. He shouted that he would rip out Gibb's tongue to make him dumb as well as blind. Then he started screaming about what he would do to me. I was sore afeart, but I had a pot of boiling water ready to throw at him if he broke in. I only wish I'd had the same today."

Antoine noted the way she spat out these last words. Perhaps this dainty woman was fiercer than he had imagined. She certainly spoke more freely than one might expect of a suspected sorceress. He almost wanted to caution her, not to incriminate herself, but instead, he motioned for her to go on. If he had been taken in by her shy manners yesterday, it was time to see her natural demeanour.

"Well, he yelled, and he swore the most terrible oaths. But eventually, his voice began to slow. It was as if the drink had doused his fire. He threatened to tell everybody that the Devil himself had taught me to read. But he was babbling by this stage, and soon he was gone. That was the last I heard o' him."

"And perhaps the last anybody heard of him," said Antoine.

Catherine opened her fist and stared at the shard of pottery she had been clutching. She stroked it rhythmically in a way that disturbed Antoine. For a moment, he wondered whether she intended to use it as a weapon, but it seemed to have a calming effect on her instead.

"That is why I said nothing to ye of the matter. When ye said he had disappeared, I knew it would look bad for me. But now ye ken the truth. And Gibb can confirm everything I've telt ye."

Antoine got up. "Well, a blind man makes a poor witness. But a dead one will serve you worse still. So you had better hope he is still with us. Come outside where we can keep an eye on you, then we will decide what to do."

They left the cottage and were met by Wilson, who had propped Gibb up against a wattle fence. "The old man lives but cannae talk. He's taken an almighty knock to the heid, so God knows whether he'll recover."

"Let me minister to him," said Catherine, clasping her hands. "Those fools have destroyed many of my herbs, but I still have ingredients which could dull the pain."

Wilson and Burnsie shuffled nervously, and Antoine immediately understood their anxiety. Even leaving aside any supernatural trickery, what if she were to poison the old man to prevent him from contradicting her story? Given her apparent affection for Gibb, it seemed unlikely, but the Frenchman's head was whirling with the things he had just heard. He decided to buy himself some time.

"You can tend to him, as long as we are able to watch your actions. But this is not a safe place for either of you anymore. So while you collect your things, Wilson will go to the nearest farm and find a cart. Then we will take you both back to our tower. You will be out of Hume's reach there and more available to help us with our investigation."

Catherine closed her eyes. She gave a long sigh and went back into the cottage to pack her belongings. Antoine gave out a deep breath, too. He was frustrated that this murder was dominating his time, but its significance seemed to swell by the day.

It was as if the torso in the river were growing arms and legs.

Chapter 11

It took a while for Wilson to procure the cart, as the farmer was suspicious of his story and haggled over the price. Even then, Catherine was not ready when he returned. She was still rushing about the cottage, gathering armfuls of jars and phials while Antoine urged her to complete her packing.

"What a mess," she moaned. "Nothing is where it should be."

As she collected the last of her possessions, the men put Gibb on a blanket and used that to lift him gently into the cart. He was drifting in and out of consciousness and looked whiter than ever, apart from the red wound blooming from his forehead. Catherine dabbed it with some sphagnum moss before climbing up beside him. The party set off, with Wilson driving the cart and Antoine and Burnsie on either side.

It was a poor road, and they were wary of the damage each bump might do to the old man, but they were keen to get back to the tower before dark. Antoine still could not believe that Catherine was capable of slaughtering a man on her own. But as he watched her tend to Gibb, it occurred to him that she might have drugged her victim first. Although instinctively drawn to her side, he would have to keep an open mind for now.

When they arrived at the tower, the other men were busy clearing more of the wreckage from the open areas – a task made easier by their new tools. They stopped to stare at the wretched arrivals, and Antoine quickly explained what had happened.

"I suppose we should put her in the dungeon?" asked Anderson. "We can repair the door bolts so she cannae escape."

Antoine shuddered. "No, it's still unclear whether she's a suspect or a witness. We also need her to nurse the old man. Put them in the storage rooms on the ground floor and have them watched at all times."

They lowered Gibb from the cart and carried him gingerly to the first room, which they had been using to stockpile some of the provisions. They cleared a space and put some straw down before laying him out as gently as they could.

Next, they transferred Catherine and her accoutrements to the other room. On the way, Antoine humoured her while she positioned some potted plants around the courtyard –the rest she took inside and arranged neatly by the wall. The men did not like the way she muttered as she moved around or the fuss she made about where things went, but Antoine told them to be patient. When she had everything the way she wanted it, she went back to minister to her friend.

Later, the men gathered around a small fire in the barmekin. Opening a barrel of their freshly delivered ale, they gossiped under the stars. Turnbull listened to them as he went back and forth to the storerooms, checking that they now had everything they needed.

"Well, well," said Burnsie. "Just when we thought this posting couldnae get any harder, we pick up a witch and a half-deid man."

"A half-deid *blind* man," said Wilson.

"Aye, All Hallows' E'en has come a fortnight early this year!" laughed a sharp-faced youth called Tait. "All we need is a warlock, and we'll have the full coven."

"Our master seems to be under her spell," continued Burnsie, who was bold with the drink. "You should've seen him at her cottage. He followed her around, like her little black cat."

"He's done the same here, ever since they got back," replied Tait. "But she seems to pay him nae attention. Nor any of us, for that matter. I sat a shift wi' her, and she behaved as if I was invisible. "

"What d'ye mean?" said Burnsie, his eyes widening.

"She just tended to the old man as if I wasnae there. Or maybe it was *she* who wasnae there – I've heard that women like her can leave their bodies in one place and let their spirits wander to another."

The men looked at each other fearfully. Their faces were distorted by the flickering orange light of the fire, and their shadows danced across the tower. Turnbull did not like the way that the mood was shifting. Despite his own scepticism, he could see that the new arrivals had conjured up deep fears. Fears that would not serve their cause well. He finished his inventory and told the others to drink up.

"You're the only ones gossiping like crones around a cauldron. Now get on your broomsticks and fly to your beds as we've another busy day the morn."

That night, Antoine's first sleep was more fitful than usual. The memories that normally plagued him in the hours before dawn came early and churned around his head like a roiling ocean. As usual, the waves came gently enough at first. He thought of Francoise and the good times they had enjoyed before he had let her slip. They had met at a tournament in Rouen, where her parents owned a modest parcel of land. Although she was not of great rank, Antoine had been smitten by her comely smile and gentle demeanour. He had planned to ask for her hand, but when the opportunity to serve in the Italian campaign came up, he had dithered and put the marriage off. What a fool, he muttered in his sleep.

Next, his memories marched off to battle, the real battle, not the one he had related to others afterwards. He had been on the winning side at Agnadello but had allowed himself to be captured by the retreating Venetians. It had been his fault: that was the verdict that he repeated to himself tonight, as with every night. As with Francoise, he had been indecisive in his pursuit, and he had let himself be taken, along with ten of his men. He turned over in his bed as he recalled being thrown into a wagon with them, to be hauled all the way back to Venice.

Finally, his nightmare dragged him down to its usual dark lair – the Pozzi dungeons under the Doge's Palace. He heard the screams of the political prisoners being tortured upstairs, saw his own men die, one by one, of illness and exhaustion, and smelled the sewage which flooded the cell and washed around his feet at high tide. Most of all, he felt the searing guilt that he alone was freed because a passing Turkish merchant took on his ransom in return for a hefty commission. And the shame that he allowed himself to be greeted as a hero on his return, for there were no witnesses to his folly.

Antoine woke up violently, as usual, drenched in sweat despite the chill air. Normally, he would get up and write until it was time for his second sleep, but he did not want to put a pen to these secret terrors. Instead, he tried to relate his fears to his current situation and understand why they had visited him so early and forcefully tonight.

Forget the tower's dungeon, he told himself. As Anderson had pointed out, there was a perfectly reasonable explanation for all that blood. No, his fear of being incarcerated had not been sparked by a single room; it described his feelings towards this entire mission. He was trapped in a foreign country, doing a job he did not want. Stuck with a red-raw assistant and a feeble collection of men. Walled in by criminals, deceivers, and dissemblers. Now he was getting tangled in the chains of this godforsaken investigation, too. As he stared up at the ceiling, his thoughts spiralled downwards. But for all his doubts, one thing was clearer than ever: he had to escape.

Chapter 12

The next morning, a strange mood hung over the tower, with everyone still lost in their fears from the previous night. The men whispered about the sorceress and her powers. Catherine fussed over Gibb and blamed herself for his condition. And for his part, Antoine ruminated over his nightmares, his desire to escape undiminished by the cold light of day. He decided to head down to Coldstream to visit the island and meet with the prioress. With luck, they might find a clue that would explain this murder, identify the killer and let them move on. There was just one problem.

"You know she's an English spy?" said Turnbull as they rode out with Anderson and Tait. "Isabella Hoppringle. The prioress, I mean. Not long ago, she helped Margaret Tudor escape over the border and now plots her return in place of Lord Albany."

"So I hear," said Antoine wearily. Over the years, he had come to accept that conspiracy was a way of life in this country. The latest struggle saw supporters of the widowed queen urging stronger ties with her native England, in opposition to Albany's French faction. "But I can also remember when Margaret and Mother Isabella were our allies. And knowing this place, a new fight might break out tomorrow, and all might be reversed. In any case, we're investigating a mortal sin, so hopefully, the Reverend Mother's desire to do God's will should trump her earthly ambitions."

"She's a traitor, so I doubt it," muttered Turnbull with uncharacteristic churlishness. Antoine reflected that, whatever the strengths of youth, nuance was not one of them.

By the time they reached Coldstream, the sun was already starting to set, so they decided to seek hospitality at the priory rather than attempt to explore the island. The surrounding countryside was even bleaker than anything they had experienced so far, pock-marked with ramshackle cottages and ruined fortifications. As the first village over the border, there was even less incentive for the people here to maintain their houses or make an honest living. However, as they passed the priory's boundary stone, the scenery brightened noticeably. They rode through beautiful orchards, where the trees hung heavy with apples, pears and persimmons. It was harvest time, and the nuns were gathering their ladders and baskets after a hard day's work.

It was the first time they had seen any real attempt at cultivation since their arrival in the Marches. The scenes reminded Antoine of his time courting Francoise in Normandy, walking through her father's orchards on autumnal evenings. If he had not overthought his advancement, they might have settled in a place like this. But instead, he had gone off to war, and she had grown tired of waiting for him. As he breathed in the perfumes of the ripe fruit, they evoked bitter-sweet memories.

"We appear to have stumbled on the Garden of Eden,"

he said, trying to snap himself out of his creeping melancholy.

"Yes – and now we must meet the snake," muttered Turnbull.

Presently, they came to a high precinct wall, which again was in remarkably good condition. They followed it to the gatehouse and dismounted, Turnbull going up to the wicket gate and pulling the string of a small bell. There were movements from within, but nobody came, so he rang it again, and once more, there were the muffled sounds of conversation and footsteps – but still no response. Then, just as Turnbull was about to yank the string for a third time, a grille opened, and a woman's face appeared. The outline of her wimple was just visible through the narrow slit.

"Greetings, strangers," said the woman, although her voice had an unfriendly edge. "I am the porteress, Sister Triduana. What brings ye here?"

"We seek a night's shelter," said Antoine brightly. "Forgive me: I am the new warden, and these are my men. We're investigating last week's murder on the river and would speak with Mother Isabella if we can."

"Aye, such a wicked business," came the reply, the words slow and deliberate. "Someone will burn in Hell for it, nae doubt. We can certainly answer your questions as best we can. But I'm afraid our guest house is full tonight, so we may no' be able to extend our usual hospitality. As for the prioress, she is unavailable as she has other visitors."

Antoine was irked by the impertinence of this response: apart from the slim chances of the place being full, his station would warrant any other travellers be turfed out of their beds.

"It's good that you're so busy with God's work," he said.

"However, I feel Mother Isabella would wish to make an exception for us, if she knew we were here. So unless she's dining with Pope Leo and all his conclave, I suggest you fetch her, and she can decide what's best for herself."

He added a little menace to the last few words, and they seemed to have the desired effect as the porteress issued a grunt of acquiescence and disappeared for a while. Eventually, the grille opened again, and a different woman appeared. She said nothing, but she had intense, calculating eyes. They flicked over the soldiers, and then the grille closed, and the main gate opened. As they led their horses through, the men were met by an unusually tall woman in a white habit and black mantle. She appeared to be in her fifties and had a confident demeanour, set out in strong features.

"Good evening, gentlemen," she said in a voice that was warmer than Antoine had expected. "I apologise for Sister Triduana's manners. She is new here and misread my intentions. We do have some other guests and their presence does present some practical challenges, which I will explain in a moment. But of course, I would be delighted to meet with you – and help you if I can."

Antoine relaxed a little. Whether or not this pleasantry was a masque, it was a welcome change from outright hostility. The men passed the reins of their horses to a couple of oblates, who could not have been much older than ten years. The girls led the beasts away, giggling as they went, while the prioress took the men into the parlour and gestured for them to sit.

"The bailiffs said you'd want to see the island," she began breezily. "So you're welcome to do that in the morn. Of course, we've already combed the area for clues and found none, but perhaps your men's eyes will be sharper than ours."

The note of humility rang false to Antoine: he did not imagine that much would escape this woman's attention. Still, it did appear that she was trying to help.

"That would be useful," he said. "But what would assist us most is a view of the body itself. I know it would be highly irregular, but exhuming the corpse might allow us a better understanding of who they were and why they died. Perhaps even who the killer was."

A shadow fell over the prioress's face. She remained cordial, but her countenance tightened a fraction. "I'm afraid that will not be possible. The poor soul has already suffered enough. Besides, don't you know these details already? I had heard that the victim was some scrivener from Dunse and the murderer a local woman?"

"I see news travels fast," said Antoine, reminding himself of the Reverend Mother's reputation as a spy. "But your informants are a little premature. The body does indeed seem to be the scrivener's, but the evidence against the woman is quite partial. Hence our desire to see the remains for ourselves."

"I'm sorry, but that really is out of the question," said the prioress firmly. "We can answer your questions, show you the island and help you in other ways, but we must draw the line at disturbing the dead."

"Even if we were to rebury the deceased with full rites?"

"Even so."

"Very well," said Antoine, whose experience as a diplomat had taught him that there was no point banging on a locked door. "We will naturally respect your judgement. But we would like to take up your offer of further conversation if the evening allows. You mentioned that there might also be a problem in that respect?"

"Not a problem, just a little challenge," the prioress said

soothingly. She was good at this, Antoine thought. "Perhaps it would be best if I explained our rather unusual situation first?"

Antoine was unsure what to make of this but nodded as Mother Isabella continued.

"Suffice to say that our priory has a unique position, being directly on the border. It means that we can minister to the afflicted of this region in a way few others can. For instance, after Flodden, we were granted safe passage to England to retrieve the Scottish dead. But on other occasions, we have ferried bodies in the opposite direction."

Antoine felt Turnbull's eyes upon him, as if he were keen to interject. However, the Frenchman silenced him with a frown. He did not want to disrupt the Reverend Mother's flow.

"This privileged position can lead to claims of collaboration. For example, even if the current truce with England fails, King Henry has promised that the priory will be spared. Some have taken this as a sign of treachery on our part. It is understandable, really – it must be hard for people to see their houses continually burnt and our home left to prosper. But the crucial point is that both sides see we have a unique role to play. Indeed, what few know is that we Scots were first to formalise this privilege."

Antoine looked at Turnbull to check for any sense of what was to come, but his aide seemed equally perplexed.

"I see this was not part of your briefing," said the prioress, with the barely disguised conceit of one who holds a secret. "Let me explain. When our late King James married Margaret Tudor, he genuinely hoped this would end the war between our nations once and for all. Hence, the Treaty of Perpetual Peace. That agreement failed miserably, and there is little point in us debating the causes. But again, one privilege has survived. Namely, our right to host up to twelve Englishmen on Scottish soil without further permission."

Antoine and Turnbull traded glances again, this time a mixture of confusion and alarm. Judging by their expressions, even Anderson and Tait had understood the significance of her words. Was the prioress really telling them that she was allowed to entertain the enemy – and that it was sanctioned by their own side? Outside these walls, there were strict laws against fraternisation, and the penalty was supposed to be death. How could this loophole possibly exist?

"Please do not be so shocked," continued the prioress reassuringly, although Antoine felt he detected the faintest trace of enjoyment in her voice. "Once you've been in the Marches a little longer, you will see the two peoples mix more than you would think. My intention is not to worry you but only to explain the challenges around us accommodating you tonight. We have some English visitors staying, so while we can certainly give you the hospitality you deserve as our warden, I need to know you would tolerate such company."

Christ's nails, thought Antoine, this thing gets worse. The enemy is amongst us right now – they might even be next door, listening to us as we speak.

"Well, I confess I find this arrangement rather strange," he said coolly. He tried to stall for time while he processed the information. "But I thank you for bringing it to our attention, and I accept that we have arrived unannounced, which may not have helped."

"Pray do not apologise – you were not to know. Now that you do, though, how would you like us to proceed? Do you still wish to stay with us tonight?"

The prioress laid out her hands as if she were submitting

to Antoine's will. Of course, the truth was anything but. He could not help but admire the guile with which she had handled this potentially awkward conversation. No wonder she had managed to wrap two kings around her finger.

"I suppose that depends on the identity of your guests and the purpose of their visit," said Antoine. "A group of monks from Durham might be fine supper partners but a party of archers from Wark Castle might tax our good manners somewhat."

The prioress gave a thin smile. "I take your point. Well, I will explain who they are and let you decide for yourself." She put her hands in her lap. "Our guests are indeed soldiers like yourselves, although they are sworn to peace while they are here."

"That's good to hear," said Antoine dryly.

"It's their leader who you will be most interested in, though. He is a man of parts, who visits us from time to time. He's here tonight on a personal mission, which speaks well of him."

"He sounds a decent fellow."

"Yes, I cannot vouch for how you will get on but at the very least I am sure that you will have a great deal in common."

"And why do you say that?"

The prioress stopped, apparently to milk the moment.

"Because he is the English Warden of the Marches. Your opposite commander, Lord Dacre."

Chapter 13

"**W**hat treachery," said Turnbull, after the prioress had left them to their deliberations. "And to think we would never have known of their congress had we not chanced upon it."

"Aye," said Anderson. "This is grim news."

Antoine was similarly dismayed but took a few moments to collect his thoughts. While the others sat muttering, he went to the parlour window. A long chain of nuns was heading off for Vespers. Novices and obedientiaries alike walked with their heads down in solemn procession. Their piety was at odds with the intrigue which was going on all around them.

"It is certainly a surprise," he said at last. "But now that we are here, we might be able to turn circumstance to our favour. After all, we have had little success in bringing Dacre to our table – now it seems that fate has brought us to his."

"Surely we cannot parlay with him here?" said Turnbull. "Dacre's visit may fall within the law, but it betrays an ill spirit."

"Of course. But therein lies our opportunity. He was no more expecting us than we were him. So he will be on the back foot, too."

"I suppose. So what is your plan, sir?"

"I think we should divide for now. He will speak more freely without an audience. I will gauge his mood and see whether we can press him for a Truce Day. Perhaps even quiz him on that murder if we've time. You three go wherever the nuns will put you. But keep your eyes out for anything odd."

The prioress agreed to this arrangement, and a hospitalless took the whole party to some out-buildings. There, she accompanied the three soldiers to the guest house while a young nun, Sister Joan, escorted Antoine and Mother Isabella to the private dining chamber. As they climbed the steep stairs, he wondered who had passed this way before and what worldly deals had been made in this house of God.

Presently, they came to a lavatorium, where they stopped to wash their hands in a stone trough. Antoine was glad to feel the cold water on his skin as he was sweating more than was seemly. Beyond was a heavy, studded door. When Sister Joan opened it, they were greeted by a thin man dressed all in black velvet. He was sitting at the head of the table but stood up to offer his seat to Antoine.

"Ah, the hero of Agnadello!" he said, raising a cup of claret. There was an empty jug in front of him; he had obviously used his time alone to good effect. "I am sorry for any confusion our visit may have caused. Hopefully, the Reverend Mother has explained the unusual status of the priory?"

"That she has," said Antoine, advancing with a firm handshake. He pegged Dacre at about fifty years, although it was hard to tell as his face was marked by deep lines. "There is no anxiety on our part. It is an odd arrangement, but one that may be fortuitous as I was hoping to meet with you anyway."

"Ah yes," Dacre said, more sombre now. "I owe you a further apology for not congratulating you on your new post.

I am afraid my beloved wife passed recently, and I have not attended to my duties as I should. Almost thirty years we had together, you know. We eloped as youngsters. Had eight children. It is a lot to get over."

Dacre's voice quivered, and Antoine was struck by the sorrow of this man, who was as infamous as any in these parts. It reminded him of his own sadness for Francoise – and the responsibility he still felt for her death. For if he had not put off their betrothal, she would not have married that merchant from Nantes and succumbed to the plague there soon after. His guilt was irrational, he knew, but then again, perhaps all grief was.

"No need to apologise. My deepest sympathies are with you and your family."

Antoine declined the offer of the top seat and took a place on the side of the table, with the prioress opposite him.

"It is Lord Dacre's sad news which brings him here tonight," Mother Isabella purred. "He is considering a generous donation to the priory in memory of his wife and in repentance for past sins. A beautiful gesture, don't you think? One which reminds us that, for all our differences here on earth, ultimately there is only one Kingdom we must all serve."

At this point, various plates appeared, and the kitcheness announced the messes in turn: soup followed by chines of beef, woodcock, blackbird and mallard. Antoine reflected that, despite the Reverend Mother's words, the priory was obviously well-served on this earth, too. However, he chose to develop her theme.

"That is a fine notion and one that is close to my heart. Our countries have spilled far too much blood over the years – all for naught. My mission is to usher in a new era of peace between our lands that will please God rather than provoke

His wrath."

"A fine notion indeed," said Dacre, taking another slug of wine. "Although you may find it harder to achieve in practice. I say that not to dampen your spirits but only to steady them with the experience of one who has grown up here."

"I understand that," said Antoine, ignoring the familiar reference to his strangeness. "But we must try, surely? I can see that your own loss has affected you greatly. Perhaps this is a chance for us to work together, to spare others from such grief?"

Dacre kept his head down, cutting at his beef. There was a pause in the conversation, and Antoine felt a look of reproach from the prioress, as if he had said too much. When the Englishman looked up, though, his eyes were moist rather than ablaze. He took another hefty draught of claret and dabbed his lips.

"As I say, it is a beautiful thought. But we have been here before. I believe you were both present at the wedding of James and Margaret?"

Antoine and the prioress nodded.

"Then you will remember, as I do, the hope that infused that fine occasion: our little princess, your noble king. I met James many times after that and counted him as a friend despite our diverse allegiances. But ten years later, I picked his body out of a ditch. Just a few miles away. On our soil."

"A day we all regret," said Antoine, clasping his hands as if in prayer. "Not least my own countrymen, for their urgings of the Scots. But things are different now. France has a new king. Scotland has a new governor. We are united in our desire for peace, and I am sure your good King Henry wishes the same."

The group fell silent as they cut their meat, and it seemed like the conversation might move on. But Dacre would not let the matter lie. His face was flushed with drink, and there was devilment in his voice, as if he were twisting a knife into the discussion rather than his beef.

"Can we trust Lord Albany, though? That's the question. Even his subjects seem to doubt it. Some say the queen should act as regent for her infant son – as was her husband's final wish."

Although his head stayed down, the words were clearly directed at the prioress, who gave a muted response. "I do not hide my long friendship with the queen. But I do not plot against Governor Albany, as some say. All I wish is peace. Like every woman in both realms..."

Antoine sensed her irritation and moved the debate to more practical matters. He leant into the table and jabbed his spoon for emphasis. "It seems we are all agreed on the end then, even if we may disagree on the means. So how can we advance things, without getting ahead of ourselves? I believe a first step would be to reinstate the monthly Truce Days, suspended since Lord Hume's arrest."

"Ah, the old Lord Hume," said Dacre, swirling the tannins at the bottom of his cup. Sister Joan moved to refill it, but a scowl from the prioress made her back off. "Another enemy who became a friend. A true Marchman, too. No offence to you, sir."

"None taken, of course," said Antoine. Again, he let the insult go. "In fact, my suggestion is based on all my years here. I know the Truce Days are not perfect, but at least they provide a forum for us to discuss our grievances."

"A fair point," said the prioress. "Talking can only improve relations, so I would be supportive of this development. For instance, rumours of smuggling disquiet me – stories of private armouries being built up. Then there is this murder on our own shore, which is so troubling."

"The Truce Days are not for trading idle gossip," said Dacre sharply. At a stroke, he sounded more sober and direct. "There are rules to follow. Bills of complaint must be filed. And the offences must involve both countries. The only arsenals being assembled are on the Scotch side, and this murder on the river does not seem to affect us either."

"I know nothing of any arms smuggling," said Antoine, trying to remain constructive. "Any such trade would be against the express orders of Lord Albany – and is more likely to be the work of factions hostile to him. But I will look into it, as well as that torso."

"Then look all you like and let me know when you have found something."

"And if we do find out more, you will meet for a Truce Day?"

"I will have to see." Dacre's eyes grew rheumy again. "As I explained earlier, I am in mourning and cannot promise my full attention. Thirty years, it was. A man does not get over that so easily."

The prioress glowered at Antoine, as if signalling that this was as good as he would get. After they had finished eating, the novices cleared the plates away, saving the guests' bread trenchers to give to the poor. Then the party retired to their respective quarters to debrief their colleagues.

Alone with his men, Antoine explained how the conversation had gone. Mindful of their need for good news, he described it in rosy terms, so he was frustrated by their muted response. When he prodded them on this, they explained that they had encountered some of Dacre's guards stationed in an adjacent block. Over some ale kindly provided by the nuns, they had briefly indulged in the universal banter of soldiers and gathered some intelligence of their own. While it was true that Dacre's wife had died, that was nearly two months ago. Since then, they had all been carousing in the brothels of Berwick and burning cottages in Scotland's Middle March. Despite the old fox's tears, it seemed that any period of mourning was long over and that this visit was highly unlikely to have been one of repentance for past sins.

Chapter 14

By the time the Scots rose, the English had already gone, and Mother Isabella was waiting in the parlour. "They thought it best to leave early and avoid any further awkwardness," she said. "However, I think we had a constructive discussion?"

"Yes," said Antoine archly. "We can only hope Lord Dacre recovers from his mourning soon."

The prioress looked at him keenly, and they both held the glance for a moment. Then she called for one of the obedientiaries to take them down to the riverbank, where the two bailiffs were waiting. The watchmen seemed more restrained on their home turf. Perhaps they did have something to hide, as Antoine suspected. Or maybe they were just used to maintaining the silence of this place. Either way, they packed the visitors into their coble and ferried them across to the island without a word.

Once they were all ashore, they set about scouring the terrain. They began at the landing point, with the bailiffs retracing the steps they had taken the morning they had discovered the torso. Antoine walked bent over while the others crawled along the pebbles. They were not exactly sure what they were searching for – a stray button, ring or amulet? – but in any case, they found nothing. Indeed, the whole island looked as if it had been tidied. It almost reminded Antoine of Catherine Gray's house in its unnatural orderliness.

"The prioress had us cut a' the bushes back," said old Thomas Heron. "And the nuns checked under every root and stane."

"I wonder why she went to so much trouble to clean up?" Turnbull said later when they were alone. "Do you think she was genuinely searching for clues or ensuring that there were none?"

"I assume the former," said Antoine, who could feel his assistant jumping onto one of his hobby horses again. "A woman like her would want to know what had happened on her doorstep before anybody else. And we haven't found any connection between her and Meikle – she referred to 'some scrivener' when we spoke."

"Perhaps that was a feint designed to put us off. We know how duplicitous she can be."

"No more than anybody else here," said Antoine, "no more than anybody else."

As they headed back to shore, a light drizzle came down, with drops so fine that they seemed inseparable from the cold air itself. They called this one *smirr*, Antoine recalled, as he wiped the moisture from his cheeks. It rendered the place even more mournful and put a shiver in his bones. Turning slightly to shield his face, he noticed two soldiers watching them on the English side.

"We have company, it seems."

"Aye, sentries from Wark Castle," said Cuddy Heron. "They're always on the lookout here."

"Interesting. I had not appreciated quite how close we

were. But I can see your point now. We really are on top of each other."

"That we are. We can watch them changing the guard. Shipping in cannons. Repairing their walls from the last war. There's no' much they can hide from us."

Antoine nodded, as a loose thought formed in his mind. "And they can see you, too, I suppose. I wonder what they might remember from that night. It would be most helpful to speak to them now that we know the Reverend Mother can host visits from our neighbours."

Cuddy reddened, and both Herons put their heads down into their rowing. So, they *were* concealing something, it seemed. But what? Antoine did not hold out any real prospect of interviewing the sentries from that night, for it would require the permission of the prioress, the Captain of Wark and possibly Dacre himself. Then, even if they were all to agree, any one of them might guide the witnesses' evidence. Still, the mere suggestion of it had rattled the bailiffs. Antoine recalled the old wives' tale about herons and how the birds were wont to defecate when flushed out. Perhaps a little more pressure would help with these ones, too.

After drying off in the warming room, the party returned to Black Rig. On the way, Antoine went over the latest developments in his mind and rehearsed how he would present them to the men without causing further unrest. However, as they approached the barmekin, his neat plan was rent asunder by a commotion from within. At first, it sounded like the usual chatter of the men as they went about their business, but he soon detected an angrier tone. When they entered, he found the soldiers had downed their tools and were gathered in the courtyard. They had formed a rough circle, with Burnsie in the centre, standing on a bench. Beneath him, Gibb lay on the ground, with Catherine kneeling alongside.

"What is all this?" said Antoine, pushing his way into the middle.

Burnsie's face flushed, and he stepped down from his perch. "We've had an incident, sir. We were just dealing wi' it."

Antoine frowned. "What do you mean 'incident'? What's going on?"

"We witnessed this woman behaving unnaturally and became feart for ourselves. We were giving her a chance to explain."

Catherine snorted. "I've no' done a thing, but they willnae listen."

Antoine sighed. It had been a tiring couple of days, but fate seemed determined to prevent him from ever resting. He nodded at Burnsie. "You should have waited for us to return. But now that we are here, tell us what has stirred you up so."

The soldier put his right hand on his chest. "Gladly – and may God confound me if I speak falsely. It happened like this. We were going about our work, clearing the last o' the rubble, as ye'd instructed us. Then Wilson came out to say that he'd had a request from our prisoner. It'd been his turn to sit wi' her, and she'd asked whether she could bring the old man out intae the rain."

Catherine moved to contest the point, but Antoine gestured for her to remain quiet, while Burnsie continued.

"It felt like a strange demand and one which might cause him more harm than good. But we remembered your orders to indulge her ministrations, as long as somebody watched. So we carried the old fellow outside and laid him right here, where ye see him."

Catherine waited her turn but was becoming increasingly fidgety. She straightened her apron one, two, three times. Burnsie cast a glance around the men as if to make sure they had all seen her strange behaviour.

"It was there that we heard her muttering. She rocked back and forth, gabbling away, and we saw that our worst fears were confirmed: she was communing wi' the Devil."

Antoine was sceptical. "What exactly did you hear?"

"They were strange words, as if she was speaking in tongues. But we could make out the word Satan, again and again. We are all quite sure o' that."

The others initially seemed afraid to confirm this but nodded meekly when Antoine gestured to them. He glanced at Turnbull, who looked unconvinced. Then, at Catherine, who could not conceal her exasperation. He motioned for her to give her side of things.

"Is there any point?" she asked. "What's my word against theirs?"

"I cannot answer that until I have heard your testimony. So say your piece, and I will see what's to be done."

She adjusted her coif and brushed a few stray hairs underneath it. As was her habit, she continued with this motion, even once it had served its purpose.

"Very well. To begin with, it's no' true that I asked to take Gibb intae the rain. That would be folly, as Master Burns suggests. I could hear the rain had stopped, and I kent the air would be fresh, which might revive him. He has been shut in that dusty room for two days."

She waited to see whether Antoine would challenge her, but he waved her on.

"Onyway, we came outside, and as ye can see, Gibb has a wee bit more colour in his cheeks, but he is still very weak. So I continued to administer certain tinctures and to dab his brow. I prayed for him as I did so – until your men mistook my intercessions for something ungodly."

She dipped her head, but Antoine waited for it to rise again before continuing with his questioning. "And to whom did you dedicate these prayers?"

She glared at him but did not answer immediately. Again, the fiddling and fussing with her clothes. Once more, Burnsie made sure that the group had witnessed this.

"Who do ye think? Our Lord, of course."

Antoine raised his eyebrows as if prompting her to be more precise. She shook her head resentfully.

"Our Lord, Jesus Christ. The Lamb of God. Our Saviour."

"So why do the men say you were praying to Lucifer? They all seem agreed that you used Satan's name repeatedly. Do you deny that?"

"I do not deny it," she said defiantly. "But only because I was beseeching Our Lord to spare us from his depredations. If your men had truly listened and not simply heard what they wanted, this much would have been quite clear."

Burnsie gave a cruel laugh. This dispute seemed to have transformed him from the shy youth who had discovered the dungeon on their first night. He addressed the crowd – and Antoine – like a much older, more confident man. Almost as if it were he who had been enchanted, not Catherine.

"What is clear is that there is a darkness to ye that we must not ignore. Ye make strange signs and movements. Ye dabble in potions. Ye call Satan's name, however ye dress it up. Only God knows whether ye killed that poor scrivener, but we cannae chance being cast in the river ourselves."

"Then let me go," whispered Catherine. "That is all I want. To go hame wi' Gibb."

Antoine shook his head sadly. It would be easy to grant her wish – and win favour with the men at the same time. But he was fascinated by this woman's strange nature and felt compelled to hold her close by. Moreover, he knew that giving in to one's soldiers could create problems of its own. Amidst much grumbling, he ordered that Catherine and Gibb be returned to their quarters and that the men resume their work.

At last, he retired to his own room to collect his thoughts. As he played over Burnsie's words, he decided that it was time to change his approach to this murder case. So far, he had viewed it as an annoying distraction – something that would prevent him from completing his wider mission and making his way home. But the more he considered it, the more he felt that the opposite was true. He would hold no sway, in his own camp or beyond, until he could solve this puzzle.

From now on, it would be his top priority. Everything else could wait.

Chapter 15

In the morning, the men lowered a scrawny lad called Waddell down the well. After much yelling and tomfoolery, he reported that the shaft was salvageable but blocked by an impenetrable jumble of timbers and rocks.

"Right then," said Anderson. "Here's another thing for your list, Master Turnbull: some kind o' winch or crane. Meanwhile, lads, I'm afraid we'll have to stick to ale."

There was a cheer from the men, but Turnbull despaired at the prospect of finding a lifting device in these parts. In the Lothians, it would be a simple matter of visiting the docks, a warehouse or a mine. However, this wasteland was devoid of such industry. He made a mental note to investigate it later, but for now, he got ready for a trip to the scrivener's house in Preston to see what they might discover there.

They skirted around the foot of Dunse Law with half a dozen men before following a winding track down through the leas of the River Whiteadder. A couple of fortified houses lay on either side of the water, but they appeared to be unoccupied, and the soldiers were relieved to splash through the ford without challenge. In contrast, the surrounding fields were busy with men attending to thorn hedges, paling stockades and ditches.

"They're preparing their defences for the winter," explained Turnbull. "The next few months are the worst for reiving. The cattle are good and fat after a summer on the high pastures. Strong enough to be driven away over long distances, too. After Christmas, the snow will make it harder for the thieves, but for now, it is open season."

"I feel sorry for these wretched people," said Antoine as they approached a group of hard-faced men clad in sheepskin rags. "They scratch a living from the dirt, only to have it stolen every year."

"I wouldn't pity them too much," replied Turnbull dryly. "As soon as they've sorted their own fences, they will be out reiving from their neighbours."

Meikle's cottage was on the edge of the woods. No smoke came from its louvre nor light from its shuttered window. The door was laced with cobwebs, but it pushed open easily, and Antoine and Turnbull ventured in while the others kept guard outside. The room was cold and stank of mildew. Wait. Something was wrong here. Very wrong. The house was not only empty – it had been completely cleared. Judging by the gaps in the floor rushes, it had once been furnished with a bed, a table and perhaps a stool or two – but nothing remained now. Likewise, the hearth had been stripped of its kitchenware. The room was so barren that it took seconds to search, without yielding a single clue.

"I had hoped to find some paperwork," said Antoine, shaking his head. "But somebody has scrubbed all traces of the man."

"Yes, there's no blood or signs of a struggle. It's as if somebody has waved a magic wand."

"For God's sake, do not say that in front of the men," said Antoine, only half-joking. "They are scared enough about sorcery already."

He crouched to the ground, hoping that some hiding place might reveal itself, but there was nothing. Scratching his head, he tried to envisage what might have happened: Had Meikle been killed here or taken elsewhere? Had he known his assailants, or were they strangers? Had the house been ransacked before it was emptied? As he pondered these things, there was a shout, and Nisbet stuck his head through the door.

"Someone was spying on us – he's made off intae the woods!"

Antoine and Turnbull ran outside. "What happened? How many of them were there?" Turnbull asked.

The men were already haring off into the undergrowth, but Nisbet did not seem in a hurry to shift his bulk. "Just one, I think. We saw a face lurking in those bushes, and when we shouted at him, he bolted."

"Did you get a look at him?"

"No, it a' happened very quickly. I doubt we'll catch him now: these woods are thick and go on for miles."

"Well, we must try, for God's sake. You mind the horses while we follow the others."

With that, they raced off. Antoine went to the left and positioned himself between the woods and the river. Turnbull took to the right, where the trees continued up a steep hill. They crept through the undergrowth, watching out for their quarry or a potential ambush. The leaves were thick underfoot and crunched as they went.

After a few minutes, Antoine could see Tait and Waddell moving towards him. They stopped and pointed silently to a thick copse to his left. The branches were tangled, and it seemed impossible that a human could be concealed there. But was that a dark shape crouching in the brambles? Antoine moved forward a couple of paces and looked again. Yes, there was the grey felt of a man's jacket and a pink hand gripping a tree trunk. The figure seemed oblivious to his presence and Antoine watched him for a short while, in the hope that he might discover further clues. In a few more steps, he would be close enough to give a good chase – but as he shifted his weight from one foot to the other, he stood on a twig.

It cracked, and the man swung round. He shot off through the greenery with Antoine in close pursuit. There were shouts from the other soldiers, too. The man switched direction as he saw them coming and scrambled back up the hill, desperately heading for the light beyond the trees. Turnbull jumped from the bushes. He seemed sure to grab the fugitive, but the fellow brushed the lad aside and ran to the forest boundary. He disappeared, but the men kept up the chase, working together like a pack of hounds.

Bursting through the trees, Antoine expected to see the runaway heading off across the river, but there was no sign of him. The Frenchman took a minute to get his bearings. There was more shouting from the direction of the cottage. A scream. When Antoine arrived breathlessly on the scene, he was relieved to find the man spreadeagled, with Nisbet sitting astride him.

"Who the hell are you?" said Turnbull.

"Who the hell are you, more like," replied the man. His face was bright red from the chase and the considerable weight of Nisbet upon him.

Antoine stepped forward to assume control. As he did so, he winced, for he had twisted his ankle in the pursuit. "I am the new warden, and we are here to investigate the murder of

Robert Meikle, the owner of that house. Now, what's your excuse for spying on us?"

The man closed his eyes, and Antoine wondered if he had fainted. But with a jolt, his shoulders began to heave. He sobbed so heavily that Nisbet relaxed his grip on the man's wrists. The tears came in violent jerks, a mixture of crying and laughter. When he opened his eyes again, they had a dark madness to them. His mouth frothed around his yellow teeth as he struggled to get out his words.

"I *am* Robert Meikle, you fools. Now let me go, for the love of Christ."

Chapter 16

For a moment, all the soldiers stared at the prostrate man.

"What do you mean, you are Robert Meikle?" Antoine said at last.

"Just what I say. I am the owner o' that house. The scrivener." He gasped his words between tears of relief and snorts of deranged laughter. "And I'm alive and well – at least I would be if this oaf got off me."

"I do not understand," said Antoine. "We were told that you were dead – or at least gone missing. How do we know you are who you say?"

"Well, ye can ask any o' the lazy carls round here – though, I doubt they'll be happy to see me again. Or if ye'd get this one off me, I could show ye your own letter of instruction."

Antoine nodded for Nisbet to let go of the man's wrists, but the sturdy trooper kept his weight on the fellow's body. "Nae tricks," he said as the captive put his hand inside his jacket. Slowly, he pulled out a letter, and Turnbull confirmed it as the one he had sent. He also pointed out the man's swarthy features, his greasy black hair matted across his face: it fitted the description Purves had given of "Blackeyed Bob".

"Very well," Antoine said. He gestured to Nisbet to let the man stand. "It seems that you are our scrivener. But now you must tell us where you have been all this time. And why you were spying on us. We still have a murder to investigate, and your Lazarus act means we are further than ever from solving it."

Meikle got up and made a great show of brushing himself down. His clothes were finer than was normal for a commoner, but they were filthy and torn from the chase.

"I have done nothing wrong," he said haughtily. "I have only tried to help. When I received your letter, I confess I was half-minded to ignore it. Instead, I decided to do my best, even though I knew it would put me in grave danger."

"What do you mean?" said Antoine. "With Hume and his gang?"

"Of course," Meikle replied. "Ye must remember that your original letter arrived just afore the execution of your predecessor, the old Lord Hume. He'd been in prison for months, and his kinsfolk were itching for news frae Edinburgh."

"So what did you do?"

"I made my initial enquiries, sent my reply to ye. But then a week or so later, somebody must have tipped them off that I was in correspondence wi' the palace as they all descended on me."

"Who, George Hume himself?"

"No, his henchmen – they were led by one o' his hardest brutes, a man named Wedderburn."

Antoine and Turnbull exchanged knowing glances.

Meikle continued. "He had me up against the wall and threatened to cut ma throat if I didnae tell him what I'd heard. Knowing him, it was no idle threat, so I telt him the truth: that the messages didnae relate to any executions but to the requisition o' a tower."

"How did he react?"

"He was angry at first, and I worried that he would carry out his threat regardless. He asked which tower it was, and I telt him Black Rig. At that, he went outside to talk to his men, and when he came back, he seemed in better fettle, merry even. Then they all rode off, and I thanked the Lord that I still lived."

Nisbet snorted. "So you caved in, at first asking?"

"I telt him as little as I could," Meikle protested, jabbing a finger. "I figured that they would find out about the tower soon enough. So I gave that intelligence away to distract them frae any suspicion that I might also be recruiting men."

Turnbull nodded encouragingly. "And did you manage to make headway there?"

"Again, as much as I could," huffed Meikle. "Some more men should join you at your tower tomorrow. Perhaps no' as many as you were after but all good fighters. True Marchmen, no' the bairns that you have brought wi' you frae Edinburgh."

Antoine let this insult go, not least because he saw some truth in it. However, the scrivener's impudence irritated him, and he determined not to let him off the hook just yet.

"That is good to hear," he said. "But it still does not explain your disappearance."

"Ah but it does," replied Meikle. "For that very afternoon, rumours o' the executions started to come through. All hell broke loose, and I feared the Humes would come back for me, so I stripped the house and flitted to my sister's up in Haddington."

Antoine pursed his lips. "So why return today? I imagine you've come to claim your reward, but you could have written to us from your safe house to explain all this?"

"I was feart that any letter might be intercepted, and my

role uncovered, so I returned here two days ago and have been camping in the woods, waiting for your visit. I ran because I thought ye might be Hume's men."

Antoine studied the scrivener again. He recalled how Hume had spoken of him, as a man with many enemies. How Purves had told Turnbull of his ill-loved manners. How Catherine had related his bullying nature. Meikle really was an unpleasant sort but in this instance, his story seemed to be straight enough.

The Frenchman produced a bag of silver coins, which he counted out in his hand. "Very well, we will let you go on your way," he said without looking up. "But we will have to make some allowances for the slighting of the castle and the shortfall in recruitment." He expected protests from Meikle, but instead, the man bore a sickly smile.

"I had anticipated this," he said. "And have something else for ye. Something ye might view as more valuable than anything I've provided so far."

Here it was, then, the real reason why the scrivener had made such an effort to meet them in person. Antoine gestured for him to go on, and the man pulled another set of papers from his jacket.

"This is a bill of complaints outlining every crime that's been reported in the district this year. Ye'll need it if the English ever agree to a Truce Day."

Antoine flicked through the document. "This is all well and good. But am I supposed to be looking for something in particular?"

"Aye," said Meikle. "Go to the last entry."

Antoine did so. "James Redpath?"

"That's it. Just as I was about to leave, this fellow visited me with his younger brother, Dand. They wanted to report a crime."

"What crime?" asked Antoine.

"A kidnap down in Swinton. They telt me that some reivers had taken their other brother, Alex, frae their hame two days afore. He's been missing ever since."

"Wait," said Turnbull. "What day was this?"

"That's the interesting bit," said Meikle with a knowing leer. "Ye'll see the man was taken on the 9th of October, the day after Lord Hume's execution and a couple o' days afore that body showed up in Coldstream."

Antoine checked the list and saw that it was true. He handed the coins to Turnbull while he digested this revelation. "Did they say who was responsible?"

"No, they just ranted that they wanted justice. I was packing my last bags onto the cart and explained that I couldnae help but that they could find you at Black Rig – if the Humes didnae burn it first."

"I see. And did they say anything else?"

"No, they rushed off hame again. But I'm sure they'll tell ye more if you visit them in Swinton. They bide in the first house on the road frae Dunse. Now, I hope I've done well to tell ye this, and ye'll let me on my way?"

"Yes," said Antoine, although he found the man repulsive. "We will give you some extra coin for this news, but you had better be telling the truth. For Haddington is an easy trip for us."

The scrivener took the money and stuffed it into his purse, as a fox might bury food. "Thank ye," he said unctuously. "It's good to see that an honest fellow like me can still prosper in this place o' cheats and thieves."

Chapter 17

The journey to Swinton passed quickly, as there was much to talk about. Antoine and Turnbull discussed whether they had finally identified their body, while the troops were more concerned by the arrival of reinforcements: they were glad to have some extra numbers, but the scrivener's words about their own inexperience had stung and they made bold promises to prove him wrong.

As they approached the rundown village, some geese honked raucously. The noise brought a woman running across the muddy track, clutching a fruit-picking basket. She was shepherded by a tall man and a gangly youth, who trotted backwards, watching them intently. They darted into a bastle house – a squat, fortified dwelling native to these parts – and slammed the door. Were these the Redpaths? They would soon find out.

Antoine drew up just before the house and steered the group towards the side of the road. Silently, he pointed out the arrow slits at the front of the building and the murder holes above the door: it would be better to approach from this angle, as the gable end carried no such threats.

"This is your new warden," Antoine called from this position of safety. "We come in peace!"

There was a pause from within, and then a man yelled,

"We dinnae want peace, we want justice. Can ye bring us that?"

Antoine frowned. He was getting tired of such petulance from those he was trying to help. "That is why we're here. I presume you are James Redpath. We've spoken to the scrivener Robert Meikle, and he has told us of your brother. We want to catch the men who took him."

A woman could be heard crying, followed by muffled conversation. The man's voice came again, more polite this time, but still with an edge of frustration. "Very well, I will open the door. But please stand back a while, so that I can get a look at ye."

The door shook as the bolts were withdrawn. When it creaked open, it revealed the tall figure they had seen on their approach. He was holding a cudgel in his right hand, but this did not seem to have imbued him with much confidence. His eyes flitted from side to side, and his left hand remained firmly on the door handle as he bade them in.

"I'm sorry for my caution," he said to Antoine as the Frenchman stooped under the lintel. "But it's only a week since those reivers stood where you are and stole my brother away."

Antoine and Turnbull followed the man into the house. The walls were incredibly thick – at an ell's depth, they belonged more to a castle than a private dwelling. Inside, the room was dark, and the air was thick with fleas. This was soon explained by the presence of a ewe, standing in the corner, next to an upturned milking pail. Beyond this, there was nothing.

Redpath ushered them into the middle of this featureless den, and then, without warning, he banged his cudgel on the wooden ceiling. The men were startled, and Waddell poked his head in to check that all was well. But before any of them could react, a trapdoor opened above their heads, and a smoky light poured into the gloom. The youth they had seen before peered down at them and began to lower a rickety ladder.

"Dinnae fret," said Redpath, spotting the alarm on his visitors' faces. "This is simply how folk here have to protect themselves. No' that it did us any good last week. If ye come wi' me, we'll tell ye everything we ken."

With this, he handed the cudgel to the youth and started to climb the ladder. Despite his reassurances, Turnbull beckoned for Waddell to come in and go next. With some trepidation, the lad followed in Redpath's footsteps, pausing briefly before putting his head above the trapdoor. Gesturing that all was clear, he lifted his nimble frame into the void, and the others followed.

The upper room was quite cosy. Apart from the slits, there was only one window, and it was shuttered. But a decent fire burned in the hearth. The youth sat by it. "My other brother, Dand," said Redpath.

On the far side of the room, two women and three children huddled on a canvas mattress. Nearer to them was a good-sized table and a couple of cracket benches. Redpath motioned for Antoine to sit and then beckoned the women over. They were dressed in black gowns and cut similar figures as they approached, but as they moved into the firelight, their faces revealed themselves as quite different. One had thin, hard features, while the other was rounder in appearance: she might almost be described as cherubic if it were not for the yellow-green markings of an old bruise around her eye socket.

"I think it's best ye speak to the women first," said Redpath. "As they'll explain, they witnessed the whole thing, while we saw only the aftermath."

Thin-face duly introduced herself as Redpath's wife, Agnes. She raised her eyes to the ceiling and began. "Well, we women and bairns had spent the summer up at the sheilings, as usual, looking after the cattle while the men saw to things down here. We were a' in good spirits, the beasts had fattened nicely, and we'd lost nane to thieves. Then our men came up to drive them hame for the winter. They stopped over for a couple of days and we a' played our part in rounding up the animals."

Agnes put an arm around the other woman's shoulders as she had started to snivel. "Onyway, our return journey passed wi'out anything o' note. Then the men went back up to help our neighbour bring down his cattle. Luggy lost his wife to the pox and has nae bairns of his own, so we always lend him a hand."

"This was a regular occurrence?"

"Aye, we've done it every year for the last five. But this time, Alex came back the next day to say that the weather had turned foul up on the hill, so the others would take a little longer."

"Did that give you any cause for concern?"

"No," said Agnes. "We were glad to have him back, at least." She squeezed the other woman's hand. "But just after sunset, we were alarmed to see two men come up the road frae Dunse."

Antoine leant forward. "What did they look like? Did you see their faces?"

"No, that was what scared us. They were wearing masks, so we kent they meant ill."

"What kind of masks?"

"I dinnae ken; we'd never seen anything like them afore."

"What about the rest of their clothes? Was there anything distinctive about them?"

"No, or at least nothing that we could see. It was dark, and by now, we were running. Alex tried to bolt the door, but one of them got a shoulder to it, and they forced their way in. Then the rest happened very quickly. We were a' screaming and trying to get upstairs. Alex put his fists up, but they came at him wi' knives. In all the stramash, they pushed him to the ground and put a hood over him. He struggled, kicked out, but they were too strong. We tried to help, but they threw me to the ground and punched Jessie here in the eye."

At this point, Jessie introduced herself with a torrent of sobs. "We did nothing to deserve this. Now look at me – a widow at twenty-two, wi' nae bairns to care for me and nae prospects either."

"Come now," said Antoine soothingly. "We have not yet established whether your husband is dead. Kidnappings are common here, and the motive is more often money than murder. Did these men mention a ransom or give any sense of why they were taking him?"

"No!" wailed Jessie. "They said not a word. Nor stole a single beast. It made nae sense. Nae sense at a' until the men came back, and we heard the news frae Coldstream, and the hounds were called, and we…"

Her words disintegrated into further sobbing, and Agnes took over again. "I bolted the door as soon as they had gone. Jessie was fighting to get back at them, God bless her, but I thought it better to protect ourselves. I checked on my bairns, who were greeting upstairs. Then I peeped through the slits to see whether the reivers were still about."

"And were they?"

"No. In faith, I didnae want to see them. So I waited a wee bit longer, until I could be completely sure they were gone. Then I ran to our neighbours to raise the alarm."

The Trail of Blood

"The house next door?"

"No, that's Luggy's, who was away, of course. One down. The blacksmith, Erchie Henderson's. He has two big laddies, and he sent them to watch over us until our men came back the next day."

Antoine was distracted for a moment as his ankle was throbbing. He refocused. "So what did you do when you discovered all this, Redpath? We know you visited Meikle, but was that the same day?"

"Aye," said Redpath. "The scrivener was in a panic himself and said he couldnae help. He telt us to wait until ye'd arrived at Black Rig. Then Dand and I raced straight back here to be wi' the others. It was a terrible day. And the week just got worse as the rumours went round."

"Rumours?" said Antoine.

"Stories about the Humes being on the rampage. Guesses about who the new warden might be. Reports of this body in the river. We heard tales about everything save the one thing we wanted – news of Alex."

"Then what? Did you make any enquiries of your own?"

"Of course," said Redpath. He beckoned Dand, who had been sitting silently by the fire all this time.

The lad came over and took up the story in a low, mumbling voice. "We waited a few days as we were still hopeful that the kidnappers would send a message with their demands. But when nothing came, I started to go round the taverns and stores, putting the word about."

"And what did you discover?"

"There was little news of him," said the youth, with a grim expression. "But we were told that the body in the river was Meikle's. I'm ashamed to say that this brought us some relief. Some hope, even. Then I met a man who owns some sleuth hounds – Cranstoun's his name – and he suggested that we put them on the trail."

Antoine's ears pricked up. He knew that the Scots bred these dogs and that they were much prized in the Marches, for their ability to track down reivers. "So, did you take the man up on his offer?"

"Aye. We took Alex's glove and let Cranstoun's hounds get the scent in their muzzles. There were two great dugs, and you've never seen such slobbering. Once they had fixed on the trail, they were off."

"Yes, yes," said Antoine impatiently. "Where did they lead? Was it anywhere you knew?"

"Aye. Along by the side of the Leet, then past the mill and Pike Rig, over Hawkslaw and down through Kincham Wood."

"I don't know these names," said Antoine. "Where did you end up?"

"By the river, sir."

"Where exactly?" Antoine bent forward as he asked the question. But he already had a sickening feeling as to the answer.

"We were upstream of Coldstream Priory, sir. Directly opposite the Truce Day Island. Where that godforsaken body had just been found."

Chapter 18

Mention of the island set Jessie off again, and Antoine judged that it would be better to leave the interview for now. He used the onset of dusk as his excuse and led Turnbull and Waddell back down the ladder, followed by Redpath. As he left, the man gripped his wrist with both hands and gave it an impassioned shake. "Thank ye for taking on our cause, sir. People like us aren't used to being listened to, by people like you."

"Things are about to change," replied the Frenchman, gently releasing his arm. He felt a pang of guilt, as he recalled that making false promises was classed as a sin of the tongue. Still, what else could he say?

Outside, the other soldiers were amusing themselves by mimicking the geese. Antoine left them to their sport and took Turnbull to the next house, where Luggy Laidlaw came out to greet them. His nickname was well-earned, as his ears stuck out from his head like the handles of a ewer. After they had introduced themselves, he led them into his bastle, built like the Redpaths' but more sparsely appointed. The mean touch of a single man, no doubt.

There was only one stool, which Laidlaw gave to Antoine, taking up his own position on the rushes. Turnbull joined him, sitting cross-legged. The fire had almost burnt out, so they drew a little closer to soak up what warmth they could.

"I suppose you're here about poor Alex," said Laidlaw. He had a rasping voice that suggested some consumptive malady.

"Yes," said Antoine. "We've heard the Redpaths' story, but we would be interested in your perspective, too."

"I'm no' sure I'll have much to add, but I'll do my best."

"That's all I ask. So, let's start at the beginning. How long have you known the Redpaths?"

Laidlaw gave a hacking cough and spat something into the fire. "We've kent each other since we were bairns and our parents afore that. They're a good family. No' saints, but you'll find precious few o' them round here."

"You would consider yourselves friends, then?"

"Aye. They've shown me great kindness since my Cate passed. Agnes and Jessie will even darn my hose if I ask nicely."

"I hear the men help you bring your cattle down from the shielings, too."

Laidlaw nodded. "This year, the rain was fair belting down, though, so it took us a wee bit longer than usual."

"And so they sent Alex back down to look after their women?"

Laidlaw gave a rueful smile. "To look after their cattle, more like. If only we had known the danger lay elsewhere."

"Yes," said Antoine thoughtfully. "It is peculiar that Alex's attackers took no beasts or goods with them when they had the chance."

"That's no' quite true, sir." Luggy coughed up another phlegmy globule and despatched it to the fire.

"What do you mean?"

"They took my cart. I suppose to take Alex away."

"That's odd," said Turnbull. "A cart would take a while to harness."

"And be a slow way to make your escape…" said Antoine.

"I know," said Laidlaw miserably. "But took it they did. It was the only thing I owned of value, too."

"I can imagine," said Antoine, glancing around the bare room again. He was conscious of the time, so he moved on. "What of the weeks before all this? Do you recall any ill omens of what was to follow?"

"Not a thing, sir. We couldnae believe the news when we returned."

"And you have no clue as to who might be responsible?"

Laidlaw's face paled as he tried to stifle another coughing fit. "No sir, it's as much a mystery to me as to you."

Antoine glowered at the implication of their ignorance. "Then we are left with a riddle. Unless there was some secret that Alex was keeping from you or his family?"

Laidlaw scratched his neck. "I suppose. He had ideas. Schemes that he didnae always share wi' me." The scratching moved to his head. "I think… no, I dinnae ken what I think. My mind is a mess."

The fire was fizzling out – and with it, the conversation. Laidlaw took a poker to the embers and began to rake them over. His convulsions grew more violent, and he put a hand to his chest to quell them. Antoine judged that he was unlikely to cough up anything more than bodily fluids at this point, so he stood up. "Well, we'll be back tomorrow, so make sure your mind is in better order by then."

One door down, Erchie Henderson was a different story

altogether. A stout man with an honest face, he seemed positively keen to talk as long as his words were taken in confidence. Antoine assured him this would be the case, and they gathered around the workshop in the basement of his house. The impressive array of bellows, hammers, tongs and swages suggested a craftsman who was doing well for himself. Even his voice had a solidity that suggested it had been fashioned on a forge.

He confirmed the Redpaths' account without any of their high emotions or deviations. When he had finished, Turnbull frowned. "You seem quite calm for someone whose neighbour has been kidnapped, probably murdered."

"No' calm, son, just experienced," Erchie said gruffly. "In my line of work, I see all sorts. Men come in wi' bent swords, buckled breastplates, horses that need new shoes in the middle o' the night. They buy manacles, axes and pincers from me, too. I ask no questions, but I can see who's on the make and who might be getting close to danger."

Antoine leant forward. "Are you saying that Alex Redpath was involved in such things?"

Erchie hesitated. "As we have discussed, this stays between us?"

Antoine nodded, and the blacksmith went on. "I dinnae like to speak ill o' the man. He wasnae the worst, far from it. But he was a chancer, and in recent times, perhaps he bit off more beef than he could chew."

"What do you mean?"

"He was too bold for his own good – gallus, as we call it. Women, fighting, robbing, that kind of thing."

Antoine scooped up a handful of nails from the workbench and rolled them in his palm. "So why did things come to a head last week? Did he overstep the mark somehow?"

"Aye, I had that feeling. He had taken up wi' some trollop in Chirnside for a start. Was seeing her a' summer while Jessie was at the sheilings."

"Could it be the husband who has taken revenge?"

Erchie's brow furrowed. "Not directly. Watt Ledgerwood's been in Hexham Gaol these last two months after being captured on a raid. It could be his confederates, though."

"Except that Coldstream lies in the opposite direction to Chirnside," said Turnbull, who seemed irked by his earlier put-down. "So it would be a strange detour to take the body there. Surely it would make more sense to kill the man on the spot – or dump him on the way home?"

"Aye," said Erchie. "I've been puzzled by that, too. So that leaves someone else. Someone much more powerful, that Alex should not have crossed."

"Go on," said Antoine eagerly. "There'll be a reward for you if you can help us solve this. And protection, too, should you need it."

An expression of intense concentration came over the blacksmith's face as if he were weighing the implications of saying more. "Ah, protection, there's a word we use a lot round here. And pay for too, more's the pity."

"I don't understand," said Antoine. "Speak plainly, as we do not have long tonight."

Erchie took a deep breath. "We all have obligations to meet, do we not? Taxes, rents, tithes and so on. But in the Marches, we must also make a special payment for our own protection. It's known as blackmail."

Antoine looked bemusedly at Turnbull, who explained with weary embarrassment. "It's a local word. It means an illegal payment to prevent your house being burnt down or injury inflicted. Paid to the very people who would commit the crime."

Erchie nodded. "Round here, we pay our blackmail to the Humes. But after the previous warden's arrest, some saw the opportunity to ease off."

"Such as the Redpaths, you mean?"

"Aye, Alex Redpath was quite mouthy about it. He and Luggy were telling all who'd listen that they wouldnae pay another penny until the situation had cleared up. After all, how could Lord Hume protect them while he was locked in a prison cell?"

Antoine stroked his beard. "Hmmm. I can imagine that argument would not play well. But the likes of Redpath and Laidlaw would not make you rich, even if you squeezed out every penny from them. Why would the Humes single them out in this way – and only one of them at that?"

"It's no' the loss of coin that would bother the Humes; it's the loss of face. If they let some small-timers like Alex and Luggy get away wi'out paying, then they would signal to the world that they were done for."

"So they made a lesson out of Alex?"

"I am guessing, that is all. I have nae evidence. But I'm telling you what I know, in the hope that it might help those poor women and all of us who yearn for a quiet life. As for Alex, please dinnae damn him on my account. As I say, he was a good enough fellow. I fear he just got in too deep."

Antoine mused that this would be a fair summary of his own handling of this mission so far. Whenever he thought he had got hold of the truth, it would slither out of his grasp, dragging him ever deeper into a mire of deceit. And yet, as he rode back to Black Rig that night, he felt like he might be on firm ground at last.

Chapter 19

Antoine used his hour of watch to capture his thoughts from the long, long day. As he scratched away at his parchment, he felt they had picked up many new leads, but there were still plenty of gaps, inconsistencies and knots to untangle. He thought of Francoise and her gift for transforming disparate strands of yarn into a beautiful tapestry. He would need to demonstrate the same patience, although he feared that the picture he was assembling might not be so pleasing to the eye.

When they returned to Swinton the next morning, Redpath and Luggy were talking in the yard. They broke off as the geese alerted them to the men's approach. In the cold light of day, it was ever clearer that Luggy was not a well man. His skin was sallow, and his face cadaverous. A hacking cough erupted once more from his weakened chest.

"We're here to see if there's anything we've missed," said Antoine.

"A good idea," said Redpath. "I'll go first, as I have some thoughts to share." He clapped his companion on the back. "Meanwhile, do not worry, my friend – all will be well; these gentlemen will see to that."

As Laidlaw went back to his bastle house, Antoine and Turnbull tethered their horses and prepared to follow

Redpath to his own home. However, he led them in the opposite direction, out onto the common land.

"Perhaps it's better if we dinnae talk in front o' the women and children," he said warily. "There are aspects of my brother's life that they dinnae need to hear."

"Of course," said Antoine. "Speak as freely as you can. We will only catch his killers if we have the whole truth."

Redpath looked out over the common and back to the house. "Aye, the truth," he said thoughtfully before blowing his cheeks out. His stale breath lingered in the air. "The truth is that Alex was like most men round here. And I count myself in that. He wasnae involved in anything too serious but rather a bit o' everything."

Antoine looked him in the eye. "Yes, we have already gathered that. I should say that we are not interested in punishing past misdemeanours. We're more interested in the names of those he wronged. People who might have wished him ill."

"That's the thing," smiled Redpath ruefully. "It might be a long list. He owed a little coin to a lot o' folk. He was fond o' a fight. I'm afraid he would also stick his pintle in places where he shouldnae. I doubt that he wronged anyone so grievously that they would come at him like this, though."

"Well, somebody clearly felt differently," said Turnbull. "Somebody with hot blood and scant fear of reprisal."

"Aye, I've been mulling that. At first, I thought a cuckold might be to blame. Men's passions run high when it comes to their women."

"That's true," said Antoine, who was careful not to betray the fact that Erchie Henderson had already pointed them in this direction. "Was Alex involved with anybody just before his abduction?"

Redpath's face coloured. "Aye, some lassie frae Chirnside called Janet Armstrong. Her man's a known reiver – as bold as they come. But I doubt he's to blame for this."

"Because he's in prison?" asked Turnbull.

Redpath jerked his head back. "How d'ye ken that?"

"We've been compiling a list of the local strongmen, and his name cropped up," Turnbull stuttered as Antoine glared at him. "Watt Ledgerwood, I think?"

"That's right," said Redpath slowly. "Well, in any case, I dinnae think he's our fellow. I'd be surprised if he even knew about his wife's treachery. And if he did, he's the sort to chop *her* up afore he got round to anyone else."

Antoine arched an eyebrow. "We will visit her later. But what about other enemies? Is there anyone else who might have wanted him dead – someone in a position of power, perhaps?"

Redpath gave them a shrewd look. "If you're hinting at Lord Hume, I'd say this doesnae bear his mark."

"Why are you so sure of that?"

"Think about it. My brother was taken just as the very first rumours of the old warden's execution started to reach the Marches. I cannae imagine that we were foremost in the Humes' minds at that moment. Onyway, I have since paid our dues and have been assured that we have no quarrel."

"What of your friend Laidlaw?" said Turnbull.

"Luggy should settle his debts, too. But Lord Hume wouldnae ken him frae Adam. No, I believe we must lower our sights to find our enemy."

"What do you mean?"

"The great and the good wouldnae stoop to deal with the likes o' us. On the other hand, some petty squabbler would think twice before taking us on in our own hame. So I believe we must look for someone twixt the two extremes."

"It sounds like you have somebody in mind?"

Redpath's eyes narrowed. "Aye, a fellow named Cospatrick Dixon. He bides over the border. His land is right on the river, overlooking the Truce Day Island."

Turnbull looked unsettled. "That's a queer thing. Where the body was found?"

"The very same." A bitter note crept into Redpath's voice. "He owns a slaughterhouse not one mile from where my brother was butchered. Uses it to supply the garrisons at Wark and Berwick but mayhap for darker purposes, too."

Antoine took a moment to mull this news. So far, the revelations about Alex Redpath had rendered him a somewhat unsympathetic character, but this latest suggestion brought home the brutality of his end. The Frenchman could not help thinking of the poor man's body, perhaps suspended on hooks on some abattoir's wall. From that image, it was a short leap to his memories of that hellhole in Venice. A shiver ran through him.

"That's a dark theory indeed. But what's this Dixon got to do with your brother?"

"They were at feud wi' each other. A long-standing one. It all stemmed from a game of cards."

Antoine cocked his head. "Let's hear it then."

They began to walk across the common, causing a flock of lapwings to take off into the pewter sky.

"Well, Alex was ever a man for gaming," said Redpath carefully. "He would place bets where no others would, bluff his way out of a bad hand. A few years ago, he was at the St James' Fair in Kelsae and fell intae a dispute over a game of picket."

"Wait," said Antoine. "What was an Englishman doing in Kelso?"

Redpath shrugged. "We relax the rules for high days and holidays. The St James' Fair is one o' the great festivities of these parts. The town is alive wi' music and dancing for three days and more."

"I see," said Antoine. It seemed the laws against fraternisation had more holes than a beggar's bonnet.

"Onyway, it was the final evening o' the Fair, and a band of us frae Swinton were there wi' some friends frae Kelsae, who we had… worked wi' afore. Our spirits were high, and when Alex spied a gaming tent, we thought it a fine way to finish the night."

Redpath stopped to blow some warmth onto his hands. "We had to wait our turn at the table, but we a' had a shot until, one by one, our coin ran out, and only Alex was left. He was playing against this big lump frae England, wi' a mouth the size of the River Tweed's: Cospatrick Dixon, we would later learn."

"He was as cocky as ye like, and when they reached the stage of declaration, he put some more money on the table and challenged Alex to do the same. My brother remonstrated wi' him as he hadnae a coin left to his name. He asked that they stick to the original wager, but Dixon wouldnae have any of it. So Alex reluctantly took out his dagger and placed it beside the purse. It had a beautiful carving of a stag's head on the hilt, and was his most prized possession."

"Cards, drink, and daggers are a bad mix," said Turnbull queasily.

"Aye," said Redpath. "So it would turn out. Dixon laid his cards out first and then sat back to enjoy the reaction frae the gallery, for he had a good hand that would take some beating. Alex shook his heid as if to confirm his loss. But when he turned his own set over, they revealed an even richer sequence. Nobody could believe it; he'd concealed his advantage so well."

"So how did it end?" said Antoine, gesturing for Redpath to hurry up.

"Alex moved for the purse, but Dixon held his wrists. He was spitting hellfire, yelling that Luggy had been sending signals through his coughing. Luggy denied it, but Dixon wouldnae be persuaded. There was a stand-off, and then the Englishman released his grip and reached for the dagger."

"Suddenly, all was mayhem. Luggy grabbed him frae behind and forced him to drop the blade. Dixon's confederates crowded in but found they were outmanned. In the chaos, we took the money and made off intae town to continue our revelry. But we kent that wouldnae be the end of it."

"Why – have your paths crossed since then?"

"Aye, a few times at similar events. Oaths have been said, though no blows exchanged."

"So why do you think he might have chosen this moment to take his revenge?"

"Who knows? When a warden changes, it's our custom to settle scores until order is restored. Mayhap, they saw their chance while old Hume was in prison and his replacement was still to arrive."

Antoine was sickened by the idea that his own appointment might have contributed to this foul crime. On the other hand, it provided all the more reason for him to solve it. He led the party back to the house to interview the others.

Before they reached the bastle, though, Turnbull turned to Redpath. "Just one last thing. *Had* your brother and Luggy been cheating at those cards?"

Redpath stopped. "I have nae idea. But I ken one thing for sure. My family willnae be cheated out o' justice."

Chapter 20

Jessie was waiting for them back at the house. She had been milking the ewe but set down her pail and wiped her hands on her apron.

"Any news?"

Her voice was raw and urgent. Indeed, her whole body seemed to be on edge. How painful this experience must be for her. Not only to be beaten in her own home but to lose her husband and her future prospects. Then, to have her man's indiscretions raked up by strangers. Antoine made a note to treat her gently. And yet, he still needed answers from her, answers that might cause her further sorrow.

"We are making progress," he said softly as Redpath disappeared into the house. Antoine feared she was about to break down again and gestured for her to walk by his side. Perhaps some movement would loosen her tongue and prevent her grief from overpowering her. Turnbull joined her other flank.

"Let us take one step at a time," he said. "Why don't you start by telling us how you met your husband."

Jessie walked with her head down and her hands clasped. She gave a great sigh before beginning. "We met at the Lammas festivities in the village four years ago. I was eighteen, and he was just a few years older. It had been a poor harvest, so the mood was dark, but Alex fair lit the place up with his fooling."

"He seems to have been a bold fellow," said Antoine.

"Aye, he was a charmer, for better and for worse. I fell for his smooth words, and we were handfasted by Christmas."

Antoine gave a kindly smile. "How did your family view the betrothal?"

Jessie paused. "Well enough. My father passed when I was young, so my brothers were my guardians. We didnae have much, and they felt Alex would take me off their hands wi'out too much trouble. It was only my mother who had any doubts."

"How so?"

Another hesitation. "She believed him to have a roving eye and feared that he wouldnae stay true to me."

"And how did that proceed?"

Jessie lifted her head for the first time. Her cheeks were wet, making her bruised face seem even more pitiful. But her voice carried a note of defiance. "As she predicted. But these things happen. He was good enough to me whenever he was with me."

"Quite so," said Turnbull awkwardly. "So you muddled on, as many do. And he provided for you, as much as he could?"

"We werenae rich, but there are many poorer. Perhaps I will join them now."

At this, Jessie started to weep again, not with the intensity of the previous evening but with the weariness of one whose emotions have near run dry. Antoine took her arm and they walked on awhile without speaking. When they reached the edge of the village, he began to wheel homewards and attempted to turn the conversation towards gathering more useful intelligence.

"As a matter of interest, do you know how your husband made his coin?" He attempted to strike a nonchalant tone, but she saw through it.

"We have the beasts that you have seen," she sniffed. "And a few crops to tide us over. Beyond that, I dinnae ken. And nor do I want to."

"You do understand that he had other enterprises, though?"

"Of course. But as long as a man puts dinner on the table, a wife should keep her neb out of his business."

Antoine nodded. "A wise policy, no doubt. But you must see that it presents us with a dilemma. For we will only find your husband's killers if we have a full understanding of his affairs."

Jessie snorted, and a bubble blew from her nose. She smeared it into her face as she stared back, with angry desperation. "I'm no' like the men, bent only on revenge. Who says I even want to find my husband's killers?"

Antoine turned her round by both elbows. "What do you mean by that?"

"What if finding them will only bring me more trouble?"

He took her wrists. "We will see that you come to no further harm. But surely you want to know who has done this and why they've acted in this way?"

"I've already telt ye – I dinnae need to ken more about my husband's business."

"Then what *do* you want?"

She looked up in exasperation before crying in his face. "For everything to go back to where it was, as if this whole cursed thing had never happened!"

Antoine held her for a moment and allowed her to sob into his chest. As he did so, he was reminded of his last embrace with Francoise as he departed for Italy. He, too, now wished that he could put everything back to where it had been. But he knew that the Lord did not indulge such fancies – and so, surely, did Jessie. They walked back up the path to the bastle, where Redpath and Laidlaw were busy stacking bales of hay.

"Oh, my dear goodsister," exclaimed Redpath when he saw the state she was in. He shouted for Agnes and, after the sound of children's complaints, his wife appeared and took Jessie inside. "Did she tell you anything useful?" he asked.

"Nothing specific, but it all helps us to paint a picture," said Antoine.

"Ye didnae tell her about the business wi' Dixon or Janet Armstrong?"

"No. In truth, she seemed strangely uninterested in finding the killers. I fear she's still in shock."

"Aye, well, no wonder. Let's let the lassie grieve while we sort this thing out."

With that, he lifted a couple of hay bales down from the stack and offered the men a seat in the yard while he followed the women inside. "You carry on wi' Luggy, and I'll bring some ale out in a while."

Antoine thought it might be helpful to keep Laidlaw waiting, so he suggested that Turnbull take some hay to feed the horses. The lad did as he was asked, and Carbonel and Fogo nickered appreciatively.

"Listen to them," Antoine said to Luggy after a while. "They're enjoying that."

"Aye, they're simple creatures. If only our lives were as straightforward."

"Very true. Well, hopefully, we will untangle what happened to your friend and get some justice for him. But we are going to need a bit more help from you."

Luggy started to hack, and Antoine remembered the story of the card game. No doubt the man's illness was real, but was his cough involuntary, or could he summon it on demand?

"As I said yestere'en, I will do what I can, but I fear I've already telt ye everything I ken."

"Come, Laidlaw," said Turnbull as he rejoined them. "You know that isn't true. You didn't tell us that you both owed money to the Humes for a start."

"That's a separate affair, which I'm attending to."

"You told us nothing of this man Dixon, either."

"I'd no' thought of that until James mentioned him. Our quarrel was a while ago."

"And not a word about Alex's philandering."

"I didnae think it pertinent," Laidlaw protested.

"Then what is pertinent?" said Antoine. "Come on man, we're trying to help you as well as the Redpaths. Whoever took Alex might come back for you next!"

Laidlaw lurched forward as he tried to stave off another convulsion. "I cannae say, I cannae say," he gasped. "I was close to him, but I wasnae his keeper."

The man's eyes betrayed a terrible fear. Whatever details he did or didn't know, Antoine thought he must have a rough sense of the forces they were grappling with. "Last night, we asked you whether Alex had any secrets, and it seemed like you might tell us something."

"I was confused, sir. It was late, and ye were pressing me."

"But now you have had longer to think things through. And you have realised that you, too, might be in danger. So let's try again."

Laidlaw rubbed his face. "I swear I dinnae ken the ins and outs of it. It's just a feeling I have."

"Then tell us about that. It will be better than nothing."

"Oh, all right," Laidlaw exclaimed in exasperation. He looked down at his feet. "As you know, Alex and I were partners in many things. That served me well. I've been poorly these last few years, so being associated wi' a stronger man has been helpful. Perhaps it helped him, too – people always underestimate an invalid."

"That's true."

"The thing is, when Alex made enemies, I made them, too. Even if I wasnae involved."

Antoine tilted his head. "Because they assumed you did everything together?"

"Aye. But in truth, Alex often left me out of his schemes until he had them more fully formed."

Turnbull rolled his eyes. "You're saying he just swept you along in his wake?"

"Aye, to a degree. Do not mistake me, I didnae complain. But I was often working in the dark."

Antoine knew the feeling. "And is that how you felt recently? As if he were engaged in secret business?"

Laidlaw nodded. "He more or less said as much – that he was working on something big and would tell me about it later, but until then, I was to stay quiet and do as I was telt. Now, my worry is that whoever took him will think I was involved. But I swear, I ken no more than you do, sir. I would tell ye if I did."

Just then, there was a bang. They all swung round. Laidlaw almost fell off his bale, his cough erupting. Antoine and Turnbull shot up and readied themselves for an attack. But it was only Redpath, kicking the door open as he brought them their ales. They retook their places, and all four men supped in silence, lost in their thoughts of the week gone by and the possible dangers of the week ahead.

Chapter 21

When Antoine and Turnbull returned to the tower, they noticed that the stable block was much busier than usual. New horses poked their heads out of every stall, and men they didn't recognise were hanging up tack. Anderson waved to them and confirmed the obvious: "Our reinforcements have arrived, thank God!"

More Marchmen were milling about the barmekin. They looked older and harder than the Edinburgh recruits: whatever his faults, this was one promise which that corrupt scrivener Meikle appeared to have kept. A group of them were throwing stones at a crow on the side of the well, trying to knock it over the edge. When Antoine introduced himself, they grudgingly stopped. "Welcome to Black Rig," said the Frenchman. "This will be your home for the next month. We all have important work to do."

The men looked unimpressed. Antoine could imagine the churlish thoughts passing through their minds, perhaps not sentiments of outright belligerence but resentment at having been picked for some stranger's doomed mission.

"What was wrong wi' that lot?" asked one of the Marchmen, leering over at Burnsie and the others, who responded in kind. "Weren't they up to the task?"

"They've done a grand job so far," replied Antoine. He looked the fellow square in the face. "And our success will depend on us sticking together. Let's see that we do."

He walked on, raising an eyebrow at Anderson as he went. If there was anybody who could meld two hostile groups into a cohesive unit, it was him. "Aye, less o' your lip, Gilchrist," the serjeant said. "We'll be early a-bed the night, and then we'll see what you're made of the morn."

Antoine and Turnbull continued their passage through the courtyard to the tower's entrance, where Catherine and Gibb sat on some sacking. The old man was wrapped in blankets, propped up against the wall. Catherine held a mortar and pestle in which she ground leaves from the plants salvaged from her garden. The pots lay in a neat row to her side. She was reaching for another handful of leaves when the men approached.

"Good evening, Mistress Gray," said Antoine. "I see the patient is faring better."

"Aye, he has a fair bit to go, but he's on the mend."

Antoine crouched down to their level. It was true: Gibb's face had regained some colour, although his head still lolled about like a fool's bladder on a stick. "It seems your potions work then."

"That and the fresh air. Thank ye for over-ruling Master Burns the other day."

Catherine lowered her eyes and returned to her mortar. She ground the pestle rhythmically, one-two-three, as she chose her words. "I hear Master Meikle is not as deid as ye thought, either."

"Yes," Antoine smiled. It was the first time she had spoken so lightly, and her cheeks dimpled pleasingly. "It's a pity in some ways. He would have made a good corpse."

"So ye'll no' need to question us further on those matters?"

"No, that won't be necessary now."

Catherine ground the herbs some more. "And Gibb and I will be able to go hame when he recovers?"

Antoine sighed. So that's what this was about. "Let's just see. It may be safer for you to stay here until we have untangled this sorry business."

He did not wait for her response, as he could guess that it would be unfavourable. Instead, he stood up and led Turnbull inside, where they retired to their quarters. The shutters had been fastened against the biting cold, but allowed an amber glow to creep through the cracks as the sun went down. Antoine felt drawn to the light and pulled back the bolt to look out over the vast landscape below, stretching all the way across the Eastern Marches to England and the Cheviots. Castles, towers and bastle houses erupted from the hillsides like dragons' teeth. Somewhere in the middle of it all was the Tweed, the source of their problems.

"We have come a long way this last week," he said. "But whether we have moved forwards or backwards, I could not say."

"Surely we've made good progress, sir?" said Turnbull, joining him at the window. "Just yesterday, we were searching for Robert Meikle's killer. Now, at least, we have the right body."

"I think so, yes. But the murderers are somewhere out there. No doubt laughing at us as we chase our tails."

They gazed over the endless valleys, mosses and rigs. It was a crooked landscape, ideal for concealment and deceit. From up here, they could see everything, yet they could see nothing.

"We have some real suspects, though, sir. And some useful evidence, too. Perhaps we are closer than we think?"

"Perhaps," said Antoine, patting the lad on the back. The sun had almost disappeared, and the chill air blew through the window. He shuddered, closed the shutters again and pulled a stool to the kist. "Let's review what we've learnt and make a plan for the rest of the week."

Turnbull walked over with a bottle of claret and two cups.

"Let's start with this fellow Dixon," said the Frenchman as Turnbull poured them some wine. "James Redpath seems sure that it was him."

"Yes, he makes a powerful case. We should find out more about him, shouldn't we?."

Antoine nodded. "That will be difficult though, without Dacre's approval, or the intercession of the prioress."

Turnbull frowned. "He might have confederates on this side of the border, though. Reivers don't care much for lines on a map when there's money to be made."

"Fair point. Let's see if we can uncover the scoundrels." Antoine steepled his fingers. "So, who else do we have?"

"This villain Ledgerwood, I suppose. He's vicious, so who knows what he might do, if he were to find he had been cuckolded."

"Except he is in Hexham Gaol, as you kindly pointed out to Redpath yesterday."

"Sorry," said Turnbull, reddening. "I didn't mean to drop the blacksmith in it. But as he pointed out, Ledgerwood will have associates who could take on such a task while he's locked up."

Antoine murmured his agreement. "I want to interview

the houndsman tomorrow, so why don't you visit the Ledgerwood place and see what you can find."

"I'll do my best," said Turnbull quietly, before taking a large gulp of wine.

"Good lad. This dismembering business still troubles me, though. Dixon has a slaughterhouse, but why would Ledgerwood resort to such butchery?"

"As Redpath said, men's blood runs hot when it comes to their women. I once heard of a fellow from Cocklaw who cut off his rival's pintle and stuffed it in the poor sod's mouth."

Antoine gave a dark laugh. "Christ's teeth. 'Cock Law', indeed. But that rather proves my point. If Ledgerwood had mutilated Alex's pintle, it would make sense. But he didn't. There must have been some point to chopping the whole body up and leaving it in the Tweed."

"Well, then that brings us back to Hume," said Turnbull. "As you know, I've been onto him from the start."

For a while, they sat quietly, turning over the evidence in their minds, which were now quite clouded by wine. Antoine let out a chuckle.

"What is it?" asked Turnbull.

"It's nothing," replied Antoine – only to let out another stifled laugh.

"No, really, sir. I hope I have not said something foolish?"

Antoine laughed again. "It's nothing, I swear. I am just tickled by that fellow from Cocklaw: the name is quite perfect for his punishment."

"Cocks are what we call wagon horses," said Turnbull priggishly. "And law means hill. There are lots of them round here."

"Forgive me," said Antoine. "I am a fool for such jokes.

Your story does make me think, though. Hume's brothers were beheaded, not quartered. And the English weren't responsible for their executions – in fact, Dacre strongly opposed them. So, leaving a single torso in the Tweed seems a strange way for Hume to make his point. If he truly wanted the punishment to fit the crime, he'd be better off decapitating the two of us and sending our heads to Edinburgh."

This time, they both laughed. But there followed an uncomfortable silence. An uneasy mood prevailed for the rest of the evening, and when they retired, Antoine already knew what image would visit him in his sleep.

Chapter 22

It rained heavily in the night, and Antoine and Turnbull woke from their second sleep to the sound of water pouring from a broken gutter. "The wind has taken a load o' slates off, too," Anderson told them when they had risen. "We'd better get the roof fixed, or you're going to get drookit." It was yet another annoyance they could do without, but at least they had more men to handle the repairs now. Antoine decided Anderson should stay behind to supervise the work while he took a party to the houndsman's, and Turnbull set off to visit Ledgerwood's wife.

Cranstoun lived just beyond Swinton, so Antoine picked up Redpath and Luggy on the way. They looked bone-weary but insisted that they wanted to come and help if they could. "We would rather keep our minds busy," said Redpath, climbing onto his black Galloway mare. Luggy followed on a scrawny bay pony, muttering to himself.

When they reached Cranstoun's farmstead, the houndsman ran out to greet them. He was a ruddy-faced fellow, with a mess of chestnut hair and an excitable manner. If he'd had a tail, it would have been wagging, mused Antoine.

"Good morning, my lord!" Cranstoun gushed. "I've been expecting you, and I'm honoured by your presence. Come in, come in, and I will do what I can to help."

They followed him into the yard, where some dogs were barking and scratching inside a shed. Antoine formally introduced himself and explained that he had come to find out more about the hounds and their capabilities.

"Ah, I'd be more than glad to tell you about them. They are marvels o' nature, these dugs. They can detect the smallest trace of any man and follow his trail long after he's gone. The previous warden wasnae a great believer in them, he preferred to follow his own instincts. But now that we have a man of learning such as yourself in charge, I hope that might change. I have been thinking o' many ways in which we could—"

Antoine gestured for him to calm down. "One step at a time, Master Cranstoun. For now, all we are concerned about is the murder down in Coldstream."

"Of course, of course. A terrible thing. Nae doubt Master Redpath will have telt ye how we have helped there. But I would gladly explain more."

Antoine's ankle was still painful from chasing Meikle, and he grimaced as he climbed down from Carbonel. The others dismounted too and soothed their animals, which were getting spooked by all the barking. "So, as I understand it, Redpath – you came here a couple of days after your brother's abduction?"

"That's right. After we'd reported it to the scrivener and asked around the taverns."

"And did you take the hounds out that same day?"

"No, sir. We didnae have the necessary coin to hand. So, we asked Master Cranstoun whether we could owe him."

Cranstoun blushed. "I explained that I couldnae offer credit. But I also reassured Master Redpath that the scent should remain trackable for a week. That gave him a little time to find the money."

"It wasnae easy," said Redpath glowering at the houndsman. "But I scraped it together on time, and then we all set off."

"'We'?"

"Myself, Dand, Luggy and Master Cranstoun. Enough to handle ourselves if we came upon the villains. Or at least to stake them out and come back wi' reinforcements."

Antoine squinted. "So this was a week after Alex was taken, but you still managed to pick up a scent?"

"Yes sir," said Cranstoun proudly. "I telt you my dugs were good. We used one o' Master Alex's gloves, and they quickly found a trail. Sometimes, that is the way, even wi' an old scent. It can come down to the weather."

"I would have thought that all this rain might have washed the scent away?"

"Ah, ye wouldnae be the first, sir," said Cranstoun. "But the rain preserves the trail. It's heat that's the problem. I cannae say why, but it clogs up their snouts somehow. I've taken them out on summer days, and the sun has—"

"Hold, sir," said Antoine, raising a hand. "I have scarce seen the sun this past fortnight, so let's not get distracted. Just tell us what the weather was like that week and what effect it might have had."

Cranstoun's face coloured further. "Of course, sir, of course. It had rained heavily, which was a good thing for us, and even better, it was bitter cold, too. The only problem was the wind, which sometimes carries the scent astray. But my dugs werenae put off by it, no' this time. They picked up a whiff straight away and went racing off to Coldstream."

"So I hear. Until the river stopped them?"

"Ah, that's the strange thing." Cranstoun puffed himself up again. "As I explained to Master Redpath when we reached the riverbank, the notion that dugs cannae track across water is an old wives' tale. I would have expected the scent to be picked up again on the island, especially as the body had lain there rotting into the ground. So we took a wee boat over. But when we got there, there was not a thing."

"Interesting," said Antoine. "And no other clues along the way?"

"No' that we could see."

"Which is odd, don't you think? The bailiffs discovered the remains two days after the abduction. They said the blood was dry, and the body had passed through its rigor. So the kidnappers must have cut him up en route, in some sheltered spot, then camped out for a day. Could you take us along the path again with the dogs, to check for clues?"

A couple of coins and much gratitude later, the houndsman headed off to the shed. He disappeared for a few minutes, and the barking increased to a great cacophony. When he emerged, he was gripping two huge, slavering hounds by their collars. "These are my bonnie lads," he said. "Egeir and Gryme. Now, boys, let's show the warden how clever you are."

They mounted their horses, with Cranstoun leading the way, the dogs roaming about and glad to be off the leash. The houndsman took them on the route Dand Redpath had described: down by the Leet waters, past the mill and around Pike Rig. It was rough land, and even the hobblers found it challenging.

"I can't imagine a cart getting through here," said Antoine as he bent his head to avoid some low branches. "Are you sure the hounds were not mistaken?"

"Upon God's flesh, sir, no. As I said, the wind may have blown the scent, and their true passage might have been over thon heath, but this was the general direction."

"Then let's keep an eye to our flanks. Gilchrist, Burnsie, Nisbet – you spread out around us so we don't miss anything."

They continued in a broad line over Hawkslaw and down the other side. The distance between them made conversation difficult, although this did not prevent Cranstoun from reciting the dogs' achievements, bloodlines and specialisms into the wind. Antoine noticed that if the hounds stopped to investigate a piece of carrion or strongly perfumed plant, he would lay great praise upon them. It reminded him of how he indulged Carbonel and how Albany had been with that lion. Why did men find it easier to express love to their animals than to their fellows?

On the other side of Hawkslaw, they came to Kincham Woods. The trail through the forest was narrow, and they had to bunch together again. While Cranstoun prattled on in front, Antoine tried to put himself in the kidnappers' shoes and puzzle out how they had gone about their business.

"This is another strange route," he said, lifting his bonnet to scratch his head. "I still don't see how they hooked up a horse and cart. Imagine: one of them must have been wrestling with an angry hostage while the other messed around with a harness. What if the women had raised the alarm and a neighbour had found them? They would have been far better tying him to the back of a horse and spiriting him away."

"Perhaps they had an accomplice?" suggested Redpath. "Our wives saw two men riding up the street, but what if a third was hiding nearby and tacked up one o' the horses to the cart while the others were inside?"

"Possibly," said Antoine. "That would explain how they got away so quickly. Did you see any other signs of intrusion at your place, Laidlaw?"

"No, but the idea of someone creeping around my house makes me sick."

Luggy drew his cloak around himself and cast his eyes nervously into the forest's shadows. Although it was only mid-afternoon, the dense canopy meant the path was dark. Occasionally, they would come upon a clearing where the bracken had been trampled down. Then they would dismount and poke about the undergrowth for some tell-tale sign.

"This is the kind of place they must have used as their camp," said Antoine as they reached one such glade. "Watch out for wheel tracks, blood marks or ashes from a fire. There may even be freshly dug soil where they buried the other parts."

He was suddenly conscious of Redpath's presence and turned round to check whether his remarks had been insensitive. But he need not have worried, for James and Luggy stood like statues, peering off into the undergrowth.

Laidlaw gripped his friend's arm. His eyes were wild, and there was terror in his voice. "There he goes again. I'm telling you. I saw him move."

"Where, Luggy?" whispered Redpath. "I'm sure you're just imagining it."

Laidlaw pointed off into the distance while he put his other hand to his chest, to control another coughing fit. "Just over there, by those chestnut trees. I tell ye: somebody's watching us."

Antoine followed the line of Luggy's finger but could see nothing. The others had stopped, too, and peered into the darkness with a similar lack of success.

"Relax, Laidlaw," said the Frenchman. "I fear we've unnerved you with talk of those reivers sneaking about your house."

Antoine turned his back on the others to show them that there was no need to be afraid. He put his foot in his stirrup, ignoring the twinge in his ankle as he did so. He was just about to push up onto his horse when he heard a fizzing sound behind him. All at once, the wind quickened, and there was an almighty thud. When he swung round he saw that an arrow had struck a tree, inches from where they stood.

Chapter 23

Turnbull wished that he was in Antoine's place right now. Accompanying the houndmaster would surely be a simple task, whereas visiting the Ledgerwoods' lair was laden with danger. As he reached the outskirts of Chirnside, he wondered whether his master had given him this job as some kind of test – and when he met two burly men on horseback, his anxiety increased. The pair carried lances and did not seem to care that they were outnumbered by Turnbull and his four soldiers.

"Stand back, we're on the new warden's business," said Turnbull. "We wish to speak to Watt Ledgerwood's wife."

"Oh aye?" said one of the men scornfully. "I'm not sure our master would like the sound o' that."

"Well, it's just as well he's chained up in England then," said Turnbull. He meant to sound firm, but he feared his voice betrayed him. "Now stand aside. We haven't got all day."

One of Ledgerwood's men glanced over his shoulder, implying they had reinforcements nearby. The horses snorted impatiently. As Turnbull worried about his next move, one of his recruits called out from behind him.

"Hey, Fat Lips, is that you?"

The spearman raised his free hand to his forehead to

shade his eyes from the low autumn sun. He squinted for a moment before breaking into a smile, which revealed burn marks around his mouth – the source of his nickname, perhaps.

"Tam Simpson, well I never."

"Aye, it's been a while."

"Since our wee expedition to Wooler, eh? We were lucky to get away."

Simpson nodded. "When that old bastard slashed my arm, I thought I was done for."

"Well, it's good to see you again, my friend." Then, more stiffly. "But what brings you here today?"

"As Master Turnbull says, the new warden has asked us to have a few words wi' Watt's wife. We willnae be long."

"What's it about, though?" said Fat Lips, leaning back in the saddle.

"It's a routine visit," interjected Turnbull. "The warden has just arrived and wishes to make himself known to all the local headsmen. Who knows, he may even be able to help your master get out of gaol."

Fat Lips gave a sly smile and shrugged. "Aye, all right. We'll take you up to the house as you've come wi' old Simmy here. But as for helping our master, there's nae need. He was released frae Hexham two days ago and should be back wi' us this afternoon. If ye want to meet him, ye could stay?"

Turnbull's chest tensed, and he made some excuse about having other rounds to make, for he had no desire to encounter the robber chief. He was already embarrassed that he had needed Simpson's help and troubled by the fellow's relationship with the gang. What other allegiances would they discover among the new recruits? Such ties were inevitable in a place where everybody knew each other, but they could complicate things. It was one of the reasons he had left the Marches in the first place.

Ledgerwood's bastle house sat on a ridge behind a wooden palisade. Half a dozen men were milling around outside, staring at them as they approached. A pig snuffled about the yard before a heavy boot kicked it out of the way. The soldiers dismounted, and Fat Lips whispered to a squat man with a bushy red beard, who was sharpening an axe on a whetstone. After some conferring, the man left his work and went inside. A long interval followed, which Simpson and Fat Lips filled with reminisces about mutual acquaintances. Then a woman appeared at the door. She was pretty, but her eyes burned with a fury that Turnbull would not forget in a hurry.

"I hear you're on the Warden's business. Can't it wait until my husband returns?"

"I'd sooner do it now," said Turnbull.

She shot him another angry look. "Need I be feart? I hope nothing has happened to him on his journey hame?"

"No, it does not relate to his release."

"Then it isnae urgent? And we're no' being singled out?"

She spoke carefully, and he realised that she wanted him to confirm the routine nature of the visit for the benefit of all present. "That is right. Perhaps it will make more sense if you come with me a while. It will not take long, I promise."

Turnbull could feel the woman's ire building as they walked in silence to a clear patch of land, where more pigs nosed about in the mud. When they were out of earshot, she turned on him. "What in God's death, d'ye think ye're doing here?"

"I beg your pardon, Goodwife Armstrong. We have no wish to cause you difficulties."

"Difficulties?" she hissed. "Ye'll get us both killed if ye're no' careful. This is about Alex Redpath's murder, I presume?"

"Yes. We understand that you were, um, acquainted. So we wanted to ask whether you might know anything about his death."

She scowled. "We had a brief friendship, nothing more. So why don't ye take your questions and shove them up your arse."

Turnbull was not used to such insolence from a woman and was glad that nobody had heard him spoken to in this way. "Friend or otherwise," he flustered, "I can imagine your husband might not approve of the relationship."

"Which is why I'm telling ye to get gone," she spat.

Turnbull took a moment to plan his next move. In the corner of the yard, one of the pigs was rootling in a pile of rotten leaves. It had disturbed a frog from its winter slumber and was trying to manoeuvre the drowsy creature into its mouth. Turnbull recalled his father warning him about the pigs in the forest and telling him that he should never turn his back if he encountered one. They would eat anything, and not so much as a bone would be left. As if to confirm the point, the pig gripped the frog in its jaw, shook its head back and swallowed it whole.

"Armstrong is not a local name," he said at last. "You'll be from the West Marches, I imagine."

He meant the question to put the woman at her ease, but it seemed to unnerve her. "Aye," she said. "From Langholm, by the Esk."

"A rough place, I hear."

She scowled. "We all come frae somewhere. I've no' lived there for years."

"So how did you end up here?"

"We Armstrongs like to travel," she said darkly. "I have

three brothers, known across the Marches. They had some business over here wi' the Ledgerwoods, and I met my Watt as a result."

"I see. So they are all in the same line of work?"

"You know they are. Why don't ye get to the point and clear off?"

In truth, Turnbull was not sure where he was going with these questions himself. While Armstrong seemed sensitive about her origins, he needed to get her talking about recent events.

"I'll be happy to go when you've told me all that you know of Alex Redpath's disappearance. So, let's start again: when did you first meet him?"

Armstrong seemed more comfortable with this line of questioning. "At the start of the summer. Watt had been captured in Hexham, and the Redpaths' women had moved up to the shielings. I met Alex at a wedding in Whitsome."

"And how often did you see each other thereafter?"

"A handful o' times. I would ride out to Swinton to see him."

"That was a little rash, was it not? Weren't you worried that your husband's men would catch you?"

"I have always gone riding on my own. They're used to it. What they're no' used to is people like you coming around, so hurry up, for God's sake."

Turnbull gathered his thoughts. "What about anybody else? Would Redpath have mentioned you to his friends, for instance?"

"As I've said, there was little to mention." She paused as if this idea had sparked another one. "Hold on. Who's telt you about me, onyway? Somebody in Swinton, was it?"

Turnbull avoided her gaze. "Let's not get into that. As

you say, we must be quick. It seems you're saying your husband is not responsible for Alex's death. So do you know who might be?"

Armstrong looked as if she was still mulling the previous question but continued, nonetheless. "I couldnae say. I heard the news along wi' everyone else and was sad, of course. But people die cruel deaths around here, and then we all move on."

"Isn't that so," said Turnbull. "Well, I am glad to see that *you* are alive. I only hope that remains the case."

She shot him another expression of pure venom. "Then get off my land, before my husband shows up."

They walked back to the house as wordlessly as they had come. The Marchmen were conversing freely with Ledgerwood's associates and seemed sorry to see Turnbull return.

As they left, something drew his eye to an old barn beside the bastle. Janet caught his glance and nodded to Fat Lips to close the door, but before he could do so, Turnbull saw the wheels of a cart poking out. Could this be the one stolen from Luggy's house? He immediately dismissed the notion, as such wagons were commonplace around here. Janet Armstrong's behaviour did prompt another notion, though: perhaps *she* had organised Alex Redpath's death, not her husband?

Chapter 24

At the sight of the arrow, Antoine ducked down behind the horses. The animals whinnied at the abrupt movement, and he had to be careful to avoid their hooves. The other men had also fallen to the ground and crawled off to cover. None of them appeared to be injured, at least. Together, they crouched amongst the bushes and waited for a further attack, but the forest was silent, save for the panting of the hounds.

A man called out. "Monsieur Warden. Where are ye hiding?"

The voice sounded familiar, but Antoine could not quite place it. It had the same sneering tone of George Hume but was rougher, earthier. Whoever it was, Luggy seemed terrified to hear him. His chest lurched, and although Redpath placed his hands upon his shoulders, he could not prevent him from breaking into one of his coughing fits.

"Ah, there ye are," came the voice again. "Thank ye, Master Laidlaw, I can see ye all now."

The men glared at Luggy, although Antoine had a feeling that their attacker had been watching them for some time and already knew perfectly well where they all were. His ankle throbbed, and he wondered how long he could remain in this position. All the while, their attacker continued to mock them.

"There's no need to be feart, gentlemen. I was hunting with my friend here and thought I saw a deer, but I was obviously mistaken. Why don't ye show yourselves and we can all go on our way?"

Antoine saw Redpath mouthing something at him but couldn't discern the words in the dim forest light. Watch your back? Where's the boy? Wait and turn? Ah, that was it: Wedderburn. At least he knew who they were dealing with now. But was it safe to stand up? Perhaps they would not be so lucky with the next shot. On the other hand, Hume's henchman could probably see them already, so they had little to lose.

Antoine rose slowly and gestured to the men to do the same. As he poked his head above the bracken, he was relieved to see that Wedderburn's bow was by his side. Another man, whom he recognised from the mob at Catherine's house, stood with him.

"What's this about, Wedderburn?" Antoine called, emboldened by his group's superior numbers.

"As I said, we were hunting. Like you, it seems – although perhaps our quarry differs?"

Antoine had no intention of explaining their business to this scoundrel. Instead, he nodded to the arrow in the tree. "You could have killed one of us…"

Wedderburn shrugged. "I apologise again. But the forest is a dangerous place. Ye need to be more careful, sir."

"If you're trying to scare us, it won't work."

"Oh, I have no need to scare ye," smiled Wedderburn. "Ye seem to be doing that all by yourselves."

He slung his bow over his shoulder and put an arm around his friend as they made off for the wood's edge. The soldiers watched them until they disappeared into the foliage.

Antoine chivvied his men onto their horses again, leaving Gilchrist to stay back and ensure that their tormentors did not return.

"That was a warning shot," the Frenchman said as they emerged on the other side of the woods. "If he had wanted to kill us, he would have brought more men."

"Aye," said Cranstoun. "And a fellow like him wouldnae miss from that range."

"The man's just a bully," said Redpath, looking at Luggy, whose face was still like death. "The more we cower, the braver he becomes. Let's give him no more thought."

Presently, they came to the Tweed, just as Dand had described. The bank on this side was steep and afforded a good view of the island and Wark Castle.

"Is this where the trail stopped?" asked Antoine.

"Right here," said Cranstoun. "We took the dugs all over the banks, but they couldnae find a thing. The same on the island."

"It's very odd. And no other signs? Cart tracks, blood or bones?"

"Nothing out o' the ordinary."

"Then let's take that path down the brae and see if we can find the river bailiffs."

They proceeded cautiously, for the steep track was treacherous after all the rain. The light was fading, too, and Luggy fretted again, that they were being followed, despite Gilchrist confirming that they were not. Antoine wished that they had not brought Laidlaw at all. Only Redpath seemed able to soothe the man. Still, even he jerked back in his saddle when they heard two voices coming from the reeds. This time,

Antoine recognised them as the Herons and motioned for everyone to stay calm.

"Good day, my lord," said Thomas Heron. The old man affected a genial manner, but his voice wavered. "What brings ye here?"

"Master Cranstoun and his dogs are helping us with our investigation," said Antoine. "We hope to have the culprits soon."

The bailiff gulped. "Good."

"Yes, we've covered the banks and are on our way to Mother Isabella to request an interview with the sentries at Wark. So if you have anything further to say, this is your last chance."

The watchman grimaced as his son rose from the reeds, glaring at his father, who went on talking with mounting desperation. "My lord, I promise we would help ye if we could. But certain things constrain us."

Antoine felt he was getting closer to the men's secret. "Look, if somebody is threatening you, I will give you the full protection of the law."

"Thank ye, sir, but it's no' that. The problem is the law itself."

Antoine was confused.

"What my father means," said Cuddy Heron slowly, "is that we could tell ye more about that night, but in the process, our account might tangle us and others in another affair."

"Holy God," declared Antoine in exasperation. It seemed that there were no innocents at all around here. "Rest assured that I will grant you clemency from any misdemeanour. Just tell me that you're not talking of another capital offence?"

Cuddy looked at his father and then back to the warden. "Perhaps it would be best if we talked alone."

Antoine dismounted and walked with the younger bailiff along the bank. With the roaring water in full flow, they did not have to go far to find some privacy. Cuddy clicked his fingers nervously by his sides. Whatever this was about, it was no small matter.

"The thing is this, my lord. We always do our job to the best of our abilities, by my soul we do. But sometimes, we must exercise discretion."

Antoine creased his brow. "How so?"

"The law can be unduly harsh. For instance, Parliament has recently decreed that the penalty for a second poaching offence is death."

"That's a high price. But I'm afraid your job is to apply the rule."

"Of course, my lord. But sometimes that sits ill wi' us. If we know a man is good but driven by desperation, it might be fairer to send him off wi' a bloodied nose. More politick, too, for if we killed every poacher we found, the people would revolt."

"That's as may be," said Antoine. "But what has it to do with our murder?"

Cuddy swallowed. "It's like this. On the night we talked of, we didnae just see some strangers poaching. We recognised them. Indeed, we caught them. And perhaps the sentries at Wark caught us, too."

Antoine glowered. "You deceived me then? I knew it. But why bother when it sounds like you simply performed your duties?"

The bailiff winced. "One of the men was a kinsman of ours. A good fellow, the husband of my sister. Their hame was burnt by reivers last winter and a' their animals taken, so they've been living hand to mouth ever since. He already has one mark against his name, so if we were to report him, they would string him up."

"I see. So what did you do?"

Cuddy lowered his head. "We took him and his cronies back to our hidey hole and roughed them up. Told him this must be the last time. But as we were doing this, we spotted the body on the island."

"And then what?"

"The rest is as we told it. My father and I rowed over and found that awful scene."

"And your kinsman?"

"We sent him and his confederates off, as fast as they could go. But they may have seen something earlier that could help ye."

Antoine leant in. Perhaps some good could come of this, after all. "What are you talking about?"

"I should let my goodbrother explain. But I believe he may have seen the murderers and even heard them talk. Please, sir, if he tells ye all, will you spare him from his punishment?"

Antoine sighed. "I will spare all of you if you tell the truth. But one more deception, and you'll be for it. Now, what's his name, and how can I find him?"

"Thank ye, thank ye," said Cuddy, clasping his hands. "I told my father that ye were cut from a different cloth. My goodbrother's name is Jock Rutherford, and he bides near us, in Lennel. He's away in Teviotdale, helping wi' the last ploughing o' the season, but he'll be back in a few days."

"Very well. Tell him that we will visit him then. Now say no more of this to anybody and take us to the prioress."

They returned for the others and continued along the

riverbank to the precinct wall, where a spiked gate blocked their way. The horses would struggle to negotiate the entrance, so Cuddy ushered Antoine in on foot. As the gate swung open, they found themselves in the cemetery. It occurred to the Frenchman that Alex Redpath's torso must be somewhere in this jumble of stone slabs, probably in an unmarked grave. James Redpath was no doubt thinking the same thing, for he hung his head in sorrow.

"Mother Isabella," said the bailiff, pointing to a solitary figure on a stone bench at the far side of the graveyard. "She always sits here at this hour."

Antoine went on alone, for dusk was falling, and he wanted to do this quickly. As he picked his way through the graveyard, he was struck by how peaceful it was, despite the violent end of so many of those interred. The birds were settling down for the night. The nuns were at their private prayers, in anticipation of Vespers. The prioress appeared deep in contemplation, but as he approached, he felt she looked troubled.

"Good evening, my lord Warden," she said quietly.

"Good evening, Reverend Mother. And sorry for disturbing you."

"Do not be sorry," she said, placing a wooden rosary in her lap. "I have just finished my prayers."

"It is a beautiful place to say them. Indeed, it feels like a sin for me to come here again, on such ungodly business."

Antoine saw her smile at the attempt to ingratiate. Whatever her heavenly musings, her feet were still firmly on the ground.

"I hear that you have been busy," she said. "And that your understanding of the murder has advanced?"

"To a point. We are now reasonably sure that the body belongs to a man named—"

"Alex Redpath, yes, I know. And if you have come here to ask for the body again, I must disappoint you. The answer is still no."

"I thought as much," said Antoine. "But we also have some new suspects. One of whom is your neighbour over the river, Cospatrick Dixon. I was hoping you might be able to arrange a meeting?"

The Reverend Mother flushed, and seizing his opportunity, Antoine explained how the card game and the ensuing feud incriminated Dixon. The prioress listened, but her interest seemed to wane at the story's telling.

"I will enquire about a meeting for you, although I am preoccupied with other matters. For a moment, I thought you might be about to connect Dixon to them, but it seems not."

"I'm not sure I understand," said Antoine. "What troubles you?"

The prioress toyed with her beads. "I have some intelligence of my own. I cannot say much more but suffice to say that I continue to be vexed by talk of arms smuggling."

Antoine frowned. "As I said at our dinner, I've seen no trace of this. I swear to you. Are you certain it's going on?"

"As certain as I can be."

"And yet Lord Dacre also says there are no signs on his side."

"Lord Dacre says a lot of things. That does not make them true."

Antoine could not resist a smile. "You were so praiseful of him the other night – I hope he has not reneged on his donation?"

The prioress scowled, as if to confirm it. "I simply state my ongoing belief that one cannot trust anybody."

"Well, I hope we can learn to trust one another," said Antoine. "After all, we share a desire for peace. And if I see evidence of arms smuggling, I will certainly investigate it."

The Vespers bells rang out, and the prioress rose. As she turned to leave, she fixed him in a piercing gaze. "Perhaps you are already doing that, monsieur?"

Chapter 25

A ntoine tossed Mother Isabella's words around in his mind as they rode home in the moonlight. Did she mean that Alex Redpath was involved in some illicit arms trade? It seemed unlikely for a run-of-the-mill chancer like him. But perhaps he was in the service of more powerful players. Could this be the grand plan he had been pursuing, according to Luggy? He thought about asking Laidlaw, but the fall of darkness had made the fellow more nervous than ever.

As they came over Hawkslaw, Luggy snapped. "This is no good. I cannae live like this."

He burst into another coughing fit, and Redpath tried to soothe him. "Hush, friend. We are almost hame."

"Aye, but what if they're lurking there for us?"

"I'll make sure they're no'. It's been a long day, and you will soon be safely a-bed."

"Then what of the morn? Next week? Next year? They might come back for me at any time."

"Who knows when Death will visit any of us," muttered Redpath. "We may all be long gone by the time my brother's killers meet their end."

Antoine felt the reproach in Redpath's voice and found he could not blame him. After all, grief could result in an excess of yellow bile that would render a man bitter and impatient. He tried to demonstrate some urgency of his own. "Rest assured, I want nothing more than to solve this case. But I need your help. Luggy, if you are so afeart, then tell us why. What do you mean by 'they'? Dixon? Wedderburn? Hume? Or some other?"

"I've telt ye, I dinnae ken."

"But you have your suspicions; I can feel it. So point us in the right direction."

"I cannae say more than I already have. All I ken is that Alex had something on his mind, a job he hoped would make him rich. But I swear, he didnae tell me what it was."

Antoine did not press him further. They continued to pick their way over the mosses in eery silence. Only when he heard the Leet babbling away to his left did he decide to take a more direct approach. Otherwise, they would be in Swinton soon, and the chance might be lost.

"You know, there's talk of arms smuggling on the border," he said carelessly. He used the faint moonlight to watch Redpath and Luggy's faces, but they gave nothing away. "Some say that rebel forces are abroad and are trying to acquire an arsenal."

"That is all we need," muttered Redpath, who seemed unaware of the dangling bait.

"Aye," said Luggy. "We have never a moment's peace."

"You don't think Alex might have been involved with it somehow? Not at the highest level but in the procurement, perhaps?"

Both men looked at each other, bemused. Then Redpath started to laugh.

"You're not being serious, are you? That's many a league beyond my brother's usual business."

"I don't know," said Antoine. "According to Luggy, he had plans above his station."

"Aye," said Laidlaw, casting incredulous side-eyes to his friend. "But I didn't mean anything of that scale. I thought perhaps he'd signed up for a big raid. Or if he was smuggling, then horses perhaps – the English have some grand nags we are forbidden to import. I dinnae see him intriguing in affairs o' state!"

The two men chuckled at the notion, and Antoine was convinced of their disbelief. Whether or not their scepticism was well-founded was another matter.

When the party entered the village, they said a long farewell to Cranstoun, who took his hounds back up the hill with another effusive display of thanks. Antoine joined Redpath inside Luggy's house to reassure him that nobody was there. They lit a torch and poked it into every corner of the man's dingy dwelling, ensuring that the shutters were firmly locked and no one could prise out the stones around the door hinges. Once they had conducted a thorough search, Luggy seemed a little calmer, and Antoine offered further reassurance by saying they would return in a couple of days.

"I still feel like he's holding something from us," the Frenchman told Redpath as the latter retired to his home. "He was on the brink of telling us, that first night, but he has since clammed up."

Redpath looked back at Luggy's house. "Ye can see how scared he is, that's why. I will see if I can loosen him, but the longer this drags on, the more danger we will all be in."

That evening, Antoine gathered Turnbull and Anderson to his chamber to share the day's news. They were tired, though, and could make little sense of their disparate reports. That cursed wind had picked up again and caused the roof to creak unnaturally. The noise seemed to mock their exhausted silence, the emptiness of their ideas. Their evidence was as shaky as the groaning rafters, it seemed to say.

Hold on. Was that the wind – or something else? The men looked at each other in astonishment. There it went again. There could be no doubt. Somebody was moving about, above their heads.

"Could it be one of the men?" asked Antoine. "They were fixing the roof today, weren't they?"

"Aye," said Anderson. "But they finished that hours ago. It's pitch black out there now."

"And no strangers have had access to the tower?"

"No, sir. We've no' seen a soul all day."

The men crept to the corner hatch, which led onto the wall-walk. The noise became louder, more easily identifiable as footsteps on the slates. Whoever it was, they were getting closer. Some light appeared at the bottom of the hatch, in the gap between wood and stone. Anderson beckoned for the others to move back while positioning himself to the side and raising his sword. They all held their breath as the little door pulled back stiffly.

Anderson drew his weapon back. He tensed and was about to bring it down – when a lamp clattered to the floor, and Carmichael's face ducked through. "It's me! It's me!" he screamed, shielding his head. "I left my hammer up there afore!"

Chapter 26

The following morning, Antoine declared the men at ease, as he was worn out by the travails of the past few days. Anderson had the idea of bringing the group together with a ball game, so he asked for a volunteer to go into Dunse and buy a pig's bladder. Carmichael raised his hand, to atone for causing such alarm the previous night. When he returned, Anderson mixed the Edinburgh recruits and the Marchmen into two teams and set up some goals on the land around the tower. The ground was too marshy to make a decent game of it, but the men seemed to enjoy it nonetheless.

Burnsie had caught some rabbits in a net, and more surprisingly, Simpson revealed that he had once worked in the kitchens at Fast Castle and was a decent cook. So that night, they all dined as kings in the hall. Even Gibb was on the mend, under Catherine's supervision. Perhaps this would be a turning point, a moment when they could start bringing the different strands together to form a coherent picture.

Antoine retired in good spirits and rose early the next morning to take a handful of men to Swinton. However, his skin began to prickle as they arrived in the village. The geese ran towards them, honking furiously, but nobody came to gather them. Instead, Redpath stood in the road, outside the entrance to Luggy's bastle house. He had his back to Antoine's party, consoling his wife. As they got closer, Agnes screamed, "This is all your fault!" and barged past them, bunching her dress in her hands.

Redpath ran over with a face like fury. "Now look what you've done. I told you the longer you held off, the more danger we would be in."

Antoine threw up his hands. "What on earth do you mean?"

"They came in the night!"

"Who did?"

"Dixon's gang. They've killed Luggy. Killed him in cold blood."

Antoine gasped and quickly dismounted. He ran into the house, where Laidlaw's body lay spreadeagled on the earth floor. The scene was surprisingly peaceful: there seemed to be no gore, Luggy just lay face-down, with his arms out in front of him. Above him, the trapdoor was open, and the ladder hung down.

"Check this floor, then upstairs," Antoine ordered Anderson, as he knelt to have a closer look. There was a small wound on the back of Luggy's head, covered by matted hair. His face was cold and stiff to the touch, limbs less so but going that way. With some effort, Antoine rolled the corpse over and immediately recoiled, for the expression on Luggy's face was terrifying. Both eyes bulged open, full of blood. There were terrible bruises around his neck. Most sickening of all, his grotesquely swollen tongue lolled from his mouth as if he were one of Cranstoun's dogs.

"When did you find him?" the Frenchman asked Redpath, who stood over him, his face utterly drained.

"A couple of hours ago, when we rose."

"And he was like this?"

"Exactly so. We could tell he was deid straight away, so we didnae move him."

Antoine cast a quick eye around the room. "How the hell did someone get in? I thought you were supposed to be watching over him?"

"I was! We said goodnight at dusk, and I helped him secure the house, just as you and I did the other night. I tell ye, this is Dixon's work, and your delay has cost us."

Antoine put his head down again as he tried to think. He feared there might be some truth in Redpath's words, even if he was less sure of the guilty party. It was terrible to think that his indecision might have cost another man his life. Still, he resented being talked to in this way by somebody of Redpath's station.

"Did you see any of the attackers?" he snapped.

"No, they came in the night, and we saw nothing. Heard nothing either."

"Then hold your tongue. We need to think coolly about how this happened."

Anderson climbed down from the ladder and announced that there was nothing untoward on either floor.

"There are no signs of a forced entry either," said Turnbull, who had gone to the doorway for fresh air.

"He must have let the killers in," said Antoine. "Then I'd say they hit him on the back of the head, perhaps as he tried to flee back upstairs. And strangled him as he lay here. You can see the marks on his neck."

"Why would he let them in?" said Anderson. "He must have known they meant him ill."

"Perhaps they tricked him?" said Redpath. He had quietened, but there was still resentment in his voice.

"Surely he would not be so foolish?" said Antoine. "Your friend was simple but not an idiot."

"They might have offered him a deal. You saw how scared he was. They might have promised to leave him alone if he let them in?"

"I suppose. Or he considered them friends, somehow. I still sense that Luggy knew more about Alex's plans than he was letting on. What if these men persuaded him that they could protect him from whoever killed Alex? Or they could give him a share of the riches if he stayed silent."

Redpath's jaw tightened. "With respect, I fear ye are over-complicating this, sir. But I will hold my counsel for now."

The men searched the ground floor again, and finding nothing, they went outside. Antoine told the men to inspect the yard while he and Turnbull interviewed the rest of the Redpaths. Agnes, Dand and Jessie sat on the bales where Antoine had supped ale with Luggy three days earlier. The blacksmith Erchie Henderson paced about beside them. Even from a distance, Antoine could feel the group's hostility.

"I am sorry to visit you again, in such circumstances," he said to Agnes.

Redpath's wife grunted and stared right through him. He tried again.

"I realise that this must be deeply painful, but we will catch your friend's killers. We just need your help."

Another snort. "We are beyond help."

"Did any of you see anyone approaching as night fell?"

"None of us witnessed anything," said Erchie. "We have given you our all. It is surely time for you to come up with the answers."

"Did Luggy say anything to you, about his fears?"

"Only that ye were taking yer time," said Jessie. "And the longer ye swithered, the shorter his life might be."

"Ye said ye would protect us," said Erchie.

"Luggy didnae deserve this," said Agnes bitterly.

"I still cannae believe it," said Dand, staring at the ground.

Antoine studied the group. The raw anger in their faces was understandable, but again, it nettled him. There was nothing to be gained from them in this mood, so he made to leave. But as he did so, he turned.

"Before I go, Redpath. Remind us exactly how you checked the house was secure."

The fellow bristled. "I telt ye, the same as we did the other night."

"Nevertheless, I want to make sure. So tell us what you did, step by step."

"Very well," Redpath said. "I went round to Luggy's just as night was falling. I asked him how he was, and he said he was fine, although I could see he was far from it. His hands shook like leaves on a tree, and his cough was even worse than usual."

"Did you inspect the outside of the house?"

"Around the yard and outbuildings, aye. Just as you and I did. There was nobody there."

"What then?" said Antoine, thoughtfully.

"We went inside and closed the door. I walked Luggy about the ground floor and showed him that it, too, was empty. Then we opened the trapdoor and climbed the ladder."

"Both of you?"

"Aye. We checked the window shutters were secure, and nobody could get in."

"And finally?"

"He followed me down the ladder again to the door. He seemed a little calmer, and we embraced." Redpath's voice broke a little. "I told him no' to worry. Then I listened as he bolted the door and I checked the outside of the house one more time, before going hame. Ye see, I did everything as ye showed me."

Antoine put his head in his hands and said nothing for a moment. Then he looked up. "Did you check the ground floor again, before you left?"

Redpath hesitated. "No, sir, I did not. We didnae either, if ye remember."

Antoine sighed. "That is because there were two of us. You went upstairs with Luggy while I stayed downstairs, remember? We had men outside the house, too."

"I'm not sure where ye're leading us," said Redpath, in a voice so hoarse it was almost a whisper.

"Did you lock the door while you were inside?"

Redpath thought about it. "No, sir, I did not. Again, I copied what you and I had done."

"So, there is a chance that somebody could have entered the house while you were upstairs with Luggy?"

"Surely we would have heard him come in?" said Redpath, desperately.

"Not if Luggy's cough was as bad as you say it was. It would take but a second for someone to open the door and hide in the shadows. Then they could wait to ensure you were gone – and spring on him."

"I suppose so," said Redpath. He ran his hand through his hair and down over his mouth as if he were preventing himself from throwing up. "My God, what have I done?"

His wife shook her head, angrier than ever, and went back inside.

Chapter 27

The men rode home in a subdued mood. Antoine felt sure that Luggy had been on the brink of telling him about Alex's secret plans, but now that chance was lost. The Redpaths blamed him for their friend's death, even though one of their own might have been more directly responsible. As for the killer – or killers – they were further than ever from catching them. When Turnbull tried to engage him on the subject, Antoine shut him down before spurring his horse and riding on alone.

As they arrived at the tower, Wilson greeted them with a message from Lord Dacre: he had consented to a Truce Day on the island at Martinmas.

"Well," said Turnbull brightly as he skimmed over the English bill of complaints, "at least we have had some good news today."

"What do you mean?" snapped Antoine.

"Dacre's finally given in to our request," stammered Turnbull. "That's a good thing, surely?"

"He's not conceded a button, for God's sake. It's the opposite. He smells our blood. Our disarray. We now have only two weeks to solve this riddle or be humiliated."

Not for the first time, Antoine regretted his sharp tone, but he had more to worry about than Turnbull's feelings.

That night, he ate alone in his room and retired to bed early. By the time his hour of watch arrived, he had barely slept – something that was becoming a regular occurrence. Even in his worst days, immediately after returning from Venice, he had usually managed to get through his first sleep, but now the torments were coming earlier and more intense than ever.

He rose from his bed and took out his quill, hoping that the act of writing might order his jumbled thoughts. The more he considered it, the more Antoine suspected that Luggy had become tangled in some bigger plot – even if it was not the arms smuggling that Mother Isabella imagined.

As he sketched out his ideas, a terrible thought occurred to him. Perhaps the two murders were not related after all? Or at least not committed by the same person? If they really were dealing with some international plot, it was possible that one side had tortured Alex in the hope of extracting information – then the other side had strangled Luggy to prevent further secrets from slipping out. That would explain why the methods chosen were so different. But it would also mean they were looking for more than one killer.

Antoine's head ached at the idea. Could this case be twice as complicated as he had imagined? He found himself feeling doubly alone and desperate.

Once more, his mind flitted between his time in that Venetian cell and his current predicament. Despite Carmichael's work on the roof, there was still a slight leak in the ceiling, and the drips reminded him of those which had fallen from the crumbling prison walls. He thought of how Albany had snared him in this job and how Dacre wished to catch him too – just as he had been trapped in Italy. Yes, this was a prison of sorts, and if he were not careful, he would be stuck here for eternity.

Everywhere he looked, there seemed to be walls hemming him in, preventing his escape. Locals who did not trust him. People who did not respect him. Powerful men like Hume and Dacre determined to bring him down.

He tumbled further into the void of despair before thinking again of Catherine. Why had he brought her to this place? He hoped that his motives had been pure, but he could not be sure. It had been a long time since he had been intimate with a woman or even enjoyed a friendship with one. In his youth, he had appreciated their company, but war had taught him that there was too much they did not understand. They asked too many questions of things he would rather leave unsaid. Perhaps that is what fascinated him about Mistress Gray: that she had her own secrets, and he was the interrogator.

It was time for his second sleep, but he did not feel able yet. Instead, he checked that Turnbull was still dozing and crept across the room to the spiral stairway. He wound his way down, taking care over the trip-step, making sure that nobody was sleeping on the middle floor.

He continued to the ground floor, peering around the stairway entrance. Once more, all was silent. A thin streak of moonlight came through one of the ventilation shafts and picked out the flour dust hanging in the air. A scrabbling sound. Antoine started – only to realise that a mouse had found its way into the pantry: another job for tomorrow.

He advanced to the two storage rooms and stopped outside. First, he listened at Gibb's door. The old man was breathing rhythmically. He sounded peaceful and did not stir. Antoine wondered what shape a blind man's dreams took and whether he, too, would be plagued by nightmares when he recovered. Would the absence of vision make them better, or more hellish?

He turned to Catherine's cell, his head swirling with the same thoughts as before: his feelings of captivity, abandonment and despair. He thought of Francoise and how he had let her down just as he had done his men at Agnadello, how he was still failing everybody to this day. The Redpaths. Luggy. Turnbull. Albany. Himself.

Putting his hand on the latch, he made to let himself into Catherine's room. He rehearsed what he might say to her, what he might ask of her. For a moment, he had a sense of utter clarity about what he wanted. Then his doubts returned, and the moment was gone. He went back up the stairs as silently as he had come.

Chapter 28

It was a bitterly cold night, and Antoine barely slept a wink. He lay under the covers, turning over his thoughts and waiting for the new day. Eventually, a sliver of light crept through the crack in the hatch, where Anderson had nearly decapitated Carmichael a few days ago. Forcing himself from the warmth of his bed, Antoine went to the main window and drew the shutters back. A hard frost had visited them: another reminder that winter was on its way and that time was running out.

Despite all his ruminations, the Frenchman still had no clear plan. But he was gripped by the idea that the tower was becoming a prison to them. With that in mind, he gathered all the men in the barmekin and announced that they would be going into Dunse that afternoon. He explained that they now had sufficient numbers to make their presence felt and restore confidence amongst the locals as news of Luggy's murder spread.

"It's the locals we need to be worried about," muttered Anderson as he organised a skeleton force to stay behind, with Catherine and Gibb.

The cruel wind chased them up the hill into Dunse, so they

were glad to reach the White Hart, where a fire crackled in the hearth and clogged the room with peaty smoke. Purves looked flustered to see them and glared at Turnbull before disappearing into a back room. While he was gone, the men sat themselves at a long trestle table and ordered ale and pottage from one of the maids. The other tables were busy, too, and the patrons stared over with sullen faces.

"Here's our Frenchie warden come to save us," came a voice from the crowd.

"He'd be better off saving himself," said another, to a rumble of laughter.

The pottage was supposed to contain meat, but there was barely a bone in the thin gruel, so the men finished early and set into their ale. The Edinburgh recruits kept to themselves while Simpson, Carmichael and Gilchrist took their drinks and drifted off to other tables.

"What are they up to?" said Antoine, frowning.

"These folk are probably their kin," said Turnbull. "Or their accomplices. It was the same at the Ledgerwoods'."

"Well, keep an eye on them and check there's no treachery afoot. Meanwhile, I think it's time to introduce myself to your Master Purves."

Turnbull flustered. "I'm not sure that's wise, sir. He seems keen to keep his distance from us, especially when he has eyes on him."

"There are eyes on all of us – which is exactly why we must behave without fear or favour. Leave it with me; I won't be long."

Antoine advanced to the counter and rapped on the rough plank that extended between two oak barrels. A group of men looked him up and down and exchanged comments under their breath. A maid caught his eye and gave him a bold smile. A little too bold, Antoine thought, but the Scottish women were often like that.

"I'm after Master Purves," he said. "Is he about?"

"Aye, my lord. But he's unavailable presently. Can I help ye wi' something?"

She leant over the counter and gave him an eyeful of cleavage.

"Yes, mistress. You can fetch him, as I've asked."

She giggled. "Oh, listen to your accent. It's as sweet as they say."

"Just fetch him here, if you will."

"He left me strict instructions, sir. Now, let me put a smile on your face."

"Find him," he said quietly.

"Suit yirsel."

The girl went off into the back room, leaving Antoine at the counter. His men were busy enjoying themselves over another round of ale. They seemed oblivious to his whereabouts, and he felt quite vulnerable. He was relieved to see Anderson and Turnbull bustling towards him through the throng, but just before they reached him, the back-room door opened, and Purves came out, red-faced. Hume and Wedderburn were right behind him.

"Bonsoir, Monsieur Warden," said Hume, moving the innkeeper to the side. "It seems we share a taste in taverns as well as towers."

"We have nothing in common," said Antoine. He was caught off guard but raised his voice for the whole room to hear.

"And yet we keep bumping into each other. I believe Wedderburn here has the same problem."

"He plays the same game as you. But you must realise that for all your threats, we will not be put off our trail. Or your trail, for that matter."

Hume's eyes narrowed. Grabbing a bottle of wine from an old codger, he poured himself a cup.

"Only the weak need to make threats," he said. "And you sound like the one threatening me. As for us, we simply protect those in need, and we punish those who deserve it."

Antoine scoffed at this. "Which category did Luggy Laidlaw fall into?" A hush had descended over the inn.

"I have never heard of the fellow. Was he a friend of yours?"

"You bullied him," said Antoine, his voice growing stronger. "Blackmail, as you call it. Just like Alex Redpath. Now, both are dead. But I am here to tell everyone in this room that we will catch those responsible and bring them to justice, no matter how high their station."

"From what I've seen, you'd struggle to catch the pox in a whorehouse," scoffed Hume. "Now, please excuse us as we have business of our own."

The warlord downed his wine and brushed past Purves, who stared at the ground. Wedderburn joined him, barging Turnbull's shoulder on the way, causing him to spill another man's ale. The disgruntled fellow cursed, and Anderson had to calm the situation before escorting Antoine back to their table. The inn gradually recovered its noisy chatter, but the mood had darkened, so they left for the tower not long after, waiting only for the Humes to disperse into the cold night air.

Once they were safely home, Anderson sent the men to sleep off their drinking for the next day. As Antoine and Turnbull entered the tower, they were met by Catherine. She seemed agitated and the Frenchman's pulse quickened.

"Good evening, Mistress Gray. We are just back from the tavern."

"So I see," she said. "I trust ye enjoyed yourselves."

"The trip was worthwhile. We are now dealing with two murders and God knows how many killers. It was important to show our faces."

She smiled, showing those dimples again. "Of course. You are a busy man."

Was she mocking him? It was hard to tell, so Antoine continued brightly. "How is your patient? Perhaps our absence has given him some peace?"

"He recovers well, sir. But there is something I wish to ask of ye."

The Frenchman sighed. "Not whether the two of you can leave, I hope? I have already told you this would be unadvisable, given all that is happening outside. Indeed, we have clashed with the Humes again tonight. It would be better to stay here until things have calmed."

"It's not that," she frowned, then raised her eyes to the ceiling or perhaps to some higher power. "Although I do dearly wish to go hame. It's a question of a personal nature."

Antoine hoped that his face had not coloured. "I see, and what might that be?"

Catherine paused, and he remembered Turnbull standing at his shoulder. "Why don't you go upstairs," he said to his assistant. "Get the fire started, and I will be with you shortly."

With Turnbull away, Catherine led Antoine to her room. He looked around to check there were no witnesses before entering and shutting the door. Although he had not supped much at the tavern, he felt lightheaded, a mixture of excitement and dread. He could not imagine what she would say to him but longed to hear it. When it came, the question took the wind from his lungs.

"Why did ye stop by my room last night?"

Her voice startled him with its intensity.

"I don't know what you mean," he stuttered. "You must have imagined it."

"Gibb heard ye at my door," she said firmly. "I know that it was you."

"That's ridiculous. There are twenty-eight men in this tower now. Any one of them could have passed by in their hour of watch."

Catherine closed her eyes and shook her head, slowly and then more forcefully. Antoine had no clue what she might do next. Or how he should act. He glanced at her hands, remembering how she had held that shard of pottery in her cottage, but they were empty. Gradually, her head slowed again, and the words dripped out, one by one.

"I ken it was you because Gibb heard ye. That ankle of yours: he recognised your limp."

So that was it. The blind man had not been sleeping after all. Antoine felt like he had stepped in a snare. But this time, it was one he had set himself.

"Very well, it is true. But it is not what you think. I came down to your room because I could not sleep. Rather, I cannot sleep. Ever. I feel ashamed, but my mind will not rest. You must think I have done some terrible things, for God to punish me so. And perhaps that is correct. But I came to you for help, nothing more."

Catherine stopped fidgeting and met his eye for the first time. "Why would ye come to me for help?"

"Because I have seen how you have cared for Gibb. I wondered whether you might have some potion to let me rest. It was probably a foolish idea."

"And why did ye change your mind?"

"It was the dead of night. Even in my wide-eyed madness, I realised you might think I had some other design. So I decided I would ask you in the daylight hours."

Catherine tilted her head and observed him for a moment. Then she spoke, more gently. "I can certainly prepare ye a posset of this kind. That will be easy. But it will not heal your wounds."

"I am not ill," Antoine frowned.

"Nevertheless, something is eating at ye. Not a canker, perhaps, but something similar. I have seen soldiers like you before and I ken the look. When I have treated them, my remedies have had little effect until those ghosts have been shaken free."

"I see no need to spill my soul to you, Mistress Gray, so if you can just furnish me with a potion, I will take my chances."

"As ye wish. I will pry no further. But then let me share a thought wi' ye."

"Go on."

"We have been at your tower for a week now. I ken ye've kept a close watch on me, but I have watched you too."

Antoine shifted uneasily as she continued.

"Ye're a man of great stature," she said, "but ye do not seem greatly content."

Her words took him aback, but still, he said nothing.

"It is as if ye are always searching for something. Not just clues for this case. Something more. Something that can't be seen."

"Now you are talking in riddles," he said crossly.

"Perhaps," she said. "After all, I am only a foolish woman. But if my work has taught me anything of you men, ye crave advancement above all else. All I say is that to progress, ye must know what ye truly want, not just what ye wish to escape."

Chapter 29

Antoine slept better than he had for a long time, helped by Catherine's posset. He was still troubled by her words, though. He woke with them on his mind and the more he considered them, the more impertinent he found them. Who was someone of her station to advise him on his life? And what could one as melancholic as she teach him of happiness? No matter. As long as her elixir worked, he would press on, as he always did.

"Get the horses ready," he told Turnbull, who was already up and griddling an oatcake on the fire. "We're going to pay the prioress another visit."

"Shouldn't we see to the Redpaths first?"

Antoine put on a fresh shirt. "We can pick James up on the way if his temper has cooled. But I feel it's time to negotiate with Mother Isabella as a stateswoman, rather than a woman of the church."

Turnbull tutted, as was his habit whenever the prioress was mentioned, but they were soon on their way, taking Anderson and Carmichael with them.

When they came to Swinton, the Redpaths' geese created their usual commotion, but what truly assaulted their senses was the smell from just beyond. The cold weather meant that the reek of Luggy's corpse had not yet become unbearable. It was even quite sweet. But it filled Antoine's nostrils as if the man were lying before him, eyes bulging, tongue lolling, his last breath still in the air. The soldiers crossed themselves as Carmichael knocked on Redpath's door and called out the purpose of their visit.

The shutters creaked open – before slamming shut. Raised voices could be heard – Agnes arguing with James, it seemed. The latter emerged, sheepish, and quickly saddled up.

"Sorry about that, sir. As ye can imagine, our passions run high right now. But I have an idea which might help us all – and make up for any damage I have caused."

"Go on," said Antoine.

"Let's wait until we're properly on our way."

They set off at a steady pace, on the familiar track to Coldstream. Antoine kept turning to Redpath to see if he might be willing to share his idea, but he seemed deep in thought. As they came over Hawkslaw, the Frenchman could bear it no longer.

"We're nearly there, so if you have some news, we'd better hear it."

"It's no' news as such," said Redpath. "It's an old idea, but one which could provide the proof ye say we need."

"Very well, let's have it."

Redpath swallowed. "I've been thinking, sir. There are no witnesses to Luggy's death. Or at least none that we know of. But what if Luggy himself were to show us the killer before we put him underground?"

Antoine could not suppress a snort. "What do you mean?"

"What if he were to point the finger? Give us a sign somehow? I've heard it said that if a murderer is brought in the presence of his victim, then the body will ooze blood. We could summon Dixon, Hume, whoever ye like, to prove themselves in front o' us."

"That is a German custom," said Antoine, sceptically.

"It's also practised here," Turnbull pointed out. "I studied it at St Andrews. It's called cruentation. For the test to be true, the accused must walk around the corpse three times, uttering the dead man's name, then he must lay his hands upon the body. The evidence for it is flimsy, though."

"Either way, it would depend on us pressing the accused to attend. I do not see us being able to do that, with the men we face."

Redpath slumped in his saddle. "Is it no' even worth a try?"

Antoine looked ahead. "It's an interesting idea, but let's drop it for now. I have a plan of my own that should bear fruit faster."

They reached Coldstream, just as the bells rang for Sext. It was an important point in the day, for noon was the hour when divine light was in its fulness, and the moment Christ was nailed to the Cross. As they passed through the orchard, Antoine was struck by how beauty and suffering coexisted in this place.

Sister Triduana, as gruff as ever, met them at the gatehouse and escorted them to the parlour. They did not have long to wait, for the service was short, and Mother Isabella came straight from the chapel.

"I thought I might see you again," she said gravely. "I hear that one of the gentlemen you brought last time is dead."

"I'm afraid so," said Antoine. "It seems we are battling no ordinary evil."

The prioress clasped her hands. "This is my worry. But let's not waste time here. Why don't you join me, and we can converse over dinner."

As on their first visit, Antoine accompanied the prioress to her private dining room while Sister Triduana ushered the others elsewhere. This time, though, the meal was a much simpler affair of bread and cheese.

"So, my lord, how can I help you?" The prioress did not look up as she attended to her trencher of food.

"It's more a question of how we might help each other," said Antoine, steepling his fingers. "It occurs to me that we both find ourselves in a hole. You with your plot and me with my murders. I still have no idea whether they are related, but if we work together, we might find out."

"I see. Well, let's start with you. I go back to my question: how can I help?"

"My hopes remain the same. I ask you for the exhumation of Alex Redpath's remains and an interview with Cospatrick Dixon."

The prioress smiled. "I've given you my answer already. Why should I change my mind?"

"Because they might yield intelligence on your own enquiries."

"Very true. But frankly, I do not need you for either investigation. We can dig up the body any time we like, and I can summon Dixon here myself. Indeed, he would be more likely to speak to me than you. So forgive me, I'm struggling to see what you can bring me that I do not already have."

Antoine nodded. "You make a fair point. But I can make much broader enquiries than you and prosecute them more vigorously, too. You have spies; do not pretend otherwise. But by their very nature, they cannot confront suspects, pursue them or bring them to justice. All they can do is report back to you. I have nearly thirty men and the Governor's whole army behind me. That's the difference."

The prioress sipped some wine. "And what if Lord Albany is himself behind the plot?" she said carefully, over the rim of her cup. "Why would I hand over intelligence to you, his lieutenant, when our loyalties might differ?"

"You said before that you have no allegiances, only a desire for peace. Well, I share that desire. And believe it or not, so does my master. It is not in his interest to inflame the Marches, quite the opposite."

The prioress rose and moved to the window. She gazed over the cemetery, where they had talked the other day. Beyond was the river, the island, the border and Dixon's land; beyond that was Flodden, where thousands lay. She kept her back to him.

"I cannot tell you everything I know, sir. Not until I can trust you fully. Nevertheless, there is something that you might help with. A matter of some urgency."

Antoine's ears pricked up. "I'm listening."

The prioress turned. "I have recently become concerned by the behaviour of some Flemish folk in Berwick. There has long been a colony of them there. They have grown wealthy off our wool, which they take to Flanders. On their return, they bring us finished cloth, claret, furs, silks and everything else you can make a coin from."

Antoine was confused. "I know of them. I hear they drive a hard bargain, but I don't see them smuggling weapons. You only have to look out that window to see Lord Dacre bringing new guns to Wark. He makes no secret of it; if he wants more, he can simply ask King Henry. As for the Scots, they have not owned Berwick for thirty years now, so it would make no sense for them to procure arms via an English port."

"Not if it were Lord Albany, for sure. But what if a rebel faction were involved?"

"Even then, they would not want the bother of smuggling them over from England. They would land them at some deserted cove on our side."

"I agree. So, I conclude that the Flemings are not involved directly. But perhaps they are providing the finance for such an intrigue."

Antoine frowned. "I'm not sure I follow you."

"There is a Fleming called Tomas Schmidt," said the prioress, lowering her voice although nobody else was present, "one of their merchants in Berwick. Until recently, we had heard little of him. But these last two Mondays, he has crossed the border into Scotland at dusk. Then he has bribed a guard to let him back through the gate at night."

"That is strange, but there could be any number of reasons for his behaviour. A woman for instance?"

"I hear not,' said the prioress. "My sources say he goes to a place called Allanton to conduct some illicit business, but I cannot get more from them."

"Cannot Lord Dacre help? Berwick falls on his plate, after all. The guards could seize this fellow."

"You heard him at our dinner. He's not interested in any plot."

Antoine gave a wry smile. "No, indeed, if it makes mischief in Scotland, he is probably happy for it to proceed unhindered."

"Quite so. Which brings me to you. I believe Schmidt is mixed up in this affair somehow. Perhaps he is involved in your murders, too. So I want you to follow him to Allanton and learn more."

Antoine stroked his beard. "And if I do, you will meet my own requests?"

"Yes. If you bring me the intelligence."

"Interesting," said Antoine as he finished his bread. It did not seem like such a great chore to secure what he was after. "When is this fellow due to pay his next visit?"

"Tonight. If you leave now, you will get there in time."

"Very well," said Antoine, putting his trencher aside. "And how far should I go, to extract the information?"

"I will leave that to your conscience," said the Reverend Mother. She looked out of the window again, across the blood-soaked landscape. "But remember that many lives may be at stake, not just Schmidt's. The end justifies the action, as they say."

Chapter 30

Antoine hurried downstairs to gather the others, escorted by the hospitalless. As they crossed the cloister garth, a young nun pushed a barrow towards them. It was Sister Joan, the novice who had escorted him on his first visit. He thought that she flashed him a glance, but as they passed, she put her head down. It must be a strange life, volunteering to confine yourself in this way. In any case, there was no time for pleasantries if they were to make this rendezvous in Allanton.

Antoine rejoined the men in the parlour, and while the hospitalless went off to fetch the horses, he explained their assignment.

"Are you sure about this, sir?" said Redpath. "We could be riding intae a trap."

"I don't think so. If we get there early enough, we should be able to stake out the land and ensure we are safe."

"Very well," said Redpath, but he seemed troubled as they collected their horses and set off. Antoine reflected that the man might be feeling churned up by the deaths of his brother and friend – and too scared for his own life – to be of much use from this point. However, by the time they rode into Swinton, Redpath had regained his composure, and he declined the invitation to stay home.

"Just let me go in to square it wi' my family. They already say that I am too close to ye and will worry that this Fleming has nothing to do wi' us. But I'll explain the bargain ye've struck."

"As you wish," said Antoine. "But don't tarry – the sun will soon be down."

Redpath assented and emerged from his bastle after a few minutes. There was a clunk as someone bolted the door from the inside, but Antoine noted that no words of affection were traded. It seemed that Redpath might be even more isolated in his camp than he was.

Into the fading light they went, over the Harcarse burn where some women were washing their linens. The goodwives knew better than to delay a pack of armed men, so they moved to the side as the soldiers splashed through. Redpath advised that the quickest route was by Kimmerghame, so they peeled off that way while Carmichael continued to Black Rig to inform the others that they would be late. Turnbull felt his muscles tense as their destination grew ever closer, and he contemplated what – and who – might lie in store.

"It's an odd place to stage a meeting," he said as they quickened their pace. "Somewhere like Paxton would make it easier for a Berwick merchant to cross the border."

"Yes," said Antoine. "I wonder if that might hold some clues: who lives round here or might find it a useful spot?"

"The Humes have land nearby. Ledgerwood is a stone's throw away, too. The only one it makes no sense for is Dixon."

"This whole thing makes nae sense if ye ask me," said Redpath grimly.

The men reached Allanton just as the sun was starting to fall. Good, thought Antoine, they still had half an hour or so to prepare. The only problem might be guessing the precise location for the meeting. There were only a few cottages, all shuttered up for the night. There was no tavern, smithy, mill or dovecote, just a broad stretch of common land.

"It feels a bit exposed to hold a liaison here," said Antoine. "But at least we should have a grand view."

"Aye," said Anderson. "There are only two roads in. The one we're on and that one, over the bridge." He pointed to their left. "Our man Schmidt should come over that, frae Berwick. Then, whoever's meeting him will likely come our way, and they'll meet in the middle. We should split up and cover either route."

"Good idea," said Antoine as he dismounted. "Get the horses under cover, then you and Turnbull put yourselves on the other side of the bridge. Let Schmidt come over it, but make no move until his friend arrives. That way, we can close in on them and take them both together."

Anderson and Turnbull went off, while Antoine and Redpath found a hollow in the ground where they could hunker down. The Frenchman looked out towards the likely meeting spot, and Redpath faced backwards to guard the road. The sun was sinking behind them, and he checked that there were no flashes of light from any buckles or studs that might give them away.

Gradually, the cottages' whitewashed walls turned pink. The air became colder. A clutter of starlings made a racket before heading to their roost. Otherwise, all was still. Antoine was starting to wonder whether they had the wrong spot when the faint clack of hooves on stone came from across the common. He nudged Redpath, and they both strained to see as two horses appeared over the bridge. But only one rider.

Antoine gestured for Redpath to guard their backs while he watched the man advance. The fellow dismounted and tethered both horses to a tree. He looked around, continuing to the far side of the common. Another glance around. It was impossible to make out his features, but he was wearing a cloak, which he fidgeted over, as if it concealed something. Once satisfied that it was in order, he proceeded more confidently – only to walk right into the ground.

Antoine elbowed Redpath again, and the two watched open-mouthed as the man's head and shoulders disappeared in front of their eyes.

"There must be a hidden fold in the land," whispered Antoine. "God knows where he's gone now."

"Are you even sure it's him?" said Redpath.

"Who else would be abroad at this hour? The only question is where his companion is. We mustn't trigger our trap too early, but let's prepare to—"

Before Antoine could finish his words, a terrifying scream rang out. He turned to Redpath, horror-stricken, and then back to the bridge. Anderson and Turnbull were racing across the common, their swords drawn. A few seconds later, there was the thudding of hooves setting off at a gallop. The Frenchman briefly considered getting their own mounts, but they had hidden them too far into the woods. Sore ankle or not, there was nothing else for it. He got up and started to run, with Redpath alongside.

By the time he neared the dip, the pain was so great that he had to give up and walk. For a moment, Anderson, Turnbull and Redpath disappeared from sight. "Christ's guts," Antoine heard one of them say as he caught up and eased himself down the slope. The others were standing by some kind of shack – a shepherd's hut, perhaps – and in front of them was a man's body. He was lying on his back, with his forehead cleft open and blood pooling all around him. Judging by his cloak, it was the person who had come over the bridge. But of his killer, there was no sign.

"I think he went that way," said Anderson, pointing southwards. "There's a third path that we couldnae see from our position. The killer must have been lurking here already and pounced as soon as this poor bugger arrived."

"As if he knew someone was watching him?" said Turnbull.

"Let's just see who this is first," said Antoine, who did not wish to encourage talk of a conspiracy just yet.

He knelt by the corpse. The man's face was frozen in an expression of utter shock, mouth agape and eyes open, either side of a deep, vertical wound to the skull, from which a gory broth continued to ooze. So it had been an axe, most likely, or perhaps a halberd.

Antoine tried to control his stomach as he leant further in. It was hard to tell in this light, but the victim looked like he might have been in his middle years, with fair, curly hair. His clothes seemed like those of a wealthy man, albeit a wealthy man who was trying not to draw too much attention to himself. He wore no jewellery, and his cloak was made of wool, not fur. Antoine rummaged around it, searching for whatever the fellow had been fussing over when he arrived. He found a sword halfway out of its scabbard and a severed cord where a purse had presumably hung. Still there was another pouch, containing a letter of safe conduct made out in the name of Tomas Schmidt.

So it was him, then. But what was he doing here, in the middle of nowhere, with a spare horse?

"Knock on the nearest door," Antoine said to Anderson, standing up. "Get whoever's there to take the body in and not touch it until we have found the next of kin. Make sure to put the fear of God in them. If they steal so much as a boot, they'll be for it. And above all, they're not to say a word to anyone. Redpath, we'll take you home now, then return to Black Rig ourselves. We'll take the man's horses, too. Then we'll pick you up in the morning and report to the prioress. Hopefully, she will be in a forgiving mood."

Chapter 31

Antoine had another poor first sleep. He tried to banish the thought of Schmidt's ruptured face, but the image would not leave him. In his dreams, the Fleming joined Luggy, Francoise and his soldiers from Agnadello in a ghastly army, rising from the river and marching on the tower. They were carrying something on their shoulders as if it were a saint's effigy on a feast day, but as they drew nearer, Antoine saw that it was Alex's bloody torso. He woke in a sweat and spent his hour of watch trying to sketch out a plan.

That morning, he gathered the men to take them through it. The challenge was pointing them forward when they – and he – still had so many questions about the previous night. Try as he might to skip over the grisly details, the soldiers kept asking what they had found and what it all meant. When it became evident that Antoine did not have all the answers, a troubled mood fell upon the assembly.

"An ill wind besets us," muttered Nisbet.

"Death seems to be following us," agreed Tait.

"Aye, doesn't she just?" said Burnsie, nodding towards Catherine's door.

Antoine lowered both hands to gesture for calm. "On the contrary, these deaths simply show that we're on the killers' trail – and perhaps they know it."

Turnbull raised an eyebrow at him, but the Frenchman continued regardless. "Anderson, I want you to take a couple of men back to Allanton and see if we missed anything in the dark last night. Check those peasants haven't touched the body. Knock on some doors to see if anyone will talk."

The serjeant rubbed his hands in a show of readiness.

"Simpson, you go to Cranstoun's. Get him to keep searching for that lair in Kincham Woods, where the kidnappers must have spent the night."

The Marchman nodded.

"Then Carmichael, you can cover off the tavern gossips. Meanwhile, Turnbull and I will go to Coldstream with Gilchrist, and the rest of you can keep watch here. We may be away for a couple of days, so see that you get up to no mischief."

Anderson clapped his hands, and the men split up into their groups. As they departed in different directions, Antoine wondered whether these fresh enquiries would pay off. Frankly, he doubted it. But until things became clearer, it was better to keep people's minds busy, including his own.

An hour or so later, they picked up Redpath in Swinton. His face was red and puffy, his eyes ringed with heavy lines.

"Please tell me that all was well with you last night?" Antoine asked.

"Aye, all safe," said Redpath. "But I fear this may have to be my last journey wi' ye. Yestere'en was too much. My family are scared, and I need to be wi' them."

"I understand. Well, I am hopeful that we will have better news for you all soon. Or at least the chance of justice."

"Thank ye, sir. That's all we've ever asked." He wrinkled his nose. "I suppose last night might make the prioress less likely to accede to our requests. Do ye think it might be worth considering my idea now? Trial by blood, I mean."

Antoine sighed at the fellow's simple faith. "No, I don't think so. That's still a long shot. Let us see what Mother Isabella says first."

They did not have to wait long for their answer as they spurred their horses and reached Coldstream just before noon. The prioress came to see them in the parlour immediately. Wringing her hands, she made Antoine rush through his account before asking him to repeat it all over again, in more detail. When he had finished for the second time, she sat back in her chair and closed her eyes. Eventually, she bent forward.

"Well, gentlemen. I think we can agree that you've not kept your side of the bargain."

Antoine's heart sank, but his brain whirred into action. "I'm not so sure. All you asked us to do was follow this fellow Schmidt and find out more. Arguably, we have done just that."

"How so?"

He took a deep breath. "Well, we can now be sure that this fellow was up to something. Even that much was not certain yesterday. We also know that he came with money; his assassin cut a purse from his belt – and who would travel to a place like that at night, with a bag of coins, if he were not intent on spending them? So a financial transaction was afoot – but Schmidt was buying rather than selling as you had thought." Warming to his theme, he raised a finger. "On top of that, we saw him bring two horses, so he either had an accomplice or hoped to bring something back with him. But not weaponry, something smaller. All that seems to be a considerable advance in your intelligence, in just one day."

The men turned to their master in astonishment,

although Antoine was equally unsure from where he had plucked these ideas. However, the prioress merely laughed.

"Well, that is a fine story. But what's to say it was not simply a robbery? Or he was meeting a woman, as you suggested yesterday – that might explain the other horse. Perhaps she was a harlot, hence the money? Then her whoremonger saw his chance to make some more coin? You see how easy this guessing game is?"

"Come, Reverend Mother, I know you don't believe any of that. No, we have advanced your enquiry a little. Moreover, we have done so selflessly, for there is nothing to connect your killing with ours. Now it is time for you to help us."

At this moment, the bells rang for Sext. It was noon again, that strange hour of light and shade, good and evil. The prioress waited for the peals to stop, then raised herself up.

"Very well. As a sign of good faith, I will grant your first request: the exhumation. But for an interview with Master Dixon, I think it only fair that you do something else for me."

"That depends on what it is."

The prioress looked at him keenly. "I will come back to you. Meanwhile, we will see to the grave after we've prayed for the deceased. Of course, you men cannot join us, but I invite you to do the same in your own way."

With that, Mother Isabella bustled off to the chapel. Outside, the cloisters filled with nuns before emptying just as quickly. Antoine closed his eyes as if to pray but found himself thinking of the previous night again and what the prioress might ask of them next. Gilchrist yawned, to Turnbull's irritation. With a mournful expression Redpath peered through the window, before taking himself outside.

As they waited, Antoine remembered how he had felt when he had first heard of Francoise's death, from some mutual acquaintances at court. They had offered solace and support, but he had wanted nothing but his own company. That night, he had gone back over the mistakes which had let her slip away from him, the words he had never got to say. Now, he wondered whether Redpath harboured similar regrets for his brother and his friend. The dead extract a heavy toll from the living, he thought.

In a short while, the nuns reappeared, some with spades and barrows. Antoine asked the hospitalless whether the men might help with the digging, but she snorted that, as Cistercians, they would make quick work of it, so they were compelled to wait again. The time dragged as the solemnity of what they were about to do sank in, and nobody felt inclined to talk. Eventually, Redpath returned, his expression no better for the fresh air. Behind him was Sister Triduana.

"We are ready now," she said. "I will take ye over."

They crossed the garth and walked around the back of the infirmary to the cemetery, where a small group of nuns had gathered. The prioress was at the head of them, clasping her hands and peering down into a freshly dug grave. She held her wimple over her nose and mouth as the smell was vile. In the hole, two nuns did likewise. Between them was a shrouded lump, two shovels on either side.

"We will need some help from this point," said one of the nuns in the grave. As she spoke, her wimple slipped away, and Antoine saw that it was Sister Joan. He motioned to Gilchrist, who reluctantly climbed into the hole and stood over the body. As he bent down, his face convulsed at the stench and the sensation of his hands sinking into the lump. He muttered a series of unintelligible oaths. Steeling himself, he straightened his legs and jerked the body up to the side of the grave. For a moment, it sat there, and nobody dared to touch it.

"Right then," said Antoine. "Let's get this over quickly so we can return this poor soul to his rest."

Kneeling beside the torso, he placed his face in the crook of his elbow to protect himself from the foul miasma. He pulled at the shroud with his thumb and forefinger so that he made as little contact with it as possible. The swaddling unravelled, and he threw the corners to either side to expose the contents. It was as the Herons had described, albeit more decayed: a human torso in a blood-stained shirt. There was a gasp as the nuns leant forward and then recoiled, like trees in the wind. The prioress ushered them back but positioned herself over Antoine's shoulder.

"Well, what do you see?"

"It's as the bailiffs told us," said Antoine, choking. "I fear we might not learn much more here."

"Then we have wasted our time?" said Redpath, gnawing at his fist.

"Not yet. Let me get a closer look."

He bent his head down, almost to the grass, to get a better view of where the limbs had been. Like Gilchrist, he had to stifle an oath. "Urgh. They cut the shirt straight through but then had to hack at the bones."

Next, he turned his attention to the neck, gingerly lifting the torso and pulling the shirt collar down at the back. "Another mess, I'm afraid. You can see it took a few blows to take off the head. There are no marks to the back, though."

By this stage, most of the nuns had turned away or even returned to the main buildings. Redpath had closed his eyes and appeared to be praying, or quelling a retch – or both. Finally, Antoine lifted the front of the shirt. "No wounds to the front either, despite all the blood. I imagine they killed him with a blow to the head, and then they set about their butchery."

He pulled the shirt down and was about to stand up when he felt something rigid under the surface. His heart quickened as he checked again. He slid his fingers under the cloth and located a thin object lying over the ribcage. He grasped it and slowly retracted his hand. Conscious of the remaining spectators, he opened his palm to reveal a small piece of paper. Its back was dark blue, and on its face was a picture of a falcon. It was a playing card, there could be no doubt.

"By Our Lady," Antoine said. "How was this missed?"

"More to the point, who left it, and what does it mean?" said Turnbull.

Everyone bent over, keening for a better view. Only the prioress straightened up. Her face was rigid, her voice harsh. "Enough of this," she said. "Sisters Joan and Triduana, return this body to its rightful place. The rest of you get back to your dorters. Work is cancelled for the day while we sort this thing out. Meanwhile, you are forbidden to speak of it amongst yourselves, do you hear?"

Chapter 32

Once the nuns had dispersed, Mother Isabella invited the men to her office. It was in a part of the priory they had not visited, up a private staircase and through a warren of corridors. Antoine was glad that the prioress said little on the way, for he was trying to process what he had just seen. There was something troubling about the torso's wounds but, for the moment, the discovery of the card preoccupied him. When they reached the dark, panelled room, it became clear that he was not the only one.

"Surely, this proves everything," said Redpath. "Dixon wanted revenge for that game of cards, and this was his way of saying so."

The prioress peered out into the corridor and then, having checked it was empty, closed the door. "It's not the only explanation," she snapped. "In fact, it makes me think that our cases might be connected after all."

Antoine was intrigued. "How so?"

"The card is unusual. Not one of your French ones, with hearts and diamonds. But a falcon."

"True," Antoine said. He examined the card in his hand. "They use these in places like Germany or—"

"Flanders?" interrupted the prioress. "Perhaps you see my point now?"

"That means little," protested Redpath in exasperation. "They are common enough round here as well."

"That's as may be, but we should consider it carefully nonetheless."

The prioress offered them a seat by her desk, and they all stared at the card. Antoine put his fingers to his temples as he tried to organise his thoughts. "First, we need to decide whether this has any significance whatsoever," he said. "If it had been a full pack, I'd say it might just be Alex's. After all, we know he was a keen player. But nobody carries a single card on their person. So we must conclude that someone else has placed it there."

"Agreed," said the prioress. She seemed happy for him to take the lead for now.

"Then there is the question of how no one spotted it when Alex was first laid to rest. You don't strike me as someone who tolerates carelessness, so I am surprised."

"I am equally perturbed," said the prioress sharply. "But leave that with me."

"So the greater issue, as Master Turnbull said earlier, is who left it and what it might mean. Master Redpath is not wrong to say that Cospatrick Dixon is the obvious candidate, so I suggest we press ahead with that interview if we can."

"I will see what I can do." The prioress raised her chin. "But if he is amenable, I want to question him with you."

Now it was Antoine's turn to hesitate. He was wary of this woman's motives, but perhaps observing her line of questioning might help him work out what she was up to.

"Very well. I take it that is the second favour you wish to ask of us?"

"Not at all," snorted the prioress. "If anything, that is a favour to you, as my presence might persuade the man to come here. No, I need something more. But if I am right, it may help you, too."

Antoine tilted his head back. "Go on."

"Go into Berwick and find out more about this Schmidt. Ask his associates the questions you would have asked him if you'd caught him. Take the card as well and see what they say to it."

Antoine was taken aback by this suggestion. "Obviously, as the Scottish Warden, I cannot go there myself. Even if it seems Lord Dacre can come here as he wishes..." The prioress gave a faint smile as he continued. "That leaves one of my men. But they would need a permit of safe conduct."

"I can arrange one. And lodging at the Ship tavern, too."

"Even so, it would be a dangerous mission as I suspect the people we are dealing with are not great respecters of paperwork. The permit might be more like a death warrant than a licence, so someone would need to volunteer..."

"I'll leave that with you then," said the prioress. "You can inform me in the morning."

The men went to their quarters, their mood as dark as jet. For Turnbull, this latest mission was yet another test that seemed ill-suited to his talents and his queasiness only increased when Redpath counted himself out. "As I said this morning, I think that's me done now. My family need me. And we should lay Luggy to rest the morn."

"Of course," said Antoine. "We will let you know if we have more news – or you can find us at the tower." He waited until Redpath was gone before telling the others. "That's no bad thing. The man's a mess and would not be up to it."

Aye, nor me, thought Turnbull. He was fumbling for his

own excuse when Gilchrist spoke up. "Given the nature of the task, sir, I suppose that I should go."

Turnbull felt a wave of relief wash over him but did not like the fellow's tone. "What do you mean: 'the nature of the task'?"

"Nothing," exclaimed Gilchrist, with an innocence that did not suit him. "Just that it will be physically demanding. Possibly dangerous, as our master says."

"And what of that?" said Turnbull. "We have all faced dangers on this mission, many before you arrived."

"Of course, of course. I mean no harm, sir. In many ways, it would suit ye better. You're much cleverer than me. Ye would ask sharper questions, pick up mistakes, and spot lies. All I'm saying is that things might get rough. In which case, our master will need someone who can handle himself."

"I can handle myself just fine," said Turnbull hotly. "But sometimes it's better to avoid a fight in the first place."

Gilchrist smiled. "Ye're right again. But if someone's determined to attack ye, ye must know how to fight back. Ye wouldnae want to be thrown out of a tavern, for instance, by someone half your size."

So that's what the sly dog was getting at. Turnbull could not remember Gilchrist from the White Hart that day, but the fellow must have witnessed his embarrassing encounter with Purves and meant to use it against him. Turnbull was relieved to see that his master was thoroughly confused, but he needed to end this conversation now.

"I don't know what you're blethering on about, but I'm sure that I'm the right man for this. As you say, I will be more suited to the main task of interviewing these Flemings. I even speak a little of their language from when I recruited some to help with our farm."

"Well, if ye insist…" said Gilchrist, raising his hands in surrender. "I suppose it might be for the best. Just take care of yourself, ye hear?"

Turnbull knew that he had been played but would not back down.

"Don't worry. I will be on my guard. And if I need to fight, I will."

Chapter 33

They informed the prioress of their decision after breakfast.

"Are you sure you're up to it?" she asked Turnbull, looking him up and down.

"Quite sure," he replied, coldly.

"Then here is your permit and a letter with my seal, to secure your lodging at the Ship. The Flemings are based in the port and should not be hard to find. Just make sure you stick to the main ways."

Once the prioress had gone, Antoine took Turnbull aside, to walk about the cloisters.

"I know you bear some grudge against her," said the Frenchman. "But she is right on this occasion. You need to take great care."

"I'm aware of that," said Turnbull, ignoring the first comment. "Indeed, I fear the same goes for you, sir. You need to watch out, I mean."

Antoine smiled. The young man might be raw and overly idealistic, but his loyalty was genuine. Touching, even. "I will be fine without you for a little while. All I have planned today is to find that Rutherford fellow. The bailiff's kinsman I told you about."

"The poacher?"

"Yes. He lives nearby and should be desperate to help us, to save his skin. Then, with a fair wind, I'll see Dixon tomorrow. That will be here so it should also carry little risk. And if anything does happen on either occasion, I'll have Gilchrist with me."

"About Gilchrist, sir..."

Antoine sighed. "I know, I know. I could see him needling you, too, last night. He's an oaf, but you should be less sensitive."

"It's not that. Well, not entirely." Turnbull glanced over his shoulder. "I just have an ill feeling about him."

Antoine cocked his head. "In what way?"

"I don't know. It's just that ever since the Marchmen have joined us, our troubles have increased. Wedderburn's attack in the woods. Luggy's murder. Then Schmidt's. Dacre calling a Truce Day when we are least prepared. I worry that somebody is working against us – somebody from within our ranks."

Antoine frowned. The idea had occurred to him, too, but he did not like to hear it noised. He looked across the garth to the parlour. Gilchrist was standing at the window, staring out in their direction. He was too far away to hear them, but the Frenchman lowered his voice, nevertheless.

"What makes you think it's Gilchrist?"

Turnbull shrugged. "He's mouthy, shows neither of us any respect. He frequents the White Hart, where Hume's men relax. Then there's the fact he stayed behind with Wedderburn that day in the woods."

"I asked him to do that. To make sure Wedderburn was away."

"Aye, but what if he used the time to speak with him? Tell him our plans. We would never know, would we?"

Antoine waved a hand. "I think you're worrying too

much, young man. Gilchrist is a loudmouth, but that rather argues against him being a spy. I will keep an eye on him, though. Now get yourself to Berwick, and I will see you back at the tower tomorrow night. Whatever we discover, we should share with each other first before handing it to the prioress."

Lennel was a small village just beyond the priory's gates, so Antoine and Gilchrist reached it in minutes. There was an abandoned tower at the top of a hill, and below were a few stone dwellings with scorch marks about the masonry. The rest of the houses were made of wood and in various states of disrepair. At the end of the street, some men were putting a new thatch on a half-finished cottage. Their heads turned to see the visitors, and Antoine could see the panic in their faces, for they were vulnerable up there, away from their weapons or any form of protection.

"Good morrow, gentlemen," said Antoine in a friendly voice. "I am the new warden, just passing through."

The men looked at each other and back to the Frenchman as he continued.

"I'm after a man called Jock Rutherford. A kinsman of the river bailiffs down at the priory. They said that I might find him here."

Again, the men traded glances. A skinny fellow with dark hair slowly raised a hand and crawled sideways across the roof, taking care not to displace the thatch as he went. He climbed down a ladder. "I'm Rutherford," he said, brushing the straw from his clothes. "My goodbrother said ye would visit, sir. Can I take ye somewhere private?"

Antoine dismounted and scanned the village for a place to talk. "Of course. Which is your house?"

"This one we're thatching. Some reivers burnt it down, along with a' my neighbours'. So we're helping each other get ready for the winter. In the meantime, we're staying at my uncle's."

He jabbed a thumb to the neighbouring house, where a woman and four children had emerged. Like him, they were desperately thin. The woman was wringing her hands, her children close to her skirts. Antoine suggested he and Rutherford go for a walk alone. Mindful of Turnbull's fears, he told Gilchrist to stay where he was.

"So you know why I am here," he said to the peasant as they took a dirt track alongside a miserable-looking cabbage patch.

"Aye, sir, my goodbrother explained, and I am eternally indebted to ye, for the mercy ye've offered me."

Antoine remained impassive. "Let's just see about that. Tell me the whole truth about this murder in Coldstream, and I will overlook your own law-breaking, but I warn you that if you dissemble—"

"I understand," said Rutherford quickly. He took a deep breath. "Well, it's been a poor year, as you can see from our crop here. This on top of losing our house and a' our animals in February. Winter was on its way, and we were starving."

"I don't need your excuses," said Antoine. "Just move on to the night in question."

Rutherford flushed. "Of course, sir." He picked some more straw from his jacket. "It was bitter cold, as I recall. I had spent the day walking round the farms, looking for odd jobs, but there were none, as usual. On the way, though, I met some woodsmen and got talking. I didnae ken them, but we had friends in common. Friends I'd fished wi' before. They said they were after an extra man for their coble and would be going out that night."

"I see. And what are their names?"

Rutherford stopped walking and turned. "Do I have to say?"

Antoine gave him a stern look. "As I said, you must tell me the whole truth."

"On God's precious heart, I will do so, sir. It's just that I barely ken them. And I dinnae want a reputation as a clipe."

"I presume you do not want a reputation as a dead man either?" Antoine softened his voice. "Look, just tell me who they are and if your account is enough, we will not bother them."

"Very well, sir." They resumed their journey. "They are two brothers frae Kincham: David and Ninian Keyne."

"Right. So you joined their band."

"Aye. We arranged to meet by the Truce Day Island at midnight. So I went hame and came out again later, wi' my leister, hidden in my cloak. That's a long fork by the way."

"So I hear."

"There was a full moon that night, but it kept hiding behind the clouds, and it was hard to find the way. Eventually, I saw the silhouette of an old oak tree they'd telt me of, and I picked my way down the bank. But when I reached the lads, they urged me to duck down."

"What was it?"

Rutherford bit his lip. "I thought it was the bailiffs and was right feart. But the boys whispered that their boat was gone from its hiding place. Even stranger, they could see the thieves, rowing back frae the island to our shore. When I followed their gaze, I could too."

"Did you get a good look at them?"

"No, it was dark, and they were too far away. But there were two of them, for sure. They were heading straight towards us, and we realised that they would see us if we scrambled back up the brae, so we crept through the rushes to a wee hollow in the bank. It was freezing to crouch in the water like that, but our minds were racing wi' what might be afoot."

"Then what?" Antoine said.

"When they reached the side, they dumped the boat in the rushes and climbed out. They didnae take out any fish. No leisters or nets either. They just stared back at the island, as if they'd come frae there."

"Did you get a closer look then?"

Rutherford shook his head. "No, they were still in silhouette." He swallowed hard. "But we did hear them say something."

"What was it?" said Antoine, gripping him by the arm.

"Something strange, which we didnae understand at the time. But we all recalled it perfectly afterwards." He shut his eyes, as if to get the words just right. "One of them said: 'Well, that's that then. No more Alex Redpath.' Then they both laughed and climbed the brae. We heard some horses stirring in the woods, and they were gone."

Antoine listened open-mouthed. The killers' words revealed nothing new, but it was chilling to hear them, in all their shamelessness.

"Did they use names for each other?"

"No, that was a' they said."

"What about their accent? Was it English or Scots?" He remembered the Flemings and added with great urgency. "Or something else, perhaps?"

Rutherford looked confused by this last suggestion. "It's hard to say. Scots, I think. But we dinnae speak so differently from the English Marchmen. They were local, for sure. No' strangers like yourself."

"So that was all you saw of them? And all you heard as well?"

"Aye, save that when we returned to the coble, we noticed that it reeked. By this stage, though, we were just glad that they'd left and anxious to get on the water, so we dragged the boat out and got fishing. Until the Herons caught us, as they told ye."

"You're quite sure that's everything?"

"I swear it, sir. I made a great mistake, and now I beg your forgiveness for it. If I can ever repay ye one day, I swear I will."

Antoine saw the desperation in the man's eyes. He cut a pitiful figure, the last person who would ever be able to repay a debt to him. But he did not deserve to be punished either.

"That's good to hear," said Antoine. "But you've done enough already. We will have no more need of you or your friends. Frankly, it would be better if we never met again."

Chapter 34

Turnbull rode Fogo hard to reach Berwick early in the afternoon. As he tracked the swollen waters of the Tweed, he thought of the maelstrom into which he was about to plunge himself. He had never visited the town before, as it had passed into enemy hands a few years before he was born. But he had heard all the stories from his father: how the English had massacred thousands of Scots there, one Good Friday; how they had displayed William Wallace's severed arm upon the walls; how they had suspended Robert the Bruce's sister from the battlements in a specially-built cage. As he recalled these tales now, the omens did not seem good. Would his old man consider him brave for making this journey – or simply foolish?

He crossed the border at Gainslaw easily enough, for there was only a light watch party, and the locals seemed satisfied with his papers. It was a different matter when he came to Berwick itself, though. Huge walls and ditches ringed the town, all guarded by an enormous castle on a hill. This created a bottleneck, forcing travellers to pass through St Mary's Gate and to show their documents all over again. There were soldiers everywhere, dressed in Tudor green and white.

"You spying on our walls, you Scotch git?" one said to him in a Southron accent.

Turnbull shook his head, although in truth he had noticed that the fortifications were in poor condition, despite their size.

"Just as well, or you'll be hanging from them. Now state your name and why you're here."

"My name is Dod Turnbull, and I come with a safe conduct from the Prioress of Coldstream, to assist in a criminal investigation. I will be staying overnight at the Ship."

The soldier scowled at the wax seal. "Who are you after?"

"I don't know yet. I simply wish to ask some questions of your Flemings."

The man laughed. "You'll be lucky to get a word out of those rude bastards." Then more seriously, "How important is your visit?"

"It relates to a murder. Possibly more than one," Turnbull replied gravely.

"No, not like that, you fool. I mean, how dearly do you want to speak to them? What's it worth to you?"

Turnbull looked around and saw other travellers handing over coins to the gatekeepers. It irked him that his paperwork was not enough, but he slipped the man some silver anyway and was allowed through. As he did so, he considered how easy it must be for smugglers and spies to pass like this. For a rich man like Schmidt, it must have been child's play.

Once safely through, he set about finding his bearings. Castle Street was chaotic, with traders calling out their wares, drunkards stumbling in and out of taverns, drovers herding pigs to market. Other narrow streets spread out on either side, like bones on a fish. He steered Fogo through the crowd, glad to be out of the reach of cut-purses and beggars. Then, catching a brief glimpse of the river, he turned down a side wynd, hoping to find the port. The overhanging jetties of the houses meant the passage was dark and oppressive. He recalled the Reverend Mother's warning to stay on the main ways, but it was too late for that now.

The alley was steep, suggesting that he was heading in the right direction for the river. But it was longer than he had expected. He found himself winding his way further and further into the gloomy back streets of the port and realised he was lost. As he began to worry, he turned another corner and was relieved to see a woman at a first-floor window. He was about to ask her for directions when another appeared in a doorway. And another still, even closer. They all had brightly painted faces and their breasts were scarcely covered.

"Who are you after, my lovely?" said the woman in the window. But before Turnbull could reply, there was a noise behind him. Shit. A man had stepped out of the shadows and reached for the pannier from Fogo's flank. In a panic, Turnbull thumped the man on his head and spurred his horse on. The women screamed abuse at him – or perhaps at the thief, he did not stop to find out – but he managed to escape down a further wynd leading into an open yard. And to his great relief, the river revealed itself.

Turnbull sat at the docks awhile, wishing he had never volunteered for this mission. Or at least that he had been more careful. As he berated himself, a man called out in the thick guttural accent that reminded Turnbull of the Flemings on his family's farm. As more men appeared from around the corner, he raised his hands. Speaking as calmly as he could, he patched together a few words in their tongue, to explain himself. The men eyed him with suspicion, then spoke amongst themselves. Turning back to him, the first man told Turnbull to dismount and come with them.

The Flemings' building was an imposing red brick structure on the riverfront. It was four stories high, with crow-stepped gables and a blue double-door. Once inside, Turnbull was led up a grand staircase into a reception room. A very tall, blond-haired man stood by a diamond-paned window. He wore a scarlet doublet, pinked to reveal a yellow underlayer. Two heavy gold chains hung around his neck. For all his obvious wealth, he appeared to be a man of few words.

"You have come about Schmidt?"

"Yes," said Turnbull. "I was there when he—"

"Who sent you?"

"My master, the Warden of Scotland's Eastern Marches and the Prioress of Coldstream. I'm sorry, I don't think we have been introd—"

"Cornelis Pauwels. The leader of our colony. Who knows you are here?"

"Just my master and the prioress. They wish to keep it secret."

This news relaxed the Fleming a little, and he took a seat at his desk, offering one to Turnbull too. "Good! Our situation is delicate."

Turnbull waited for Pauwels to elaborate, but he seemed reticent. The young man thought a show of goodwill might loosen him up. "My master and I were there at Allanton when your fellow Schmidt was killed. We did not see it happen and were too late to catch the killer. Or killers. But we have secured the body and wish to return it to you."

Pauwels moved his head very slightly, from side to side, as if he were weighing up his response. He gestured to one of his assistants. "Send it to Zoetaert here. He will deal with it."

Turnbull looked at the man, hoping that he might be

more forthcoming, but his expression was equally stony. He decided to be more direct himself. "Obviously, we wish to find the murderers and bring them to justice. But we will need your help."

Pauwels stared at him. "As I say, our situation is delicate. You must promise to be discreet."

"I'm not sure I understand," said Turnbull. "But yes, I swear by the holy rood that you can trust me." He seized the moment. "Why don't you start by telling me how Schmidt found himself in Scotland. We know he had been visiting these last few weeks, but who was he seeing?"

Pauwels pursed his lips as if he had tasted something sour. "Forget Schmidt. This is firstly about Willem de Bruyn, my deputy. He handles the day-to-day running of our affairs down at the quayside: liaising with ships' masters, loading and unloading, paying the harbourmaster. Or at least he did. But three weeks ago, some men took him. Extortion."

Turnbull's eyes opened. "When exactly was this?"

Pauwels consulted a ledger. "Monday the 6th of October."

"And do you know who the men were?"

"No, they wore masks. Two of them. Took him after close of business, so we did not see them. All except Morkart."

He gestured to another of his men, who explained in broken English. "I tidy the yard when I see them drive off in cart. They tell me not to follow or they kill him. Said to bring £100 to Allanton at sundown next Monday."

Turnbull's mind raced to the parallels with Alex Redpath's kidnapping, just three days later, but he did not wish to disrupt the flow.

"So did you?"

"No. It was too much," said Pauwels. "We sent Schmidt to negotiate instead."

"I see," said Turnbull. "Wasn't that rather dangerous?"

"No. Just good business. We have dealt with kidnappers before. They are not uncommon here. It is important not to give in straight away. Otherwise, they ask for more. Think of de Bruyn as a commodity. They have possession, and so most of the power. But we are the only buyers interested. They must know that we can walk away if we are not happy. So we must talk."

Turnbull was disturbed by the merchant's cold, calculating mind – but fascinated at the same time. "How did you fare?"

"Schmidt went to Allanton as agreed. When he arrived, the two men were waiting. Still in masks. They took him to a little hut. He gave them £20. Explained that we needed proof de Bruyn was alive."

Turnbull raised his eyebrows. "What did they say to that?"

"They would bring evidence the next week. This seemed reasonable. So next Monday, they met again. Schmidt gave them another £20, and they gave him this." He opened a drawer and produced a white handkerchief with the initials WdB embroidered on it.

"I suppose it's his," said Turnbull. "But it's hardly proof of him being alive."

"You're right," replied Pauwels. "So Schmidt asked for a signature. But these men said they had no writing materials. Next he suggested asking a question that only de Bruyn would know the answer to. But they were impatient. Said enough games, they would bring de Bruyn to the next meeting, if Schmidt brought another £40."

"That must have sounded like a bargain?"

"Yes, we thought we had saved £20. But as you know,

when Schmidt turned up, they killed him and took the money. Probably de Bruyn is gone, too, otherwise why not bring him or hold out for more? Anyway, it looks like we have wasted £80. We can write off the hard cost. But we are anxious the news does not spread."

So that was it: rather than mourning his associates, the merchant was worried about the Flemings' commercial reputation. Although it was distasteful, Turnbull sought to reassure him. "Clearly, we have no desire to promote the use of kidnapping. It is in everybody's interest that this is dealt with quietly. Do you have any idea who might be responsible?"

Pauwels sucked his teeth. "Our only business rivals here are the Germans. They are also based in the port and would profit greatly from our disarray."

"Have you confronted them? Or alerted the authorities?"

"No. We don't want either of them in our affairs. If it is the Germans, we will find our own revenge."

Turnbull kept pushing. "What about other local enemies? We are investigating the abduction of a man in Swinton, which bears certain similarities to this. Alex Redpath: he was kidnapped three days after de Bruyn, by two or three masked men, also using a cart. His friend was murdered a week later, too, by the name of Laidlaw."

Pauwels seemed genuinely non-plussed. "I have never heard of them."

"If it helps, this card was found on Redpath. You'll see that it is Flemish?"

"Or German," said Pauwels sharply. "Either way, it means nothing to me."

"Then, finally, could this be part of some greater plot? We are looking into reports of arms smuggling. Could this abduction be tangled up in it somehow?"

"Certainly not," said Pauwels. His face reddened, and for the first time, Turnbull detected emotion in his voice. "Let me tell you something, sir. Our community has had a base in Berwick for hundreds of years. In that time, the town has changed hands between Scotland and England thirteen times. But we have stayed on throughout. We have learnt the hard way to stay out of your wars. So please do not suggest that we are engaged in some plot or intrigue. That would be bad for business – the greatest crime of all."

Chapter 35

"You were talking in your sleep last night, sir!" Gilchrist laughed as he opened the parcel of warm breads which the nuns had brought them for breakfast.

"Was I?" Antoine said casually, but he dreaded the notion that he might have disclosed some secrets about his past or the investigation.

"Aye, it was all in French so I couldnae understand a word, but you werenae happy wi' someone."

Probably myself, thought Antoine. However, he was relieved that whatever had tormented him remained a private melancholy. He made light of it. "That does not narrow things down. Now make haste, or my unhappiness will be directed at you."

Gilchrist grinned and readied himself as he had been told. They both went over to the parlour, where Mother Isabella was waiting for them.

"Good morning, gentlemen. How went your business yesterday?"

"There's little to report," Antoine answered quickly. "We took another trip to the river in search of clues but found none."

"Oh," said the prioress innocently. "One of the Sisters

thought she saw you heading towards Lennel?"

Antoine did not blink. "We made a wrong turn at first."

She eyed him carefully. "Well, 'tis easily done. I just hope Master Turnbull has not been so mistaken in Berwick."

Gilchrist smirked, and Antoine waited for Mother Isabella to pick further at his story, but she did not pursue the matter. Instead, she said that Dixon would be there within the hour and that they would interview him after chapter.

When she had gone, Gilchrist shot Antoine a sly look. "You deceived her nicely over our trip to Lennel, sir. I take it that you got something tasty out of that Rutherford fellow?"

"I'm still mulling it," said Antoine.

"What about Dixon, then? Redpath's sure it was him."

"I will see to him shortly," Antoine snapped. He remembered Turnbull's warning. "Now keep your questions to yourself, as I can't be updating you every minute."

Gilchrist sulked at this rebuff and they both sat in silence until Sister Triduana came to announce that Dixon had arrived. "He is fearful of stepping too far intae our precinct, so the prioress suggests we conduct the interview here. Master Gilchrist, I am to take ye to the warming house."

"Fine by me," the soldier responded. Then, sarcastically, "I look forward to hearing all about it later."

Cospatrick Dixon was a toper, judging by his ale-belly and florid features, but he was clear-eyed enough as he entered the parlour to account for himself.

"Good morrow, Monsieur Warden," he said. "I'm told ye wish to speak to me, but I'm afraid I've little to tell ye. I only came out of respect for my neighbour, the Reverend Mother."

Antoine nodded and offered him a chair on the other side of the desk. "I appreciate your candour and only ask that you maintain it when it comes to my questions."

"*Our* questions," the prioress corrected the Frenchman as she took a seat alongside him. He began to say something, but she was already off, like a dog at the hares. "Why don't you start by telling us of your relationship with Alex Redpath?"

Dixon waved the question away. "What relationship? As I'm sure ye know, he cozened me over a game of cards a few years back, but since then, I've barely thought of him."

"Are you sure?" said Antoine. "His brother says you crossed paths at various fairs and race meets."

Dixon sneered. "Aye, once or twice. We may have exchanged the odd word, but that's it."

"And how did you hear of his death?" said the prioress.

"Same as everybody. I heard that a body had been found on the island. And then a few days later that it was him." Dixon inspected his nails, as if this whole exercise were beneath him. "I was surprised when folk said ye were after me."

Antoine bristled at the fellow's manner. "It would be a surprise if we were *not* after you, given the body was found opposite your land."

"Which would make it a right stupid place for me to leave it then, wouldn't it?"

"You tell me. Was it also stupid to use one of your butcher's carts to kidnap him?"

"Many men have carts. Besides, I thought they took his friend Laidlaw's?"

Antoine gave him a sharp look, for this fact had not been made public. "How on earth would you know that?"

Dixon kept his face quite rigid but drummed his foot on the floor. "People talk."

"So it seems," said Antoine. He let the foot-drumming continue for a while. Tat-tat-tat. Tat-tat-tat. With every beat, the fellow's cocksure manner seemed to fade. "So have you also heard that Alex Redpath's body had a card on it, when we dug it up?"

"No," said Dixon, quite rattled now. He folded and unfolded his arms in quick succession. "But again, it would be stupid of me to leave such a sign, would it not?"

Antoine shrugged. "Sometimes, the truth is stupidly simple. Certainly, James Redpath believes it so. He reckons that you kidnapped his brother as revenge for your gaming dispute. Then you took him to the island – right by your land. There, you butchered him as though he were one of your animals, and you left him with a card by way of a signature. Finally, you did away with Laidlaw, as Redpath's ally. Not a bad theory, I have to admit."

Antoine felt like he had Dixon where he wanted him: not ready to confess perhaps but at least prepared to offer up an alternative explanation. He was minded to leave him sweating for a while, so he was annoyed when the prioress intervened.

"Alex Redpath is not our only interest though. So cast your mind's net broadly. Have you witnessed anything strange over the last few weeks?"

Dixon's face lit up at the change of direction. "As a matter of fact, I have. We've suffered a number o' trespassers on our land. People showing up after dusk and then disappearing afore we could catch them."

"When was this?" asked Antoine, cursing that he'd not been allowed to press his point.

"Afore Redpath's body was found. The visits stopped soon after."

"Could they have been going to the island?" urged the

prioress.

"I suppose," said Dixon, furrowing his brow. "There was one other thing too. A couple o' days after the body was found, my men saw a young fellow standing on the Scotch side as night fell. Just staring at the island. The light was poor so they didnae get a good look at him. But it struck me as odd when they told me of it."

It struck Antoine as odd too, and he was about to ask for further details, but he was too late: the prioress had diverted the conversation yet again.

"What of Berwick? Does your business ever take you there?"

Dixon sagged back in his seat. "We are regular visitors, of course. We help to provision the garrison and have done for many years."

Mother Isabella nodded. "And the Flemings?"

"Do I really have to go through a list of everyone in Berwick who buys meat? We work with victuallers, innkeepers, tanneries – all sorts."

"So the only bodies you know of have hooves and tails?" It was Antoine's turn to adopt a mocking voice, for he was sure that Dixon was hiding something.

"That's correct."

"And you would swear by it, in our chapel?" asked the prioress.

"That I would."

There was a pause as both interrogators searched for further questions. In the lull, Antoine remembered Redpath's strange idea of trial by cruentation. It seemed like a silly obsession, but he wondered whether it might flush something out.

"What about swearing over Luggy Laidlaw's body?" he

asked.

"What?" exclaimed Dixon. "Isn't he buried yet?" He fiddled at the hair around his ear.

"No," lied Antoine. "I could take you there now, and we could get it done before he's laid to rest."

Dixon's face tightened and he got up to leave. "I'm no' going another step intae Scotland, thank ye sir. And certainly no' to Swinton. If ye wish to charge me with any o' this, then submit the forms to Lord Dacre and I'll see ye at the Truce Day. But I warn ye that your case willnae hold. And then ye'll be the one looking stupid, no' me."

Chapter 36

The Ship was used as a billet for Berwick's garrison, and Turnbull woke to the sound of troops going back and forth. Boots stomping, armour clanking, men laughing. He felt uncomfortable being so close to English soldiers, so he decided to keep to his room until they dispersed. However, by midday the racket had not let up, so he went downstairs to check on Fogo before setting off to visit the Germans on foot.

After yesterday's misadventure in the backstreets of the port, he was determined to avoid further trouble, so he kept to the main ways. A fierce wind was picking up and he heard the creak of the town's rickety wooden bridge before he saw it. The Flemings' red house was to the North. Closer to him was an equally large white building emblazoned with the double-headed eagle of the Hanseatic League. As he approached it, the rigging on the ships whistled for his attention, but he kept his eyes on the men bustling around him, wheeling barrows, unpacking crates, stirring barrels of stinking hot tar.

Turnbull explained his business to two guards, who took him into a reception area on the ground floor. It was more modest than the Flemings', the only decoration being an enormous tusk mounted on the wall. It was longer than a man and required three iron brackets to hold it up. Turnbull was inspecting the way it spiralled when a short man entered the room. He was perhaps sixty years old and was wearing a thick overgown with a fur mantle and a simple cloth beret.

"Ah, you are admiring our unicorn horn. A fine specimen, don't you think? A present from the Baltics."

"Yes," said Turnbull, who was encouraged by the man's friendly tone. "It is much longer than I thought it would be." Then, not wishing to sound inexperienced, he added: "The ones I have seen before have been smaller."

The old man smiled and ushered him into his office, which, in contrast to the reception area, was cluttered with the paraphernalia of trade: sea charts, ledgers, sets of scales, scrimshaw ornaments, and a telescope. He sat at his bureau and offered his visitor a chair.

"Welcome, sir," he said spreading his arms. "I am Jakob Ritter, and my people say you are called Turnbull. That is a strong name!"

Turnbull smiled. "You would get on well with my master. He enjoys such plays on words."

"Ah yes, the new warden. A stranger like myself. Perhaps such jokes are our way of showing we are not so foreign. At any rate, it is good to meet you. Now, how can I help?"

The German's voice was rich and fruity. Turnbull immediately warmed to him but reminded himself not to be deceived.

"It is about your neighbours, the Flemings. As you may know, one of their number was murdered in Scotland a few days ago. And now we hear of a kidnapping."

"I see. And this affects us how?"

"There is some suggestion that your countrymen might be involved. I make no such accusation, of course, but I would like to hear your side of it."

Ritter laughed. "Well, I was not expecting that, but I might be able to help." He settled back in his chair and cleared his throat. "Let me begin by painting you a little picture."

"As you wish."

"This place was once one of the most powerful towns in these isles. But look at the state of its walls, its castle, its bridge. It has been on the slide for years. So have the Flemings. And so, I am pained to say, has our league. In Berwick, we are like two bald men fighting over a broken comb."

"There seems wealth enough to me," said Turnbull, who was suspicious of such modesty from a merchant.

"But nothing compared to what we once had – or the gold now pouring into other places from the New World." Ritter gestured to the charts on his desk. "We are on the wrong side of the map, and the wrong side of history. Anyway, that will be your generation's problem, not mine. For now, we must do our best in a shrinking market. And that means keeping a close eye on our competitors."

"Spying, you mean?"

"I prefer to call it monitoring," the German chuckled. "Nothing illegal, I assure you. But whenever a Flemish ship docks, I like to know about it – size, cargo, port of origin and so on – to ensure we are not missing out. I have men on this by the quayside, but sometimes there is no substitute for one's own eye. Which is my long way of explaining how I found myself at that window a few weeks ago, with my telescope pointed at their harbour."

Turnbull followed his gaze. The creamy sails of the Flemish ships stood out against the ever-darkening sky. "When?"

"The day that Master de Bruyn was taken." Ritter licked his lips as if reliving the drama. "I saw it happen."

The revelation had the desired effect. Turnbull's eyes opened wide as he leant across the desk. "What exactly did you see?"

"A horse and cart came down to the quayside. I thought it was odd because we had closed up for the day, and there was nobody around apart from de Bruyn, who was completing an inventory. He was ever the first to start and the last to leave. He had his back to the cart and did not turn round, so I watched as three men alighted, donning masks. Then they rushed him. They beat him savagely with clubs and bundled him into the cart. That fellow Morkart ran out, but they brushed him aside and made off."

Turnbull's mouth hung open. "Wait, there were three of them? The Flemings only saw two on the cart."

Ritter gave another knowing smile. "Two rode at the front. The third climbed in the back with their prisoner."

"And you saw them put their masks on. Does that mean you saw their faces too?"

Ritter's good humour receded for the first time. "I misspoke," he said bluntly. Then more brightly again: "I saw only the masks. But I can tell you exactly where they got them: they sell them near the spittal, for those visiting the lepers."

"Interesting! But, as for the men, you have no idea who they were?"

Ritter pursed his lips. "I could not say."

"And did you tell the Flemings?"

"No, I think it might be rather awkward to explain how I saw them, don't you? Besides, they have said nothing of this to us. They are embarrassed, I think."

Turnbull nodded. "Apparently kidnappings are bad for business," he said, before reminding himself of the gravity of the situation. "Jests aside, why do you think the Flemings have pointed the finger at you?"

The German shrugged. "They cannot see beyond our rivalry. If they opened their eyes they would see how these straitened times have made us both vulnerable to other forces. We have attempted to diversify by offering loans, funding building work, general provisioning. Local folk pass through our doors now who we would never have entertained before. Our neighbours would be better looking in that direction if you ask me."

"Does anybody spring to mind?"

Ritter fiddled with a brass astrolabe on his desk. "I make a general point."

"Well, here's one in return. Have you heard any talk of arms smuggling through the port?"

Ritter put the astrolabe aside and waved a hand. "No, and I very much doubt it could be happening. Neither we nor the Flemings would profit from a war. The opposite, in fact."

"How about the murder of Tomas Schmidt in Allanton?"

"I know nothing of that either."

"Luggy Laidlaw in Swinton?"

"Never heard of him."

"How about Alex Redpath, then? You must have heard of his body showing up on the island in Coldstream?"

Ritter nodded. "A terrible story."

"That it was. You know, we found a playing card on his body?" Turnbull took it out of his pouch and laid it on the desk. "German, as you can see."

"Or Flemish," said Ritter, his lip curling. For a moment, it looked as if he might say more, but he seemed to check himself. "You know, I fear my usefulness has come to an end.

But perhaps I might leave you with one last thing. Some advice to your master, from one stranger to another."

A rumble of thunder caused the window shutters to rattle on their hinges.

"Tell your master that if he hopes to solve this mystery, he must simply follow the trail of blood."

Turnbull waited for more, but nothing was forthcoming. "That's it?" he said, placing his hand on one of the German's maps as it flapped in the wind.

"That's it," said Ritter. He went to the window and closed the shutters. "Now, you'd best be gone before you get caught in this cursed weather. Another thing which we strangers must put up with here."

Chapter 37

The wind howled like a sea wolf as Turnbull went back up Castle Street. Shopkeepers wound in their awnings and started to pack up their stalls for the day. A goodwife called her children inside with threats that they would be blown off to Denmark. Turnbull put his head down and walked as fast as he could. He pictured the hearth at Black Rig and mused that things had come to a pretty pass for him to miss the tower's meagre comforts.

By the time he reached the Ship, the weather was even fouler. Shielding his face, he ran the last few steps to the door before pushing it open and diving inside. He brushed himself down and located the innkeeper. The man was sitting by the fire with some off-duty soldiers and seemed to be drunk on his own ale. Turnbull quickly paid him for his stay and asked him to send a stable boy for Fogo.

"Ye're never leaving in this storm?" slurred the innkeeper. "Why not keep your room for another night and I'll do ye a deal?"

"Thank you," said Turnbull. "But I need to be somewhere else."

"Very well. But the lads have a' buggered off. A man gave them a penny to make themselves scarce while he entertained some harlot down there. Ye'll have to get your nag yourself."

He pointed to a side door, and Turnbull followed his direction despite his irritation at the fellow's manners. The wind was so strong, he struggled to open the door. The men behind him laughed, no doubt happy to be holed up for a night of drinking by the fire, while this fool battled the elements outside. "Ye sure ye want to leave?" called the innkeeper. "Ah well, it's your funeral."

Turnbull went back into the yard to the stables. A torch flickered on the wall, illuminating flecks of straw in the cold air, but otherwise, all was gloomy.

"Hello?" he called, anxious not to disturb the harlot and her beau. There was no reply. He peered through the dim light. Fogo's neck craned out of the end stall, and the horse gave a whicker of recognition as he approached. Or was it something more?

The animal jerked its head back and began to kick at its gate.

"Steady boy," said Turnbull, although he felt the hair on his own neck rising. He cast about himself and up to the hay loft, but there was nobody around. He quickened his pace.

Just as he reached the stall, the horse let out another whinny and reared right up so that its legs extended over the door. It was stuck and beginning to panic. Its nostrils flared. The whinnying became more shrill. Turnbull had never seen Fogo in such a state and tried to stroke his head, but he could not get close enough because of the flailing hooves. He thought about distracting him with hay and looked behind himself for a feeder. As he did so, he saw a man heading towards him. A masked man. Carrying an axe.

Christ's nails. Turnbull fumbled for his sword, wrestling it out of its scabbard just as the man reached him. But now what? He waved it in an arc in front of him but knew he had little clue how to wield it beyond that.

"Who are you?" he asked, hoping he could talk his way out of this. However, the fellow did not respond. Instead, his eyes flitted to Turnbull's side, where another man's arm was reaching over the door of Fogo's stall, grappling with the bolts. Only the horse's wild movements prevented him from undoing them. Turnbull knew it would not be long though. He had little enough chance against one but would be doomed against two. He would have to fight.

Heart racing, he lunged at the axeman. The fellow read his move and stepped back out of the blow. Turnbull made another swipe, but his opponent parried it. When he came at him a third time, the man leapt to the side, causing Turnbull to fall on one knee. God, what an idiot he was!

The attacker raised his axe and prepared to deal the final blow, but Turnbull somehow managed to duck to the side. The blade came down with enormous force and landed in a stable door. It was well and truly stuck, and as the man tugged at it, Turnbull saw his chance. Using both feet, he kicked him in the stomach and sent him flying backwards.

Now he had the upper hand. Or so it seemed. For although his first assailant was unarmed, Turnbull had dropped his own sword too. More foolishness! Worse, the other man had managed to free himself from Fogo's stall and was coming at him with a dagger. Turnbull heard him chuckle behind his mask.

He had one last chance.

As the man lurched forwards, he tore a feeder from the wall and hurled it at him with all his remaining energy. The fellow staggered back, and, in the confusion, Turnbull was able to wrestle the dagger from him. But his triumph was again short-lived, for his first assailant now had his sword.

By this point, Turnbull had nothing left to give. He was out of breath, outnumbered and outarmed too. He wondered what his father and brothers would make of the fight he'd put up. Ah well, he could soon ask them.

But before he was reunited with his kinsfolk in the otherworld, the door behind him banged open and half a dozen men rushed in with the wind: soldiers from the tavern.

"What goes on?" one shouted angrily.

The two assailants looked at each other, and the one who had originally held the dagger shouted "Run!" The duo went full pelt for the exit by Fogo's stall. Turnbull tried to stop them, but they warded him off with his own sword. The soldiers gave chase, but when they reached the door, they clearly had no desire to follow the strangers into the storm. Instead, they turned back to Turnbull.

"What was all that about?" growled one.

"It's a long story," Turnbull gasped. "I am here on behalf of the Scottish Warden, investigating a murder. Those two must have been the killers."

He fumbled for his papers and the leader of the troops gave them a cursory glance.

"We could have ye for affray, ye know? Possibly attempted murder."

"But they were the ones attacking me," cried Turnbull. "That's surely obvious from their masks."

"Or ye were picking on some poor leper's family," said the soldier.

At first, Turnbull thought that he was joking, but the man's granite face told him that he was deadly serious. He was dumbstruck for a moment. He put an arm around Fogo's neck, as much to calm himself as the animal.

"They were waiting for me, when I came for my horse."

"We have only your word for it."

"They came at me with that axe and this dagger."

"When we came in, ye were holding it."

"Because they took my sword!"

The soldiers crowded around him. They had not put their own weapons away just yet. Their leader spat on the ground.

"Listen, friend," he said. "We can do this two ways. We can take ye to the tolbooth for the night and ye can explain yourself to the justices in the morning. Or we can escort ye to the gate. What's it to be?"

"The second one," groaned Turnbull. "All I want is to go home."

"Fine. But we're supposed to be off duty. We're not going into that storm for nothing. No' wi' those two men after ye."

Spotting a familiar pattern, Turnbull gave the man his final coin. With that, they all saddled up and set off on the short journey to St Mary's Gate. The wind was screaming, and there were no other travellers on the road. Seeing the escort, the sentries did not even bother to leave their gatehouse. Fogo's reins were cold and wet, and Turnbull felt his hands shaking as he tried to hold them. As he set off into the wild night, he vowed never to set foot in this awful town again.

Chapter 38

Turnbull followed the Dunse road as the storm raged all around. He passed unchallenged at the border as the watch parties on both sides had clearly agreed to desert their posts. However, the return to Scotland did little to steady his nerves. Instead, his mind spun with fresh worries. How had his attackers known where he would be? Where were they now? Could they be waiting for him on this very road?

He had been in such a rush to leave that he had not considered any of this. Nor had he questioned the innkeeper about the man who had paid off the stable boys with that story of the harlot. It dawned on him that this must have been one of his attackers and that he had lost a golden chance to find out more about him. It had been a foolish mistake, one he would not include in his report to his master.

"Sweet Mary, you look like death," said Antoine when Turnbull staggered back into their quarters at Black Rig hours later. "Come sit by the fire and we'll get some wine in you."

The young man collapsed on a stool and said nothing while Anderson poured them out three cups. He waited for his blood to warm up before telling the other two all about his adventures in Berwick. He was still on edge so they had to ask him to slow down and repeat himself at times. When he had finished, Antoine talked through his interviews with Rutherford and Dixon. Anderson completed the circle, although in his case he brought much slimmer pickings. For all his excellence as a soldier, he was no investigator, it seemed.

"I found nothing new in Allanton: those peasants were shitting themselves about Schmidt's body and will be glad to give it back. Simpson says that Cranstoun and his hounds havenae found the kidnappers' lair, either. As for Carmichael, he's still at the tavern so God knows what we'll get out o' him."

When they were all done, Antoine got up and paced the room with his hands behind his back. "Follow the trail of blood," he said, repeating Ritter's words. "It's usually good advice for anyone sleuthing a murder. But in this case, it's impossible!"

"What do you mean, sir?" said Turnbull, shivering as he nursed his drink with both hands.

Antoine raised a finger. "Think about it. Alex Redpath's body left no trail, as the blood had already dried by the time he was left on the island. Luggy Laidlaw was strangled. Schmidt was killed with one blow of an axe, and then his attacker left on horse. We don't know what has happened to this fellow de Bruyn – and not a drop of blood was spilled in your own attack in the stables!"

"I don't think Ritter meant it literally. He seemed to like his word games, as you do."

Antoine scratched his head. "I know, it just bemuses me. Do you think he would tell you more if you returned?"

"To Berwick?" spluttered Turnbull. "I doubt it. Perhaps he simply meant us to go over the evidence methodically, one step at a time."

"Then let us do that," said Antoine. He returned to his

seat and took out his parchment and quill. "Can we begin by agreeing that this Flemish riddle is somehow connected to our own?"

The others nodded. "It all seems too much of a coincidence otherwise," said Turnbull.

Antoine scribbled some notes. "I agree. So the next question is who – or what – connects the cases?"

Anderson scratched his head. "It strikes me that the killers must be Scots. All the negotiations wi' Schmidt were held in Allanton. And according to Rutherford, the men he heard dumping Alex's body in the river had Scots accents."

"He couldn't be sure though," said Antoine cautiously.

Turnbull wrinkled his nose. "And I am fairly certain that when my attacker said 'Run' he spoke with an English voice. 'Run' not 'rrrun'."

"I see," said Antoine, completely baffled by the distinction, or lack of it. "So perhaps we are looking for a mixed gang? As you keep telling me, reivers do not care much for the border."

"That's true," said Anderson. "But what does any of this have to do with Mother Isabella's theory, that it all revolves around weapons?"

The men retreated into their own thoughts for a while. They drank their wine and stared into the fire, as if the flames might yield some explanation for this hellish sequence of events.

Suddenly, Turnbull clicked his fingers. "That's it. Weapons."

The others stopped and waited for him to explain, but he said nothing more. Instead, he rummaged in his pouch and pulled out the dagger he had recovered from the stables. He turned it over in his hand, to reveal the silver hilt engraved with a stag's head.

"I think this is Alex Redpath's dagger," he said breathlessly. "Look, it's just as his brother described it when he told us of that game of cards. He said Cospatrick Dixon grabbed it during their fight, then they wrestled it back off him."

"So you're saying Alex is still alive?" laughed Anderson.

"No, you dolt," said Antoine. "He's saying that whoever killed Alex took his weapon and also tried to kill him." He looked at Turnbull, briefly doubting his interpretation. "Aren't you?"

Turnbull nodded enthusiastically. "I'd say it puts the matter beyond doubt. But more than that. I think it might explain why Alex was killed in the first place. I think he might have been one of de Bruyn's kidnappers in Berwick."

Antoine was dumbfounded. "How the hell do you jump to that conclusion?"

"Bear with me, sir. I don't have it all worked out yet. But what if kidnapping de Bruyn was the grand plan he mentioned to Luggy? The venture that would make him more money than all his previous schemes put together?"

"How would he get involved in something of that scale?"

"I don't know. But we know he was ambitious. Suppose he chanced upon the plan of some more powerful player? Lord Hume, for instance."

Antoine frowned, but Turnbull would not be deterred. "Anyway, let's say he served his initial use, so then the reivers did away with him. Or something went wrong. Either way, they fell out and they decided to kill him – but not before finding out who else knew of their scheme. That's why they kidnapped him, rather than killing him on the spot. They tortured him as you have suggested, he gave them Luggy's name – and they came back the next week to silence him. By this point, they realised we were after them too, so they killed Schmidt and tried to murder me."

Antoine rubbed his forehead. Turnbull was talking so quickly that it was hard to keep up. He worried that the attack in the stables might have unbalanced the lad's humours and tried to slow him down. "If I remember right, Alex was up at the shielings with James and Laidlaw when de Bruyn was kidnapped."

"Unless he slipped away from them, for a while. He could easily have made some excuse about rounding up the cattle."

"It's a full day's ride frae the shielings to Berwick," said Anderson sceptically.

"Perhaps that's how Luggy became suspicious. Maybe he found out, then covered for Alex, to keep it from his brothers?"

"What about this talk of arms smuggling? I don't see how any of that fits with your notion?"

Turnbull shrugged. "I don't know. I suppose the kidnappers may have wanted the ransom money, to buy an arsenal? Look, I don't have all the details yet. But everything starts to add up. Even the variation in the gang's numbers. When de Bruyn was kidnapped, there were three of them. But when Alex was taken, there were only two. The same when Rutherford and the poachers saw the men in a boat. We don't know about Luggy's murder because there were no witnesses, but Schmidt also told the Flemings he was meeting two men. And that's how many came for me too."

"So Alex was the third man," said Anderson slowly.

"Aye. And now there are only two."

Antoine wanted to point out all the holes in the story. The timings and distances. The carts. The playing card. The whole business with the torso in the river. But he felt Turnbull was getting overwrought. "Let's get a-bed," he said. "We can quiz Redpath on all this when next we see him. Until then, let's keep it to ourselves. Whatever their numbers, it seems the killers know our moves. It's time for us to surprise them, instead of the other way round."

Chapter 39

Despite all that Turnbull had been through, he slept soundly, and Antoine spent his hour of watch observing him with envy. While Catherine Gray's potion had softened the edges of his own night terrors, it had not eradicated them. It was as if he were bailing out a sinking boat: he had scooped out some of his old fears, but new ones had poured in, faster than he could cope with them. As he prepared to get up, he remembered that today was that strange festival known as All Hallows' E'en. The Scots set great store by the notion of the dead walking amongst them for one night, but he mused that this was a daily occurrence for him.

He went downstairs to the kitchen, leaving the lad to his slumber. The storm had blown through overnight, and rays of golden light came through the arrow slits. Simpson was making bannocks on the hearth, while Anderson dished out chores for the other soldiers.

"How's Master Turnbull?" asked the serjeant.

"He sleeps off his troubles. I trust he will be better for it."

"Aye, he went through a lot yesterday. Still, at least he's back, which is more than can be said for Carmichael."

"What do you mean?"

Anderson grimaced. "He didnae return frae the Hart last night. It might be nothing. Some woman or other. But we ought to take a look-see don't ye think?"

"I suppose," said Antoine uneasily. "You don't think he's deserted, do you? Or something worse?"

"We'll find out soon enough, sir. I'll get some men together."

Antoine added the missing soldier to his list of worries and continued to Catherine Gray's room. She was rearranging some small bottles on the floor, her face drawn.

"That's me out of chamomile now. I can only make two more draughts of your potion."

Antoine bit his lip. Although the medicine had not been entirely successful, he hated the idea of giving it up now. "Couldn't you use something else?"

"It willnae be the same. My plants are not prospering outside my garden."

"Well, we can't take you back there, if that's what you're getting at. On top of all these murders, I've just heard that one of our men is missing."

She gave a little twitch. "Into town then? There will be a market today where I can buy some fresh supplies."

"Why not make a list and we will find them for you?"

She started to fidget. "Ye'll no' get the right ones."

"Could you dilute the dose, to stretch it out for a while?"

"What with? We're running out of water, and ale would spoil the remedy."

"We will fix the well in time."

Catherine threw out her hands. "Ye're no' listening, sir. We're already out of time. I cannae help ye if you dinnae help me first."

Antoine sighed. "Very well. A party of us will be going this afternoon. You can join us. But you will need to assure me that this is not some scheme to escape. We are keeping you here for your own safety, and we do not need further trouble."

A few hours later, Catherine was waiting in the barmekin with Antoine, Anderson, Burnsie and a newly revived Turnbull. She had been given the smallest pony; a grey mare usually ridden by Wilson. The men watched to see how she would fare without a side-saddle, but they need not have bothered. By the time they were a hundred yards from the tower, they could see that she could ride as well as any man. They rattled down the hill and then up Dunse Law, taking care over the fallen branches and detritus left over from the previous night's gale.

As they entered Dunse's main street, they saw that the All Hallows festivities were already in full swing. Stalls had been set up along the way, where men dooked for apples and women had their kale leaves read to divine their marriage prospects. Children roamed about with sooty faces, swinging grotesquely carved turnip lanterns from wooden poles. At the top of the Law, away from the houses, the townsfolk were building a huge bonfire. The crowd appeared to be in good humour, but Antoine felt an underlying menace to proceedings. He remembered what Turnbull had said as they crossed the Lammermuirs that first day. Something about bringing the candle of wisdom here. Now it seemed like they had stepped out of Christendom's light altogether, into a darker, more primitive realm.

At the mercat cross, they divided in two. Antoine and Burnsie went to the White Hart while Turnbull and Anderson escorted Catherine to the market. The tavern was heaving, and they had to push their way to the counter. As they did so, the Frenchman noticed that, despite the crowds, a spare place had been set aside at every table. "In case a kindly spirit wishes to join us," explained Burnsie. But the expression on his face suggested that he feared less friendly visitors.

"We are looking for one of our men," said Antoine to Purves, who had made a beeline towards them on the pretence of doling ale from a tray. "Local fellow named Carmichael."

"Yes, he was in here last night," said the innkeeper under his breath. "What of it?"

"He didn't come home."

"No' surprised, the way that storm was blowing. Most likely slept his ale off at one of his friends' houses."

Antoine was confused. "What friends?"

"I dinnae ken their names, but he left wi' two men. Some fellows I hadnae seen afore."

Antoine's mind raced back to Turnbull's theory from the previous evening. "What were these two fellows like? Did they say where they were going?"

"No' sure. Both big men, hair as red as a fox's. Ye can check the tavern for them if ye like. But take an ale, for Christ's sake, so ye stand out less."

Antoine and Burnsie took a cup from his tray and walked around the hall but found neither Carmichael nor a pair meeting the description Purves had given. Despite their best attempts to be inconspicuous, hostile stares followed them. After completing a full circuit, they slipped back out into the fresh air.

Revellers packed the square. In the middle, a group of young men had placed a cat in a basket and the ringleaders were tormenting it by aiming kicks at it. It was a French custom, thought Antoine. Trust the people here to import this tradition out of all the ones on offer.

Antoine and Burnsie walked around the jeering, clapping, throng but still found no sign of Carmichael or his two friends. After a while, though, they did come across the

239

others. Catherine had filled some panniers, and the men were loading them onto the grey mare.

"Did you get everything you need?" Antoine asked Catherine.

"Just about," she muttered. "Enough for now, anyway."

"What about Carmichael?" said Anderson.

"He's not in the tavern," replied Antoine. "But he was there last night. And left with two men. Big men with red hair."

"God's teeth. Do you think they might be the ones we're after?"

"I don't know," said Antoine. "Turnbull, does it sound like your attackers?"

His assistant grimaced. "Mine were big enough, but I didn't see their hair."

"Well, I don't like it," said the Frenchman. "Let's do another sweep and then get out of here."

This time, Antoine and Turnbull took Catherine off one way, while Anderson and Burnsie went the other. The crowd was getting more and more boisterous, fuelled by hours on the ale. The youths started to kick the cat's basket as if it were a football. Others joined in.

"You should be ashamed o' yourself," said Catherine to one man after he had placed a boot to the wicker and sent it spinning through the air.

"Get it up ye, ye dumb hoor," he snarled back. "Or ye'll be next in line."

Antoine frowned at her. He did not enjoy such entertainments himself, but he knew better than to pick a fight over them. He pulled her away by the elbow and through a line of food stalls selling roast pork, black pudding, tripe and chestnuts. The vendors' braziers enveloped them in a delicious, warm fug, but the light was fading, and the smoke made it hard to see. Antoine tried to quicken their pace, but the crowd was too dense. He felt hemmed in.

As he searched for a way through, he saw two redheads bobbing about, twenty yards in front. Their shoulders were visible, too, so they must be a decent size. It was not clear whether they were travelling together, but they were close enough for it to be possible. He nudged Turnbull and they tried to squeeze past the group before them.

"Watch yourself," growled a shaven-headed fellow over his shoulder. "There's time for all of us."

Thwarted, Antoine looked around to see if there might be a way to bypass the crowd. There was a path behind the stalls, but the street vendors were using it to prepare their wares. Ducks were roasting on spits. Cauldrons bubbled. It would be equally difficult to navigate: they were stuck. Still, there was no way of losing the men either, as the crowd was moving in one direction only. Always upwards, on to the bonfire at the top of the Law.

"Can't we go now?" said Catherine, who seemed uncomfortable in the throng.

"I'm afraid not," said the Frenchman. "We may be close to making our breakthrough. But once we have checked it, we will be off."

They continued to make slow progress along the muddy path, shuffling along as if chained to those in front. They heard raucous laughter behind them, but the crowd was pressed so tight that they could not turn round to see what it was about. Eventually, the noise came closer, and they saw that something was being passed above their heads, to the front of the throng. Antoine was reminded of his nightmare, where Luggy and Schmidt's ghosts had carried Alex Redpath's torso on their shoulders. He was relieved to see that it was only the cat's basket but felt queasy all the same.

At the top of the Law, the road opened up, so the press of the crowd reduced. The bonfire had just been lit and the revellers spread out around it. Antoine scanned them urgently. He thought he saw one of the redheads again, but it was a smaller fellow with his wife and children. The family threw their turnip lanterns on the pyre and laughed as the flames lapped about the macabre, carved faces.

Antoine was searching the crowd afresh when a hand touched him on the shoulder. He whipped around. Anderson and Burnsie. They had Carmichael and the horses with them.

"We found another way round the back," said Anderson. "This one was coming up there too."

"Where in God's name have you been?" said Antoine. "And who were those fellows you were with last night?"

Carmichael clasped his hands. "I'm sorry, sir. As I've just explained to the serjeant, I went to the tavern as ye telt me. Then the storm hit so bad that I feared for the journey back. So I got talking to two men from Cranshaws who were visiting their kin. We all stayed at their cousin's house."

"You had never met them before?"

"No, but we have acquaintances in common. They're shepherds, like my own folk."

"And are they here right now?"

"No, we parted company a good hour ago."

"Sir, I fear these men are a distraction," interjected Anderson. "Quick, Carmichael. Tell our master what ye discovered in the taverns."

Carmichael took a deep breath. "In my visits, I heard that three men from the West are abroad. Bad men, intent on mischief. They robbed a trader on the Kelsae road last week, then ransacked the priest's house in Birgham three days ago."

"That's near Coldstream, isn't it?"

"Aye," said Anderson. "And here's the rub: they all wear masks."

The men looked at each other fearfully. Antoine moved to speak, but before he could say a word, a huge cheer went up. The bonfire was fully ablaze. The wood crackled, and smoke jagged at their throats. The clamour continued to build as the cat basket was passed to the front. Then a man took it by the handle and swung it in the air. Once, twice, thrice it went – each time provoking whooping and chanting. The man tossed it right onto the top of the pyre, to great applause. For a moment, they could do nothing but watch as the creature was consumed by the flames, surrounded by ghastly lantern faces.

Amidst the merriment, Catherine pushed her way to the front. "Shame on you all!" she shouted.

Antoine grabbed her arm again, but she would not be quietened. "What harm did that little thing ever do to you?"

The crowd jeered at her as the fire continued to rip through the basket. Some shadowy figures moved towards them, silhouetted against the leaping flames. Antoine nodded to the others to ready themselves for trouble. When the figures got closer, they turned so that they were illuminated by the orange glow. To Antoine's alarm, he realised it was Hume, with Wedderburn at his side. The warlord stood directly in front of the bonfire, like Lucifer himself. He spread his arms out wide, his cloak flapping behind him, and addressed the crowd.

"Well, well. Look who has come to our All Hallows fire. Our very own witch, come to save her cat!"

Chapter 40

The crowd closed in on them, like a tightening noose. People craned to see what was going on, who these interlopers were. Behind them, the flames rose higher and higher.

"Leave it, Hume," said Antoine. "We're just here to make some enquiries."

From the corner of his eye, he was glad to see that Anderson was quietly untangling the horses' bridles. As he did so, the warlord continued to play to the crowd, sweeping his cloak around himself, as if gathering up all those in attendance. "Talking seems to be all you've done since you got here. Meanwhile, the bodies pile up, I hear."

"We are doing plenty, as you will find out in a fortnight's time."

The warlord shook his fist. "I told you we do not like waiting here. There is a killer in our midst. If you do not catch him – or her – then others will!"

These words met with roars of approval. The crowd surged forward as if to seize them. At the same instant, Antoine saw that Catherine had placed her foot in the stirrup of the grey mare – only for Burnsie to drag her off.

"What are you playing at, you treacherous culroun?" cried Anderson, wrestling the lad away but knocking

Catherine off balance in the process. A free-for-all ensued. Antoine and Turnbull quickly got themselves into their saddles and wheeled their horses around. Catherine scrambled onto Burnsie's hobbler. Anderson pushed Burnsie over and pulled some assailants away from Antoine before taking his own mount. There was mayhem as the revellers tried to get close to their quarry, only to be repelled by the wild swings of the panicking horses.

In the melee, Fogo bolted. The memories of the stable attacks were no doubt fresh in his mind, and he raced off down the other side of the Law, with Turnbull struggling to control him. The other horses followed, urged on by their riders. Bystanders tried to block their path, but the beasts were not for stopping. Only Catherine's original nag remained – until Wedderburn leapt into the saddle and gave chase.

They pelted down the far side of Dunse Law, with taunts ringing in their ears. Soon the blast of a horn added to the cacophony, as other riders were summoned. Antoine knew that while they had benefitted from a head start, their pursuers would not have to take the long way round. Sure enough, by the time they had reached the foot of the Law and swung round towards home, half a dozen men had retrieved their horses from the square. They were thundering straight down the hill, with others running behind them on foot.

Anderson was at the front of the pack by this stage and just managed to squeeze through the grasp of their pursuers. Carmichael followed, with two of Hume's riders on his tail, but the others stood their ground and formed a blockade. To his horror, Antoine realised that they had been divided and would not be able to make it back to the tower. Glancing behind him, he could see Wedderburn gaining on them too.

"This way!" Antoine shouted and galloped off towards

Earl's Meadow instead. It was dark, and Dunse's bonfire was well behind them, but other pyres burnt from every hilltop for miles around. Antoine looked at Turnbull and Catherine, expecting to see fear in their eyes, but they had passed that stage. Their faces were set in rigid expressions of determination, concentrating on every step and leap their horses took.

After a while they came to the Swinton road, and Antoine wondered about seeking sanctuary at Redpath's bastle house. But if Wedderburn were still chasing them, he would easily find them there. Moreover, the building would not stand up to a sustained attack. Instead, he urged his companions onwards, through the village and on to Kincham Woods. They were going dangerously fast for this time of night, but the journey still seemed to take forever. Antoine remembered how Wedderburn had ambushed them here the previous week and how difficult the woods had been to pass on horseback. He guided them round the edge, hoping that the crescent moon would soon grant them a glimpse of the priory. Only when they reached the precinct wall did he dare to turn round.

Nobody had followed them, which was just as well, for they were so utterly exhausted that they could barely escape their saddles. Turnbull staggered to the gatehouse and banged on the door.

"We're no' staying here, surely?" asked Catherine. Their arrival seemed only to have increased her anxiety.

"We've got to stop somewhere, or we'll end up in England," Antoine said. "It will just be for one night, then we can make a plan."

The slit opened and a pair of eyes appeared. Their owner

gave a gasp. After some hurried fumbling at the bolts, the gate opened to reveal Sister Joan.

"My lord! What are you—? I mean, why are you—?" She was trembling, as if she were the one who had been hunted these last few hours. Or as if she had seen a ghost.

"We met with some difficulties in Dunse and require beds for the night while we regroup. I trust that will be possible?"

"Of course," she said nervously. "You will be off in the morn?"

"I hope so."

"Then if you wait in the parlour, I will fetch the hospitalless for you gentlemen. As for you, my lady, I will take you to your quarters."

When the hospitalless had left them, the men collapsed on their shared bed and said nothing for a while. Turnbull stretched out his lanky frame and pondered the events that had led them here. This was partly Antoine's fault, for indulging Catherine so. For the first time, Turnbull wondered whether his master was up to this job.

"What do you think, sir?" he said at last.

"About what?" said Antoine wearily.

"What we do next."

Antoine pinched the bridge of his nose with his thumb and forefinger. "We need to get back to the tower, of course. But I don't know how, if Hume has men on the roads."

"Do you think he's behind all this, then?"

"I do not know. He's up to something, for sure. And he's determined to see us fail. But he seems to delight in taking us on, face to face, so why would he send three men about in masks?"

"True. So what did you make of Carmichael's story? These men from the West?"

"They seem more likely suspects, don't you think? But we have no clue who they are. That is where we should focus, if we ever get out of here."

Suddenly, Turnbull sat up. He squinted as his weary mind went over the facts. "Hang on. Ledgerwood's wife is from the West," he said slowly. Then his words picked up pace. "She said she had three brothers too, all reivers by the sound of it. She seemed reluctant to talk of them."

"But why would they be here?"

"She said they had business all over the Marches. Perhaps they came to conspire with Ledgerwood, now he's out of gaol?"

Antoine nodded. "Except he was still in gaol when de Bruyn was kidnapped and Alex Redpath was killed."

"Then perhaps he is not involved, but his wife is?"

"How so?"

"Go back to my theory of the other night. It looks like I was wrong about Alex being one of de Bruyn's kidnappers. But let's say that was the Armstrong brothers, our three men from the West. Then suppose Alex discovered something of the plot, through their sister, his lover. Perhaps she also wanted him gone, so that her husband did not find out about their affair. So it suited them all to get rid of him. But first they needed to torture him, to find out if anybody else knew. He told them about Luggy, so they got him too. Finally, they eliminated Schmidt, to cover their tracks."

Antoine smiled. "I'll say one thing for you, young man. You have a good imagination."

Turnbull frowned, for he was sick of being patronised. "I am trying to help, sir. It is not my fault we're in this mess."

He felt his master's hackles rise. "Very well," said the Frenchman. "Help me with this. How did these Armstrong brothers know that we would be going to Allanton, to intercept Schmidt? How did they know that you would be in Berwick and staying at the Ship? How do they always seem to be one step ahead of us?"

"I've told you: I believe we have a spy somewhere in our ranks."

"Yes, another of your fancies. But I saw no sign of it in Gilchrist. He is not clever enough for that."

"Then Burnsie? He showed his true colours tonight."

"His quarrel was with Mistress Gray alone. I cannot see how he could be passing on news to the Marchmen. He's an Edinburgh lad."

"Still. Something is not right."

Antoine shook his head. "By the martyrs, you'll be accusing Anderson next."

It was a ridiculous suggestion, and Turnbull glowered at the crude attempt to belittle him. "All I know is that we are being watched. And when we find out who it is, we should make sure we—"

Just then, there was the slightest of sounds outside their room. A footstep. Then others, fading away. Both men leapt from their bed and raced to the door. They flung it open but there was nobody there.

They sprinted down the corridor, but it was dark as they had left the lamp in their room, and the torches on the wall were fading. As they rounded the corner, they came upon some stairs. A hooded figure was hurrying down them, a nun, by the looks of it. Antoine bounded down the steps two at a time, to catch her. But his ankle buckled on the second leap, and he crashed into the wall. Turnbull raced past him and blocked the nun's way. She cowered away from him before slowly lifting her head.

"You!" said Antoine, climbing to his feet. He shook with indignation.

Chapter 41

"It's no' what ye think, sir," Sister Joan snivelled.

"Oh no?" said Antoine. "You were not listening at our door?"

"I confess I was. But I swear I meant ye no harm."

"Rubbish," hissed Turnbull, jabbing a finger at her. "I bet you'd be straight off to the prioress if we hadn't caught you. Or whoever else you've been trittle-trattling to."

"By my fay, I would not," she sobbed.

"Then what were you up to?"

"I hoped to learn your plans, 'tis true. Though not to hand them to someone else, but for my own sake."

"What?"

She lifted her chin to reveal her tear-streaked face. "I wish to go wi' you the morn."

Antoine and Turnbull looked at each other, confused. Sister Joan clasped her hands, which seemed to increase her conviction.

"I didnae choose my life here, my family did. And although I've tried to serve Our Lord as best as I can, I find I am ill-equipped for it. Since that man's body was found on the island, the constant politicking here has worsened, and my desire to escape has only grown. Now, seeing Sister Columba tonight has given me the strength to make the leap."

"Sister Columba?"

"Mistress Gray." She wiped her cheek. "That was her name when she was here."

Antoine gasped. "Wait, you are saying that Mistress Gray was once in Holy Orders?"

Now it was Sister Joan's turn to be taken aback. "She was a novice here, yes. Hasn't she telt ye?"

"No, she's not said a thing."

The nun dabbed her eyes with her sleeve. "Oh dear. Well, she was our beloved Sister in Christ, until ten years ago. I never thought I would see her again, but it seems Our Lord has brought her back to us."

Antoine rubbed his forehead as he tried to take in this news. If it were true, it would show how little he really knew Catherine Gray. And also explain her agitation upon arriving here. "Why did she leave in the first place?" he asked at last.

"Ah," said Sister Joan. "I think it's best she tells you that herself. But meanwhile, I beg you: please grant my wish and take me wi' you."

Antoine peered down the gloomy corridor to check they had no other company. "Why should we do that, when we already have enough troubles on our hands?"

Sister Joan's face hardened. "I can tell ye things about our Reverend Mother. Things she's hiding from ye."

Antoine tutted. "Whatever it is, we could shake it out of you now if we wanted."

"But ye won't, sir. I know ye are good men."

"Good men do bad things when they are desperate," said Antoine. "And believe me, we are very desperate. We are far from our tower. There are likely men watching for us on the roads. Now you hint that Mother Isabella might be working against us too. If we wanted to escape, it would be much easier to squeeze the intelligence from you and then slip out alone at dawn."

"How far would ye get though? The three of ye would be sitting targets as soon as ye left the precinct walls."

"Well, we can't stay here either. So what would you suggest?"

"A cart, sir. The priory has a fleet of them, for the carrying of our wool and fruit."

Antoine and Turnbull exchanged glances but said nothing.

"They are kept in a barn by the gatehouse. I could get the oblates to have one ready for us, wi'out alerting the others. Then I could sit up front and drive the horses while ye hide in the back, under cover."

Antoine stroked his beard. "Have you discussed this plan with Mistress Gray?"

"No, we had only a little time to make our reacquaintance. But I can pass by her room tonight and get her aboard."

Antoine felt Turnbull staring at him in disbelief, an expression that only became more pronounced as he agreed to the plan. "Very well. It will be slow-going in a cart. So let's meet in the parlour at dawn and leave as the Lauds service begins. Then we'll take the Dunse road and aim to get back to Black Rig before noon. Once we're there, what you do next will be up to you. Now be off with you before I change my mind."

Turnbull was still exasperated at Antoine as they climbed into bed. Angry even, as he felt that his master would have ridiculed this plan if he had suggested it. "Are you sure this is wise?" he said. "She now knows our exact route and timing. If she really is in communication with our enemies, she could arrange to have men waiting for us. And why take the Dunse road in any case? Isn't that the very place they'll look?"

"Leave all that with me", said Antoine irritably. "Now try to get some rest if you can. It's been another difficult day – and tomorrow will be no easier."

Turnbull did as he was told, although he found it impossible to sleep. His body ached with exhaustion, but his mind kept returning to Antoine's recent behaviour. Judging by the way his master tossed and turned, he harboured his own doubts too. Turnbull had noticed this restlessness before, but tonight, the man seemed to be unusually disturbed. At one point, he even called out a name. Francis, perhaps? Turnbull feared the French King would not view their current situation kindly. The more he watched his master roll about, the more his own worries grew.

When the Lauds bell rang the next morning, it came as a relief to both men.

"It's All Saints' Day," said Antoine, pulling back the covers. "So the Mass should be of a goodly length. Let's give it a minute before we make our move."

They waited for the last bell to ring before creeping out of their room and down the corridor. The guest house was empty. Quietly, they opened the front door – only to shut it again when they saw some stragglers heading off to chapel. Another few moments passed, and they were outside. They headed over to the main buildings, taking care to go round the cloisters instead of across the garth. There was nobody abroad – until they bumped into the hefty figure of the hospitalless, running from her office.

"Watch out, sir!" she complained angrily. "I am late for Mass as it is."

"We are sorry," said Antoine.

The hospitalless eyed them with suspicion. "Why are ye up at this hour, anyway? Ye cannae join us in the chapel."

"No, we were going to the warming room."

She snorted. "If you found our blankets lacking, you should have said so. In any case, it's back that way."

The men pretended to follow her directions, before doubling back on themselves when she had gone. They hurried into the parlour, where Sister Joan and Catherine were waiting for them. Antoine caught the latter's eye. He thought of challenging her for not divulging her secret past but decided that it was more important to get moving.

"You two have spoken?" he said urgently.

The women nodded.

"And we are all agreed?"

Another nod.

"Then let's be off."

Without saying another word, they made for the gatehouse, where the oblates had rigged up Carbonel and Fogo to a cart. They unlocked the main gate and headed off through the orchards, with Sister Joan at the reins and the others in the back. It occurred to Antoine that he had not travelled this way since that terrible journey back to Venice. The track was bumpy, and the pain in his ankle was excruciating.

After a few minutes, he guessed that they must be at the priory's boundary stone, and he poked his head through the cover. "A change of plan," he said to Sister Joan. "Take the Lennel road, not the Dunse one."

"Are you sure, sir? We will get to your tower much quicker this way?"

"We're not going to Black Rig anymore."

"Then where *are* we going?"

"Never mind for now. Just take the right turn and keep going until I say so."

Antoine tried to gauge the nun's reaction, but she did not turn around. She simply steered them in the direction that he had requested.

"What's going on?" asked Turnbull when Antoine brought himself back in.

"A tactical shift. You were right about not taking the obvious route. We'll go to Dunbar instead."

Catherine gasped. "But that's miles away – this is not what we agreed!"

"Calm yourself, Mistress Gray. It's only a temporary adjustment. We will pick up reinforcements and come back over the hills in a couple of days."

They rumbled through Lennel and across the Simprim Burn. The jolts of the cart were so violent and noisy that nobody attempted conversation. It was all that they could do to hang on to their places and not crash into each other. Antoine kept an eye on their progress through a hole in the cover. After they had been travelling for a couple of hours, he stuck his head out again to issue Sister Joan with new instructions.

"Head through Swinton next, and on to Allanton."

"If you're headed to Allanton, it's quicker to go by Whitsome."

He paused to think about this. "Then go that way. And keep up your pace until we get through Chirnside."

They continued like this into the afternoon, not daring to stop until they had passed their enemies' strongholds. Antoine remembered Ritter's words to Turnbull. Was this rutted track the 'trail of blood' they were supposed to follow? If ever they needed some guidance from those above, it was this All Saints' Day.

After a while, they began to climb a steep hill. This made conditions in the back even more uncomfortable, and Antoine asked Sister Joan to stop. They had cleared the places where Luggy and Schmidt had been murdered and where Ledgerwood and Wedderburn lurked. They would soon be leaving the Humes' territory altogether.

"Let's have something to eat and let the horses rest," said Antoine. "Then Turnbull, you can change places with Sister Joan when we resume."

Again, he watched for any reaction from the nun, but she did not seem unduly perturbed. It was Turnbull who frowned at the decision. Antoine took him aside as they ate a parcel of bannocks which Sister Joan had liberated from the kitchens.

"I think we can trust her," said the Frenchman. "If she were working against us, she'd want to steer us back into trouble, but she seems content to go wherever we ask. On the other hand, we're now so far from the priory that it will look strange for a nun to be guiding the cart. If you go up front, it will make all of us safer."

"All of us?" muttered Turnbull as he took his place. But Antoine did not take the bait, and they soon continued on their way.

The going was very hard from this point as the hills rose and dropped sharply on their way to the sea. Antoine studied his companions. Turnbull hunched his shoulders in grim determination. Catherine straightened her gown in irritation every time they went over a bump. Only Sister Joan showed any lightness of humour. Antoine realised this was a true escape for her, in a way it was not for the rest of them. He wondered if he would feel that way when this business was done, and he was shot of this country. He hoped so, but he did not know any more.

On they went, over flimsy wooden bridges, through gorges and ravines. The air began to take on a salty tang, and the crash of waves against rocks could just be heard in between the clanks of the cart's wheels. When Antoine peeped out to their right, he could see the cliffs of Cockburnspath, dropping straight into the German Ocean.

For the last two hours, they had to rely on the horses to pick their way through the dark. The gibbous moon proved no help as it lured them over to the sea like a malevolent siren. Occasionally, Antoine would worry that they were straying too close to the edge, only to realise that his fear was misplaced. Perhaps the horses were the only creatures to be trusted here.

Finally, they entered Dunbar. Antoine clambered through the cover to sit with Turnbull up front. He breathed a great sigh of relief to see the massive walls of the castle loom ahead. It was a truly enormous structure, built on a series of rocks and sea stacks connected by a series of walled passages. Antoine had substantially reinforced it in recent years, and although those changes were not apparent in the dark, the light shining from various windows and arrow slits gave a sense of its scale.

"It's incredible," said Turnbull as they mounted the causeway, which curled around the outer walls. Antoine smiled as he contemplated the comforts which lay in store. They rolled slowly up to the gatehouse, where some sentries rushed to meet them. One was holding a torch while the others brandished spears.

"My lord! I am sorry. We were not expecting you!"

Antoine grinned. "I was not expecting to be here either. But get that portcullis lifted before we freeze to death."

"Of course," said the man. He waved to the gatehouse, then turned back to his master. "I'm sure Lord Albany will be glad to see you."

"Lord Albany?" said Antoine, bemused.

"Yes, sir, he arrived yesterday. I'm afraid he's in a temper."

Chapter 42

This was the last thing Antoine needed: an audience with his master, while his affairs were in such disarray. Technically, the castle was Albany's, but he had entrusted its running to him these past two years. Why then would he turn up like this? As he entered the gatehouse, Antoine wondered how much the Governor knew about his travails. The sooner he spoke to him, the better.

He strode through the courtyard in search of a familiar face. Most of the garrison were French, and he quickly found a serjeant he could rely upon. He spoke briskly, in their common tongue.

"De Brézé, take this cart and horses to the stables. And make sure that these ladies are made comfortable."

Then, turning to Catherine and Sister Joan: "We will speak in the morn."

If his words sounded threatening, he was in too much of a hurry to care. He led Turnbull through the outer ward and then into the North Tower. Here they climbed a spiral staircase all the way to the roof. Next they took the vertiginous walkway which linked the castle's two great rocks. A gale was blowing, and they were lashed with sea spray as they raced to the other side. From here it was two more flights up to the solar. They were breathless as they approached the sentry on the door, who grimaced as if to warn them of the mood inside.

"The Chevalier de Lissieu," he said, ushering them in.

Albany stood in the middle of the room with sheaves of papers in his hands. His face was red, as if he had been shouting. One of his secretaries, a weaselly figure by the name of Pentland, was gathering other documents from the ground. He scrambled to his feet as they came in. Antoine's own deputy at the castle – a Portuguese officer named Ferres – watched on. He, too, looked flustered.

"I am sorry if we interrupt, sir," Antoine said, bowing deeply to the governor. Turnbull followed suit and introduced himself to the other functionaries. Albany smiled, but his expression seemed forced.

"Do not worry, it is always good to see you. I just hope you bring me better news than these two."

"Why, what goes on?" said Antoine. He already dreaded the prospect of explaining himself, but perhaps there might be some broader context he could use to his advantage.

"It is more a case of what does not go on. The peace talks move like a snail, so I have come here to clear my head. Anyway, enough of my troubles. What brings you back here so early? I trust all goes well in the Marches?"

"It has been an interesting first month…" said Antoine slowly.

"Interesting is not good," said Albany. He walked over to the hearth, where a great fire burned. "I would rather that you brought me boring."

"And so I shall, my lord. But it is still early days."

"That is very true, forgive me. Well, why don't you both bring up a chair and tell me all about it."

The men followed their master's lead and gathered around the fireplace. Antoine thought that he saw Pentland smirk, no doubt relieved that the focus was on someone else. The Frenchman began to talk, but before he could get a word out, Albany waved him silent.

"No, my friend. Let's hear it from Turnbull. After all, he's the only one of us who is from the Marches."

Turnbull looked over at Antoine. "I am not sure I am the right person to—"

"Nonsense, lad. But no sugaring your words. And no conferring with your master. Just tell me everything that has happened since your arrival."

Turnbull tried to keep his account brief, but it was difficult, given all the twists and turns. Antoine winced as the lad stumbled over the order of events, tied himself in knots trying to avoid talking of their mistakes. All the while, Albany tugged at the details, like a dog with a bone. Antoine waited for the reaction.

At first Albany said nothing; he just stood up and warmed his hands on the fire. The sound of men's laughter rose up the chimney from the Great Hall below. It seemed to irritate him.

"So let me get this straight. You have been there less than a month. Early days, as you say..."

Antoine nodded, although he sensed a blow was coming.

"...and yet within that time, you have managed to alienate the locals, collaborate with a spy, befriend a witch and now kidnap a nun?"

Pentland started to chortle but stifled it when he saw the expression on Albany's face. Antoine bowed his head.

"With respect, sir, it is more complicated than that."

"Are you saying I have it wrong?" said Albany, his face purpling.

"Certainly not, sir."

"Then Turnbull has not told the truth?"

"No, he speaks straight. Although, he may have over-egged certain aspects. After all, he is young and naïve."

Albany raised an eyebrow at Turnbull, who sat sullenly in his chair.

"Well, I am neither of those things. And nor are you. So let me tell you what I think of it, as one old friend to another."

He walked behind Antoine and leant over his shoulder.

"I think you have become caught up in these murders at the expense of everything else. I think you should deal with them swiftly and move on. Most of all, I think you should forget this talk of arms smuggling, for that's the kind of rumour that can start a war!"

Antoine knew he had to choose his next words wisely. "Thank you for your counsel, sir. As ever, you are quite right. I will increase our pace forthwith." He paused. "Though it is a challenge when the culprits move like ghosts."

"Christ's passion!" said Albany, looming over him. "I said deal with these crimes, not solve them. If the wrong folk swing, it will not be the first time. Just pick some likely targets and be done."

"As you wish, sir. But what if the likeliest target is someone powerful? Lord Hume, for instance?"

Albany glowered at him. "That would be very unhelpful, and I would urge you to look elsewhere."

"Then what of the prioress?"

"Much though it would please me to take her down, it would bring King Henry's wrath on us. Another dead end!"

"And if Lord Dacre is involved?"

"By the saints, are you going to list names all night? All three are rogues, but they are rogues of high station. Take any one of those others you mention whether they be witch or watchman. It. Does. Not. Matter. Who. You. Pick!"

Albany jabbed his finger with each word, as if he were scolding a child. Then he walked back to the fireplace and stood with his back to the group. Without warning, he kicked a set of fire pokers, sending them flying across the stone floor. Ferres quickly picked them up, while the governor retook his seat, taking a moment to collect himself.

"Listen, my old friend, I do not wish to beat your back. I am trying to help you. Help you from yourself and that over-active conscience of yours!"

"Of course, sir. I understand."

"Good. Also, I know this task is difficult. That is why I chose you for it, remember? You above all others."

The praise seemed hollow, but Antoine bowed respectfully.

"So what I propose is this. You will spend two days here to restore yourself. Eat well, relax, get some warmth in your bones. We will give you some fresh food supplies and that winch you say you need. Then on the third day you will return to the Marches – and sort this whole thing out."

"Thank you, my lord. That is very generous of you." Antoine decided to chance his luck. "And extra men? We are greatly outnumbered and might not make it home without them."

"That won't be possible," Albany said curtly. "But I will send a message to Hume tomorrow, encouraging him to stop his games."

Antoine was disappointed at the lack of reinforcements but knew better than to complain. "Very well, sir. I am sure a little menace will do the power of good."

"You would think so, wouldn't you? Although it has not

so far, from what you say. So I am going to give the Humes a little carrot instead of a stick: some lands at Manderston in return for their good behaviour. It sticks in my throat, after all that they have done, but it seems the only way."

Antoine could not believe that Albany intended to reward the Humes for their lawlessness. However, he bit his tongue, in the hope that one of the others might raise an objection. He turned an eye to Turnbull, but the lad seemed to be in a sulk. Nor did Ferres come to his assistance. As for Pentland, he had already picked up a parchment and was reaching for his quill. Albany dictated the words to him in a monotone. As he finished, a bell began to toll.

"Well, I daresay we have all had enough of this for one night. And I must to the chapel, for the All Souls' vigil begins." He stood, causing all to rise. On the way to the door, he gripped Antoine's wrist and looked him in the eye. "You have a week to get this right, you hear? Now, get some sleep. You look like you need it."

Albany swept out, with Pentland and Ferres trailing behind him. When they were gone, the Frenchman gestured for Turnbull to join him at the hearth, but the lad went straight to wash himself at the basin.

"The Governor is right; we need some sleep. Even I – a young and naïve fool – can see that."

Chapter 43

The bells for All Souls continued through the night, making Antoine's slumbers even more fitful than usual. He had been without Catherine's medicine for the last two days and felt its absence greatly. His ankle still ached. Indeed, every muscle throbbed from their recent travels. As he lay in the solar's main bed, he observed Turnbull on the truckle and felt sure that he was feigning sleep. Very well, he would let him stew. He pulled on his outer clothes and went downstairs.

The Great Hall was full of men, heading off to Mass. They bowed as he passed through, and he noted that it had been a long time since he had received such respect. It seemed of little import now though. As he made his way to the adjacent chapel, Albany slipped off through a side door: he had clearly decided that the night's vigil would excuse him from the morning's service – and from the risk of further conversation. Catherine and Sister Joan were kneeling with the other women. Antoine took his own seat at the front, alone.

The Mass for All Souls was one of the longest of the year as prayers were said for all the departed, to speed their path through purgatory. Antoine thought of Francoise, whom he had lost through his indecision; the men that he had served ill at Agnadello; and the victims of these foul crimes, whom he had let down so far. Once the service was over, he stayed behind to light some beeswax candles for them. They smelled sweet and he hoped they would help bring all these souls closer to the purifying joy of God. However, he also feared for the time when he himself would have to enter the cleansing fire. Or something worse.

As he contemplated this, a voice whispered behind him. "I was right: ye're a good man, sir."

Turning, he discovered Sister Joan. He frowned and looked forward again.

"I will have to make my own peace wi' the Almighty," she continued quietly. "But I am sure that bringing me here was the right thing to do."

Antoine still did not reply.

"Now I wish to repay ye for your kindness."

This time, he turned fully round. In the flickering candlelight he could see that her eyes were red, but her expression was determined. He wondered what intelligence she might have for him.

"It is not right to have such discussions here," he said. "Take the first left after the Great Hall and meet me on the battlements."

She nodded and left while he finished his prayers. A few minutes later, they were both standing in the fresh air, gazing out to sea.

"I have never seen the ocean before," said the nun. "It is much more beautiful than I imagined."

"It can be dangerous too," said Antoine, looking over the castle wall to the foaming mess below.

"Of course," she said. "Still, there are perils in every place. Even in the house of God."

Antoine looked at her keenly. She was still wearing her

habit, but it now seemed little more than a plain white gown, devoid of any innocence or mystery. "If you have something to say about your time at the priory, then let me have it."

"I do, sir. It's about Alex Redpath's exhumation."

"Yes?"

The nun eyed him, uneasily. "When the Reverend Mother instructed us to bring him up, she emphasised that she would like to see the body afore anybody else."

Antoine was puzzled. "But we were all there when it was unwrapped. Gilchrist brought it out of the grave, and I took off the shroud myself."

"That is how it appeared," said Sister Joan hesitantly. "But the truth is that after Sister Triduana and I had removed all the soil around the body, we lifted it onto the side of the grave. Then we went off to fetch the prioress. When we returned, she asked us to turn our backs, lest we be upset. She conducted a brief inspection, said a quick prayer and asked us to put it back. Only then did we come for ye."

"So she was acting when we revealed it?" Antoine said in astonishment.

"Yes, I am afraid so."

He processed the news. "And she could have tampered with it too?"

"Yes, although she did not have long."

"Long enough to put that card there, though, if she had wanted?"

"I suppose."

Antoine felt his anger rising. "And you went along with it, knowing that you were deceiving me? Playing games with the dead? And with the poor man's brother standing there, a bag of nerves and grief?"

"I'm sorry, my lord. I knew it was wrong, but the Reverend Mother was insistent."

"Well, I fear you may have to light a candle of your own today. For your silence may cost further lives."

Sister Joan began to cry. "Oh, sir. Please do not say that."

"We will have to see," Antoine said curtly, only to feel a twinge of pity at the young woman's distress. "But what's done is done. Now, for the love of all that's holy, have you any more to say?"

"No sir, I promise," she sniffed.

"Then get back to your quarters. And send down Mistress Gray, for I would speak with her as well."

While he was waiting for Catherine, Antoine pondered the implications of Sister Joan's confession. On the one hand, it was not certain that the prioress had interfered with the body. But the very fact that she had behaved this way showed she was not to be trusted. Antoine wondered how she might have profited from planting the card. Why would it suit her interests for the Flemings to be collared for this crime? Had she invented the whole idea of arms smuggling? And if so, what was really going on?

Catherine interrupted his musings with a cough. "You asked for me, sir?" She held her arms straight down, her fists in balls.

"I did, mistress. I am sure you can guess why."

She lowered her head. "Sister Joan told me, yes."

Antoine waited for her to say more, but she simply looked at her feet. "Why didn't you tell me that you had been in Holy Orders?"

"It was a long time ago, and I didnae think it relevant."

"Yet we have spoken of the priory many times. You know

enough about our case to realise it is of interest to us. Of increasing interest, I should say."

Catherine looked up. "I've no' been there for over ten years. I know nothing of its workings now."

"You know the prioress though. And some of the other nuns."

"I was young then. And the little I know of my time there, I have tried to forget."

"I see," said Antoine. He softened his tone. "Well, for the sake of all the souls we pray for today, I wish you to remember just one thing: why you left. Then I can decide whether it might help us."

Catherine's fingers started to twitch by her sides. A gull landed on the battlement but flew off straight away, as if sensing the tension in the air. "Very well," she said. "I left the orders all those years ago because I was… afflicted."

"Afflicted, how?"

Catherine's face coloured. "By a malady o' the mind. There, are you happy?"

"I'm sorry," said Antoine. It was not what he had expected.

"It started soon after I arrived at the convent. The more I learnt of the terrors of Hell, the more I worried that I would end up there."

"That is quite normal," said Antoine. He remembered his own thoughts at Mass. "A good thing, indeed."

"This was different," Catherine said forcefully. "The notion wouldnae leave me for a single moment. I began to hear the voice o' the Devil mocking me in everything I did. Whether I was at chapel or working in the fields, he taunted me wi' my fate. The more I struggled against him, the more persistent he became."

This still did not seem so strange to Antoine, although it

explained some of her behaviours. The constant fussing, the self-blaming. He searched for something to say. "Did prayer help?"

Catherine smiled wearily. "It only made things worse. I increased my devotions ten-fold, a hundred-fold, but still he laughed that it was no' enough."

"And what of the prioress?"

She paused. "I know you would like me to speak ill of her. But she was good to me. She urged me not to chase perfection in an imperfect world."

Antoine gave an appreciative nod. Not for the first time was he forced to acknowledge Mother Isabella's wisdom. Whatever she lacked in spiritual purity, she made up for in earthly pragmatism. "That seems like good counsel."

"It was – and it helped me for a while. Until a priest from Melrose came to visit. He said that I suffered from an excess of scrupulosity and that if I were to stay, I might infect the others. So that was that." Catherine wiped her cheeks. "I left, or rather, I was made to leave."

Antoine was confused by her account. Her malady did not seem so different to his own melancholy – or the normal doubts that everyone must surely harbour. And yet the church obviously viewed her differently to men like him. Perhaps her mistake had been to speak of her pain. He resolved to keep his own worries to himself.

"You have had naught to do with the priory since then?"

"Not a thing. I have thrown myself intae my work instead. Helping others if I can."

Antoine nodded. So that was *her* escape. "And does your malady still affect you?"

Catherine looked down. "I have learnt to keep it at bay, using the Reverend Mother's advice. But this past month has roused it again." Her chin trembled. "Oh, what if the Devil was right all along? What if I am to blame for these deaths, as they say? Perhaps I should confess to you and throw myself on the fire, as everybody seems to wish?"

Antoine felt sick. Not just at her willingness to condemn herself but at the thought which flickered through his own mind. It was only a fleeting idea but one which horrified him, nonetheless. What if he followed Albany's order to close the case – by pinning the blame on her? He looked at the sea again and imagined himself sailing over the horizon, free from all this. No, it was unthinkable. He took Catherine's shoulders and gripped her tight.

"Do not say such a thing, Mistress Gray. You have contributed nothing to this, nothing at all. Just stay quiet, while I work out what to do next."

Antoine spent the rest of the day in the solar, turning over his dilemma. Surely there must be a way to solve these crimes without harming the innocent or plunging the country into war.

He realised that he missed Turnbull's counsel on such matters, naïve though it sometimes was. But when the lad came back that evening, it was clear that he was still in a state of dudgeon. For the second night in a row, they went to their beds in silence.

Antoine listened to the sea, crashing against the rocks below. He hoped it might send him over but instead it pulled him back through the riptides and eddies of his imagination. Round and round his ideas swirled. Every time he thought he had a firm hold of them, they were swept away like flotsam and jetsam. He thought again about sailing over the horizon

– or just letting himself drown. But there was still some life force within him which pulled him up towards the light.

The light. He thought of the candles he had lit in the chapel. And of the dangers of eternal fire. He knew he had to do the right thing – even if it might harm himself. Indeed, perhaps he *needed* to harm himself to atone for the wrongs he had done to others. He put his head to the pillow with a new determination to solve these crimes, despite what Albany had said. And if he had to do it on his own, he would.

Chapter 44

Afer a day of rest, it was time to return to Black Rig. Antoine stood in the outer wards of the castle as soldiers loaded their cart with fresh provisions. Wiping a fleck of brine from his face, he tried to catch Turnbull's attention, but the lad kept his back to him, fiddling with the panniers on Fogo's back. How long was he going to keep this up? If it was about Antoine suggesting that he was immature, this was a fine way to prove it.

Earlier, Sister Joan had declared her wish to stay at Dunbar, while she planned the next steps of her life. Antoine had agreed that this was wise, and he was glad to bid her farewell. They had both proved useful to each other, but he did not need another passenger on this journey. Catherine hugged her before stepping up to drive the cart, pausing only to complain that the cellarer had not been able to replenish her herbs.

And so, after all this, the three of them were off. They left the causeway and proceeded carefully around the edge of the harbour. Fishermen were mending their nets and loading their boats with wooden crates. Women and children sat on their doorsteps, patching up sails. Judging by their great industry, the winter cod had been sighted off the coast. The men would be hunting them in the icy, black waters that very night.

"It could be worse," Antoine said, in an attempt to lighten the mood. "Imagine going on their journey instead of ours."

Turnbull looked ahead.

"I said it's not a job for faint hearts, eh?" said Antoine.

"What do you mean by that?" said Turnbull.

"Just that I'm glad our feet are on dry land. Aren't you?"

"I suppose."

"You should see this place at the end of summer. When the herring come, there are as many folk as fish. Thousands of them. The Lammas Drive, they call it."

"Good for them, sir," said Turnbull.

Antoine mused that it was going to be a long ride.

At Innerwick, they cut inland over the moors. This way to Black Rig should have been much quicker than their journey from Coldstream. However, the ground was marshy, and the cart kept getting stuck. After a couple of hours, Antoine pulled them up.

"Are you sure this is the right way?" he asked Turnbull.

"I believe so, sir. Unless you have a better idea?"

Antoine was irritated by this latest impertinence but did not wish to argue in front of Catherine.

"Come with me," he said to Turnbull, and they guided their horses towards a dip in the land. The wind blew through the marram grass and carried their voices away from the cart.

"Are you going to tell me what's wrong?" he asked.

"It's nothing," Turnbull replied. "I'm just tired from all our travelling."

"We all are. But I hope you are recovered soon. I'm going to need you these next few days."

"Of course, sir."

"You know, when I said you were young the other night, I did not mean it as an insult."

Turnbull's face reddened. "You called me young and naïve, sir. It could hardly be a compliment."

"You lack experience, is all I meant," said Antoine, showing his palms. "But you have fresh eyes. And I have a feeling those will be more useful than years this coming week."

"Then I wish you had said so to the governor, sir."

Hell's teeth, that was it. They were in enough trouble already without falling out. "You are nobody to lecture anybody on how to speak to their master," Antoine said sharply and geed up his horse. "Forget this foolishness by the time we get to the tower, or I will put Anderson in your place."

The Frenchman wheeled Carbonel around and started to move back towards the cart. But after a few steps, he felt the ground give way. To his alarm, he realised that they had strayed into a peat bog. The horse whinnied as his feet began to stick in the thick, clagging mud. Antoine soothed the beast and tried to guide him back onto firmer land. However, Carbonel stumbled further into the glaur. The beast threw its head back and shrieked as its legs were almost completely submerged.

"Don't move, sir!" shouted Turnbull. He had dismounted and was running over.

"I'm not sure if I even can," Antoine replied, a tremor in his voice. He felt Carbonel strain his muscles in an effort to budge himself – but to no avail. "Perhaps I could jump off to that rock, then we could pull him out together?"

"No, I think it's too far. You're better staying with him for now, to keep him calm."

Just then, Catherine called over to see what was happening. Turnbull shouted at her to stay where she was. Picking his way back to her, he uncoupled the carthorse and rummaged about for a length of rope. He led the beast back to Fogo and soothed them while he took out his dagger and started to hack at the rope.

"We will need two pieces, one for you and one for Carbonel. Get yours on first, sir – so we know you are safe, whatever happens to the horse. Then we'll try to loop the other round the animal's body."

He continued to saw at the rope, but it was hard going. Carbonel started to panic. He thrashed about, trying to climb out of the bog, but only succeeded in miring himself even deeper. It reminded Turnbull of Fogo's terror when he had been attacked in the stables.

"Try to steady him, sir. If he keeps panicking, he will tire himself to the point when we'll never move him."

"I know!" said Antoine. "I am doing what I can!"

Eventually, Turnbull made it through the rope. He threw one piece to Antoine, waiting for him to tie it around his waist. Then he threw the other section over. The movement made Carbonel jerk his head and go into another frenzy of exertion.

"Easy boy, we are trying to help!"

Once the horse calmed a little, Antoine bent to see where to attach the second rope. Turnbull told him it needed to be around the chest and over the withers. But Antoine could not see how to loop the rope around. He gripped the pommel of his saddle with his left hand and leant over Carbonel's shoulder, swinging the rope in his right. Again, he felt the horse straining against the thick, cloying mud. He wobbled and almost fell in.

"Holy God," he said, bobbing up again. "I cannot get far enough around. If I bend over any further, I'll be done for."

Turnbull scratched his head. "Right. Let's see." He raised a finger. "I know. Make a bowline and throw it under as far as it will go. Then use your sword to pull it through from the other side."

"I will try," said Antoine, although his fear was growing alongside Carbonel's.

He slipped his foot back into his right stirrup and, leaning over as far as he could, threw the loop under Carbonel's barrel. The horse tossed his head wildly, and Antoine had to cling on for dear life. As soon as he steadied himself, he switched to the opposite side. The pain in his left ankle was excruciating, but he lowered himself until he could see the bowline in the mud. Oh God, it was starting to sink!

Desperately, he poked the sword into the quagmire and jabbed about in search of the loop. He felt his arm cramp from holding on to the pommel and thought he would have to let go. But just as he was about to give up, the rope snagged on the sword and he managed to draw it up.

He sat back in the saddle and tied the knot before throwing the other end to the side. His heart was thumping. "Now what?"

Turnbull attached the rope to the carthorse's harness and used the remaining section to hitch up Fogo alongside. He walked both animals forwards, so that there was no slack. He slapped them to get them started and took a length of rope himself, slipping and sliding as he tried to dig his feet into the clart.

Carbonel thrashed about at the new sensation of being dragged. For a moment, he veered to the left, and it looked like he might take them all into the depths of the bog. Then

Antoine managed to correct his course, and a combination of heaving and coaxing allowed horse and rider to stagger out of the morass. They had been stuck for over an hour, and when they emerged, they were both exhausted and caked in a thick layer of black slime.

Once they had recovered from their ordeal, they resumed their journey. The land became more navigable, and Turnbull began to recognise the way. It took them down through the backroads of Bonkle, past the scrivener Meikle's house at Preston and over the Whiteadder. As they neared Dunse, they kept an eye out for Hume's men, but the roads were surprisingly quiet. Perhaps Albany's bribe of land was working after all.

At the tower, Anderson was shocked to see them arrive – especially in such a state – but they waved away his questions and went straight to their chambers.

"It was touch and go back there," said Antoine as he changed out of his filthy clothes. "You might have just saved my life."

"Thank you, sir. I did my best."

"Yes, you did. But how did you know what to do?"

Turnbull pulled out his truckle. "I'd seen my father do it many years ago. Remember me saying our land was once like a bog?"

Antoine nodded. "Well, it seems you are more experienced than I thought."

Turnbull smiled. "I suppose so, sir."

"Your father would be proud of you too."

"Perhaps."

They climbed into their beds and blew the candles out.

Although the room was cold and damp, they were glad to be here and not in Dunbar. They lay in the darkness for a while, each reflecting on the day's events.

"By the way, it's drave," said Turnbull lightly, just before he drifted over.

"What?" said Antoine wearily.

"That herring shoal you talked of. It's the Lammas Drave, not Drive. I've been wanting to tell you that all day."

Chapter 45

In the morning, Antoine brought Anderson and Turnbull together to debrief each other on the last couple of days. He related what Sister Joan and Catherine had told him in Dunbar. In return, the serjeant told them that Burnsie had stayed on in Dunse and that Gilchrist had deserted too. Perhaps they had been the spies after all, thought Antoine.

After breakfast, they went out into the barmekin, where the soldiers were assembling the winch. Anderson reckoned that they would have it ready by the end of the day and could clear the well tomorrow.

"Let us hope it is a wishing well," said Antoine.

"Why, what would you wish for sir?" said Turnbull.

The Frenchman had been praying for his escape for so long that the answer almost came out automatically. But he was surprised to hear himself say something else instead.

"The answer to our case, of course. Or at least more time to solve it."

"Aye, but time's the one wish God never seems to grant," said Anderson.

"Then we have exactly one week to crack it. With or without divine intervention."

As they contemplated this prospect, a voice called down

from on high. It was Carmichael, who was on sentry duty on the wall-walk.

"Visitors coming!" he shouted. Everyone in the barmekin stopped what they were doing and stared up at him. "There's four of them, sir. I think... I think two of them are... nuns?!"

Perplexed, Antoine ran to the gate. Sure enough, four riders were coming up the hill. The first two were easily recognisable as Mother Isabella and Sister Triduana. Alongside them, they could now make out Thomas and Cuddy Heron. They stopped a short way from the entrance.

"Good morrow, Monsieur Warden!" cried the prioress.

"Good morrow to you too, Reverend Mother. This is a surprise."

"I can imagine. You left without a word the other day."

"I am sorry. We were in a hurry."

"Yes, but I noticed you had time enough to take one of my nuns. And an old acquaintance too." She smiled. "Do not worry, I'm not here for them. I think it would be good to talk though."

Given everything he had learnt in the past few days, Antoine was wary of entertaining the prioress. However, something in her voice intrigued him, as if she carried news. He told Turnbull to take her inside while Anderson detained the others in the barmekin.

As they went through the courtyard, Catherine passed by. Her face was as white as a Cistercian habit.

"Sister Columba," said the prioress softly.

"Reverend Mother," Catherine whispered back.

Antoine ensured they were alone before joining them at the trestle table on the ground floor. He steepled his fingers. "So, Mother Isabella, what brings you here?"

The prioress spread out her hands. "Well, to begin with,

I am still waiting for your report from Berwick. We did have an arrangement, you remember?"

"You certainly made an arrangement for me," said Turnbull fiercely. "Two men almost killed me at the Ship."

"What?" said the prioress. She seemed genuinely shocked.

He snorted. "Enough of this act. Only you knew I was there."

"You must have told the guards at St Mary's Gate," Mother Isabella protested. "Or perhaps the Flemings. Are you sure you did not let some detail slip?"

Turnbull made to reply, but Antoine waved him silent.

"Reverend Mother, it would be better if you explained yourself, before asking us any further questions." He stroked his beard. "You can start with the way you deceived us over Alex Redpath's body..."

"Ah, that." The prioress took a moment to recover. "I wondered if Sister Joan would tell you. Very well, I apologise. But it was simply a little overcaution on my part."

"A little overcaution?" said Antoine. "You interfered with a man's body. And misled us by placing that card there."

Mother Isabella jerked her head back. "What's this? I fear we misunderstand each other."

"You placed the card on that corpse," Antoine repeated. "To further your claims against the Flemings."

"Is that what she told you?" said the prioress indignantly. "I swear on all that's holy, I did no such thing. I merely wished to see the body before anybody else did. Beyond that, I did not touch it."

"Then how did the card get there?"

"I presume the killers placed it there when they dismembered him, but we missed it the first time round. That was Sister Joan's fault. I chastised her. Now she is covering herself." The prioress ran a finger over her lips. "Look, I can see why this discovery would trouble you gentlemen. But I beg you to put it aside. It was a foolish error on my part, nothing more. Let me share something of greater import, and you will see why I am so anxious."

"We are ready," said Antoine.

"But be straight with us," added Turnbull.

"Very well." She leant across the table. "You'll recall I told you we found nothing when we searched the island – but that wasn't strictly true."

"No?"

"No. The day after the torso was found, we crawled over the island, in search of clues. We cut back the bushes, lifted every rock. And as we did so, we found a hollow in the ground, which had been covered by a flat stone."

"A hiding place?" said Antoine, his eyes widening.

"Yes, but more than that. There was a letter inside. This one."

The prioress drew forth a crumpled piece of paper with a series of crude symbols drawn on it. A dog. An eagle. A cat. The number 1.

"What does it mean?" asked Turnbull, holding it up to the dim light of the ventilation shafts. This revealed nothing further, so he put it back on the table.

"I don't know. But someone was using the hole as a place to exchange messages."

Antoine looked at her keenly. "It is all very persuasive and in line with your theory about some grand plot on the border. But forgive me, Reverend Mother, why are you only telling us this now?"

She shrugged. "I was hoping you would discover

something on your travels that might explain these symbols. But it seems not…"

She pushed the letter across the table, inviting them to scrutinise it again. For a moment, Antoine wondered whether the pictures might be heraldic devices. Hadn't Turnbull mentioned a double-headed eagle on the Germans' house in Berwick? But he could think of no local clans with dogs or cats on their arms. At any rate, the prioress interrupted his deliberations.

"I have now told you everything I know, gentlemen. As you say, it strengthens my belief that something is afoot. Something which could prove disastrous for all of us. Perhaps we can still prevent it. But only if we are honest with each other."

Antoine chuckled. "With respect, Reverend Mother, you have not been honest with us so far. How do we know you are not making this whole thing up?"

"You don't. Any more than I can trust everything you say." She paused. "Like when you went to Lennel to see Master Rutherford – but told me you were on the river…"

Damnation. So she did know about that, after all. Antoine rubbed his temples. "More overcaution, as you put it. My turn to apologise."

"Apology accepted. Now, let's put our games aside. Pray tell me what you've learnt and we will see if we can work this out together."

Antoine considered the offer. Although he was still wary of the prioress, he figured that if she were responsible for any of this, she could hardly profit from any intelligence he had. On the other hand, if she were as innocent as she claimed, she would be a useful ally. With time running out and a potential disaster looming, he decided to take a leap. He took her through all the discoveries of the last few days and encouraged Turnbull to do the same.

When they had finished, the prioress sat back from the table and exhaled deeply. "Well, I confess I am more confused than ever."

"Whoever we are up against is devilish cunning," said Antoine.

"That does not rule out many here," said the prioress.

"Perhaps they are not from here," said Antoine. He looked up to the vaulted ceiling, in search of inspiration. "I have a feeling that those three strangers from the West might hold our key."

The prioress nodded. "Yes, but how do we find them?"

"We should try to anticipate their next move," said Turnbull. "Why have they come here? If we knew that, we could guess where they might turn up next."

They fell into silence, each trying to fathom the minds of their deadly adversaries.

Suddenly, the prioress winced, as if in pain.

"What is it?" asked Antoine urgently.

"I've had a dreadful thought," she said. "About what they might be up to."

"Well?"

"The reivers of the West make ours look like angels. Some of them have set up a robbers' statelet, the Debatable Lands. Neither Scotland nor England. Even the March Laws do not apply there. What if they mean to carve out the same in the East?"

Antoine felt sick. "You mean, with the Humes unseated and our own authority challenged, they might seize power here?"

"Yes! And create the same kind of havoc they do at home. Ten times worse than anything we are used to."

"Then how would this explain the things we have discovered?"

"Just say the three men from the West are on a scouting mission, with this plan in mind. They use our island to communicate with allies in England. Then they kidnap de Bruyn to raise a ransom and fund their scheme. Alex Redpath finds out about it somehow, so they kidnap him to discover what he knows. Under torture, he says that Luggy has an inkling, so they take him too. This clears their path to put their scheme in motion."

"Not quite," said Antoine. "Even if they came back with a horde of riders, they'd be hard-pressed to take Black Rig. And they'd be no match for the governor's cannon."

The prioress maintained her pained expression. "What if they were able to obtain their own guns? So they could take this tower down and defend the area from the governor's attack?"

Antoine sat in stunned silence. He did not like the notion, but it had a chilling ring of truth to it. With the country so unstable, opportunists would always seek to exploit the chaos. Perhaps he and his men were sitting targets now, for some outlaw force intent on mayhem. He tried to remain calm.

"Procuring cannon is no easy business. Just bringing them here to besiege us would be a huge undertaking. Each one needs at least a score of oxen and the same number of skilled men. Even the ground here is unsuitable: it is so boggy that the wheels would stick."

"Unless they are procuring lighter guns?" ventured Turnbull.

"Do such things exist?" asked the prioress fearfully.

"They do," said Antoine. "They call them…"

"What?" Mother Isabella said. She was sitting on the edge of her seat. Antoine shook his head bitterly, as he contemplated what he was about to say.

"Falcons."

"As in the bird?" the prioress asked, bemused.

"As in the card on Alex Redpath's body."

Chapter 46

Antoine reached for his pouch and took out the card. He had kept it there ever since Turnbull's return from Berwick. He placed it on the table beside the letter and stared at both objects, hoping that some pattern would emerge. Unfortunately, there was no obvious similarity in their design. Nor did there seem to be any connection between the creatures depicted: a falcon, a dog, an eagle and a cat. So much for Ritter's advice about following the trail of blood – all it seemed to be doing was leading them in circles.

On the other hand, perhaps looping back on themselves was exactly what they needed to do. Antoine raised a finger. "You know, Turnbull, perhaps I was too hasty to dismiss your theory from the other night."

"Which one?" the lad said.

"The idea that these three strange men are the brothers of Janet Armstrong. You said she was reluctant to speak of them, or her origins in the West."

"Aye, and you picked holes aplenty in my theory," said Turnbull. He smiled, but Antoine detected an undertone of smugness in his voice.

"That I did. But perhaps this latest news makes more sense of it. We should visit Watt Ledgerwood's lair in Chirnside tomorrow. Speak to him and his wife. Search for these brothers, if necessary."

"It would still leave your challenge of how they knew so much about our plans."

Antoine thought about it. "Maybe you were right about that too, and it was Gilchrist after all? That would explain his desertion. Either way, we should be particularly cautious about our movements from this point."

"What about alerting Lord Dacre?" asked the prioress. "Whatever his taste for mischief, he would not welcome this kind of anarchy on his doorstep."

"Not yet," said Antoine, although he admired her shrewdness. "Let's think about him when we have some real evidence. The same goes for Albany. Meanwhile, it's not safe for you here. Get back to the priory as soon as you can. Stay there unless we call for you, and otherwise, we will visit you for the Wardens' Congress on the eve of the Truce Day."

The prioress gave them the letter before accompanying them to the barmekin where the others were waiting. Catherine fidgeted in the background, head down but watchful. "Take good care on the road," Antoine said to the Herons, although he suspected that Mother Isabella and Sister Triduana would be more than a match for most men. "You do the same for Sister Columba," said the prioress, glancing backwards at her former charge.

When they had gone, Antoine explained the latest developments to Anderson, only for the serjeant's face to cloud over.

"What's the matter?" asked Antoine. He had noticed that the man seemed unusually on edge recently.

"Black Rig is no' set up for cannon fire," Anderson replied. "The tower is high and easily hit. The outer walls are thick but made o' stane, not brick. Even smaller shots will cause them to shatter."

"Well, we cannot do much about that now. Could we dig a ditch beneath the wall, to deflect the fire?"

Anderson thought about it. "No, the rock's too hard. I think we may be better off creating some earthworks further out. A falcon's range is a mile or so, but the further we can push them back, the less accurate they will be."

"Good idea," said Antoine. "Let's have a look now."

They went out of the gate and walked down the hill. As they surveyed the terrain for a potential line of defence, Antoine remembered his first impressions of Black Rig. With a sinking feeling, he realised that the very things which had once made it seem so daunting now made it utterly vulnerable. It no longer loomed over the barren landscape but was terribly exposed: a fortress which was formidable at close quarters but could be obliterated from afar.

He was kicking himself for not bringing some guns down from Dunbar when he spotted a lone rider coming over the hill. He nudged Anderson, and they readied themselves, only to relax when they saw it was James Redpath. He waved at them, and they let him approach.

"What are you doing here?" asked Antoine. "Is everything all right?"

"Aye, sir, as much as it can be. We buried Luggy last week and are trying to get on wi' things. It is hard wi' the Truce Day looming though. I came to see if I could help."

"Of course. Come with me, and I'll tell you where we are. Anderson, you keep at this, and we will make a plan afterwards."

Antoine and Redpath walked back to the tower and picked up Turnbull, who had been supervising the clearing of the well. The job was almost complete. The ground floor was busy with men, so they climbed the spiral staircase to the kitchen.

"Watch the trip-step," Antoine started to say, but Redpath had already passed it unscathed. Carmichael followed them up with a basket of logs to revive the fire.

For the third time in as many days, Antoine and Turnbull shared what they had discovered. Redpath listened to their account open-mouthed. It was clear he was struggling to take it all in, and when they showed him the letter found on the island, he signalled that he had heard enough.

"I cannae believe my brother would be involved in something like this. Secret codes. Weapons smuggling. Insurgency. It is madness."

"That isn't what we are saying," said Antoine gently. "It seems more likely that he simply discovered it through his lover and paid the price. Perhaps he thought he could claim a share of it – but found the Armstrongs were not for bargaining."

"No, no, it cannae be. What about the card they found on him?"

"We believe the falcon refers to a type of cannon."

Redpath shook his head. "What about their accents? Ye said your attackers in Berwick spoke like Englishmen, didn't ye?"

"I only heard one word," said Turnbull. "But Rutherford thought the voices on the river were Scots."

"So ye think Dixon is telling the truth? Despite all the evidence in front of ye? The card, the placement of the body near his land, the butchery?"

Antoine hesitated. He remembered Dixon's caginess, especially when he had asked him to attend Luggy's dead body: how the fellow had known some details that had not been noised in public. The Frenchman did not wish to indulge Redpath's imagination at this point though. He watched Carmichael stoke the fire but decided he should smother this one.

"I'm sorry, Redpath; I know you seek a simple solution to your brother's case, but it seems it is more complicated than we thought. All we can say with some confidence is that the people who killed Alex and Luggy went on to kill again – and now wish to kill us."

This truly confounded the man. "How can you be so sure?"

"Because of this dagger," said Turnbull, withdrawing it from his belt. He put it beside the letter and the playing card on the table. "Taken from your brother, I believe? It was used on me at Berwick too."

Redpath looked utterly bewildered. He rubbed his face. "But... that's not... his dagger."

He picked it up and turned it around. "Look," he said. Reaching into his jack, he took out another knife and put it beside the other one. It was very similar, but the stag on the hilt was in profile, not head-on. "This is."

Turnbull gasped. "I just assumed—"

"That the killers wrested it frae my brother?" said Redpath bitterly. "No. If he had been wearing it when those cowards came for him, he would still be here. But he was unarmed. I carry it with me now."

Antoine picked up both daggers and turned them over. They were the same length, weight and colouration. He cursed himself for allowing Turnbull to jump to conclusions but did not wish to open old wounds by chastising him.

"I suppose this design is common round here," he said.

"Aye," said Redpath. "Like those cards are. Falcons and stags: we are simple countryfolk, that's all."

Antoine sighed. Perhaps he *was* over-complicating this.

It was hard not to, though, when the path seemed to take so many twists and turns. He collected himself.

"Dixon may still have a role to play in all this. And we have summoned him to the Truce Day, just in case. But for now, we must investigate these men from the West. They are our only new lead, and we have but days to go."

"As you wish, sir," said Redpath, reluctantly. Then, more brightly: "I'll do whatever I can to help."

By now, Carmichael had the fire going well, and the flames filled the hearth. He headed back downstairs, and the men moved closer, to warm their hands.

"You know, we *could* do with some help right now," said Antoine. "How long could you stay for?"

Redpath shrugged. "I told Agnes I might be here for a couple of days."

"And how did she take that?"

"She wasnae best happy," he said sheepishly. "But Luggy's brother has stayed over since the funeral. Between him and Dand, the women should be safe."

"I didn't know he had a brother?" said Antoine.

"Aye," said Redpath archly. "It's been a while since I've seen him too."

Antoine gave a knowing smile. If his time here had taught him anything, there was nothing like a body to bring long-lost kinsfolk out of the woodwork. For all their clannishness, the Scots were not so different from any other folk.

Blood might run thicker than water, but gold was the strongest bond of all.

Chapter 47

That night, Antoine woke with an intense pain in his stomach. He hoped it might pass, but it seemed only to grow. He tried to get up, thinking that standing might help, but the room swam before him, and he quickly sat down again. Leaning right over, he put his head in his hands and his elbows on his knees. He retched, bringing up a mouthful of thin, watery spew. It spattered over the rushes between his feet.

"What's happening?" said Turnbull, waking up and rubbing his eyes.

Antoine didn't say anything; he just wiped the traces of vomit from his beard.

"Are you all right, sir?" Turnbull raised himself and sat beside his master. He put a hand on his back and peered round to see his face, but it was impossible in the darkness, so he fetched an oil lamp. When he returned, he shone it by Antoine, whose face was a contortion of misery and pain. It reminded him of those paintings of the condemned souls in Hell.

"What's the matter, sir?" he said. "I have noticed you are often troubled in your sleep?"

"It's not that," said Antoine weakly.

"Then what?"

"I don't know. I have not felt like this before."

"Could it be a fever?" Turnbull touched his master's forehead. "You are very hot, although the room is cold."

"No, not a fever," groaned Antoine. "It's my stomach. It feels… it feels like I've been poisoned."

Turnbull recoiled at the idea but was not sure what to do. He persuaded Antoine to lie down again while he ran to the barracks to get help, but from whom? He searched for Anderson, but he could not find him, despite the early hour. He did not wish to alarm the others, so he took Redpath and Nisbet aside and asked them to come with him. At last, he remembered Catherine. He ran back to the tower and banged on her door.

Amidst much consternation, they all rushed upstairs. Antoine seemed oblivious to their presence; lost as he was in some awful trance.

"He's burning up," said Catherine. "He needs water to cool the fire."

Turnbull spun round. "Nisbet, run down and get some. And take these dirty rushes with you."

The man disappeared.

"What do you think?" Turnbull asked Catherine quietly. "Could it be poison?"

"I dinnae ken," she said slowly. "Either way, it looks serious. Did he speak of aches in his neck or limbs?"

"No, he talked only of his belly."

"Then it's no' the sweats, thank God. More likely something he ate. What did he have last night?"

Turnbull racked his brain. "Stockfish, same as all of us. Some bread, some wine as well."

"And could someone have doctored it?"

"I shouldn't have thought so. What would they even use?"

Catherine rolled her eyes impatiently. "There are plenty of poisonous plants round here. Deathcaps, foxglove, cuckoo pint…" She counted them out on her fingers before seeming to check herself. She dipped her head. "My point is that anybody could have done this, if they had half a mind."

Downstairs, Turnbull instructed Nisbet and Redpath to keep this to themselves.

"Aye, sir," said Nisbet, his big, doughy face knotted with worry. "You don't think it could have been the woman, do you?"

"No," said Turnbull. "But I cannot think who else it could be either. We did not eat with the prioress, so that counts her out. Burnsie and Gilchrist are no longer here. Mayhap another of the Marchmen?"

"But who?" said Redpath, scratching his head.

With a burst of inspiration, Turnbull clicked his fingers. "Nisbet, find Simpson and send him to me. Redpath, you try to find out where the hell Anderson is. We must postpone our visit to the Ledgerwoods until we solve this."

After a short while, Simpson arrived. He stood with his hands on his hips despite the offer of a seat. Turnbull felt his displeasure at being summoned, so he tried to ease his way in.

"You were a cook at Fast Castle, were you not?" he said pleasantly.

"That I was," growled Simpson. "Although it was a long time ago now."

Turnbull nodded. "It's one of the Humes' castles, isn't it?"

"It was until recently, aye."

"And you also know Watt Ledgerwood's gang in Chirnside."

"Ye ken that. I made no secret of it when we visited there."

"What about his wife's family?" Turnbull asked casually. "The Armstrong brothers?"

Simpson waved a hand. "I ken they're hard men frae the West, but I've never met them. Look, where are ye heading wi' all this?"

Turnbull fumbled for his words. "Our master has fallen ill, perhaps from something he ate. So naturally, I must speak to you, as our cook."

Simpson gave him a dark look. "It seems ye're more interested in *who* I serve than *what* I serve."

"I'm interested in both," Turnbull said as calmly as he could, although he found the man's physical presence intimidating. "So if you have anything to disclose..."

Simpson snorted. "I have no idea what you're talking about. I prepared a' the food as usual yesterday, and I've had no complaints from anyone else. Now, if you'll excuse me, I need to get on wi' dinner."

He shook his head and stomped out. As he did so, Nisbet came back from the barmekin. "How was that, sir? D'ye get what ye wanted?"

"Not exactly. Have you found Anderson?"

"No sir, it's quite strange. He seems to have completely vanished."

Turnbull screwed up his face. The serjeant had been cagey recently, but surely he could not be involved with any of this?

"Try outside, he was checking our defences yesterday. Perhaps he's gone out again."

298

"Why," asked Nisbet warily. "Are we threatened by attack?"

"Just take a look," Turnbull said. "And put someone else on cooking duties: I'm giving Simpson a rest."

When Nisbet had gone, Turnbull tried to arrange his thoughts. His master was afflicted, and Anderson had vanished. That put him in sole command of over twenty men, many more experienced than himself. They would soon be seeking orders. One or more of them might be a traitor. Their enemies circled outside and, all the while, the time until the Truce Day was running out. His head spun as he tried to make sense of it all.

At this moment, he heard a noise behind him. He swung round and was relieved to see it was only Gibb.

"God's wounds, I thought I was alone," Turnbull cursed.

"I'm sorry," said the old man. He was shuffling out of his room. "I gather you have a problem."

"It is nothing. I am dealing with it."

"That's good. But have ye thought—"

"Later, Gibb. I don't have time for this. Whatever it is, tell Mistress Gray, the next time you see her."

With that, Turnbull returned to see how Antoine was getting on. He was troubled to see that his master seemed to be even worse than before.

"It's no good," said Catherine. "I give him only water, but he doesnae revive. Have ye discovered anything frae the men?"

Turnbull shook his head sadly and lay flat out on his truckle. What if he had to complete this mission on his own? What if his master did not survive at all? For several hours, he waited for some sign of recovery, but there was none. He cursed himself. He should be downstairs, organising the men instead of hiding up here.

He was just about to leave when Nisbet shouted up the spiral staircase.

"Come quick, sir! Something's happened!"

What now? He jumped up and ran back down the stairs. The trip-step almost caught him out, but he managed to stop himself just before he went over. He raced past the middle floor and arrived in the basement, where he was met by Anderson and Carmichael. They both had cuts about their face. Redpath and Nisbet watched them warily.

"I've found our spy," said Anderson triumphantly. He grabbed Carmichael by the arm and gave it a jerk. "Although no' wi'out a little fight."

"What do you mean?" asked Turnbull, putting both hands to his head.

"I've had my eye on this one for a while. When I heard him leave last night, saying he was gathering kindling, it didnae ring true to me, as he took no panniers. So I followed him frae a distance. I tracked him a' the way to the White Hart, where I found him wi' a fellow frae Leitholm, by the border. He's been using him to pass messages to Cospatrick Dixon."

"Cospatrick Dixon?" said Redpath, his face a strange mixture of confusion and vindication.

"Aye, it all made sense when I thought about it. I recalled him on the roof that time – he said he'd left a hammer there, but he must have been listening to us: he volunteered to go to town for supplies the next day. Then on All Hallows' E'en, we shared our plans wi' him and sent him round the taverns: he stayed out all night, remember? And just yesterday, he eavesdropped on us as he stoked the fire. Again, he found an excuse to escape and pass on his news."

Turnbull stared at Carmichael. He cut a wretched figure.

"Is this true?"

The man looked at his feet. "It's no' how it looks," he said, dejectedly. "I'll admit passing on our news to Dixon. He's an old associate o' mine. But he swears he's innocent o' these crimes. He fears ye have it in for him."

"This is surely the final proof against Dixon," said Redpath angrily. "Why, now I think of it, did ye no' ride back wi' us on the night that Schmidt was killed, but leave us at the Harcarse burn?"

"I came straight here, to warn the others." Carmichael protested. "I know nothing about any Flemings."

"But you made sure that Dixon was well briefed on everything when our master interviewed him at the priory," said Turnbull.

"As I say, he fears a false trial. I simply evened things up for him."

"Well, he's not the only one who might need to worry about a trial now. And woe betide you if our master passes from this poison."

"I know nothing about that either!" said Carmichael. He clasped his hands in desperation, but his pleas were met with silence. Turnbull realised that the others were waiting for him to say something.

"We'll keep you under lock and key for now. But before you go, tell me about these three men from the West. Were they a fiction too, designed to put us off Dixon's trail?"

Carmichael put his hand to his heart. "No, sir, I swear they are real. I was telt about them on my travels, and their crimes are as I described, although—"

"What?"

The man's shoulders slumped. "They didnae wear masks. That was something I added as it seemed to be what you were after."

Turnbull shook his head in disgust. "So there are three hard men from the West, but they might not be our suspects after all."

"It sounds like it," said Anderson.

"And Dixon can't be trusted, whatever this carl says."

Redpath nodded. "I knew he was to blame."

"Then let's get him locked up. Mistress Gray will continue to tend our master. Anderson, you should join me in our room tonight lest there is further mischief. Nisbet and Redpath, you take guard on the stairs. Hopefully, that will get us through the night, and he will be well enough in the morning to make a plan."

"What if he isn't?" asked Nisbet, his eyes like cartwheels.

"Everything will be clearer in the morning," said Turnbull. However, there was little conviction in his voice.

Chapter 48

Antoine continued to toil through the night despite Catherine's ministrations. "This is my fault," she muttered, tilting his head back for water. "I should be curing him, but I seem to be making him worse."

"Don't say that," said Turnbull, who remembered Antoine's account of her strange malady. He nudged Anderson awake.

"You ready for your watch?"

"Hmmm?"

"Anderson, are you waking?"

The serjeant yawned. "I… what… give me a moment. What's afoot?"

"Our master makes no improvement. We must press on with our visit to the Ledgerwoods, without him."

Anderson grunted. "But I need everyone I can lay my hands on to dig these defences."

"That will have to wait a day," said Turnbull. "I'll need fifteen men to secure that place; that still leaves you a dozen to defend Black Rig."

"More like half that, myself included. Burnsie and Gilchrist are gone, remember? Carmichael's locked up. Simpson needs watching."

Turnbull rubbed his face. "It will have to do, I'm afraid. Let's get our second sleep, and I'll set off early. I promise we'll be back by the afternoon to help you with the defences."

As they came to the outskirts of Chirnside, Turnbull recalled his previous visit to the Ledgerwoods' lair. That had been uncomfortable enough, but now he would have Watt himself to deal with. Strangely, though, he felt less scared. Whether he had grown braver or simply got used to the threat of death, he did not know. Somehow, coming face-to-face with their enemies was preferable to all this groping about in the dark.

As it happened, there were no lookouts, as there had been last time. Instead, the cavalcade snaked its way up the hill to the Ledgerwoods' palisade and into the yard. There, they came face to face with a small group of men. They looked as if they were in the middle of something.

"Who the hell are you?" asked one. He was an enormous fellow, bursting out of a quilted jack. He wore an iron gorget around his neck.

"My name's Turnbull. The new warden's deputy."

Simpson's friend, Fat Lips, called from the back of the group. "That's the one who came to see Janet, chief."

"And the other one's Alex Redpath's brother," piped up another voice. Turnbull immediately regretted bringing him, but it was too late now.

The veins in the giant's temples seemed to throb. He cracked his knuckles. Then he broke into a toothy grin. "I thought ye might pay a visit. But ye've come at a bad time. My wife's just gone missing."

At first, Turnbull assumed the man must be jesting. He waited for his explanation, but Ledgerwood threw his head back instead, shaking his long greasy hair over his broad shoulders. "We were just talking of it when ye arrived."

"That's a shame," said Turnbull, still sceptical. "We were hoping to speak to both of you. When did she disappear?"

"Just last night. Why don't ye all dismount, and I can tell ye about it?"

Turnbull hesitated. He thought he saw some movements behind the arrow slits in the bastle house. And was that more men closing in behind them? Stay calm, he told himself.

"That would be useful. We can help you look for her. Why don't my men search the farmstead while we converse?"

Ledgerwood's nostrils flared like a dragon's. It looked as if he might explode, but he seemed to control himself. "As ye wish," he said. "Ye're obviously looking for something else beyond my wife, but ye won't find anything either way. Now hurry up and come wi' me."

The soldiers dismounted and tied their horses to a rail in the yard. They spread out, looking around the outbuildings. While they did this, Ledgerwood led Turnbull up some stone stairs into the bastle house. "Not you," Fat Lips told Redpath when he tried to follow them. "My master doesnae like big meetings." Redpath lowered his eyes and slunk back to the horses.

Inside the bastle, the reception room was dark and smoky. Ledgerwood drew up a stool for Turnbull, before settling himself on a large, ornately carved chair, with a red velvet cushion. It had presumably been stolen from some grand house. Other loot hung from the walls – a tapestry, a tattered flag, two battered shields. Turnbull wondered about the stories behind them. But mostly, he used them as an excuse to look about the room and watch out for an attack.

"So what happened to your wife, Ledgerwood?" Turnbull asked at last.

"Vanished!" the reiver replied. "She went out riding yestere'en, as she often does, but she didnae come back."

"Did you send out a search party?"

"Of course. Last night and again this morning, but there is no trace of her – or her horse."

Turnbull cocked his head quizzically. "It's very strange. You don't look worried though?"

"We'll find her soon enough," said Ledgerwood, shifting awkwardly on his giant's throne. "But get to the point. Why are ye here?"

Turnbull felt his host's eyes boring into him. He did his best to return the gaze.

"We're looking for Janet's brothers."

"Her brothers?" repeated Ledgerwood, confused. "Why would they be here? They live out West, ye ken."

Turnbull sat back, arms folded. "When was the last time you saw them?"

"A couple of years ago. Look, tell me what this is about, then get lost, laddie."

Turnbull marshalled his words carefully and watched for Ledgerwood's reaction.

"Very well. We believe that Janet's brothers might be involved in arms smuggling. Perhaps something even bigger than that."

Ledgerwood's face darkened, and he thumped his hand on the arm of the chair. "What stupid talk. Ye've come and turned my house upside down for this?" He got up. "I've no more to say to ye. Just finish your search and be on your way."

Well, that had touched a nerve, thought Turnbull. "We will go when we're ready," he replied and went outside.

The soldiers continued their search through the morning but found nothing out of order. Turnbull reflected, ruefully, that even if the brothers were there, they would be impossible to identify because of Carmichael's tomfoolery. His mind returned to Janet and her potential role in all this. Was she involved in this intrigue, rather than her husband? Had she been abducted, or had she gone somewhere of her own accord? He remembered those brutish pigs he had seen on his first visit and instructed his men to search the sty.

By noon, Ledgerwood was getting increasingly irritated. However, Turnbull was determined to give the place a thorough going over. As the men moved on to the barns, where he had glimpsed those carts last time, he had another idea.

"We should get Cranstoun's dogs to look for Janet," he told Redpath.

"What?" said Redpath, who did not seem keen to prolong this visit.

"Aye. Janet's disappearance is too much of a coincidence. The hounds are only a couple of miles away, so you could be back with them in an hour or so."

"Me?" Redpath ran a hand through his hair.

"You know where he bides. And it will get you out of Ledgerwood's way for a while."

It was a clever argument, but Redpath still looked worried. "Shouldn't we be returning to Black Rig soon? What if Janet is a decoy? What if our enemies wish to lure us frae the tower?"

Turnbull hadn't thought of that. He remembered his promise to Anderson as he left him with six men that morning. The idea of being duped so easily made him queasy.

Still, they were here now, and surely another few hours wouldn't make a huge difference. He decided to double down on his gamble.

"Just go as quickly as you can. I'll tell Ledgerwood, then we'll give ourselves until dusk to find something, afore we go home."

By early afternoon, the men had searched every inch of the farmstead and sat around the yard with Ledgerwood's men watching them. Turnbull tried to make small talk with his troops, but they were anxious to leave. He was relieved when Redpath returned with Cranstoun and his dogs.

"You must be Master Turnbull," said the houndsman, rushing over. "I am sorry to hear o' the warden's illness. And now, another disappearance. What a terrible business. I am happy to help, and I believe we—"

"We are short of time, Master Cranstoun," said Turnbull, remembering his master's description of the man's babbling. "This is Master Ledgerwood, the woman's husband. He has a ribbon of the lady's for your hounds to work with."

Cranstoun gave Ledgerwood a fearful look and advanced gingerly with the dogs.

"That is very helpful of ye, sir. I will do whatever I can. If ye could just give—"

Ledgerwood tossed the ribbon to him, but the houndsman fumbled the catch so that it floated to the ground. He quickly picked it up and pushed it to the dogs' muzzles. They drooled over it, panting. It was as if they were devouring the scent rather than inhaling it. Cranstoun let them have their fill, until they strained at their leashes. He smiled proudly.

"They are ready to go, gentlemen. I suggest we form a small group and proceed on foot."

Turnbull picked half a dozen men, leaving the others to look after the horses. He calculated that this would still let them outnumber the gang at the bastle house. He told Redpath to come too. Ledgerwood completed the group. Turnbull noted a certain anxiety creeping into the man, as if it were dawning on him what might be discovered. He could not dwell on it, though, for the dogs picked up a trail quickly and led the party out through the gate, down the hill and on towards Allanton.

Presently, they came over the bridge which Schmidt had crossed the night he had been murdered. Turnbull remembered the man's shriek as he met his killer, the blood that had oozed all around his body. He mused that the axe used on the Fleming might have been the one which his own attackers had swung at him in the stables in Berwick. Or was this a further coincidence, like the two daggers with the stags' heads?

They climbed down the embankment and passed the shepherd's hut where Schmidt's killer must have lurked. It looked the picture of tranquillity now. Then they headed South, on the track to Whitsome. Rabbits scattered ahead of them, but the dogs were not interested, they were wholly dedicated to the trail. On they went, through a series of burns. Cranstoun was right: the running water did not put them off.

It was only as they reached the banks of the Tweed that the hounds began to slow down. Cranstoun told the group that this was natural: it was hard work for them, and the day was coming to an end. But after a while, they became listless. As they neared the old tower at Lennel, the dog named Egeir stopped and lay down. The hound was breathing unevenly, and its muscles twitched.

"That's odd," said Cranstoun, crouching down. "My boys have never done this afore."

He ruffled Egeir's head, but as he did so, the dog vomited on the ground. The other dog, Gryme, sniffed the mess before emptying its guts too. Both hounds lay down with each other and whimpered. Their eyes were bloodshot, and Turnbull was reminded of Luggy's terrible expression as he lay on the floor of his home.

"They must have eaten something," said Cranstoun anxiously. "Either way, we cannae continue like this. I must take them hame and tend to them."

"Eaten something or been given something?" said Turnbull, looking at Ledgerwood. "It seems like bad luck for them to go down, just as they might show us where your wife is."

The reiver's face contorted into an expression of pure contempt. "I've got nothing to do wi' this," he said. "But perhaps the almighty is telling ye to stop looking for things that dinnae concern ye."

"Well, we'll have to talk about that, back at Black Rig," said Turnbull. He surprised himself with the firmness of his words and waited for Ledgerwood to resist, but he obviously thought better of it, outmanned nine to one as he was. Reluctantly, he let Turnbull take him back to Chirnside, where he conferred briefly with Fat Lips and accompanied the soldiers back to the tower.

It was dark when they arrived, and Turnbull was relieved when Anderson greeted them at the gate.

"I thought ye said ye'd be back by afternoon," huffed the serjeant. "What's taken ye so long?"

Turnbull gave a wan smile. "Oh, just another missing person. And more poisonings. And seizing the one who might be behind it all, as well."

Chapter 49

Anderson put Ledgerwood in the dungeon's second cell while Turnbull climbed the stairs to see how his master was doing. He found Antoine still fast asleep, with Catherine beside him. Despite the dim candlelight, he could see that she was upset.

"Forgive me, sir,' she wailed. "This is all my fault."

He sighed. "Not this again, Mistress Gray. I want to sleep."

"But, sir, it truly is my doing. It's me. I've poisoned the warden."

Turnbull was exasperated. "What are you talking about? Don't say these things out loud."

"It's the truth," she gabbled. "I think the potion I've been giving him has made him ill."

Turnbull stopped mid-boot removal and looked at her intensely. "What potion?"

Catherine avoided his eyes. "The warden finds it difficult to sleep," she said.

"So?"

"So for the last fortnight, I've given him a potion to settle him."

Turnbull did a double take. "What potion?"

"A mixture of herbs," she snivelled. "Catswort, bryony,

chamomile and the like. But my supplies have run low recently, so a few days ago, I adjusted the mix."

Turnbull gasped. "In what way?"

"I added some wild lettuce," Catherine sobbed. "It's normally quite safe, but now I realise I must have misjudged the dose." She put her head in her hands and rocked back and forth. "I swear I did not mean this. Or perhaps I did? Oh Lord, what have I done?"

"Christ's eyes," said Turnbull, shaking his head. "If this is true, just thank the Lord that he still lives." He threw his boots across the room. "Now make sure he sticks to water, and we will see how he is in the morn. Oh, and say nothing of this to the men. It will do you – and us – no good, d'you hear?"

He climbed into his truckle, but despite his overwhelming exhaustion, he could not sleep. He thought of the irony of this. As he tossed and turned, he mused that if Catherine were right, at least they did not have a wilful murderer in their midst. Perhaps the dogs' sickness might be the result of an accident as well. After all, hadn't she said there were poisonous plants all around the countryside? The idea comforted him somehow. Gradually, the unbearable heaviness of his body took over and he drifted off.

In the morning, he rose to find Antoine still dozing; Catherine remained over him, her eyes red-rimmed, and her face drawn.

"How does he fare?" he asked.

"No better," she said sadly.

He leant over Antoine's bed and saw that it was true: his master looked gaunt and sweaty. He was still hot to the touch. "Keep an eye on him, and I'll return at noon to see if there's any change."

He went downstairs and helped himself to a bannock from the kitchen before continuing to the ground floor, where he exchanged pleasantries with the troops and updated them on Antoine's condition. As he prepared to leave for the dungeon, he heard Gibb call from his doorway.

"Is that you, Master Turnbull?"

He grimaced. "Aye, but I'm just off to conduct an interview."

"I'll be quick then," Gibb said, and he hobbled into the hall. "It's about the warden's illness. And Mistress Gray's role in it."

Turnbull checked that nobody else was listening. "Hush, old man. I know about that."

"About what?"

"The sleeping potion. Her mistaken dosage."

Gibb was close to him now. He gripped Turnbull's wrist. "But that's just it. She blames herself for using the wrong dose. But she would never do that: she couldnae be more precise."

Turnbull weighed the idea in his mind. It was true now that he thought about it. "What could it be then?" he said uneasily.

"It's the water that's to blame. The water she uses for the potion."

Turnbull frowned. "If it's the water, wouldn't we all be ill?"

"Who else drinks water here? We're all on ale or wine."

Turnbull was still not convinced. "So why has he just fallen ill now?"

"Until this week, Mistress Gray had been using the barrels o' water that Purves provided. Now she has switched to the well. Your soldiers mustnae have cleaned it properly."

"But we winched out all the debris just the other day."

"Then there must be something smaller at the bottom. One o' those poor crows the men have been throwing stanes at, perhaps. I'd get it dredged again."

Turnbull thought this made more sense as his master had been on nothing but water for the last two days.

"I will do that. But how did you think of this?" He had a vague notion that those who were blind could be gifted in other ways. "Could you smell something in the well?"

Gibb smiled. "I'm no' one of Master Cranstoun's dugs, sir. I used my head, no' my nose. Now please tell my friend that she's no' to blame. Or at least no' in the way she thinks."

While the old man groped his way back to his room, Anderson appeared looking for some tools. Turnbull instructed him to double-check the well and to tell Catherine to switch back to the barrelled water. The serjeant looked puzzled but did as he was told. Turnbull set off for the dungeon as initially planned. He decided to start with Carmichael, who had looked close to breaking yesterday. His instincts were confirmed as he peered into the cell at the man sitting dejectedly on the cold stone floor.

He slid the bolts open and went in. He offered Carmichael the rest of the bannock.

"Don't worry. It's not poisoned."

The man winced but took the food eagerly. "I ken nothing about that, sir. Honest to God, I was only passing messages."

"Messages which may have helped a murderer."

"Dixon swears he's innocent, sir. If that's no' true then I'm guilty of stupidity, but nothing more."

"We'll see. But meanwhile, the charge list grows ever longer. We now have a missing woman on our hands, you know. Watt Ledgerwood's wife is gone."

Carmichael nodded awkwardly. "Aye, I heard Anderson bring him in last night."

"Do you know them?"

"Only what I've heard you say."

"Could Dixon know them?"

He thought about it. "I can't see how. They keep pigs, don't they? And Dixon's got an abattoir. Perhaps they've met at market."

"What about—"

Turnbull was about to ask Carmichael whether the Dixons had other associates in Scotland when there was a scream from outside, followed by a great deal of shouting.

"By Christ," he said. "Don't move an inch." He made for the door, turning quickly to bolt it again, before running upstairs and into the barmekin. The men were gathered around the well, in a loose gaggle. As Turnbull advanced, they turned to him, their faces frozen into expressions of horror and disgust.

"Bloody hell," said Nisbet, turning away.

"What is it?" Turnbull asked desperately but nobody replied.

The men parted to reveal Waddell bent over, retching violently. In front of him was what looked like a pile of rags. Redpath sat on the ground beside them, shaking.

"What is it?" Turnbull repeated, gesturing for someone to speak up. Anderson ran to him, ashen-faced. He held his hands out, to slow their progress until he could explain.

"Waddell went back down the well as ye asked," he said breathlessly.

"And?"

"He's found something terrible. I think ye'd better see for yourself."

Turnbull's legs turned to lead. Everything around him slowed down, and the men's voices seemed muffled. It was as if he were underwater. He continued to the well and put a hand on Waddell's back. Leaning over him, he looked at the dredged-up bundle.

It was as gruesome as he had feared. Lying in front of him was a human head, two arms and two legs. The flesh on the limbs was half-rotten and fell from the bones. The head was further gone: melted and misshapen. It reminded Turnbull of the turnip lanterns the villagers had thrown on the All Hallows' E'en bonfire. Maggots were crawling out of every orifice, busily devouring the face, the eyeballs and nose already taken. Only the patch of damp, fair hair on the skull suggested that this had once been a living, breathing person.

Turnbull blenched at the putrid smell. He looked at Redpath and knew he did not need to ask if this was the man's brother, but Redpath confirmed it, through violent sobs. He lifted a finger as if he were about to say more, but no words came. His eyes were vacant, his mouth empty, as if he, too, had been hollowed out from within. Turnbull took his hand and helped him up.

"Get those wrapped up and put them in a shallow grave for now," he told Nisbet quietly. "We will deal with them properly, when we are ready."

He took Redpath back to his quarters, the man clinging to his elbow.

"You should get some rest while we deal with this," said Turnbull, setting him down on a pallet. "If it is any small consolation, this discovery might bring us closer to Alex's killer. We just need some time to think it through."

Not for the first time recently, Turnbull did not believe his own words. Perhaps this was what leadership was about:

exuding confidence while being eaten by doubt. He wondered whether his master ever felt the same way. As he mulled this, he returned to the tower, where he brought Catherine up to date.

"So you see, you were not to blame at all," he said.

Catherine looked relieved but still on edge. "I gave him the water."

"But you could not have known its state. I urge you, Mistress Gray, do not chide yourself. You cannot control these things. But you can make our master better now that you are informed."

Only upon retiring did Turnbull find the space to take in what had happened. Redpath had not emerged from the barracks all day, although Tait reported him to be stable. Catherine was nursing Antoine, who seemed to be slowly improving as they had hoped. Anderson sat with him, looking more tired than Turnbull had ever seen him.

"What I dinnae understand," said the serjeant, "is how we didnae notice this afore."

"The well's been blocked for a month," replied Turnbull. "All that time, none of us drank the water. Until our master, a couple of days ago."

"Yes, but why was there no stink until now?"

"The body parts must have been pushed down, by all the debris. They wouldn't rot as quickly in that icy water as they might in the air. Only after we cleared those great timbers did the pieces float up and start to foul."

"Christ, it makes me sick to think they've been there a' the time."

"Aye, what that means, I do not know. We've been

chasing all over the country these past few weeks, but the trail seems to have led us right back to Black Rig."

Just then, Antoine stirred for the first time in two days. He opened his eyes, although he seemed to be in some waking dream. Lips trembling, he managed to force out a few words.

"The trail… the trail… follow the trail of blood."

Chapter 50

Antoine continued to improve through the night. At first, he uttered little that made sense: a jumble of names, places and exclamations with no apparent thread. He remained that way all morning. But by mid-afternoon, his mind seemed to bring itself into an order of sorts. He gradually began to sound more like himself, albeit enfeebled and befuddled.

"Have you caught my poisoner?" he croaked as Catherine dabbed his brow.

"There was no poisoner," said Turnbull gently. "It was the well water. Alex Redpath's other parts were lying at the bottom."

Antoine grimaced. "But how did they get there?"

"We're trying to work that out. They must have been left there before we arrived."

"And our spy?"

"That was Carmichael. He was passing messages to Cospatrick Dixon. He's in the dungeon now."

Antoine shuddered. "The dungeon," he repeated. Turnbull noted that his face clouded as if his mind had wandered to some secret place.

"Aye," said Anderson. "Watt Ledgerwood's in there too. His wife's gone missing. We were about to find her when Cranstoun's dugs were poisoned. We think he's to blame."

"Wait, so there *was* a poisoner?" said Antoine, his brow furrowing and causing a bead of sweat to trickle down his face. Catherine wiped it away and gave the men a stern look.

"That's enough, gentlemen," she said. "You can speak to him again this evening, but for now, he needs to rest."

Turnbull nodded meekly and went downstairs with Anderson.

"What do you think?" the serjeant said as they entered the barmekin.

"I think our master will be of little use today. So we must hurry."

"Aye, the Truce Day is the day after tomorrow. What if he doesn't recover in time?"

"I don't know," said Turnbull. "But we can't rearrange the meeting at this late hour. I suppose we must keep going. You dig those ditches, and I'll see if I can squeeze more out of Ledgerwood. It might be our last chance to find anything new."

He turned towards the dungeon, but as he did so, he spotted Redpath kneeling beside a rectangle of freshly dug earth in the opposite corner of the barmekin. Turnbull's instincts took him over. When he reached him, though, he found his tongue was tied. It wasn't just the pitiful state of Redpath: he could not help thinking of his own father and brothers, whom he had never been able to bury. Mother Isabella's nuns might have brought back the bodies of various gentry from Flodden, but they had not bothered with the likes of his kin. It was why he could never forgive her, despite her recent help.

"We will get whoever did this," he said, faltering for the right words.

Redpath did not reply straight away. Instead, he stood up

and brushed the dirt from his hose. He looked shattered. "I'm away now, sir. Come round to ours the morn, afore the Truce Day, and we'll see where we are."

Before entering Ledgerwood's cell, Turnbull looked through the grille. The robber chief was sitting on his pallet and secured to the wall by leg irons. The room's cramped space only seemed to accentuate his enormous size.

"You've taken your time," he said sourly as Turnbull entered.

"We had an unpleasant discovery."

"Oh aye?"

"Aye, we found Alex Redpath's body parts at the bottom of the well. That's what poisoned the warden."

Ledgerwood gave a dark laugh. "That just about sums up that culroun. As poisonous in the afterlife as he was in this one."

"You were not a friend of his then?" Turnbull asked innocently.

Ledgerwood's eyes narrowed. "You know fine well I wasnae. Unlike my wife."

Turnbull was wrong-footed. So he *had* known about Alex and Janet all along. Could he have done away with both of them? Ledgerwood seemed to read his mind.

"I'm no' an idiot. I've kent about their trysting all summer. I would have killed Redpath myself if I wasnae in gaol. I wouldnae touch Janet though, no' with her brothers being as mad as they are."

"I thought you had not seen the Armstrong brothers for years?"

"Aye, and that's how I'd like to keep it."

"So you have no idea where your wife is now? Or who might have taken her?"

"I have some thoughts," sneered Ledgerwood. "If ye'd let me go, I could see if they are right."

Turnbull ignored his plea. "We were on the brink of that yesterday when our sleuth hounds fell ill. What did you make of that?"

"That Cranstoun misfeeds his dugs?" Ledgerwood waved a hand dismissively. "I dinnae ken. It was nothing to do wi' me."

Turnbull noted that he did not seem troubled by any of these questions. He allowed the silence to linger before changing direction.

"In that case, let's turn to something else: your involvement in this arms smuggling business."

Ledgerwood flushed at this, as he had the other night. "I've telt ye, I ken nothing about that either."

Turnbull thought he saw the man strain ever so slightly at his leg irons. Ah, he was right: this was the place to push. He decided to bend the truth a little.

"The trouble is, we have untangled everything now and know precisely what you've been up to."

Ledgerwood curled his lip. "You're talking out your arse."

"Not according to Mother Isabella," Turnbull said. It felt ungodly to involve the prioress in his lie, but she was not above deceit herself. "She has told us of your plot. And the name of your conspirators. In turn, we have sent warning to Governor Albany."

Turnbull was warming to his ploy now. Every embellishment made Ledgerwood more uncomfortable, but still, the man was not for folding.

"I have no idea what ye mean. I came here to help ye find my wife. Now I wish I hadnae."

"Ah well. You can tell the governor that in good time. He will be with us in the morning, with an army for the Truce Day. He plans to hang anybody involved with this treason, so feel free to take your chances with him if you don't want to strike a deal with me."

Turnbull got up and made his way to the door. As he turned his back, he heard the chains being pulled taut as Ledgerwood launched himself from the ground. He braced himself, but when nothing happened, he knew he was out of reach. He turned to see the prisoner wild-eyed and boiling with frustration, like a dog that knows it cannot escape its leash.

"You wish to talk?" Turnbull said.

Ledgerwood gave him a filthy look. "I want my safety guaranteed first."

"I can do that. But only if you tell me everything you know."

Ledgerwood threw his head back. "Who says ye even have the authority for this? If the warden was here, I would be more assured."

"But he is not," said Turnbull. "So it's me or Albany. Take your pick."

He hovered, hoping that Ledgerwood would call him back, but the man seemed determined to hold his tongue. This was Turnbull's last opportunity: perhaps the last opportunity of the entire mission to explain events before the Truce Day. When there was still no response, he put his hand to his purse and took out the letter the prioress had given them.

"We have this, you know." He showed the paper to

Ledgerwood, without unfolding it. The man swallowed hard. "The nuns found it on the Truce Day island. It gives us everything we need already. The nature of the plot. The names of the conspirators. All I wanted from you was some further detail. But without it, this will still see you swing."

Ledgerwood's bravado seemed to desert him. Turnbull opened the letter and pretended to read it before folding it up again. He gave a smug smile, as if it contained all he needed.

"Last chance. And then I'm off."

The reiver stretched, before lowering his great weight onto the pallet.

"Very well. Ye've got me. But be careful what ye're getting intae. Are ye sure ye want to hear this, laddie?"

Turnbull remembered the man's words when the dogs were poisoned: his suggestion that the Almighty was telling them to stop looking. He dreaded what he might be about to discover but knew that he could not go back. Not now. Not after all they had been through.

"Just tell me your side," he said. "And I will check that it tallies with our intelligence."

Ledgerwood rubbed his face and began. "Right. Well, it looks like you already know of our little letterbox."

Turnbull nodded and tapped the folded letter in his hand. "Yes, it's a clever idea. Typical of its inventor."

Ledgerwood took the bait. "Dacre is a wily one, for sure. He knew he couldnae reach Hume through the usual messengers, as the risk of interception was too great. So the island was the perfect middle ground."

Turnbull's heart raced. This intrigue was between Dacre and Hume? The two most powerful figures on either side of the border? He remembered Albany's advice not to aggravate either of them, but here they were, directly plotting some awful treason. Surely that counsel could no longer hold. He reminded himself to remain calm and talk in general terms that would allow the truth to out.

"The perfect spot indeed. And you were the perfect person to lend a hand."

Ledgerwood looked at him suspiciously. "I was only the messenger, I swear. Not even that. When I found myself in gaol, Dacre visited me and promised to release me if I got my men to act as couriers."

"So that's all you did."

"Aye, I never even went there myself. My men took the letters frae Hume and deposited them there. Some English fellows took them to Dacre and left others for us."

"Ah yes, Cospatrick Dixon," said Turnbull, with a flash of inspiration disguised as nonchalant assertion. Ledgerwood frowned, and then his face lit up too.

"Aye, I think you're right. Cospatrick Dixon was the name."

Turnbull felt Ledgerwood was just agreeing to hurry the conversation, but he had more to ask. "The Armstrong brothers were not involved in this at all then? They have no plan to set up here?"

"No," said Ledgerwood impatiently. "I keep telling ye that."

"And their sister, your wife?"

The reiver bared his teeth. "I believe Lord Hume has taken her to ensure I keep up my work somehow, now that the letterbox is found."

"Blessed Mary," said Turnbull. "The man's an animal."

"Aye," said the reiver, "but perhaps even Hume is in too deep."

Turnbull tried not to show his interest, but it was too late, and Ledgerwood gave a knowing grin.

"Ah, I see you do not have the final piece. Lord Dacre's end game."

"Try it on me, and I will confirm it."

Ledgerwood snorted. "You're bluffing, but no matter. Let this be the favour that secures my safety." He waited for Turnbull to signal his agreement before explaining. "I heard in gaol that Dacre plans to double-cross Hume at the last. He has dangled cannons afore his eyes that he might use on ye – and against Governor Albany. While Hume waits to receive them, Dacre encourages him to disrupt your work and make himself a nuisance. But here's the twist – when Dacre delivers the guns, he will claim Hume procured them himself, for use on England. That will give Dacre the perfect pretext to invade."

Turnbull could not believe what he was hearing. It was the worst possible news. Not just an internal rebellion but the threat of all-out war.

"There's no chance King Henry would sanction such an adventure now," he spluttered.

"I doubt the king's heard anything of this. By the time he does, though, Dacre will have made himself a hero."

"But it would break our truce. And plunge us all into war."

Ledgerwood laughed. "Since when have truces mattered here, laddie? And besides, this one runs out on St Andrew's Day: The 30th of November. And as ye'll know frae that letter, the guns will be delivered on the first of December."

Turnbull felt the cell spinning around him. He took out the paper again and unfolded it in plain sight. He heard Ledgerwood protest as he realised that he had been tricked, that the letter contained nothing but a code. However, he was too busy staring at the symbols to listen to the complaints. Dog. Eagle. Cat. 1. God's blood – the initials formed a date. December the first. The start of a new war. The end for all of them, perhaps. He snatched the paper away again and raced up the stairs, with Ledgerwood screaming blue murder behind him.

Chapter 51

Turnbull burst through the upper door at such speed that he sent Nisbet flying.

"Send Anderson to our master's quarters," he called, without looking back. He ran around the base of the tower, his mind whirling. As he passed through the barmekin, he dodged men carrying pick-axes and spades. They had been digging the outer fortifications in preparation for an attack from the Armstrongs. All for nothing now, he thought. The men from the West might have been imaginary, but the English army was very real. It would destroy this place and everyone in it, ditch or no ditch.

Up the stairs he went, brushing past more soldiers on their way to supper. He cursed himself for not trusting his first instincts that this had been the Humes' doing. The discovery of Alex Redpath's remains here confirmed it. He had presumably stumbled on the plot, so they had taken him here to torture him, thrown his pieces in the well and then slighted the place. But why had Cranstoun's dogs followed a trail to the river, rather than here? And where were the Flemings in all this?

So many aspects of this affair still did not make sense. And there was so little time to work them all out.

With his anguish rising, he arrived panting at the top of

the stairs. There, he was relieved to see Antoine sitting up in bed. Catherine was feeding him a bowl of pottage – his first food for days – but she put it down when she saw the look on Turnbull's face. A moment later, Anderson barged in. Time seemed to stand still as Turnbull caught his breath, and the others waited to hear what on earth had happened. He sat down on the kist and, as calmly as he could, set out everything Ledgerwood had told him.

"Well, this is our worst nightmare," said Antoine when Turnbull had finished. He propped himself up at the edge of the bed. "It looks like Hume and Dacre are behind all this, but Albany has forbidden us from touching them."

Anderson furrowed his brow. "Does the scale of their treachery no' mean we should move differently?"

"Differently, perhaps. But not by force. Both sides outnumber us greatly and would crush us in an instant."

"Then what?" asked Turnbull. "Do we call in the Governor's army, as with my lie to Ledgerwood?"

"That was a good ruse. But in truth, there is no time. Our meeting is a day away, and an army would take weeks to raise."

Anderson stood open-mouthed. "Ye cannae mean to go ahead wi' the Truce Day, sir?"

"Why not?" said Antoine tetchily, as if the very act of speech still pained him. "If we go ahead with the meeting, we might show our weakness. But that risk will be a certainty if we postpone it now."

Turnbull put his hands to his cheeks. "So we go to a meeting surrounded by our enemies?"

"I don't see that we have a choice."

"What if it's a trap? They might mean to clear us out first, before proceeding with their plan?"

"Not at the Truce Day. It would be too public."

"Sir, this does not matter to these folk. Wardens have been murdered at these events afore."

"Then we should consider ourselves forewarned."

Turnbull shook his head. His master must still be ill to act with such poor judgement.

"What will we even say at the Truce Day?" asked Anderson. "We are nowhere on these crimes. And what we do know points at those we cannot collar. If we dinnae have answers, we'll do more harm than good."

"That's what I'm trying to think of now!" said Antoine sharply. "If you two would stop your worrying, that is."

They fell into a gloomy silence, each attempting to untangle the knot in which they found themselves tied. Eventually, it was Catherine who broke the impasse. She had been lighting the oil lamps for the night but had clearly been listening to every word.

"Forgive me, gentlemen, if I intrude," she said, her head bowed low. "But I am minded of something a wise woman once said to me." She raised her eyes briefly to meet Antoine's. "Do not chase perfection in an imperfect world."

All three men stared at her, in confusion, as she explained herself.

"These last few weeks, I have heard ye talk of nothing but this mission and its great complexity. Ye've sought to solve it all at once, tie up every loose end, bring justice to the victims, punish the guilty, establish law and order, bring peace to the Marches and much more besides. Ye've chased perfection, in other words. But what if that is no longer possible, if indeed it ever was?"

Catherine turned her back and returned to her final preparations for the night. After folding the blankets, fastening the shutters and clearing up the pottage bowl, she went downstairs. Once she had gone, Anderson pulled a face of derision but retracted it as he saw his companions were in no mood.

"By the Lord, that woman speaks the truth," said Antoine. "We must focus on what we can achieve for now and accept it will not be perfect."

"So what do we let go of?" said Turnbull, struggling to keep up.

"Dacre and Hume, for a start. It pains me to say it, but we cannot take them on now. What we can do is let them know that we're onto them. And perhaps set them against each other while we buy time."

"How so?"

"Hume will not be happy to hear of Dacre's plan to double-cross him. And Dacre will not like to be caught red-handed either."

"For Hume, it could mean death," agreed Anderson. "And perhaps even the same for Dacre, if he makes King Henry look a fool."

"Exactly," said Antoine. "We cannot put an end to all their mischief, but we can stop this one scheme. Let's send a letter to Hume inviting him to the Wardens' Congress tomorrow."

"I'll see to it," said Turnbull.

"So we deal with the plotters behind closed doors," said Anderson slowly. "But what about the Flemings? One man murdered in front of us and another kidnapped – likely deid as well. Surely we cannae turn a blind eye to them?"

"I'm afraid we may have to," said Antoine. "We've found no connections to the other crimes. Not a single witness, apart from Master Ritter, has had a word to say about them. Even their own people desire to hush it up. So for now, we lose nothing if we put them aside."

"It does not seem right," said Turnbull.

"I agree, but we can't do everything."

"So what *do* we do? There's no point calling the Truce Day if we have no charges to make?"

"The very fact of calling the meeting shows the Marchfolk that we are serious about maintaining the law. There is value in that itself. Then, there are dozens of minor infringements on our list: sheep rustling, menaces, affrays and the like. We will not contest the Scottish offences, and we will urge Dacre to do likewise with our side's complaints. This will clear the way for us to focus on the two crimes that have reared their bloody heads most publicly: the murders of Alex Redpath and Luggy Laidlaw."

"And who will we accuse for those?" said Turnbull. "I hope you are clearer in your mind than me."

"We will agree that in the morning," said Antoine, sitting back down on the bed. He looked exhausted by the discussion and the impossible choices it entailed. Anderson took it as his cue to leave, for he would need a plan of his own, to guard the tower and its prisoners while the others were at the Truce Day.

When he had gone, Turnbull noted how frail his master looked. As if the mission had aged him, made him less sure-footed. He dreaded to think how he would fare on the journey to Coldstream tomorrow, let alone at the meeting the following day. Putting his hand on his wrist, he spoke gently, like a son to his father in the winter of his years.

"You are determined to go ahead with this then, sir?"

"I am sure," came the hoarse response. "Think of all the ordinary folk to whom we have promised change: the

Redpaths, Laidlaw, Catherine, old Gibb, the Herons, Rutherford, Henderson, Purves and more. None of them are perfect, but all deserve better. What would it say to them if we swerved the meeting? That law and order matters little? That justice cannot be had? That hope is just a dream? On our journey here a month ago, you talked of the need to bring a little light to this region. We can do that for now, even if there are dark days further ahead."

Turnbull sighed. Not so far ahead, he thought.

Chapter 52

There was a tense atmosphere at the tower the next morning as Turnbull and Antoine prepared to leave for Coldstream. Tait had already set off with a message for Hume. Anderson had halted the digging and had charged the men with readying their weapons instead. Although none were aware of the latest developments, they could all feel that they were hurtling towards some form of confrontation, for better or for worse.

Later, as they rode out over the mosses with four men, Turnbull asked Antoine whether he'd reached a view on the murders. The Frenchman didn't answer straight away. It took all his strength to stay upright on Carbonel. But as they neared Swinton, Antoine summoned up the energy to speak.

"I say it's Dixon. I have my doubts, don't get me wrong. But with a day to go, he's our best hope."

Turnbull frowned. "What's the case?"

"The same as it's always been. We know he wanted revenge on Alex and Luggy because of that game of cards and that he has spies like Carmichael in this area. Now we hear he might have been involved with Hume and Dacre. Perhaps they told him Alex had rumbled their plot, through his lover, Ledgerwood's wife. So he saw the chance to settle a private score and gain favour with their Lordships."

"I suppose it does add up." Turnbull scratched his head. "Except why would Dixon's men leave the body on the island if they used it as their secret letterbox? Would that not draw attention to their intriguing?"

"Who knows?" said Antoine. "Because they're stupid? Reckless? We cannot fathom these people any more. The important thing is to press our case. Give the families the best chance of justice they will have. And leave the rest to God."

For a while, both men remained lost in their thoughts. But as they entered the village, they noticed something strange. An eerie silence had descended that was quite unlike anything they had experienced on their previous visits. Suddenly Antoine realised what it was.

"No geese," he said. And indeed, it was true. Or at least it was until they approached the Redpaths' bastle itself. For there, over the door mantle, the family's old gander hung by its neck, its throat slit and a pool of blood spilling into the mud of the yard. The scene was grotesque, but worse was to come: three children ran out screaming, with blood-streaked faces and hands, pushing the bird's corpse out of the way as they tumbled into the road. The surviving geese looked on, in silent accusation.

Antoine thought he must be in a trance again, for the vision was like those he suffered in his dreams: utterly visceral in its violence. He feared he might fall from his saddle, only to feel Turnbull's hand upon him.

"Don't worry, sir," he explained. "It's just a local habit. On Martinmas Eve, some kill a goose and let the blood flow over the threshold, to keep bad spirits out. Then they daub it on the bairns too, for good measure."

"Holy God, that's all I need today."

The children ran off to play upon the common, and

Redpath himself emerged, followed by Jessie, Agnes and Dand. After them came another fellow, a big man who introduced himself as Luggy's brother, Edward. He had none of his sibling's nervous ways or frail disposition: if only he had been there for his brother when he needed him, thought Antoine. Not that he himself had always been there for others when it mattered.

"Forgive us, sir," said Redpath, coming forward to greet them. "They say that if you do not spill blood on Martinmas Eve, the blood shed on Martinmas will be your own."

"A little caution is fair enough after all you've been through," said Antoine.

"Fair enough is all we want," said Jessie. The young widow seemed to have gained strength since their last meeting.

"But can ye get us it?" said Agnes.

"I believe so. We have dropped our interest in the Flemings and the other business with the guns. Instead, we will focus all our attention on your own losses – the deaths of Alex and Luggy."

Redpath clasped his hands. "That comes as a relief," he said. "But do ye know the killer?"

"And can ye prove it by March Law?" added Dand sharply.

"Again, I think so."

"Well?" said Luggy's brother.

Antoine took a deep breath. "We will be charging Cospatrick Dixon with both killings."

The kinsfolk exhaled as one, as if a great burden had been lifted from them. Jessie started to cry a little.

"I knew it," said Redpath. He punched his fist in his palm. "All this time, I've been saying it."

"We had to explore all trails," said Turnbull. "And still we may be challenged."

"Even so. The evidence is there. You'll win the case, I know it."

"We cannot promise that," said Antoine hastily. "But we'll give it our best."

He smiled, but the family's giddy optimism unsettled him. He dreaded to see these poor folk again if their hopes were crushed tomorrow.

After saying their farewells, they continued on the path to Coldstream. Antoine occasionally let out a groan of pain on the way. His ankle was still tender, and his illness had left him with his humours out of kilter. His stomach lurched as they passed more houses decorated with gruesome carcasses, the blood seeping into the soil.

Upon reaching the priory, they made straight for the gatehouse where Sister Triduana awaited them. For once, she seemed glad to see them, although there was anguish in her features too – as if she sensed the grave importance of this meeting.

"The Reverend Mother told me to bring ye as quickly as possible. She's with Lord Dacre in her dining room. Keeping him busy until you arrive."

"That's good. And Lord Hume?"

"Yes, him as well," she said as they hurried. "Your doing, I suppose?"

Antoine nodded. "We invited him but did not dare to send you a message explaining why, lest it be intercepted."

Sister Triduana sent the four soldiers to the guest-house while rushing Antoine and Turnbull through the precinct to the dining room. The prioress greeted them with relief, but again, there was an edge to her manner. Antoine considered taking her aside to explain what they had discovered but realised that she must be seen to protect her neutral status in front of her guests.

"Good evening, gentlemen," he said, taking the place at the top of the table this time. "And, of course, you too, Reverend Mother."

"Bonsoir, Monsieur Warden" said Hume, smugly. "I was surprised to receive my invitation here."

Dacre smiled. "Perhaps our French friend wishes to give you his job, George? Being a warden is not to everybody's taste."

"On the contrary," said Antoine. "I find it much to my liking. But enough of such small talk. Let us dine and we can plan the morrow's business."

The prioress signalled to the hospitalless, who stood at the back of the room, and within minutes, the messes arrived, having been kept warm until all were ready. They were heavy dishes, created especially for Martinmas: goose, pork cheeks, black pudding and the like.

"You go first," said Dacre. He exchanged a smirk with Hume. "After all, you called this Truce Day. And invited my old friend along tonight."

"Very well," said Antoine. He helped himself to some pork. "I will start with why we are all here. We have a shared interest in enforcing law and order in the Marches. Whether as wardens, headsmen or servants of God."

"Of course," said Dacre, putting his hand on his heart.

"Nothing more important," said Hume, sardonically.

The prioress remained silent, watching the others with her sharp eyes.

Antoine continued. "This is particularly important when there is so much trouble in the world. We may have our disagreements, but it is vital that our people see the law applied." There were more murmurs of agreement and clinking of spoons on platters. "So it's with great disappointment that I have learnt of a plot on the Marches involving both your Lordships." Antoine watched the faces of the accused. The men exchanged sideways glances while the prioress looked at him in astonishment.

"As you don't deny it, I will explain it for the Reverend Mother's benefit. It seems that your guests are behind the plot to smuggle guns from England into Scotland. They had been using the island to trade messages, so the letter you found was theirs. It conveyed that the weapons would be delivered on December the first, as soon as the latest truce runs out."

The prioress thumped her hand on the table. "Is this true, you two? You would imperil all of us with your games?"

Dacre's face tightened into a ferocious scowl. "He's talking nonsense, Reverend Mother. He has no evidence."

"Actually, we have written proof," said Turnbull, pulling out the letter the prioress had given them. He placed it, folded, on the table.

"Some silly code means nothing," scoffed Hume.

"We said nothing of any code," said Turnbull, unfolding the letter. "But you guess right. It does contain one, which we have deciphered, with the help of a witness we hold under lock and key."

Dacre shot Hume an anxious look.

"Yes, he's a very compelling witness," continued Antoine. "One who has seen everything at close quarters. Perhaps that's why you've taken his wife as security?"

Hume laughed dismissively and dug about the messes with his spoon, shaking his head as he did so. "You've gone mad, sir. This whole thing is folly."

"A folly indeed. But I fear the mistake is yours," said Antoine. "For our prisoner also tells us that Lord Dacre planned to betray you – and use it as an excuse to invade Scotland."

This time, Hume did not look up, but his compact frame quivered with indignation.

"So that's why you visited me," said the prioress, jabbing a finger at Dacre. "To find out what I knew, not to make a donation at all."

The Englishman's eyes flickered nervously between his fellow diners. For a while, there was silence. Then Hume took the surnap from his shoulder and dabbed his lips. He cleared his throat and smiled disconcertingly.

"Who says I didn't know Dacre's intentions all along?" he asked smoothly. "Perhaps I meant to trick him and then alert you and Governor Albany, to win favour for myself?"

Dacre visibly relaxed. "A good point, sir. And who says I did not aim to do the same? To warn my neighbours of the threat within. Perhaps we have both been trying to catch each other out, but all in the name of peace?"

Antoine rolled his eyes at their shamelessness. "I doubt Governor Albany will think much of those excuses."

"Or King Henry," said the prioress. "Remember, I have his sister's ear. Both sides will see this poorly."

"Only if they find out," said Hume, his eyes narrowing. For a moment, Antoine feared the warlord might lunge at him, but the reiver sat back in his chair instead. "So how do we prevent this little misunderstanding becoming a greater trouble?"

Antoine studied his adversaries' faces. He had them then: not on the run but prepared to cut a deal for now.

"We must all ensure a successful Truce Day tomorrow."

Dacre sneered. "What does that mean?"

"We must hold a meeting which inspires faith amongst the local people. Demonstrate that we can work together across the border and apply the March Laws properly."

"How noble," said Hume. "And how exactly do you propose we do that?"

"Well, for a start, each side will agree the charge list without contest. Hume, all the English complaints stem from your family's time in office, so you can stump up the initial compensation. Dacre, you will pay for the Scots' complaints. Then we will recoup the coin from those responsible later, as is the normal custom."

Dacre took a large draught of wine. "How much are we talking about?"

Turnbull drew out the accounts and ran his finger down the figures. "I suggest you each bring £200 sterling on the day. That should be enough for the first tranche. We can work out the other details later."

"That's a small fortune," said Hume sourly. "And we don't usually pay out on the day…"

"Well, tomorrow will be an exception."

Dacre's jaw tightened, but he thought better of complaining. "Very well, it's done. But tell me, sir, if we agree on this now, what business will we conduct the morn?"

Antoine took a deep breath. "The trial of Cospatrick Dixon for the murders of Alex Redpath and Luggy Laidlaw." He watched for a reaction, but there was none. "I suggest that you and I decide his fate, to underline how our two realms will work together in future. If we disagree, the prioress will have the casting vote." Again, no response. "Oh, and while we're at it, I need your absolute guarantee of safety; otherwise, all these arrangements are null and void."

Hume and Dacre began to protest until the prioress leant forward and eyeballed them. "I strongly suggest you agree, gentlemen. If you cannot protect the Warden, he cannot protect you from your betters."

"So be it," said Hume through gritted teeth. "I can guarantee you on the Scottish bank."

"And I on the English bank," Dacre muttered.

"Then we are all in line," said Antoine. "Now, excuse us while we retire. It shapes to be a busy day tomorrow."

Antoine and Turnbull returned to their quarters, where they collapsed exhausted on their shared bed. The room was cold and dark, and the rain had started to batter down outside. They took their boots off quickly and climbed under the covers.

"That was quite the spectacle," said Turnbull enthusiastically. "The way you ran rings round them, sir."

"I suppose," said Antoine. Perhaps the meat had caused his bile to rise, or maybe he was just weary from the day, for he felt a deep melancholy gathering within him. "Or is it they who have made idiots out of us?"

"What do you mean?" asked Turnbull.

"We have secured some concessions for tomorrow. But have we lost the long game? Are we right to let them get away with their treason? Should we forget the Flemings and move on? Perhaps we have lacked ambition."

"Do not chide yourself, sir. You have done your best. And that is something nobody else has done for the Marches before. As for the rest, we may never know what happened. It reminds me of that old saying: if only the dead could talk."

Antoine grunted in agreement and rolled over. His body ached, and he longed to be rid of this quest. He grabbed his side of the blankets and drew them up to his chin. Then his eyes opened, as wide as an owl's.

"Oh, Good God, that's it. I see it now."

"What?"

Antoine sat bolt upright. "I–I must be losing my mind. Or have we been fools all along?"

"I don't understand, sir. Tell me what it is."

The Frenchman spoke deliberately, drawing on every ounce of strength he still had left. "As you say, these past few months, we have followed blind alleys. Wrong turns. False clues. All has been deception. But now it is time for the truth. And you are right Turnbull. You are so right. We must look to the dead to reveal it."

Chapter 53

By the time Antoine arrived at the river the next morning, there were already hundreds of people on both banks. Stalls of all manner were being assembled. Food vendors, brewsters, card sharps and tinkers vied for the best pitches while peasants gossiped about the feuds that might be settled. Antoine was relieved to see that a dozen of his soldiers had already arrived from Black Rig, the rest remaining with Anderson to guard the tower and the prisoners. But only a few would be allowed onto the island with him. And besides, they were vastly outnumbered by Hume and Dacre's men. He hoped their Lordships would keep to their guarantee.

As he looked around, he saw that Redpath and Luggy's brother were there too, looking anxious about their day of reckoning. Antoine waved to them but did not go over, for he was still mulling his thoughts from the night before. He remembered Ritter's words and prayed that the trail of blood was about to lead them all to justice. But what if he had gone mad and was about to make a fool of himself in front of all the Marches?

His worries were interrupted by Cuddy Heron. "All ready, sir?" he asked, as he helped his father steady the coble. Dacre, Hume and Mother Isabella were waiting in the boat.

"I'm sorry for the delay," Antoine said, clambering in.

"No Master Turnbull today?"

"He'll be joining us later," the Frenchman said vaguely. "I have sent him on a little errand."

The prioress gave him a curious look as they pushed off to the island. In the middle of the boat were two large bags: the money for the claims. Dacre and Hume eyed them resentfully but said nothing to each other. An icy wind blew in, causing all to shield their faces.

Once the main party was safely on the island, a flotilla of other boats crossed from either side. Earlier, they had agreed to a hundred men from each country, so it took a while for them all to arrive. As each group disembarked, they swore to keep the peace until sunrise the next day "and not offend by deed, word or countenance". Despite this, every new arrival seemed more heavily armed than the last.

After an hour or so, everybody was assembled. Mother Isabella sat at a small desk which had been specially shipped over. The two bags of money lay before her, all counted and correct. The spectators and aggrieved family members lined up on either side, Scots behind Antoine and Hume and English behind Dacre. Antoine recognised a few faces here and there: Wedderburn leering at him from behind Hume; Redpath and Luggy's brother fidgeting at the front; Wilson and Waddell looking somewhat bewildered; Cranstoun gabbling to his neighbours; and there, on the English side, a furious Cospatrick Dixon.

"You're about to make a fool of yourself," he hissed as Antoine approached the front.

"We will see about that," replied the Frenchman as he

scanned the horizon. But the object of his search was not forthcoming.

The stalls on the banks were in full swing, and the crowds there did not seem to be paying attention: in this wind, they would not be able to hear proceedings either. The folk on the island were fixed on him though – and on the bags of money, waiting to be claimed.

Antoine checked the Scottish riverbank again and cursed under his breath. He could tell the crowd was growing restless, but he wanted to give it another couple of minutes. Another glance, still nothing. He felt Hume and Dacre's eyes upon him, enjoying his discomfort, even if they did not know its cause. Straining his eyes for the last time, he accepted that he could delay no more. He cleared his throat and clapped his hands for order.

"Friends," he said as loudly as he could, given his lingering infirmity. "It has been too long since we have had a Truce Day in these parts. But as the new warden on the Scottish side, I am determined that we will serve justice better from now on. And I know my good Lord Dacre feels the same."

The Englishman gave him a look that flatly contradicted this.

"Indeed, as a token of goodwill between our nations, we have agreed to resolve all the disputes listed on the bill of complaints and pay the compensation according to the Laws of the Marches."

A ripple of excitement ran through the crowd as aggrieved claimants realised they would not have to go through the usual rigmarole of proving their cases. The prioress looked at him encouragingly.

"Meanwhile, though, we have one case before us that

deserves our special attention. A case that has become notorious, even in these parts, for its depravity. Lest anybody is in any doubt, I refer to the murders of Alex Redpath and Luggy Laidlaw."

He looked over to the victims' brothers and saw that they were hanging onto his every word. Waiting for their moment of vindication.

"As most of you will know, Cospatrick Dixon stands accused of these terrible crimes. He was engaged in a feud with the victims. He had the means. And he had the opportunity."

It was Dixon's turn to shoot him a look that could kill.

"But I no longer come to charge him. For in the last few hours, it has become clear to me that we have been hoodwinked by a great deception. A deception of which the Devil himself would be proud."

A wave of confusion spread through the gathering, nowhere more so than across the face of Cospatrick Dixon.

"Do not mistake me, the man is a knave. No doubt he is guilty of many things. But he is not guilty of the crimes we are interested in today. That dishonour lies with someone else entirely. Someone I would have never doubted until a few hours ago. Someone who stands in front of us right now."

He swung round to his left.

"That person is Alex Redpath's brother, James."

There was a great intake of breath as the crowd parted around the accused man. Even Luggy's brother took a step to the side. Redpath stared back in disbelief.

"What is this madness, sir?"

"Don't come the fool with me, Redpath. That's an act you've played so well for weeks. But I now realise you're no simpleton, you're the mastermind behind all this.

Kidnapping, theft, extortion, murder. Including that of the poor soul left on this very island."

Redpath appealed to the crowd. "Our warden's been ill – and it seems his mind still ails him. Anyone who knows me knows I'd never kill my brother."

Antoine felt his sinews stiffen. It was time to commit. To say out loud the outrageous thought that had occurred to him the previous night when Turnbull had wished that the dead could talk. The idea which had forced him to turn this whole case upon its head.

"That much is true. For your brother is still alive. The greatest of your deceptions!"

Chapter 54

At this accusation, Redpath looked around as if he might bolt. But he was well and truly trapped on the island. He'd seemingly brought no supporters, for nobody stepped up to his defence. As he considered his options, Luggy's brother gripped him from behind. "Don't even think of it," he growled. "Let's hear what the warden has to say. And God help you if it's true."

Antoine shuddered at the memory of Luggy's swollen face as he lay on the muddy floor of his bastle house. It disgusted him but fortified him at the same time. "Thank you, Laidlaw. Your brother was an innocent victim in this. Indeed, his trust in his supposed friends provided both the start of this whole enterprise – and the end of his own life. Now let me explain, for your sake and all present."

He massaged his temples, as if straightening all the twists and turns of the story in his mind. Keeping his eyes firmly on Redpath's outraged face, he went on.

"This sorry tale began just over a month ago, when you hatched a scheme to get rich, with your brothers Alex and Dand. The idea was that you would kidnap a Flemish merchant from Berwick and extract a ransom from his people: Willem de Bruyn, wasn't it?"

Mother Isabella gasped at the mention of the Flemings, then gestured for him to continue.

"To carry out this crime, you used your neighbour Luggy Laidlaw as your cover. You didn't inform him of your plans, I am sure of that. But you did ask him to support the story you'd fed your wives, that you'd gone up to the shielings to help him bring his cattle down. Instead, the three of you went into Berwick. You took Luggy's cart with you, without telling him. That puzzled me for a long time because I believed it was taken in the rush of Alex's kidnapping. I couldn't see how it was harnessed so quickly. But now I realise you took it at your leisure, several days before. Of course, Luggy was away all this time, so only noticed it was missing on his return."

Redpath shook his head in silent protest.

"Anyway, you and your brothers went to Berwick, bought masks outside the leper spittal and stole Master de Bruyn from the quayside. Then you bundled him into the cart and took him back to Black Rig. The tower had been deserted after the recent forfeitures and you meant to use it as your base. I thought it odd when you visited us last week and seemed familiar with the trip-step."

"Your plan was to hold de Bruyn there until the ransom was paid. But you'd battered him so badly – yes, we have a witness to this – that he must have been dead on arrival or shortly after. Now you had a dilemma: you had killed your golden goose. But you came up with a fiendish solution. You would continue to extort money from the Flemings, who remained ignorant of their comrade's fate. But you would also mutilate the body and pretend that it was your brother Alex. That way, you could make further coin under the March Laws. Blaming an old enemy for this would make your victory all the sweeter."

Antoine looked at Dixon, whose face had turned to puce.

"The first step was to dismember the body so that it could not be recognised. You hacked up de Bruyn in the dungeon – the blood is still all over that floor – then threw the leftovers in the well. There they would stay hidden for a whole month. For someone else would later pour debris over them while wrecking the castle."

He glared at Hume, but the reiver did not respond.

"This weighed down the pieces in the icy water and prevented them from rotting – until we cleared the well the other day. The water made me ill, but I'm sure that the discovery must have turned your stomach too, for my friend Master Turnbull described the head as having fair hair, quite unlike any of your kin. Still, false grief can be convincing."

Antoine looked from Redpath to Dacre, recalling the latter's own pretence of mourning at the priory. Again, no response.

"But wait, I've jumped ahead. Before all this, Alex went home and told your womenfolk that the weather would delay you. This allowed Dand and you to stage his kidnapping. You kept the masks so that even your own families would not recognise you. You took care to say nothing. You even hit Alex's wife, Jessie, for good measure. Then you took Alex back to Black Rig. Presumably on the back of one of your horses, for he was no prisoner but a willing accomplice."

Redpath moaned pathetically. "Sir, I beg of you. You embarrass yourself with these wild claims."

Antoine would not be stopped though. "The next morning, you went back for Luggy at the shielings. He knew you'd been up to something, and Alex said he'd tell him about it later. But you kept him in the dark for now. That way, he could be genuinely shocked when you returned to Swinton and found Alex gone. And he *was* shocked, for he trusted you, little realising that you were simply using him."

Luggy's brother tightened his grip around Redpath's body as Antoine continued.

"You went through all the motions of searching for your brother. Visited the taverns, approached the houndsman Cranstoun to conduct a search—"

"Aye, a search which led from our house to this river, not Black Rig," Redpath interjected.

Antoine curled his lip. "I'll come to that later. The point is you made sure you were seen doing all the right things. You even visited the scrivener Meikle to make your complaint official. Unfortunately, while you were there, he told you that the Humes were heading to Black Rig."

The Frenchman allowed himself a bitter smile. "That must have sent you into a panic, as de Bruyn's dismembered body was still there in the dungeon. So you and Dand rushed to the tower and took the torso to the Tweed, while Alex made off elsewhere."

He scanned the horizon again and frowned before going on.

"Your plan was to leave the body on this island to make it visible and incriminate Dixon. You found a boat that had been left by some poachers, but little did you know that they were watching you from the rushes. They heard one of you joke that it was the end of Alex Redpath. I bet you couldn't believe your luck when I told you of that later. But at the time, you had to make completely sure that the body was identified as your brother's. Which takes me back to Cranstoun."

The houndsman looked up, confused. This was one trail he could not follow.

"As I said, you visited him early on, on the pretext of

mounting a search. But really you wanted to find out when Alex's scent would disappear. Otherwise, he could be tracked straight to Black Rig. On that first visit, you pretended not to have the money so that you could delay a while. Then a week later someone laid a fresh trail to the island with some item of Alex's. Whoever it was went on foot, to ensure the trail was as strong as possible. That let him get through Kincham Woods. Again, this confounded us, as we had imagined a cart, which could not pass that way. Dixon's men described seeing a young lad over there, so I assume that was Dand."

Antoine stopped to point to the Scottish side. As he did so, he saw a coble setting off. Could it be Turnbull? If so, he would be just in time, but would he have what he hoped? What if something had gone wrong? Had he been mistaken? It was too late to worry about that now. He must keep talking until the boat's arrival.

"Dand's only mistake was not to go over to the island – for he believed, as I confess I did, that the trail would not continue across water. Later, Master Cranstoun explained to me that this was not the case. Indeed, it baffled him because the torso had lain rotting on the island all night. If anywhere should have had Alex's scent, it was here. But the truth was that only you and Dand had ever been on this island. Alex had never been here, dead or alive."

The houndsman flushed with pride and exalted the dogs' capabilities to the crowd. Antoine was about to hush him but felt it might help to waste more time. He let him ramble a while before picking up the story again.

"Now you were set up nicely: all the evidence pointed to this being Alex's body: there were witnesses to his kidnapping, the hounds had traced him to the river, and nobody else was missing. You were free to turn back to the Flemings. Until you hit some more bumps in the road."

"Firstly, Luggy started to panic as you would not tell him what had happened. He began filling the gaps in his own mind, imagining that he was in danger from some great men of these parts."

Antoine glowered at Wedderburn, who spat on the ground.

"In truth, the threat was much closer to home, wasn't it Redpath? You knew Luggy was on the verge of telling me about your absence from the shielings. That time we sat on the hay bales, and you appeared with drinks, you'd been listening, hadn't you? So you decided to silence him. He let you in one night, and you strangled him in cold blood."

Was that remorse which contorted Redpath's face or the force of Luggy's brother on his body? "I did no such thing," he said shakily. "Perhaps I left him unprotected when I closed the house up for him, but that was an honest mistake. Ye concluded that yourself."

"No, I suggested it, and you jumped on it as your excuse. Another fine deception on your part." Antoine craned over the heads of the crowd to check on the coble's progress. It was halfway across the river, unseen by all. "You now had two murders on your hands, but a third one was soon to come, for the prioress asked us to investigate another Fleming, a man named Schmidt. She mistakenly believed him to be involved in some other plot when, in fact, he was negotiating with you, for de Bruyn's release."

"Hold on. Schmidt?" exclaimed Redpath. "I was with you when he was slain!"

"Yes, but you were initially reluctant to join us. That's why you stopped off at your house, on the pretext of warning your family. In truth, you told Dand of our liaison. You then made sure we took the longer route to Allanton – I realised this when we travelled to Dunbar last week: Sister Joan said it would be quicker to go by Whitsome. This detour gave Dand long enough to get himself in place, kill Schmidt and escape."

Mother Isabella put her hand to her mouth in shock.

"I unwittingly caused that poor man's death?" she said.

"Not really," replied Antoine gently. "They planned to kill him that night anyway."

She nodded thoughtfully, before giving another gasp.

"What about the attack on young Master Turnbull?"

"I'm afraid that was all our doing. Redpath was there when you briefed us to go into Berwick and told us of the inn. But I allowed Turnbull to go there – and let Redpath go home, as he said he needed to be with his family. In reality, he and Dand went to Berwick and lay in wait. You even affected an English accent once you knew Turnbull would survive, didn't you?"

Redpath shook his head. He seemed to have given up on his defence. Or had he?

"I don't know what's come over ye, sir," he said at last. "Only yesterday, ye visited my house and promised my poor family that ye would help us. Ye agreed that it was Dixon who had killed my brother. Now ye say Alex is alive." He licked his lips. "I say the idea is ridiculous. But if it's true, where is he?"

"It's a good point," said Hume coldly.

Dacre nodded. "Even by the March Laws, there must be proof."

A rumble of agreement seemed to pass through the crowd. But then Antoine realised that the people were jeering at something behind them. He looked at Wilson and Waddell in the hope that they might have a better view of what was going on, but they simply shrugged. As the noise spread, the spectators parted to let a ragged group come forward: Turnbull, four soldiers, Janet Armstrong and a tall, dark-haired man with a striking resemblance to James Redpath.

"We got him," said Nisbet breathlessly, dragging the stranger by the elbow.

"And her," said Tait, manhandling Janet.

"Thank God," said Antoine. "I was beginning to worry. Well, you're here now, that's all that matters. So why don't you tell everyone what you've been up to. I've already given them the gist."

Turnbull looked round at the expectant faces. "All right," he began falteringly. "We have come from the tower at Lennel, another one of Lord Hume's deserted castles. Our master sent us there at dawn this morning with the idea that Alex Redpath might be hiding there with his lover Janet Armstrong. That turned out to be so, as you can see."

The prioress wrung her hands. "And the Armstrong brothers?"

"No, they were not there. It seems our three men from the West were but a dream. Not that these two came easily, mind you. They put up a hell of a fight, raining stones down through the murder holes, the lot. Eventually, we took them and confirmed what you had thought, sir: that Janet had not been kidnapped after all but had gone willingly to her lover."

"This is your victory, not mine," Antoine said with paternal pride. "Last night, when you wished that the dead could talk, it made me consider whether Alex might be alive. Then you pointed out that Cranstoun's dogs were tracking Janet to the tower at Lennel when they fell ill."

"Aye," said Turnbull. "Doctored by Redpath, who had

heard Mistress Gray list the most common poisons in these parts."

Antoine looked at the wretched couple of Alex and Janet and mused that their expressions were more venomous than any toxin. The prioress caught his eye and beamed with admiration. Slowly, the crowd burst into a round of applause.

When the noise had died down, James Redpath's demeanour changed completely. He no longer made any pretence at denial or contrition. "Well," he said. "It sounds like you have worked it all out, monsieur." He looked round at Luggy's brother, still holding him tightly by the arms. Then beyond, into the crowd. "I always knew ye were a clever man. And so ye've proved to be. But I'm afraid ye've made one very big mistake…"

Chapter 55

In one fluid movement, Luggy's brother let go of Redpath and grabbed Antoine around the neck. A second later, he held a dagger to his throat. At the same time, two burly men emerged from the depths of the crowd, brandishing swords. They bore a strange resemblance to Luggy's brother. Except Antoine now realised that none of them were any such thing. How could he have been so stupid? The three Armstrong brothers were real enough, after all.

All hell broke loose on the island. In the stramash, Alex kneed Nisbet in the groin and shoved his heavy body aside. One of the brothers threw him a knife and he caught it, unsheathing it in a flash. Meanwhile, Janet jerked her head backwards into Tait's nose, leaving it splattered all over his face. He bent over in agony, allowing her to take his sword with ease.

"In the name of God, somebody do something!" cried the prioress, as James Redpath swiped the money bags from her desk. "Hume, Dacre – remember your oath!"

However, the two headsmen stood still.

"I only swore to protect the warden on the Scottish bank," said Hume, gesturing for his men to stay where they were. "I did not speak of the island or the river."

"And I did the same for the English bank," said Dacre.

359

Turnbull was exasperated. "Then who will help me take them?" But as he cast his eyes about, the answer seemed to be nobody.

"Do not risk yourself, Turnbull," spluttered Antoine through his stranglehold. He had no wish to add to the list of men he had sent to their graves.

The brothers laughed. "That's good counsel from the warden," snarled one. "Make a move and he'll be the first to get it. Then you! Now get out of our way."

The six renegades grouped themselves together, and holding their weapons out before them, they carved their way through the crowd. In moments, they were down at the water's edge and climbing back into the coble on which they'd arrived. James Redpath slung the two bags of money in before dragging Antoine aboard.

"Yes!" shouted James, punching the air as they pushed off. "Christ, but that was close."

"We've got much more than we were after too!" hooted Alex. He started to pour the coins from one bag into the other, to make one big sack.

"Be quiet, lads," said the brother holding Antoine, the one who had pretended to be Edward Laidlaw. "Let's celebrate when we're done. Davie, Clem, you take the oars. Janet, you go up front. Alex and James, help me look after him."

"Right ye are, Will," said Alex. Leaning over, he took Antoine's sword and handed it to James. When he was satisfied that their captive was unarmed, he nodded to Will, who relaxed his grip.

"That's better, sir," he said. "Now don't do anything stupid if ye ken what's good for ye."

The other two brothers put their backs into the rowing, although they were not natural oarsmen, and the coble yawed about in the swirling water. Antoine wondered what they had in mind for him. Or indeed whether they had a plan, for events had turned so quickly. He decided his best hope was to keep them talking, perhaps to sow some seeds of doubt as well.

"There's no escape for you," he said quietly.

"Doesnae look like that to me," scoffed Redpath.

"There will be search parties everywhere. You'll never get out of here alive."

Janet snorted from her position at the bow. "Hume and Dacre didnae seem in any rush to catch us. Whatever ye have on them, they'd obviously prefer ye deid than get their money back."

"So what will you do? Float off to sea? Just disappear? What of your family, for God's sake?"

"Agnes left for the West wi' the bairns this morning," said Redpath smugly. "Dand's waiting at Lennel wi' more horses. As for Jessie, she kens nothing of this, poor cow. She can have our houses once we're gone."

They continued to steer haphazardly down the river. The Martinmas festivities were in full swing on both banks. Nobody would notice the little coble going by, or grasp its significance.

"So where did all this come from?" said Antoine, determined to keep the gang talking. In truth, the fugitives did not require much encouragement as they were still jubilant at what they were about to pull off.

Redpath shrugged. "Last year I borrowed some money frae a German in Berwick, the leader of those people. Seeing how rich he was, I saw the chance to make some coin out of him. But when we reached the harbour, the only one around was that Fleming."

So Ritter was the original target, thought Antoine. And

the merchant had recognised Redpath after all. If only he had been more direct rather than messing about with his cryptic advice.

"You must have been disappointed when de Bruyn died on you?"

"Aye, he only lasted a day, but it turned out to be a blessing in disguise."

"And a good disguise too," said Antoine archly. "It can't have been easy, chopping up a man though?"

"It was easy enough when we thought of the money," said Alex, turning round. "He was already in the dungeon, so we butchered him down there and burnt his clothes in the yard. Then we put my spare shirt on him, cut the sleeves off and wiped the gore about to make the story fit."

"Ah, I wondered about that," said Antoine. "The shirt did not seem to match the wounds. I was too distracted by the playing card though."

"That was my idea," said Redpath proudly. "When I heard ye aimed to bring up the body, I came prepared. As ye waited in the parlour, I said I needed time alone. Then, when the nuns went to fetch the prioress, I slipped in."

"The falcon meant nothing then?"

"Of course no'. It was just the first card that I found."

Antoine kicked himself. He had overthought the elements that required no further explanation – and not given enough time to others. Perhaps he was guilty of doing the same again right now? He should be plotting his escape, but he felt compelled to learn more about how he had been deceived.

"What about the attack in Berwick?"

"It was Dand and I, as ye suspected."

"And was it Alex's knife?"

"Aye, he gave it to me when he went intae hiding. Then I lost it in the attack, but I had a week to make another before I next saw ye. Living next door to a blacksmith has its benefits."

Antoine shook his head. Turnbull had been right, after all. "And Schmidt's murder in Allanton?"

"Ye got all that correct as well. We only chose that shepherd's hut because Janet and Alex used to meet there, for their trysts."

Antoine nodded. "And so we come to Luggy. You almost tricked me with your suggestion that Dixon should attend the body. You guessed rightly that he might refuse, for folk are superstitious in these parts, even when they are innocent."

Redpath did not respond, so Antoine continued. "You had no such qualms though. You killed your friend in cold blood and then stood over your work."

"Nobody wanted that," said Redpath quietly, trailing his hand in the water. "But it had to be done."

"Ye're right," Janet told him. "Dinnae let it trouble ye, whatever others say."

Alex shot them both a dirty look before turning his back again. Luggy's murder had been a point of contention within the family then. Antoine wondered whether he could exploit this division.

"Is that why Agnes was so upset the next day?" he probed. "When I heard her say 'This is all your fault', I thought she was accusing me, but now I realise she had just rumbled you. She was berating *you*, wasn't she?"

"Just leave it," snapped Redpath. "The poor man was very ill. Perhaps I did him a kindness. Now keep your thoughts to yourself, as our journey's almost done."

They passed the priory, where a group of nuns were

working in the garden. It would be pointless shouting to them: they were too far away, and besides, what could they do? Antoine determined to reach firm land and then try to strike a deal.

He was about to steer the conversation in that direction when Davie Armstrong stopped rowing to point behind them. "Look, lads. There's someone after us."

Antoine craned over Alex's head to see another coble coming round the river bend. There were three figures in it.

"God's guts, it's your wee lapdog, Turnbull," said Redpath. "And the river bailiffs, too, by the looks of it."

"I told you you'd be chased," said Antoine.

"They will not trouble us," said Will Armstrong darkly. "James, how far are we now?"

"We'll be there in a few minutes."

"And Dand will have the horses ready?"

Redpath hesitated. "Only three," he said. "He's no' expecting all of us, remember. Only Alex and Janet."

"Of course," said Will, thoughtfully. As his brothers rowed forward, he leant in and whispered to them. They remained locked in hushed conversation as the boat coasted in the current. Antoine turned and saw Turnbull and the Herons catching up.

"Right," said Will. "No point in keeping his Lordship if we cannae take him wi' us for a ransom. So let's get rid o' him here."

"What?" cried Antoine. He looked around in desperation. "This will only make things worse for you."

"No. Worse would be getting caught," said Will. "And we have no intention o' that."

He put his dagger to the side and lifted Antoine by the elbows. The boat rocked, and for a split-second, Antoine thought he might be able to move for the weapon, but Clem put his oar down and picked the dagger up.

"Help me, lads," said Will. Antoine felt the Redpath brothers' arms around him, trying to heave him over the side. The boat lurched again, and Davie Armstrong shouted: "Be careful, for Christ's sake – or we'll all be in the water!"

The little boat rocked wildly as four men wrestled for their lives and two tried to row through it. Janet screamed, not for them to stop but to "get the bastard over!" Davie swung his oar like a club, hitting Antoine on the back of the head, and his knees dropped a little. He began to fall. Another blow connected, this time with his shoulder.

Antoine toppled over the side to a great cheer from his captors.

But as he fell, he managed to grab the money bag and take it with him, down into the icy waters of the River Tweed.

Chapter 56

Lightning. That's what it felt like as he hit the surface. As if he had been struck by the most excruciating bolt of pain. Freezing him, burning him, stabbing him all at once. In his state of shock, Antoine let go of the money bag and saw silver flash before his eyes. So Albany had been right, that he would have more coin than he could carry one day. But he did not care. Could not think. Had to do something.

Struggling for breath, he tried desperately to pull himself to the surface. However, there was a fierce undercurrent on this stretch of the river, dragging him down into the black. His limbs would not obey his commands. His chest was on fire. He tried not to give in, but it felt like he were being torn open from within.

Eventually, he could bear it no longer, and he began to gasp uncontrollably. At first, each gulp of water was agonising, but after a while the pain just washed over him. It was pleasant, even. His mind was suffused with an incredible feeling of lightness. He had failed in his mission but tried to do the right thing. And whatever guilt he bore for Francoise and his men had surely been assuaged. It was time to surrender himself to God and His mercy. He shut his eyes and thought of sleep. But, for once, he did not want to sleep.

Something deep within him made him kick, back up

towards the light. He continued to gulp down water, but now he was screaming as he did so, channelling all his anger and frustration into the idea of survival. He roused his arms and legs from their icy stupor and thrashed them about for all they were worth, more like he was battling a beast than trying to swim.

For a moment, his head broke the surface. It brought another shock, but a more welcome one this time. The taste of fresh air brought him a new burst of energy, a new desire for life. He managed to stabilise his position, then float downstream with the current, numb with cold and exhaustion. As he passed a fallen tree trunk, he grabbed hold of a branch and stayed there for a while. From there, he was able to pull himself to the side.

Antoine lay shivering in the rushes, teeth chattering. His vision was hazy, and his ears were still full of water. Where was he? As he came to, he could hear voices close by – voices he recognised, with a feeling of fresh dread.

"You cannot leave us," James Redpath was saying angrily. "What kind of trick is this?"

"There's only three horses," replied Will Armstrong bluntly.

"Aye, our horses. Just as this was our idea."

"The idea was to make money," said Clem. "Now that chance is gone, it's everyone for themselves. Sister, are ye coming?"

Janet Armstrong unleashed a torrent of invective that Antoine could not make out, but as he raised his head from his hiding place, he could see her climbing onto the back of Clem's horse. She held Alex's hand as he beseeched her to stay or take him with them. However, her brothers were having none of it. James and Dand stood raging at the injustice of it, but the Armstrongs spurred the horses and disappeared into the greenery.

As they left, Antoine breathed a sigh of relief, only to realise that he was in danger all over again: he was now the only hope of three increasingly desperate men. They started to look around. Redpath pointed in the Frenchman's direction. Antoine ducked down, thinking he had been spotted, only to realise the fellow's gaze was directed behind him.

"Give yourselves up," shouted Turnbull as he leapt out of the coble and splashed through the water.

"Nae chance," said Redpath.

"Then the Devil take you. Or we will!"

At this, Turnbull rushed at Redpath, swinging his sword with both hands, just past the man's ear. His enemy skipped to the side and returned with a deep lunge, also missing his target. They parted before going again, goading each other as they fought. As Redpath thrusted and parried, Antoine saw that he was using his sword, taken from him on the boat. He felt sick but could do nothing save watch and pray.

While this went on, Cuddy tackled Alex, leaving them both rolling around in the dirt. It was desperate, primal stuff, and in the chaos, Thomas Heron tripped backwards over his son, with Dand upon him. They, too, grappled on the ground, each pressing their dagger ever closer while holding the other's wrist. Antoine could barely follow what was going on, let alone predict who might win.

Peering from his hideout, Antoine saw Redpath standing over Turnbull with his sword – yes, Antoine's very own blade – raised high in the air. The man's face contorted into a devilish, spit-flecked smile as he pulled the weapon back and prepared to bring it crashing down on his prone victim.

Then nothing.

Redpath hovered in position, mouth agape, before collapsing forward in a heap. In his back, there was a long fork, attached to a rope. It was one of those leisters that the bailiffs had described the poachers using. At the other end of it was Jock Rutherford, standing with the other Lennel men. They raced to secure the other renegades, and Antoine could finally raise a feeble call from the rushes.

Epilogue

FOUR DAYS LATER

Antoine sat in the White Hart at Dunse. That morning, he had woken from his best sleep in a long time. His ankle still gave him trouble and he now had a throbbing head and shoulder to match, from the fight on the boat. His lungs ached from his near-drowning too. But these pains were softened by a warm glow from deep within his soul that he had not experienced for many years.

Two days earlier, they had released Carmichael and Ledgerwood from the dungeon at Black Rig – and replaced them with Alex and Dand. It was the first time that Antoine had visited the cells since mistakenly thinking he was trapped, and when he returned to the surface, he felt strangely liberated – as if the shackles of his own past had been loosened. He told Nisbet to scrub away all traces of de Bruyn and to treat the Redpaths well. They would find out what true justice was like soon enough.

The following day, news came that Hume's men had taken the Armstrongs too – after a fierce battle on the road to Kelso. He had handed them to the Warden of the Middle March, who promised to transfer them to the West. It was a clever move, Antoine thought: it allowed Hume to say that he had kept to his guarantee, while getting them off his plate. He hoped that he would never hear from them again.

As for Agnes Redpath, she and the children had been picked up at an inn by Leitholm. Antoine had decided that she should avoid punishment, for she had played little part in the crimes, beyond covering for her husband. Her life would be hard enough without him – and living alongside Jessie, given all that had passed between them.

As Antoine nursed his ale, he took out a letter and put it on the table. "I received this from Lord Albany today," he said quietly.

"Ah, yes?" said Turnbull, leaning in.

"As you know, I sent him a heavily edited account of the Truce Day, and he has replied with gratitude and appreciation to all."

"I see, so what does that mean?"

"Well, for you, it could be a plum role back in Edinburgh. If you want it, that is."

Turnbull flushed but did not answer. "And what will you do, sir?"

"I am not sure. The Governor says that talks with England and France go better. There may be a job for me in Paris soon."

"I see," said Turnbull, his shoulders falling. "And will you take it?"

"I'm not sure yet," said Antoine. He remembered Catherine's counsel that escape must have a purpose. "It's what I've long desired. But I feel there is still unfinished business here. For instance, the Herons believe they can bring up the money from the riverbed, and if so, it should be distributed to the small claimants as we originally intended."

"That would be fair," said Gibb.

"And on top of that," said Antoine, "Mother Isabella has pressed Dacre and Hume to make further donations to the priory. Some will go to Jessie and the rest as alms for the poor on both sides of the border."

"Another good solution for an imperfect world," smiled Catherine.

"She's a woman of remarkable ability," replied Antoine. "It seems to be a local trait."

Catherine dipped her head, and he regretted his forwardness. Mistress Gray had already made it clear that she wished to return to her quiet life in the forest, so whatever the future might have in store, this was not a matter for today. He moved the conversation on. "Then there's the ongoing job of running the garrison. We must let the Marchmen go home in a week, under the terms of their procurement. So we'll need to get some new troops in to replace them."

"I can organise that if ye like, sir," said Anderson.

Antoine smiled. "That's good to hear. I can think of nobody better."

"And the Flemings?" said Turnbull. "What do we do about them?"

"A fine question," said Antoine thoughtfully. "They will be anxious to keep this matter quiet, so perhaps we offer to return the ransom money that the Redpaths took – and if they do not accept it, we will add it to the alms."

Turnbull nodded. "I'll go into Berwick to tell them," he said. "If you'll keep me on, of course."

Antoine marvelled at how the lad had grown since their first meeting in the Red Office at Holyrood. He had feared that he might wish to return to his desk job, but here he was, volunteering to revisit the scene of his near-death. Antoine thought of what they had already achieved together and what they might yet do.

"Gladly," he said. "Actually, if you are going there, perhaps you could visit Master Ritter again?"

"I don't see why not," said Turnbull. "Why, what's on your mind?"

"The one remaining puzzle," Antoine murmured. He ran his finger around the rim of his cup. "I'd like you to thank Ritter for his help and ask him what he meant by his advice."

"Follow the trail of blood?" said Turnbull. "Wasn't that exactly what we did? Work backwards from the crimes, trying to make sense of all the clues."

"I suppose so," said Antoine. "I just had it in my mind that he meant something more."

"That may have been my fault," said Turnbull. "I told him that you enjoyed plays on words and he seemed to take a fancy to that, as a fellow stranger. Perhaps I overthought it though."

"You've spent too long with me," laughed Antoine.

"Does it even matter now?" said Anderson. "We solved the case and lived to tell the tale."

"True," said Antoine. "I just wish Ritter had spoken more clearly. We now know he had identified Redpath from his previous dealings. If only he had told us that."

He motioned to Purves, who promptly arrived with another round of drinks. The innkeeper placed them on the table. For a while, the group sat in quiet contemplation.

Then Antoine put his hand to his mouth. "Oh, Holy God."

"What?" said Turnbull fearfully.

"Ritter *did* speak clearly. Or at least as clearly as he dared."

"What do you mean?"

"He sent us a message, as clear as water from a rock. We've paid no heed to it all this time."

"What was it then?"

"A play on words, from one stranger to another. Telling us exactly who the murderer was. For what is a trail of blood – if not a red path?"

The table stared back at him in astonishment, and he took a long draught of ale. As he did so, he mused that it had been exactly a month since they had come down to this wild border region, on the edge of the civilised world, forever on the brink of war. It was a strange, liminal place, where life and death, good and evil, truth and deceit were sometimes indistinguishable. So it was fitting that the path through it had been both invisible and plain for all to see. But was this the end of the trail – or just the beginning?

Antoine folded up Albany's letter and resolved not to overthink his decision for once.

Thank You

Thank you so much for reading this book. It would be wonderful if you could take a minute to leave a review on Amazon.

If you'd like to learn more about the locations mentioned in this story, you can get a free behind-the-crime-scenes guide when you visit AKNairn.com

Historical note

As with any historical novel, this story combines fact and fiction.

In particular, the character of Antoine de Lissieu is based on the real-life French diplomat Antoine de la Bastie. He was, by all accounts, a good and chivalrous man who fought as a tournament knight, before being captured by the Venetians in the Italian Wars. As the representative of the French cause in Scotland, he supported the Duke of Albany's bid for power and was "rewarded" by being made Warden of the Marches in the Autumn of 1516. Sadly, he only lasted a year in his post before being murdered by the Humes, just outside of my hometown of Duns (or Dunse as it was back then). *The Trail of Blood* is my attempt to make amends.

John Stewart, Duke of Albany, was the Governor of Scotland intermittently from 1514 to 1524. As a result of feuding amongst his fellow Stewarts, he was brought up in Paris and probably spoke French rather than his mother tongue. His rule was plagued by internal turmoil and conflict with England, but he did achieve some success, by bringing in experts from all over Europe. He also had a notorious temper – with several contemporaries relating how he would throw his bonnet in the fire when enraged. A minor confession: I have invented his creation of the menagerie at

Holyrood Palace, actually introduced four years earlier, by King James IV.

The Humes (often spelt "Home", but I have used the phonetic variant for simplicity throughout) were one of Scotland's most powerful families in the 1500s. Alexander, the 3rd Lord Hume, was a formidable operator who was executed for treason in Edinburgh on the 8th of October 1516. His brother William was beheaded the following day, and his other brothers went into hiding. George eventually emerged to become the 4th Lord Hume, albeit a few months later than I have suggested here. The family lost many towers, as a result of their treachery, and routinely sabotaged them – including their wells – to prevent them being reused.

David Hume of Wedderburn was a violent warlord, even by the standards of the Marches. After hacking the real Antoine de la Bastie to death in 1517, he decapitated the warden and stuck his head on Dunse's Mercat Cross. A few years later, he caused further outrage by kidnapping the French Ambassador Denis Poillot and then murdering the Prior of Coldingham. He escaped justice and, by 1523, had defected to Albany's side.

Lord Thomas Dacre was Warden General of the English Marches from 1509 to his death in 1525. He was a constant meddler in Scottish affairs and supported multiple plots by the Humes and other rebel factions. Although his beloved wife died in August 1516, this did not diminish his appetite for mischief-making over the border.

Isabella Hoppringle was the Prioress of Coldstream Priory from 1505 to her death in 1538. She was a remarkable woman who variously spied for the English and agitated for the Scots when it suited. I have been faithful in recording the privileges she secured from both sides, particularly her close friendship with Margaret Tudor. Isabella would be sad to know that little remains of her precious priory today.

Catherine Gray is my creation, although her mental affliction – related to an excessive scrupulosity or religious compulsion – was known in this period. A few decades later, Scotland – and the Borders in particular – was responsible for some of Europe's worst crimes against women in the fight against "witchcraft".

Likewise, Dod Turnbull and the Redpaths are entirely fictional, although based on the truth that the carnage of Flodden (where over 10,000 Scots died) threw up opportunities for idealists and criminals alike. Incidentally, the defeat was more commonly known as the Battle of Branxton Moor back then, but I have used the more familiar modern label to avoid confusion.

Finally, we come to the Armstrongs (including Janet, who would not have changed her name on marriage, as that did not become the Scottish custom until much later). They were perhaps the most notorious of all the reiving families. A few years after this story is set, they moved into the Debatable Lands in the West as a base for their murderous activities. Despite regular attempts by the authorities to exterminate them, they terrorised the whole region for the rest of the century.

Acknowledgements

I've drawn on a host of experts to write this story. As ever, any mistakes are entirely mine, not theirs.

In terms of a general grounding in the history, I read extremely widely, so I won't try to mention every reference here. Instead, I will call out four great books, above all others: *The Reivers* and *The Borders* by Alistair Moffat, *The Border Reivers* by Godfrey Watson, and *The Steel Bonnets* by George MacDonald Fraser. Of these, the first was particularly instructive and inspired several scenes in my story, including the cat burning and the miring of Antoine's horse.

For more specialist advice on the March Laws, Dr Cynthia Neville, Professor Emeritus at Dalhousie University, was very generous with her time and advice. As was Dr Kimm Curran of St Andrews University, regarding the history of the Cistercians and the role of Isabella Hoppringle. I also drew on Andrew Spratt's fantastic reconstructions of Dunbar Castle, Professor A. Roger Ekirch's ground-breaking work on medieval sleeping behaviour, and Professor Neil Murphy of Northumbria University's understanding of the various peace treaties and truces between Scotland and England.

Local historians and librarians are a fabulous breed. I am indebted to the Dunse History Society and its counterpart in Coldstream for all the resources that they have made freely available. Dr Hanita Ritchie of the East Lothian Library Service and Pauline Smeed at Dunbar and District History Service also deserve great thanks for answering my questions on the Lammas Drave so comprehensively. And Keith Ryan's *Bloody Berwick* was really helpful regarding the story of that remarkable town.

Turning to the science of all this, Sue Procter of Think Forensic gave me a good overview of all matters related to decomposition, while Kat Albrecht-Thiessen of Missing Animal Response Network furnished me with some great insights on the wonderful abilities of tracking dogs. And Professor Kamil Hakan Dogan of Selcuk University helped me with the peculiar forensics of bodies left in wells. (Thanks to my family for not being alarmed whenever these gory topics popped up in my search history – and for all their support along the way.)

When it came to the writing itself, J.B. Mylet and Barbara Henderson gave me invaluable advice after looking at early drafts. Dauvit Horsbroch of the Scots Language Centre was similarly helpful with the Medieval Scots (ah wish ah couldae yaised mair but ah feart ither fowk widnae unnerstaun). And, of course, I am forever grateful to the super-talented Kari Brownlie for giving me such a great cover, to Alex Kidd for the imprint design, to Lynne Walker for proofreading and to Lorna Reid for the interior formatting.

Finally, to the real experts: the people of the Borders. Thanks to all of the wise folk I learnt from growing up. I hope I've done you proud, just as I am proud to hail from this extraordinary part of the world.

Printed in Great Britain
by Amazon

43765811R00219